Chasing
Shadows

Chasing Shadows

C. Paradee

RENAISSANCE ALLIANCE PUBLISHING, INC.
Austin, Texas

ISBN 0-9674196-8-9

First Printing 2000

9 8 7 6 5 4 3 2 1

Cover art by Linda Callaghan
Cover design by Mary Draganis

Published by:

Renaissance Alliance Publishing, Inc.
PMB 167, 3421 W. William Cannon Dr. # 131
Austin, Texas 78745

Find us on the World Wide Web at
http://www.rapbooks.com

Printed in the United States of America

For Maribel Piloto, without whom the process would have been twice as hard and the results half as good.

The Agent

Chapter
1

Quantico, Virginia

Tony Viglioni stretched fluidly as she stood at the window waiting for dawn to arrive. It was her favorite time of the day. She had spent the better part of a month at the FBI barracks at Quantico for debriefing. Tony didn't have a home in the real sense of the word. Her job had been infiltration and, when necessary, termination. This required ingratiating herself into the enemy's camp. Not much need for a home since her assignments lasted anywhere from days to months. For the first time in years she allowed herself to think of civilian life and wondered if she could survive it. Tony muttered, "Damn, damn, damn," and paced restlessly around the room, wondering where she would be sent, and in what capacity.

Her thoughts flickered to the meeting with her boss six months ago. She'd approached him and said she wanted out. If he was surprised, he had hidden it well, simply asking why. Tony told him she was burned out and wanted to put roots down somewhere. She wasn't asking to leave the Bureau, *yet*, she had silently added, just transfer to a visible job.   He never questioned her answer, indicating instead, she was lined up for another mission.   Upon its completion, if she'd had no change of heart, he would arrange the transfer.

Tony thought of the real reason why she wanted the transfer and smiled self-depreciatingly.   On her previous mission, she had accidentally found out that, although her report indicated this particular militant group was no threat to the government, the leader had mysteriously died of a heart attack within a week of her departure.   Tony had learned the hard way that coincidence did not exist in her realm.   So pulling in a few markers, she had confirmed her suspicions.

That had started an unending rush of questions in her mind regarding every undercover operation she'd been assigned.   How many times had groups and organizations she reported as no threat been dealt a deathblow?   How many terminations had she participated in that maybe, just maybe, should not have been terminations?   That thought still made her blood run cold.   Her mind tried to reason, *It was always for the greater good.*   Her cynical voice taunted, *Whose greater good?*

The debriefing had been intense.   Tony, ever the master of deceit and deception, a true chameleon in the corridors of power, had simply stowed her conscience and emotions into neat compartments of her mind, and convinced the FBI shrinks that she was carrying no excess baggage from her years undercover.

Looking inward, Tony snorted derisively at the deception she had pulled off.   She continued to prowl around the room and shook her head, sighing.   *What's wrong with me anyway?   It's a little late to be developing a conscience. Time to go for a run.*

Moving gracefully across the floor to the dresser, Tony threw a silent thanks to whatever cosmic entity her share of the gene pool had come from, as she looked into the mirror.   Tony was undeniably beautiful.   Tall and lean, her body was muscular but supple.   Her high cheekbones and full sensuous mouth were offset by a golden complexion with black hair gently outlining her face, falling loosely over her shoulders and down her back. Her most striking feature was a pair of magnificent blue eyes. She exuded an essence that was powerful and physical in its impact, an aura dangerous yet exotic. Both men and women fell to her charm, and Tony had been quite resourceful about using that to her advantage. It was just one of the many reasons why she was so successful in her line of work.

Tony dressed quickly and glided down the barracks steps. Running usually relaxed her, and since her meeting with the Director wasn't until 9:00 am, it would help pass the time. Setting an easy pace, Tony's mind swirled with unbidden images and, in the nanosecond before the power of her will could shut out these thoughts, she realized with sudden blinding clarity, that she was scared of leaving the familiarity of the dark corridors behind.

Tony poured on the speed. Faster, faster, faster. Her mind was now unable to focus on anything except the rhythmic breathing required to keep the grueling place she had set for her body.

Cleveland, Ohio

Megan rolled over and hit the snooze button on her alarm clock for the second time. She forced herself awake by asking the same question she asked every day. *Why does morning come so quickly?*

After languishing in bed another five minutes, she dragged herself up before the alarm could go off yet again. Megan ambled slowly out to the kitchen, and turned on the coffee maker. She thought, *If the darn timer hadn't quit working it would be ready.*

Megan loved her job, but acknowledged wryly that it did cause her to lose a lot of sleep. Getting called out in the middle of the night wasn't exactly conducive to a good night's sleep. Megan knew that her body required at least seven to eight hours a night, and lately she hadn't been getting it because it was her week on call.

To make matters worse, a serial killer had apparently decided to pick Cleveland as a base of operations. The killings began about four months ago and were becoming more and more frequent, with the lapse only lasting two weeks this time. The police were stymied, they just had no clues to go on. The Coroner, Dr. George Whitehouse, had been handling the case. *But then he always handles the high visibility cases*, she thought. That's why she had been so surprised to get the call last night telling her there was another victim with the same M.O. and that Dr. White-house was unavailable. Megan's mood perceptibly darkened as visions of the body she had been called out to examine came flooding back in vivid detail, the bruises around the neck, and the face frozen in terror. Shaking off the dark images, she headed for the shower.

She dressed quickly and enjoyed a breakfast of coffee, orange juice, and English muffins while quickly perusing the sports page for the Cleveland Rockers' basketball game highlights. When she read they lost the night before, she threw down the paper in disgust and headed to the parking garage.

Megan piloted the car through the orange barrels on the innerbelt that had traffic almost at a stand still as she reflected on the unexpected turn of her career a year ago. Who would have thought she'd be the Assistant Coroner at the ripe old age of 27? Always an optimist, Megan had started medical school with the altruistic idea of being able to help people, until that fateful day when a classmate of hers had become the victim of a senseless, violent murder. It was almost as if some unseen piece of a puzzle fit into place in her mind, and she realized she could accomplish much more good by doing her part to stop the senseless killing. From that day forward there was never a doubt in her mind that forensic pathology was the way to do that. She remembered her parents' reaction to her proclamation and smiled. They had been shocked, pure and simple. It's not that she was that close to her parents anyway, but her mother's approval had always been important to her. Her father, well that was another story. She wasn't about to entertain it now and ruin a perfectly good day.

Megan hated the wanton violence. If she could find evidence to link someone to that violence, then the cycle wouldn't be repeated. *At least not by the same perpetrator.* After completing her training and residency in record time, she was offered a job at the Coroner's office. She accepted and became single-minded in her quest for evidence. Things overlooked by the other pathologists didn't escape Megan's close scrutiny. The quantity and quality of evidence the police received from the Coroner's office took a drastic upward swing that didn't go unnoticed by the police or Dr. Whitehouse. As a direct result, Megan was promoted over her co-workers.

There had been some resentment from her coworkers, but Megan felt if they had been more diligent, she wouldn't have been the one that got the promotion. Megan stayed so totally immersed in her work, that she never really noticed that Dr. Whitehouse was a political creature and, by promoting the young woman, he was actually covering his own back. Since Megan was the golden girl of the media and police, she was the logical choice, and it gave him a scapegoat should the need ever arise.

Megan parked and exited the car, proceeding to the door of the squat brown building that housed the Coroner's office and morgue. The early morning sun accented the red highlights in her blonde hair causing her hazel eyes to appear green. She was totally unaware of the eyes that tracked her small lissome body, noting the slight bounce to the beautiful woman's step, while dispassionately taking in her attributes.

Quantico, Virginia

Tony arrived back at the barracks in total control once again, feeling pleasantly tired and relaxed after the run. She quickly showered and changed into a simple black

suit, the skirt accenting her body but not outlining it, with
a white blouse open at the neck complemented by a gold
rope chain and matching earrings. She judiciously applied
a touch of makeup and headed out the door to for her meeting with the Director.

* * * * * * * * * * *

Huey Straton sat at his desk drinking coffee and con-
templating the upcoming meeting with one of his most talented agents. Raking a hand through his thick gray hair, he
thought about Tony's request and wondered if she understood the implications of it. He would grant the request,
she had certainly earned it, but he questioned her ability to
adjust to the mundane daily existence of an ordinary FBI
agent. It wasn't unusual for an agent to burn out. They all
did sooner or later, but the reasons she had given for
requesting the transfer just didn't ring true. Tony loved
the excitement of the chase. She lived her part until she
believed it herself. The real person was buried under years
of alternate identities and role-playing. *Does she even
know who she is anymore?* He knew she had passed the
psychological debriefing with flying colors, but he'd
expected no less. This was not just any agent. This was
Antonia Viglioni, master of the game. He sighed, wondering what was really up with her. When his secretary
announced her arrival, he told her to send the agent in.

"Hi, Tony." Huey smiled, leaning back in his chair
and taking in the agent's beauty with an appreciative look.

"Hey Huey. How's it going?" Tony flashed a quick
smile in his direction, strolled over to the chair facing the
desk, and lowered herself into it.

"Good. You have any second thoughts about your
request to transfer out of covert operations?" he asked,
pinning her with his eyes while unconsciously drumming
his fingers on the desk.

"Nope. This is something I really feel like I need to
do." She crossed her legs and quirked a crooked little half

smile. "Change of pace, ya know?"

Smirking, Huey replied, "That has to be the under-
statement of the year." Standing and walking around the
desk, he leaned against the front of it, peering intently at
Tony. "Do *you* understand just how big a change of a pace
you're looking at here?"

Tony winked to ease the tension. "Now, Huey, have
you ever known me to fail? Anyway, this will be easy considering my past assignments." *You have no idea how
much I realize what a big change I am jumping into, and
how out of control I feel. I just hope I can handle it.* "And
besides, I know you're going to give me a really good job
to get my feet wet in, right boss?" she teased.

Huey grinned at the confident young woman sitting in
front of his desk, smiling sassily, making a career move
that would have a major impact on her life, and acting like
this was something she did every day. "As a matter of fact,
yes. I have a perfect opening for an agent in the Cleveland
office..."

"Cleveland? What's wrong with LA or San Francisco
or even the Windy City? Why Cleveland? What's in
Cleveland?" Tony grumbled, raising one eyebrow so high
it was lost under the cover of her bangs. *Surely he's joking.*

Huey pretended not to notice the incredulous look on
her face and continued, "Look Tony, Cleveland's been
ignored for too long. I need some talent there, and you're
it." He smirked, and then added, "Besides they do have the
Rock and Roll Hall of Fame."

"Oh please, spare me," she replied with an exasperated
sigh.

Laughing, Huey continued, "You'll start off by working with the locals on a serial killer case. With your background, you're perfect for the job. You get into the heads
of the bad guys better than anyone I know, and they are
having a real problem there. It appears our killer isn't
leaving any clues. I've arranged for you to report tomorrow to Michael Braxton. He is the head honcho. He'll go

over the case with you, and then introduce you to the locals. Any questions?"

Tony almost rolled her eyes at the notion of her tracking down a serial killer. *This is what you asked for, right? This is what a regular FBI agent does, right? OK, so what's the problem?* Her mind taunted. "No questions." Tony stood to leave.

"Okay, good luck and..." Huey began.

"Yeah?" Raising an eyebrow in question, she turned back towards him.

"If you change your mind, just call me."

"That isn't gonna happen." She paused and said, "But thanks anyway," and waltzed out of the room.

Huey shook his head behind her. He realized that even though he'd known her for several years, he still wasn't immune to her charm. He silently wished her well. If he had to lose her, at least the Bureau would get some leadership ability in the Cleveland office.

Cleveland, Ohio

Megan walked into her office and checked for messages. There were two, one from Dr. Whitehouse, and one from Sgt. Brian Davies of the Cleveland Police Department. She picked up the phone and quickly dialed.

"Dr. Donnovan calling for Dr. Whitehouse."

His secretary, Hilda, placed her on hold, and she started humming along with the canned music. Megan knew she couldn't carry a tune if her life depended on it. A musician she wasn't, but that little detail wasn't about to stop her from contributing to the vocal.

"How are you this morning, Dr. Donnovan?" asked Dr. Whitehouse in his polished voice.

Somewhat startled at how quickly he answered, Megan replied, "Fine, Dr. Whitehouse. What's up?"

"I've decided to assign you the Shadow case. My schedule is too busy to handle it personally. Stop in and Hilda will give you all my files on the case. I understand there was another body found last night."

I wonder what the deal is? "Yes there was. It appeared on gross examination at the site of the crime scene to be the same perpetrator. I'll go ahead and do the autopsy this morning. Do you want me to copy you my findings?"

"No, I'll access your report from the computer. I've got enough paperwork covering my desk without adding more to it. Do you have any questions?"

"Not right now," she replied with a small frown creasing her forehead, "but I may after I look at the files."

"My files are very concise. I really don't think they will need to be expounded on," Dr. Whitehouse stated pointedly.

Whoa...are we testy or what? "Ok, fine. Anything else?"

"No. Good day," he said shortly.

"Bye."

Wonder what his problem is? I guess I know why I got sent out last night when everyone knew it was Dr. Whitehouse's case. Mm, it's not like him to turn over a high profile case. I wonder what gives.

Megan returned Sgt. Davies' call while powering up the computer to take a look at the four previous autopsy reports filed by her boss.

"Hello, Dr. Donnovan," said Sgt Davies in his deep, gravelly voice. "I understand you're handling the Shadow case."

"Yes, as of this morning, it is my case." *Interesting that he knows that already. Dr Whitehouse sure didn't waste any time.* "What can I do for you?" she asked, propping the phone on her shoulder.

"I'd like to meet with you to discuss your findings on the victim found last night."

"I'll be doing the autopsy this morning. You're welcome to attend. Otherwise, I'll call you when I'm finished," Megan absently replied while scanning the computer for the autopsy reports on the previous victims.

"Fine. I'll be expecting your call."
"Goodbye."

* * * * * * * * * * * *

Each of the four autopsy reports showed suffocation as the cause of death. Each victim had extensive bruising around the neck, and the neck had been broken. There was no evidence of sexual assault. Megan just didn't understand. Why hadn't any of the victims fought back? There were no hair or clothes fibers. Nothing at all to link the perpetrator to the victim.

She decided the "Shadow," which the press had dubbed the killer, was appropriate. It was like a shadow appeared, killed the victim, and then disappeared. She knew how unrealistic this illusion was, but she had a vivid imagination and had no problem putting it to good use.

This is going to be a tough case. So what else is new? Besides, when did I ever let that bother me? With that thought in mind, she went to the locker room to change into scrubs so she could get started.

Once the autopsy was completed, Megan did a gross examination of tissue samples. Like the other four cases, there was no apparent evidence to be gleaned. The fingernails were clean. There were no hair or fabric fibers, and no unknown substances, nothing.

She sat on a stool looking at the Scanning Electron Microscope (SEM) that had so far failed her. There just had to be something she was missing, but what? The only thing she could think of to do that Dr. Whitehouse had not done was order a complete toxicology work up. He had ordered the usual abbreviated one. She really didn't expect this to show anything, but was ready to grasp at straws. Megan knew she was likely to incur the wrath of Dr. Whitehouse for wasting taxpayers' money with the expensive test, so she decided to make it worthwhile and added a Gas Chromatography Mass Spectrometry (GCMS) test also.

She changed back into her street clothes and returned to her office to prepare her preliminary report.

"Hey Doc..." A teasing voice called from her doorway.

Smiling, she looked up. "Mark, how many times do I have to tell you it's Megan?"

Grinning easily, he winked at her and replied, "Okay, okay. So what tidbit do you have for this lowly reporter struggling to survive his purgatory on the crime beat?"

Megan rolled her eyes. "Since when haven't you loved the lure of the police scanner? I think you beat the police to the scene half the time."

"Guess I'm busted," he laughed and continued, "I heard the Shadow case is now yours. How'd that happen?" Mark Potter was handsome in a rugged sort of way. He was somewhere around 6 feet tall, with wavy, chestnut brown hair trimmed to a fashionable length. He had an easy smile and a charming manner. His chin was square, and he was always sporting a five o'clock shadow no matter how many times a day he shaved.

Megan answered absently, "Just lucky I guess." She was still wondering why herself. And she particularly didn't like the fact that everyone in the city seemed to know it was her case almost before she did.

"So what did the autopsy show?"

"Mark, you know very good and well I can't discuss that with you." Megan smiled to take the sting out of her words.

"Oh, come on. I'll just quote an inside source."

"Oh, that's just great. Everyone in the city seems to know I've been assigned this case, and you're going to quote an inside source. Get real will ya?" Megan said exasperatedly.

"Sorry, you're right. I was really being inconsiderate. Can I make it up by taking you to dinner tonight?" Mark asked hopefully.

Glancing at the figure in her doorway, Megan silently sighed. She liked Mark and considered him a friend, but knew he wanted more. Going to an occasional movie or out to eat as long as she paid her way was okay, but she wondered if he was ever going to understand that their relationship would never proceed beyond friendship. God knows, she had told him enough times. If nothing else he was tenacious. "I know you didn't mean any harm. You're just doing your job. So dinner isn't necessary and, besides, I already have plans for tonight," she said, feeling guilty about the little white lie.

"You can't blame a guy for trying. If you do find out anything you can let me have, would you give me a call?"

"Sure, Mark, I always do."

"Later," he replied and sauntered out of the office.

"See ya, Mark."

Megan turned her attention back to the report she was working on. She wasn't looking forward to calling Sgt. Davies and telling him the autopsy results were negative. Finishing the report, Megan placed the call, "Dr. Donnovan here. I just wanted to let you know that the preliminary autopsy report hasn't yielded anything new. Death was by strangulation, and then the neck was broken. Time of death was between 2300 and 0300. Preliminary reports on the blood, toxicology, and tissue samples won't be back until tomorrow."

"Okay, thanks. I guess I wasn't really expecting much on this one either," Brian said. He had hoped the killer would make a mistake, though. "Seems our killer is extremely clever, but then the organized serial killers usually are. Be sure and let me know what the tests show."

"I'll fax the results tomorrow..."

"Oh, Dr. Donnovan," he interrupted, "one more thing. Apparently the Mayor decided we weren't making enough progress on this case so he called in the FBI. I thought you should know because you'll probably get a call from them. The Mayor made it perfectly clear we are to cooperate fully."

"Thanks for the warning." *I wonder if that's why I got this case? Dr. Whitehouse hates working with the FBI. They always tell him what to say or not to say to the reporters. He hates being told what to do.*

Approaching Cleveland, Ohio

Tony was glad to see some of the outlying suburbs of Cleveland approaching as she drove her new 1998 Buick Regal GS westbound down I-90. Buying the car during her stay at Quantico, she had opted for something with soft lines but not overtly sporty. She wanted something that would be fairly nondescript, and, with that thought in mind, she chose jasper green metallic. She had tested the ability of the turbo charged engine during the day and been pleased with the results. *Yeah, it would do.* She popped out the CD and turned the radio on.

The thought of going into this assignment blind made her distinctly uneasy. When doing infiltration, she had always been provided a complete dossier on the target. So when the game began, she knew the players intimately. Their likes, dislikes, families, friends, job, hangouts, amount of money they made, what they had claimed on their IRS forms over the years, previous military or law enforcement experience, basically *everything* about them. With this information provided, it was easy enough to either befriend someone in the target organization or stage an incident that would call her to their attention and wait until they made contact. And they always did. Even on wet operations, the information only provided on a need to know basis, it was still always sufficient to get the job done.

Tony reminded herself that she was not working undercover anymore, and that she didn't need the support system of the infrastructure to find a serial killer. Somehow that thought did not ease her concern.

Driving along the Lake Erie shoreline, Tony noticed the boats and yachts docked at the various piers along the lake. *Maybe there are some redeeming features in this town after all.*

Tony sang along with the songs on the soft rock channel and exited the freeway. She easily followed the directions she had been given to the Marriott and parked her car in the underground garage. She grabbed her luggage and headed for the elevator.

When checking in, she was given a message from Mike Braxton requesting that she call upon her arrival. Stuffing it in her pocket, she quickly took in her surroundings, falling into the old habit of checking the layout. The locations of the doors, stairs, and elevators were of primary importance. This attention to detail had saved her life on more than one occasion.

Tony returned her attention to the desk clerk. "The pool is open 24 hours a day, and on the Club floor there is a fitness center that is open from 5:00 am to 11:00 pm. The dining room closes at 10:00 pm but the sports bar is open until 2:00 am. Handing her a key card, he said, "You're in 305. Just go down that hall to the elevators, go up to three and turn left. The room is near the end of the hall. Do you need help with your luggage?"

Shaking her head no, Tony thanked the clerk and went to find her room. All she could think of was a nice hot shower to wash the road grime off, and then perhaps a martini and Caesar salad for dinner. Might even get a chance to start that book she'd been carrying around for over a year. *What was it? Oh yeah,* The First Wives' Club *by Olivia Goldsmith.*

Relaxing after her shower and dinner, Tony picked up the phone to call Mike as she downed the last of her martini. "Agent Viglioni calling for Mike Braxton."

"Hi, mind if I call you Tony?" Mike didn't wait for a response and continued. "Welcome to Cleveland. How was your drive up?"

"Not too bad," she automatically responded while trying to get a fix on the character behind the voice. "I'm looking forward to getting started."

"Well, we're glad to have you aboard, Tony. We've been very shorthanded lately. You will be handling the serial killer case. There was another victim last night,

same M.O. I'll brief you on it in the morning." He
silently hoped this agent would last longer than the last
one. That agent had only lasted three months before getting caught in the cross fire of a gang war. For some reason no one took a Cleveland assignment seriously. "I'll
meet with you at nine tomorrow morning in room 640 in
the Federal Building." Mike was unaware that Tony had
already ascertained the location of the FBI office.

"I'll be there," Tony said before hanging up the phone.
Walking over to the bar, she fixed another martini, picked
up her book, and gracefully lowered herself to the sofa,
totally relaxing for the first time all day.

* * * * * * * * * * * *

Megan finished up her workout and decided to stop for
Chinese on the way home. She always went to the same
place because the food was good, and they didn't use
MSG. Arriving home, she parked in the parking garage
and started making her way to the elevator. Suddenly she
could feel her neck prickling, and the hairs on the back of
her neck stood up. Megan stopped and turned around,
scanning the garage carefully. There was no one there.
She could have sworn someone was watching her. Megan
hated deserted parking garages. She had autopsied too
many cases that were the result of them. But lately the
garage seemed almost malevolent. Clearly her overactive
imagination was at work again. *But this wasn't the first
time,* a small voice in her mind spoke. Ignoring it and trying to shake off the feeling, she proceeded to her apartment.

While she was eating her dinner, Megan's thoughts
drifted back to her conversation with Mark. She never
lacked for dating opportunities, but she turned most of
them down. She thought about her two engagements, both
to the same guy. She had loved Ray, but something had
been missing from their relationship. She was the one who
broke off the engagement both times.

She still wondered why she had felt so threatened by the idea of marriage to him. She just knew it wasn't right for her. What she had never figured out was why. Now when she dated, she always stopped short of a relationship. Being a romantic at heart, she guessed she was just waiting for someone to sweep her off her feet.

Well you better quit turning everyone down or it's never going to happen, her mind voiced her unspoken thoughts. Not knowing why she felt so melancholy tonight, Megan decided to lose herself in a book. She picked up *Montana Skies* by Nora Roberts and was quickly captivated by the story.

* * * * * * * * * * * *

Bolting upright, the pounding of his heart in his chest threatened to explode as his lungs struggled for air. He ripped the tangled sheets away from his sweat-covered body before realizing it was only a dream. He finally caught his breath and slowly gained control.

It was wrong. It was too soon. The nightmares shouldn't be back yet. Panic reared its ugly head, and his mind fought for control. *Get a grip. Panicking isn't going to help.*

With an effort that was almost physical in its intensity, he was able to shut the panic down. He walked over to the sink and filled a glass with water, drinking deeply. There would be no more sleep for him this night.

Chapter
2

Tony was up early after spending a fitful night. Donning a pair of shorts and T-shirt, she headed to the fitness center. A couple of hours later, feeling the pleasant tiredness associated with a good workout of well-toned muscles, she reentered her room.

Tony knew that today was important in setting the tempo at her new job. Deciding on the subtle power approach, she showered and blew dry her hair. She donned a blue slack suit, offset with an ice blue blouse, and sparingly applied makeup. The color of the suit and blouse offset her eyes giving them an incandescent look. *What else? Oh yeah, the not so subtle height intimidation thing.* Smiling, she donned three inch spiked heels.

On the taxi ride to the Federal Building, Tony looked out at the city noting things that might be useful. She rode the elevator to the 6th floor, located the FBI office, and entered. Cubicles divided the large room. She headed to the closest desk and asked to see Director Braxton.

John Austin looked up to address the woman speaking to him and had to consciously struggle to keep from gaping. He took in the image appreciatively, and thoughts best left unspoken ran through his mind. "It's right down there on the left."

"Thanks," Tony answered, smiling easily. She was well aware of his eyes following her as she followed his directions down the aisle. Tony entered the office indicated and asked the secretary to see the Director. Taking a seat, she waited.

Mike Braxton had carefully gone over the file on Tony Viglioni. The problem was that it had revealed very little. The picture showed an attractive brunette. She was 30 years old and had graduated *Summa cum laude* with a major in Political Science and a minor in Criminal Justice. Immediately upon graduating, she had entered the FBI Academy at Quantico. She had graduated at the top of her class breaking many of the previous records in self-defense, infiltration, hostage negotiation, and marksmanship. It was here that things became sketchy. Her file indicated she had been assigned to the Washington, D.C. office for the last eight years.

Mike was not a fool. *This record has been cleansed.* That could mean one of two things. Either the agent had been involved in some major screw-up, or else she had been involved in top-secret covert operations. Whatever the case was, apparently Headquarters didn't think he had a need to know. Mike wasn't entirely happy with this lack of information, but he'd worked for the government too long to question the decisions of the higher-ups.

If there was such a thing as a stereotypical FBI agent, Mike Braxton fit the mold. Average height, brown hair cut short, clean shaven, conservative dark blue suit, white shirt, blue tie, black wingtips, a slight bulge under the jacket indicating a shoulder holster, and no particularly distinctive features.

He called his secretary and told her to send the new agent in. Mike rounded his desk to meet Tony. Holding out his hand, he said, "Hi. Please call me Mike." He shook her hand, feeling slightly intimidated, and decided the picture in her file did not do her justice.

Tony smiled engagingly and said, "Hi, nice to meet you."

"Have a seat. Once again, we're glad to have you. When you are finished here, see my secretary for an in-processing packet."

Walking back and forth he continued, "We are currently very short staffed. Some of the operations we are involved with include a computer scam targeting old people, a counterfeit ring, and several bank robberies. One of our agents is out on disability and a gang war is looming. Monday the Mayor asked for our assistance in the serial killer case. In the interest of good relations with the local law enforcement agencies, we cannot refuse."

Continuing to appraise her new boss, Tony raised an eyebrow and asked, "Your point is?" *This is definitely a company man. What a wus. Well, did you really expect to be impressed? It's not like Huey didn't kind of warn you, and if he doesn't quit pacing back and forth in front of my chair, I'm gonna have to hurt him.*

Feeling control of the conversation slip away when she interrupted him, Mike replied, "I don't have anyone else to assign with you on this case. So you're on your own. I expect to be kept informed of all developments as they occur. Of course you will have access to all the FBI resources through the computers here in the office. Our job is to assist the locals, not take over their operation. I know I don't have to tell you how important it is to maintain good working relations with them. Your point of contact is Sgt. Davies. My secretary will give you the number." *God, she has presence, a very powerful presence. I'm glad we're not on opposite sides.*

"Fine. Anything else?" she inquired in a bored voice, just anxious to be out of this meeting.

"No, that will be all. The only agent in the office right now is John Austin. Come on, I'll introduce you."

Tony turned to follow him thinking, *Must be the guy by the door.*

After the introductions were made, Tony received her

in-processing packet and was shown to her cubicle, which included a small desk, a PC, and a filing cabinet. Laying the in-processing packet aside, she picked up the phone and called Sgt. Davies.

"Sgt. Davies, this is Tony Viglioni of the FBI. I've been asked to assist you in the serial killer case."

"I've been expecting a call from someone in your office. I have had a file made up with copies of the progress of our investigation so far. I have also included all the crime scene photos. I'll have a squad car drop it off. Once you review it, if you have any questions, I'll do my best to clear them up. Otherwise we will provide you with new information when we get it and will expect the same from you. What number can you be reached at?"

Tony gave him her number and hung up. *Nothing like getting blown off by the locals,* she mused. It was obvious the FBI was not very popular with the police department, but she didn't create that little problem and she would be damned if people were going to keep blowing her off.

Pacing around the cubicle, she slowly emptied her mind and thought, *Focus.* It was a technique that she had taught herself over the years. She was aware of her quick temper and knew that success in this endeavor relied on her controlling it.

When the packet from Sgt. Davies arrived, Tony quickly scanned the contents. Paying particular attention to the crime scene photos, she tried to lock into the mode the killer must have been in, but there really wasn't enough to go on. All the victims had been killed between 2300 and 0300. All were of similar body type and age. All were killed near the Cuyahoga River. The autopsy reports indicated death by strangulation, with the neck broken post-mortem. There were pages of interviews with people in the area at the time, but no one had seen or heard anything.

Looks like I'm gonna have to start from scratch. The file indicated that the Assistant Coroner, Dr. Donnovan, was in charge of the case. The autopsy report for the latest victim was not in the file. Wanting to talk to someone who had been at the crime scene, she decided to start with the Coroner's office.

"Dr. Donnovan," answered Megan, while absently twirling a piece of hair in her fingers.

Tony thought the pleasant voice sounded young to be the Assistant Coroner. "Dr. Donnovan, this is Agent Tony Viglioni with the FBI. I would like to talk to you about the serial killer case. I can be there in thirty minutes. It won't take much time."

Megan took in the low-pitched voice, thinking, *God, what a voice. It's almost, sexy.* She loved to play a game with herself of what someone she hadn't met would look like in person based upon what the voice sounded like on the phone. She smiled to herself remembering an exposé on TV about the women that talked on sex chat lines. Many of them worked out of their homes while tending husbands and children. Interestingly enough, most of them did not look anything like the voice would lead you to believe. This woman had one of those kinds of voices. With this in mind, Megan drew a picture in her mind of a frumpy, dour woman, 30 to 40 years old, dressed in a severe business suit, probably gray, *after all everyone knew the FBI didn't have any imagination*, with her hair in a bun, and wearing wire rim glasses.

Smiling at the image, she replied, "Agent Viglioni, I am getting ready to go to lunch and will be tied up the rest of the day. How about tomorrow? I'm free at three-thirty." The FBI had a reputation for coming in on a case, using the locals, and then taking all the credit for solving the case. So she wasn't about to interrupt her schedule to accommodate the agent, especially since she hadn't even asked for time, but instead demanded it.

Tony was slightly taken aback. She couldn't believe the nerve of the woman she was talking to. She had a case to solve, and no one wanted to give her the time of day. Thinking quickly, she drawled in her most compelling voice, "Dr. Donnovan, I really need to see you before tomorrow. I would be so grateful if you could find some time for me today."

Against her will, Megan was now thoroughly intrigued by the voice on the phone. Her inquisitive nature overcame her desire to make the FBI agent wait, but still wanting to control the situation, she replied, "I'm going to the Chef's Diner for lunch. I can meet you there in fifteen minutes. Just tell the hostess you're meeting me. I'll do my best to answer your questions then. Otherwise, I'm sorry, but it'll have to wait until tomorrow."

Don't piss off the locals...don't piss off the locals...don't piss off the locals, Tony's mind chanted, remembering the words of her boss that morning and thinking just how much she'd like to throttle the pompous woman she was talking to. She thought, *Focus,* and felt the control slip back in place. *Just do whatever it takes.* She replied, "I'll be there," and hung up the phone.

Megan stared at the phone in her hand. *That was abrupt,* and wondered if her curiosity about the woman behind the voice was wise. Snaring her purse on the way out the door, Megan left for lunch. She figured she would find out soon enough.

Tony sighed. She was not having a good day. Everyplace she turned, she hit resistance. She was used to getting her way and couldn't believe she had literally had to beg for a meeting with the doctor, shutting the door on the more descriptive words that came to mind.

Now where is this Chef's Diner? What was that guy's name. John? Yeah, that was it. Calling his name as she walked toward him, Tony asked, "Do you know where the Chef's Diner is?"

"Sure. It's over on Rockwell and East 6th. When you leave here, turn right, and go up to Rockwell. Turn left. It's right at the corner of East 6th. Take you fifteen to twenty minutes depending on how fast you walk," he replied, wondering how she could possibly have a luncheon date already. She had just arrived in town yesterday. *Talk about a fast worker.*

"Thanks. I was wondering if you could do me a

favor?" she inquired innocently, flashing him a beguiling smile.

John said, "Sure," willing to do anything she asked.

She relayed her request and thanked him again. Turning to leave the office she thought, *If I'd have known I was going to have to go waltzing around downtown, I sure wouldn't be wearing three inch heels.*

* * * * * * * * * * * *

Megan was absently watching the door as she drank her iced tea. Several people had entered after her, but none had been directed her way. She noticed the hostess leading a tall striking woman down the aisle. *Nah, couldn't be.* She directed her eyes back toward the door.

"Dr. Donnovan?"

Recognizing the voice, she drew her attention from the door, automatically answering, "It's Megan." Looking up, she found herself gazing into a pair of the bluest eyes she had ever seen. The sight rendered her momentarily speechless. *No, no, no, it can't be. FBI agents don't look like this,* her mind told her as her eyes disagreed. Gregarious by nature, it was disconcerting to her to find she had trouble finding her voice. "Please have a seat," Megan said, a smile touching her lips.

Megan's thoughts continued to run wild. *She's,* and for the first time in her life couldn't come up with a word to describe what she saw and finally settled on, *beautiful.* As she tore her eyes away from the mesmerizing ones holding them, she finally broke the trance.

Megan felt the quiet power that surrounded the woman. She didn't understand her body's strong reaction to the agent, and felt it was probably because of the disparity between the image she'd created in her mind, and the person standing before her.

Realizing the tall daunting woman was still standing, Megan knew she had one of three choices. She had been raised in a house where her father ruled by intimidation.

She could be cowed or ignore it as she had when a child, or she could face it head on, which she chose to do. "Are you going to stand there and keep trying to intimidate me, or are you going to sit down?" she asked in a level voice, keeping a smile on her face to ease the impact of her words, not really sure what to expect.

"Sorry." The word slipped out before Tony even realized she had spoken. She sat down and thought with amazement, *I can't believe I'm apologizing to the same person I wanted to throttle less than an hour ago.*

Actually, Tony hadn't been trying to intimidate Megan. Expecting to dislike the woman and be greeted with hostility, she had found instead an open, friendly face smiling up at her. She was so surprised that the vision in front of her could be the same woman she had spoken to on the phone that her body had automatically taken over with the persona she was most comfortable with. Thoughts continued to run rampant through her mind, *She looks so young, what a little wisp of a thing, what gorgeous eyes. She's so attractive, no, beautiful,* before she was drawn out of her reverie by Megan's voice.

Megan smiled and said, "You aren't exactly what I pictured an FBI agent to look like."

Still somewhat off balance, a sarcastic comment flew to her lips but gazing at Megan's face and seeing only friendly curiosity, she bit off the retort and replied with a half smile, "And you don't exactly look like a coroner."

Megan laughed easing the tension. "You know the cold lobster salad is really good," she suggested while discreetly studying the woman across from her. Once she got over her initial reaction, her curiosity was sorely piqued. *Goddess,* she realized in a flash. *A dark goddess,* her mind added. That was the word she couldn't find when first confronted with the appearance of the agent.

Tony really hadn't intended to eat lunch. She merely agreed to the meeting to find out what she could about the Shadow case, but maybe eating lunch wasn't such a bad idea. The young woman seemed friendly enough, and she clearly expected it. "Sounds good," she replied to the suggestion.

After they placed their orders, Megan asked, "What exactly would you like to know?"

"Start with the crime scene. I've seen the photos, but a first hand account would be much better," replied Tony, drawing her attention back to the reason she was here.

Megan's voice took on a clinical detached tone as she began her recital. "The body was laying lengthwise across the pier. At first glance it was obvious by the unnatural angle of the head that the neck was broken. The position of the legs and arms indicated that she was probably dead when she hit the ground. The clothes were also skewed in such a manner to support this. There was no indication of any struggle. I bagged the hands and checked to make sure that no one had moved the body, and then began my examination. There was extensive bruising around the neck. Other than that, there was just nothing else."

The frustration obvious in her voice, she continued, "I did the autopsy yesterday. It confirmed my suspicion that the cause of death was strangulation. Similar to the other cases, the neck was a broken postmortem. I did send out a complete toxicology test including a GCMS." Megan then added for clarification, "It'll show any unusual chemical strands. The preliminary results should be back this afternoon. I really don't expect it to show anything, but I just don't know what else to do."

Studying the young woman across from her, Tony listened to her description and actions at the crime scene. Young or not, this woman was obviously very knowledgeable and committed to her work. She actually seemed upset at not finding anything. Tony found this unusual. She had dealt with her share of coroners, and most did their job, turned over any evidence found to the police, and moved on. She seemed to be blaming herself for not finding anything.

Always pragmatic, Tony knew that evidence was not always easy to come by. Feeling a pang of sympathy, she decided to try to ease the doctor's burden. Although why she cared was not within her grasp at the moment.

"Megan, you can't find something that's not there."

"I know. It's just so frustrating. I wish there was something else I could do."

"You've done everything you can. Now it's my turn. That's why I'm here. I want this case solved just as much as you do. Tell me about the other three victims."

"I'm afraid I can't tell you too much. This case was just turned over to me yesterday. Dr. Whitehouse was handling it until this last victim. I know where the victims were found, and I read the autopsy reports he posted. They were basically the same as the one I did."

Smiling ruefully to herself, Tony thought, *So she got this case dumped on her, too.*

"And Dr. Whitehouse is?"

"The Coroner. I thought everyone knew that." Megan was puzzled by the agent's apparent lack of knowledge.

Ignoring the comment, Tony asked, "Isn't it a little unusual to have the Coroner hand off a high profile case like this right in the middle of it?"

"It is very unusual." Twirling the straw in her iced tea, she decided not to elaborate.

"Do you have any idea why he would do that?" Tony persisted.

Now how do I get out of this one? Do I lie and say no? Or do I tell this very imposing FBI agent that he doesn't like the FBI? Oh well, she'll just have to get over it. "I think he doesn't like working with the FBI very much." Megan waited for the reaction she felt was sure to come.

To her surprise, the agent laughed. "That's certainly not a novel concept."

At that moment their food arrived, and Tony decided to relent in her questioning until they ate. The doctor was correct. The food was excellent.

Giving her mind a break from the murders, Megan found herself totally fascinated by the woman sitting across from her. *She's so intense, and she seems almost dangerous. I wonder why she became a FBI agent. Guess I'll have to ask if I want to know. She seems perfectly content to sit there and eat, and not say a word.*

"Uh, Tony?" she began, waiting until she had her attention. "Have you been an FBI Agent long?"

"Almost ten years," Tony replied, not liking the turn of the conversation.

When it was obvious she was not going to elaborate on the answer, Megan continued, "Did you always want to join the FBI?"

"What is this, twenty questions?" Tony snapped, regretting the words the instant they were out of her mouth. Seeing a shadow flicker across the face in front of her, Tony realized it really bothered her that she was the cause of it. Forcing the memories the question had conjured up back into the recesses of her mind, Tony silently berated herself. *That was really smart. All you've done is bitch about everyone blowing you off, and then when someone tries to be friendly, you bite her head off. Real bright move.*

"Sorry," Megan quietly replied, looking down at her food. *Guess I should've minded my own business.*

Oh God, now what do I do? It's not her fault. "Megan," Tony began, waiting for the doctor to meet her eyes before continuing, "*I'm* the one who should be sorry. There was nothing wrong with your question. I just don't like to talk about myself."

"No, it's ok..." Megan interrupted.

Tony held up her hand and said, "Please, let me finish. Your question deserves an answer. I've wanted to be an FBI agent since I was seventeen. So I went to college, and as soon as I graduated, I was accepted into the academy." Tony vehemently hoped that the young woman would leave it at that, because she couldn't tell her anything more and didn't want to hurt her feelings again.

Steering the conversation away from herself, Tony asked, "What about you? Did you always want to be a forensic pathologist?"

Megan realized the agent was more a mystery than ever. She obviously was not a talker, but she was making an attempt, and her apology seemed sincere. Megan knew she had just received a peace offering. She also instinctively knew the agent didn't make many. So despite the earlier rebuff, she gave into her intuition about the woman sitting across from her as it dictated that she accept the offer.

"Actually, no." Megan paused at this point unconsciously making a decision, and continued, "I wanted to be a writer when I was a child. But things change." She was unaware of the slight hardening of her voice at the last comment. "I decided I wanted to be a doctor in high school. Medicine seemed like a good way to help people. Then in the last year of medical school one of my classmates was brutally murdered. It was senseless. She didn't deserve to die. I made my mind up then to devote my life to helping find the perpetrators of violent crime by finding evidence to link them to the victims. I knew I could do that in forensic pathology. So here I am."

Listening to Megan, Tony sensed an inner strength belying her appearance. She had not missed the subtle change of tone during the recitation and wondered what could have happened to make a potential writer turn to medicine. However it was obviously something she did not wish to talk about, and Tony understood that very well indeed.

"It seems you have been very successful." Tony said and noticed a slight blush appear at her words. *She's modest, too.* That thought was filed away for contemplation later.

A little uncomfortable, Megan changed the subject. "Do you have any other questions about the Shadow case?"

Again, surprised at her reluctance to turn her attention away from Megan and back to the case, Tony answered, "What are your impressions? Not your clinical findings. Your *gut* impressions. Is there anything that doesn't fit, or that you're not comfortable with?"

"The only thing I can think of is that the victims seem to be dead before hitting the ground. When someone is strangled, there are always signs of a struggle of some sort. The shoes may be scuffed, the clothing torn or dirty, fingernails broken, that sort of thing. There were absolutely no signs of a struggle, and I just don't see how that's possible when someone is fighting for their life. It's as if they are lifted up into the air, killed, and dropped onto the ground. Sounds silly, huh?"

"I'll admit it's puzzling, but, no, it doesn't sound silly at all. Is there any possibility the victims may have been killed somewhere else and then moved?"

"No. There was no indication that they had been killed elsewhere. The thing that's really weird is how can someone be murdered in the Flats, of all places, without anyone seeing anything? I find that amazing."

"The Flats?"

"You never heard of the Flats?" Raising her eyebrows with an amazed expression on her face, Megan asked, "How can you live in Cleveland and not know what the Flats are?"

Tony narrowed her eyes slightly. She hated looking stupid. Obviously the police hadn't bothered to put that little tidbit in the files. With a nonchalance she wasn't feeling, she said, "I just arrived in Cleveland yesterday. Apparently the file I was given on this case is a little lacking."

"I'm sorry, I had no idea." With a chagrined look, Megan continued, "The Flats refers to the flat land on both sides of the Cuyahoga River. All the victims were found there."

Still smarting a little from the look on Megan's face when she had first mentioned the Flats, Tony said, "I find it surprising that it's so common a phrase here in Cleveland when it just refers to the land by the river."

"Oh, no. It's much more than that. It is one of the most popular nightspots in Cleveland. Businesses range from the very best in dining to places that are nothing more

than meat markets. It's divided by the river into the West
Bank and the East Bank. The West Bank sports a little
older crowd, late twenties and up. The East Bank caters to
the younger, wilder crowd and those out to prey on the less
experienced. It has a pulse of its own and is really quite
fascinating. All the victims have been found on the East
Bank. The place is rocking at night. That's why this case
is so frustrating to me. It doesn't make sense that no one
has seen anything."

Tony remained silent enjoying Megan's animated
voice as she absorbed the information. She had already
planned to visit the crime scenes. The fact that it was a
teeming nightspot just made it more interesting.

Megan realized she could help the agent. With that
thought came the insight that she also wanted to know
more about her. Once she left, the opportunity might not
present itself again. So risking rejection, she took the first
tentative step and said, "You know, Tony, since you're new
in town, I could show you around down there. I know
where the victims were found. It's not like a regular place.
There's no parking in most areas, and it really is easier if
you go with someone who's familiar with it."

"Why would you do that?" Tony asked, surprised at
the offer, studying the open earnest face across from her.

"Because I want to see this case solved, too, and I
thought it might save you a little time since you're new
here." *And because for some reason I can't define I don't
want to lose contact with you.*

Tony quickly thought through her options. She had no
doubt she'd be able to maneuver in the Flats on her own,
but it would take less time with someone who knew the
area. The sooner this case was solved the sooner she could
get to her own agenda, she justified to herself instead of
just acknowledging she liked this attractive woman. "Ok,
but I really need to do it soon."

"No problem. How about tomorrow afternoon around
three?" *Yes, yes, yes!* Megan still had no clue as to why it
was so important for her to see Tony again. She just knew

it was.

Smiling at her, Tony replied, "That'll work."

"It would probably be better if I drove. Where should I pick you up?" Megan smiled back agreeably.

"The Marriott on the Square. You know where it's at?"

"Yes," Megan replied. "You parked around back, too?"

"No, I walked."

"You walked all the way from the Federal Building?" Adding incredulously, "In those shoes?" Not waiting for an answer, she said, "Come on. I'll give you a ride." Tony wanted to be angry, but the look on Megan's face was so comical, she started chuckling and followed her.

Megan used the keypad to unlock the doors to a blue Mercury Sable. Tony got in thinking it was a good thing the car had bucket seats because with her long legs, she would never have been able to fit in the front seat with the short woman driving.

Tony discretely watched Megan expertly maneuver the car through the downtown traffic. She drove with the same confidence and poise Tony had noticed throughout lunch.

Never one to remain quiet for long, Megan began pointing out various buildings and naming them for Tony's benefit. As far as Megan was concerned the short drive was over all too soon. She'd have been surprised to find out Tony's thoughts mirrored her own.

Chapter 3

Megan returned to work and found David waiting for her in her office. "Hi."

"Hi, Megan. Where ya been? We got another case to do."

"At lunch. What's it to you?" she teased the blond morgue assistant. David was usually assigned to help her with the cases she autopsied, and they had developed a close friendship during her short tenure. Not only was he good at his work, he was just a delightful person to be around. "What kind of case?"

"A wire," he replied, grinning mischievously.

"I'm sure, David. A wire?" she inquired with her eyebrows raised.

"How about a piano wire wrapped around the neck?" he replied innocently.

"Oh, great. Now they're getting creative." Megan pushed dark thoughts aside knowing David's gentle bantering was necessary to their sanity when dealing with the grim results of suffering and death, day after day.

"What do we know?" Her high spirits were replaced by the clinical detachment that best suited her line of work.

"Male, 30-35, clothes indicate he was most likely homeless. Found on the West Side near the gang hangouts, probably an initiation killing. Jerry went out to the scene, but since he's already working on two other cases, you got elected."

Megan's forehead creased at the mention of Jerry. He was one of the other pathologists on staff, and she knew he was still angry about her promotion. More than likely he just didn't want the case. Knowing what a sneak he was, she figured he went to Dr. Whitehouse to have the case assigned to her. Not that it was a problem, but she'd been getting more than her share of cases lately. Jerry managed to make his cases last longer than she thought was humanly possible. She knew it was all a front to get out of work, but that was up to Dr. Whitehouse to notice.

David looked at her sympathetically. He was very fond of Megan and would do anything he could to protect her from the treachery of the morgue staff. He knew Jerry and his assistant, Dwayne, had nothing but hatred for the little doctor. He had to give her credit, though. She ignored it for the most part and treated them with professional respect that they did not deserve, as far as he was concerned.

David and his partner, Mike, had invited Megan over to dinner several times and had enjoyed her company immensely. She was absolutely endearing and he wished there was something he could do about the situation at work. More than anything, he wanted to see her happy.

David knew she was lonely. He also knew it was something that she had not really acknowledged. Instead, she had become so dedicated to her job that he wondered if she ever really left it behind. David knew from experience that once she met the right person that would all change.

"Earth to David." Megan had noticed her friend go off to la la land and hoped everything was okay. She knew if it weren't, he would come to her when he was ready to talk.

"Just visiting with my spirit guide," he replied grinning. "I guess you're ready to start."

"Might as well get it over with. Has the body been prepped?" she asked, knowing the answer.

David rolled his eyes, pretending to be indignant. "Of course."

It was almost five o'clock before they finished and Megan returned to her office. Once there, she noticed the preliminary toxicology results were in her inbox. The screen was negative, but the GCMS had shown some abnormal chemical patterns. Megan felt a quick rush of adrenaline, but she also knew determining what these patterns represented could take from a week to a month. Megan faxed the results to Sgt. Davies.

* * * * * * * * * * *

Tony returned to her office, and once again began reviewing the case file the police department had provided. After soaking in every detail, she turned her mind loose to identify anything she might not have noticed. Something about the bodies tried to surface, but the more she concentrated, the more elusive it became. Frustrated she looked for something else to turn her attention to.

Walking around the office, she noticed some paperwork sitting in the fax tray. Curious, she picked it up and saw it was the background checks she had asked John to run before she left. Tony was a creature of habit and had decided to create her own dossier for this case. The background checks were on Sgt. Brian Davies and Dr. Megan Donnovan.

Returning to her desk, she read over the information provided on Brain Davies skipping what wasn't pertinent. He was 39, born in Madison, Ohio, and moved to Cleveland as a child. He entered the police academy in 1979 after being awarded an Associate's Degree in Criminal Justice. He had done well on the police force with a 75 percent of conviction per arrest ratio. In 1983 he was wounded in the line of duty while protecting a fellow officer during a domestic violence call.

He married Jennifer Sheridan, age 33, in 1985. They had three children, two boys, twelve and ten, and a girl, seven. In 1986 he was promoted to Detective and had been assigned to homicide. His record indicated he was very successful in homicide, having been credited with solving some cases almost single-handedly. Tony finished reading wondering why he was still a Detective Sergeant when his record was so outstanding. Looking at the picture provided, Tony smiled when she saw the height and weight.

Next she picked up the file on Megan Donnovan. Picturing the attractive woman, a slight twinge of guilt was quickly displaced by intense curiosity. Megan Donnovan, 27 years old, was born on September 25, 1971 in Cleveland, Ohio. Her father, Charles Donnovan, was an attorney with Hughes, Smith, & Donnovan. He specialized in corporate law. Her mother, Barbara, had a part time career in real estate. She had two sisters, Ashley 30, Taylor 24, and a brother, Charles Jr., 28. All were married, and Ashley and Charles each had two kids.

Tony read on. While in high school, she was a member of the National Honor Society and the Literary Club. Sports included the intramural field hockey and swim teams. She had been accepted into the high school/college preparation program and completed her first year of college at the same time she graduated in 1987. *Wait a minute. That made her only 16.* Tony thought with admiration. She graduated in 1990 with a degree in chemistry and was accepted into a joint M.D./Ph.D. program, graduating in the top ten percent of her class in 1994. She completed a short residency and began work at the Coroner's office in 1996.

There was no record of any marriage. The remainder of the record was just the usual: no arrest record, no participation in student unrest, no evidence of drug abuse, no moving violations, no warrants, no military service, and no adverse credit.

An image of the young doctor planted firmly in her mind, Tony found herself wanting to know much more about her than the basics provided by the background check.

* * * * * * * * * * *

Megan was bored. She thought of a number of things to do, and nothing interested her. She didn't want to go to Bally's or a movie, didn't feel like cooking dinner, even the book she had been reading held little interest. Pacing back and forth, restless, she finally decided to go online. She quickly answered a couple of emails from some of her professional friends before she decided to go surfing. Wonder what the FBI had on their website?

Finding that URL, she read the pages with interest. A short time later, after reading everything from the history to what the profilers did, she perused about the services offered by the FBI laboratory. As Megan continued to read she realized her interest was in one particular FBI agent, not the Bureau itself.

The phone rang interrupting her thoughts. "Hello."

"Hi, Megan. I had to work late tonight. Let's go to dinner. John is watching the kids."

Smiling at the voice of her sister, Megan asked, "Okay, where, and what time?"

"How about I meet you at the Stone Hedge at seven thirty. I'll call for reservations now."

"Ok, Ashley. See ya then."

* * * * * * * * * * *

Tony stayed late at the office entering the few facts available on the case into the FBI database. There wasn't much point in contacting the profilers yet, she didn't have enough information to give them.

Once Tony arrived back at her room, she began wandering around aimlessly, feeling trapped. She was going to have to find some place to live. The hotel was already getting to her.

Her thoughts once again turned to a certain young woman. Frustrated, Tony sighed. *God, you'd think I was a high school kid with a crush.*

Knowing she needed a distraction, Tony decided to go explore. This was a new city, and it was important to learn the layout. Opting to get some exercise at the same time, she donned a set of lightweight sweats and departed.

Jogging toward the huge lights of the baseball stadium, Tony took in the downtown businesses as she passed them. She noted that most of the streets went east and west, or north and south, except for a few that diagonally crossed others. The layout was much simpler than the array of streets she was accustomed to in Washington, D.C.

Tony leisurely moved along with her senses fully extended. She quickly assessed people she passed on the streets. While Cleveland was certainly not the crime capital of the world, it had its share of crime per capita. Tuning into the night life around her, she created a surreal image with her long hair flying behind her head, a single woman alone, daring to breach the dark domain of gangs, drugs, sex, and violence.

Rounding another street corner in her lazy loop around the downtown area, she saw three young men swaggering abreast heading her way. Thoroughly enjoying her night sightseeing, she decided to go around them, and jogged off the sidewalk into the street.

The men, dressed in the dark garb of predators of the night, were both surprised and pleased that they had found prey so quickly. The three lowlifes stepped into the street to block Tony's passage.

Tony's entire demeanor changed as she coldly reviewed her options. She could simply keep running. With her athletic body capable of gymnastic moves that would awe the judges at world sporting events, she could easily maneuver around them. On a sustained run, there was absolutely no way they would ever come close to her speed or stamina. She could stop, tell them she was an FBI agent, and to get lost before she decided to find a reason to haul them in. She chuckled at this thought. *Like they would believe that*, or she could disable them and call the police.

None of these solutions particularly appealed to Tony. From the moment they had blocked her path, she'd felt the familiar rush of adrenaline, and now she wanted to kick some serious ass. With the exception of lunch, *where'd that thought come from*, this had been the most boring day she could remember, and she was ready for some action.

Tony began waging a battle with her conscience. *Overt FBI agents do not go around kicking butt. Maybe not, so I guess I'll be covert for about the next five minutes. Besides, there's no doubt these guys are going to harm some innocent citizen somewhere tonight. You're just making excuses for your behavior. All right I'll compromise. I'll advise them I'm a FBI agent and if they take off, fine, but if they don't*...knowing full well she'd get her wish for some action, conscience be damned.

Drawing to a stop about four feet from the thugs, Tony's entire body tensed, ready for action, under the guise of relaxation. Her narrowed, hooded eyes took on a glacial hardness and a cold smile covered her face. "Something I can do for you, boys?"

"Oh, yeah, baby." The middle thug leered at her while grabbing his crotch suggestively as the other two began moving sideways.

Tony kept them in her peripheral vision as she gave a warning that she considered a total waste of time. "I am an FBI agent, and I suggest you move on before I find a reason to haul you in."

Were these thugs any less used to preying on women and other innocent, harmless beings, they might have sensed the aura of danger that rolled in waves off the tall woman standing in front of them. But they had become so used to taking what they wanted, when they wanted, the danger never permeated their brains.

As all three began hooting derisively, the one in the middle guffawed, "Yeah, and I'm the President..."

Another interrupting, "No, man, I'm Elvis..." and doubled over laughing.

The third offered, "No, I got one better, I'm Superman." Lowering the timbre of his voice until it became threatening, he added, "And we know he always gets what he wants."

Moving closer, knives appeared in their hands.

"I have a better one," Tony drawled ominously.

"Yeah?" the one in the middle snarled, tiring of the game.

"I'm your worst nightmare," growled Tony. Her body became a flurry of motion, one foot slamming into the groin of the middle thug, a fist simultaneously slamming backward into the nose of the thug to the right. She grabbed the third man's wrist in an iron grip causing him to drop his knife, while spinning her body and connecting with a bone-breaking sidekick to his ribs. She pivoted toward the only attacker still standing. Warily circling her, blood dripping from his nose, he feinted in and out with his knife. With a feral smile Tony taunted the thug. "Are we having fun yet?"

Lunging forward, determined to slice this crazy arrogant woman open, he met only air as she deftly sidestepped at the last moment. She grabbed his wrist rendering the knife useless and turned her body into him. Stretching his arm over her shoulder and driving her other hand palm up under the elbow, the snapping of bone echoed through the night. She thrust him away. "You're lucky I was in a good mood tonight."

Tony looked with disdain at the scene and watched them scuttle away, feeling no remorse, but rather vindication, knowing these three would not be targeting anyone else soon. Quite satisfied with herself, she continued her slow leisurely tour.

* * * * * * * * * * *

Megan was thoroughly enjoying her dinner with Ashley. She very seldom got to see her sister one on one. She knew how many things Ashley had to juggle to take care of John, the children and a career. It wasn't that Megan minded visiting with her brother-in-law and two nieces; she just felt that their world was so far removed from her own. So the infrequent times when just she and Ashley could get together were that much more enjoyable.

Ashley had brought her up to date on Kimberly and Kristine, Megan's five-year-old twin nieces. Then she had continued on about John and his career, and how her own was progressing. "So now that I've monopolized the conversation, what are you doing these days?" Ashley smiled over at her younger sister.

"Oh, you know. Work mostly. They assigned me the Shadow case."

"Yeah, I heard. I read the article that reporter you know did. Mark something. Are you still going out with him?"

"Ashley, I never was going out with him. We're just friends. We go places together sometimes. That's not the same as going out," Megan said with a sigh.

"Megan, I didn't mean anything." She continued, "You know Mom and Dad ask about you all the time. You don't visit them very often."

"I know. But every time I do, they want to know who I'm dating, when I'm going to get married, and I have to hear all about how my biological clock will run out if I don't do something soon. I'm only 27. When I meet the right person, they'll know. In the meantime, I just wish they'd give it a rest."

Ashley wisely decided to change the subject. "Want to have some dessert? We've got time." She chuckled at the delighted look on Megan's face. *Some things never change.*

Ashley's thoughts turned back to their childhood.

Megan had always been such a dreamer. She was always reading and practically lived in her books. That was before their father found out how intellectually talented she was, and decided that he wanted her to follow in his footsteps and become a lawyer. He had done everything he could to belittle all her interests except for those related to the textbook.

Ashley remembered the day her father had finally put an end to Megan's dream of becoming a writer. He ruled with an iron hand, and Megan was often at the receiving end of it. After that, Megan did what he wanted and excelled at every academic challenge. He never could take away her genuine concern about other people though. Ashley remembered the two times Megan had stood up to him, consequences be damned. The first time she told him she was going to medical school, not law school, and the second time when she had announced she was going to be a forensic pathologist. Their father had been so flabbergasted he was actually speechless, and that had to be a first because the man could talk. She just wished Megan hadn't given up on her other dream.

"What are you dreaming about over there?" Megan asked watching her sister.

"Oh, just thinking about when we were kids," Ashley replied, quickly changing the subject. "I called you earlier today, but you were out to lunch. Did you get the message?"

"No." Megan smiled remembering lunch. What a challenge that had been, but in a good way.

"Now it's my turn. What are you smiling at?" Ashley asked, pleased with the mood change.

"I had lunch with the most interesting FBI agent. She was really different than what I expected. I've never met anyone like her before. I'm going to show her the crime scenes in the Flats tomorrow. She's new in Cleveland. She's probably the most beautiful woman I've ever seen, and she must be close to 6 feet tall. She was really intimidating at first, but, well you know with Dad, you get used

to handling that." Megan stopped, realizing she was bab-
bling.

Ashley listened to the whole exchange with interest.
Megan's entire demeanor changed as she talked about the
FBI agent. *Now isn't that odd...or is it?* It would certainly
explain a few things. Megan was Ashley's favorite sibling,
and whatever made her happy was fine with Ashley.

"Sounds like an interesting friend." Ashley smiled
over at Megan.

"Well, I'm not sure you could really call us friends.
It's more like business acquaintances."

Ashley smiled to herself and thought, *Not if you have
anything to say about it, dear sister of mine. I know ya.*

As they parted ways, both promised to try to get
together more often.

Chapter
4

Dwayne Hudson glanced at his reflection in the mirror as he finished shaving. He ran a comb through his dark brown hair studying his face. His chin could be a little stronger, and his brown eyes could be a little bigger, but overall not bad. He looked at his muscular body and knew that it was his strongest suit.

Posing before the mirror, he combed his hair straight back. Studying his reflection, he smiled, and then combed it toward the side. *Oh yeah, much better.* Dwayne did not consider himself vain, merely accurate.

Looking over at his rumpled bed, he was glad he had insisted on separate bedrooms. It was so much simpler that way. Dwayne listened to the sounds coming from the kitchen and smiled affectionately. Gloria was making his breakfast. He knew it would be a perfect meal. After all he had taught her well, just like his father had taught his mother. Granted, the first couple of years had been rough, but that was before she had learned The Rules. She just hadn't understood that a wife's place is to serve her husband. Now her whole purpose in life was to please him, just like it was supposed to be.

Putting on blue pants and a striped sports shirt he went downstairs. He knew he could wear jeans and a T-shirt since he just changed into scrubs at work anyway, but his ego would not allow him to go to work dressed in jeans. Smiling, he said, "Smells good, honey."

"I hope you like it," came the quiet reply from the small woman who knew if he found anything wrong at all she would pay dearly.

Gloria knew how to play by The Rules, and continued, "You look really nice, Dwayne," knowing that if she played on his vanity, he was less likely to find something wrong. She knew he had been preoccupied lately, and this did not bode well for her. Perhaps if she could find out what was bothering him, she would be able to avoid a confrontation later. So feeling braver now that she had a plan, she asked, "How's work?"

Dwayne stopped eating and stared at his wife. She had unerringly gone straight to the source of the problem. His thoughts turned toward work, and his face darkened with rage when an image of Megan flickered through his mind. How dare she enter the world of forensic pathology in the first place? Any decent woman knew that it was a man's field. That was why he was in it. He was sick of all the hussies who thought they were as good as men and took their jobs. What really infuriated him was that she had been promoted to Assistant Coroner over his friend, Jerry Calhoun. Although it had taken him a long time to decide what to do about that, lately everything had fallen into place. Thinking about his plans for her, he smiled a cruel smile.

Shuddering, Gloria watched her husband's face change first to rage and then to a cruel smile. She had only wanted to ward off any action against her. She hadn't meant to make him mad. All she had done was ask him about work; what was wrong with that? But she knew she was not allowed to make him mad, it was one of the Rules.

Dwayne looked at his wife coldly. "I'll talk to you when I get home." He stood and walked out the door.

Gloria, noticing his unfinished breakfast, knew just what a "talk" entailed, and she put her head down on the table and cried.

When Gloria's despair reached the bottom of her soul, her instinct for survival forged a tiny crack in it, allowing a tendril of courage to course to the front of her brain. She only took her purse and the small amount of money she had been able to scavenge each week from that allotted for groceries, and headed to the women's shelter. She had taken the first small step. There would be no turning back now.

****

Detective Sergeant Brian Davies was an imposing figure crossing the squad room to his desk. Measuring in at 6'7", he had the body of a linebacker and the weight to go with it at nearly 275 pounds. When he was a beat cop, his appearance alone had often thwarted crime about to be committed as petty criminals regarded the wisdom of their acts. Having nearly 18 years on the force, he was a cop's cop. Brian Davies refused to kiss ass. He was not willing to play politics and would never be promoted any higher because of it. He protected his officers from the day-to-day power plays of the chain of command, while following the age-old adage of working right along side of his subordinates. The few officers that had chosen to invoke Brian's wrath had quickly learned that while he would protect them from the upper echelon, if he could, they would still have to deal directly with him for any misconduct. Most wisely chose not to do that. His willingness to go out on a limb and protect his officers had inspired a fierce loyalty among those under his command.

Brian hated task forces. At best, they were just political attempts to appease the public. The "task force" still consisted of the same members that had been working on the case all along, while allowing outside interference from the FBI, and the addition of some of the upper echelon as figureheads.

Right now he was going to have to deal with one of the products of this particular task force, and he wasn't looking forward to it. He had been informed the FBI agent assigned to the case was here to seem him. Brian, along with many of his fellow police officers, had no use for the FBI since the Fielding case two years ago.

Watching the FBI agent approach his desk, he noticed several sets of eyes cut toward the woman. Word traveled fast through the precinct, and most of the officers were aware that this was the FBI agent assigned to the task force. Brian had been a cop long enough to have seen it all, but even he was surprised at the agent's appearance and deportment, although it did not show on his face.

Arriving and standing in front of his desk she exuded confidence and poise. "Sgt. Davies?" Tony asked, appraising the man.

He stood to greet her. "Yes, and it's Brian. Have a seat." He waited for her to take the lead in the conversation, knowing instinctively this would be a powerful foe.

"Tony Viglioni." The agent could feel the latent hostility directed her way throughout the squad room. "I have a problem with the file you sent me. It's not complete. There are no copies of any interviews with the family members of the victims. The crime scene paperwork is missing, along with a list of what evidence was recovered. Those are the apparent things that are missing. I have no way of knowing what else may have been left out."

Brian thought to himself, *Shit. I should have checked the file before it was sent over. Deliberately leaving out part of the case file was serious. Well, I'll deal with that later.* "I'm sorry that happened. I'll see that you get a complete file. Anything else I can do for you?"

"Yes, as a matter of fact, there is. As a member of this task force I intend to be included in the task force meetings. It's quite obvious," Tony paused, glancing around, "there is some hostility toward the Bureau. At least I suspect it's against the Bureau since none of you know me personally. Since it does affect me, I want to know what the problem is. The air needs to be cleared if we are going to work together to solve this case. We don't have to like each other, but our goal is the same here."

Brian studied the agent's expressionless face knowing it spoke volumes about the woman behind it. He recognized the wisdom of her words, and although they had been delivered in a cool, even tone, he did not underestimate the intent behind them. He also sensed the alternative was that she would attempt to solve the case herself, and that did not bode well for the police department. She was challenging him as a law enforcement official, and he knew he had to rise to the challenge.

"I'm not going to try to justify the hostility directed toward you. Whether or not I feel it is warranted isn't the issue here. As you astutely pointed out, it's not personal. Simply put, there is bad blood between the police department and FBI. It stems from a kidnapping case a couple of years ago. A tip from one of our informants came through the squad room. The FBI agent assigned to the task force answered the phone and didn't bother informing the task force that the phone call had revealed the location of the child. He chose to call on a few of his fellow agents and affect the rescue. The upside was that the child was rescued successfully. The downside was the betrayal of the task force." He paused, trying unsuccessfully to gauge her reaction to his words before continuing. "So if you're expecting to be welcomed with open arms, it ain't gonna happen; however, I can assure you that there will be no repeat performance of what happened with the file."

"The task force meetings?" she countered, absorbing the information he had delivered. Tony knew there were FBI agents who liked to hot dog for their day of glory and gave no thought to the consequences of their actions.

Brian always paid attention to his gut, and it was telling him that this was not a woman who could be easily intimidated. Most people he met for the first time were cowed solely because of his size. Many would have been surprised at how gentle the man normally was. Brian felt like the agent had seen right through his veneer. "The entire group meets every Monday and any other time something major breaks. Informally, I meet with the officers each morning to direct their part of the investigation."

Tony studied the behemoth of a man sitting at the desk. His short cropped, brown hair was combed straight back. A pair of steely gray eyes and a heavy mustache offset his grizzled face. The small lines around his eyes indicated his face could erupt quickly into humor or ire. He could be a worthwhile ally or an awesome foe. She sensed his strength of conviction but felt he was no threat.

While Tony noted the last thought, she also knew she could handle him if it became necessary. It was his choice really. All she was doing was the job she had been assigned. The sooner it was done the better. She still had her "agenda" to deal with, and she wouldn't be able to give it any attention until this case was solved.

"Have you met yet this morning?" Tony countered, watching Brian carefully for any sign of reluctance at having her attend.

"No. Everyone is waiting for me now. Let's go. I'll introduce you." Brian stood up and headed toward the conference room, Tony following behind him.

* * * * * * * * * * *

Brian and Tony walked into the conference room. Five officers were seated around the large table in the center of the room, and all turned their gaze to the stranger walking in. Brian informally called the meeting to order. "All right, listen up. This is Tony Viglioni, the FBI agent assigned to the task force." Sighs and rolled eyes greeted the announcement. He continued, "We are going to bring her up to date on the case. I expect everyone to cooperate fully with her. I know quite a few of us have hard-ons for the FBI. Get over it. You can't judge everyone by the actions of a few. Now I know I sound like I'm preaching, and I am, because I know I'm guilty of that, too. So I ain't asking you to do anything I ain't going to do. So set it aside, and let's focus on solving this case."

Tony noticed the respect all the officers showed toward Brian. He was obviously a very effective leader. She would have to prove herself, it went with the territory, but she was used to it from her covert days.

"Dr. Donnovan faxed over the autopsy report yesterday afternoon. It didn't show anything that can help us out."

Tony drew out of her quiet appraisal of the task force members when she heard the words, "Dr. Donnovan," accompanied by a mental image of the Assistant Coroner. Turning her attention back to the case, she listened to Brian's briefing.

"The victim's family doesn't know of any reason why anyone would want to harm their daughter. To the best of their knowledge she was not dating anyone on a regular basis. As you all know, this doesn't mean shit. Since when do 24 year olds tell their parents what they are doing in the first place?" Laughter spread around the room as the officers agreed. Tony remained silent but was impressed with the easy camaraderie the small group displayed.

"We are still trying to locate one of her neighbors to determine if they can tell us if she had a regular boyfriend other than the casual friends we've uncovered so far. There are a couple more people in the apartment building we've been unable to locate, and we're still trying to recreate her movements from the time she left. You all know since the press dubbed the serial killer, the Shadow, the phone has not stopped ringing with people calling in tips. The calls have included everything from confessions to offers of psychic help. Each and every one needs to be checked out. So today we are going to focus on finding the missing neighbors, look for a steady boyfriend, and the phone tips."

"Jack, you and Chuck get the apartment building again. Kris, you and Dave get the neighborhood. Mike, you get to check out some of the phone tips." Casting his eyes toward Tony, Brian said, "Mike could really use some help with the phone calls." He almost sighed with relief when she nodded her head, recognizing his silent message.

* * * * * * * * * * * *

Megan woke up in an extremely good mood. Since she usually always wore a suit to work, she set aside a pair of casual beige slacks, a white blouse, and a comfortable pair of loafers to take with her. She wouldn't have time to go home to change before meeting Tony at three o'clock.

Once she arrived at her office, Megan checked for messages and then went looking for David to find out what cases they had scheduled for the day. Walking into the autopsy suite, she saw Dwayne first. "Hi, Dwayne." Megan had greeted him like she always did and was totally unprepared for the fleeting look of rage that crossed his face. Looking around for David, she felt a faint tremor of fear run through her body, and she found herself wishing someone else were in the suite with them.

Just then David came barging through the double doors. "Sorry, I'm late. Traffic's a bitch."

Megan smiled, inwardly relieved. "I know what you mean. I'll go see what came in overnight." She didn't think Dwayne would ever physically harm her, but that look was one of pure hatred and it still unnerved her. Only one of the new cases was assigned to Megan. After they finished, she went to her office to catch up on work that had sat for far too long, already.

Megan discovered she had no interest in paperwork. She was looking forward to the trip to the Flats with Tony too much. She was glad for the distraction when David came in and sat down. Ignoring the file on her desk, she turned her attention to David. "So how's Mike doing? Does he like his new job?"

"Yeah, he really does. The boss seems to really like him, and he's off to a great start." Megan and David continued to chat until it was time for Megan to change and leave.

"Where are you going so early?" David asked, curious.

"I'm meeting the FBI agent assigned to the Shadow case. I'm going to show her where the victims were found in the Flats."

"What are you going to do that for? I'm sure someone else can do it," David asked, puzzled.

"Because I WANT to. Is that okay with you?" Megan shot back, surprising herself with the sharpness of her retort.

"Ok, ok, sorry," David answered with a wide-eyed look.

"Look, David, I'm sorry. This case is just getting to me," she said not understanding why she had become so upset at him for suggesting someone else show Tony around.

Chapter
5

Tony had returned to the hotel to change into clothes better suited for walking, and donned a pair of a walking pants, a long shirt, and her running shoes. She ran a brush through her hair, checking her appearance more carefully than usual, and went down to the hotel entrance.

Megan arrived at the Marriott, parked the car, and then went looking for Tony. Finding her out front, she said, "Come on."

"We're walking?" Tony enjoyed walking, but she hadn't gotten the impression the Flats were within walking distance.

"Just to the Tower. Then we'll catch the Water Front Line. It's part of the public transportation system. We'll get off at the stop in the East Bank." Megan was thoroughly into what she perceived as her job of a tour guide.

Entering the Terminal Tower, Megan led them to the escalators going down to the lower level giving a running commentary on how a city once on the verge of bankruptcy had now developed the downtown area into a major shopping area where businesses once again thrived. As they walked past several stores, she told Tony they were in a new mall called The Avenue which extended through several buildings and featured many of the big store chains, as well as a six-movie cinema. She paused her commentary long enough to tell Tony the fare was $1.50. She pulled the fare out of her purse, explaining the pass was good for four hours. When she looked up at Tony for the first time since they entered the Tower, Megan noticed a small smile on her face and wondered what she had said that was funny.

Tony was content just to let Megan talk. She was enjoying the lilting tone of her voice and, when she became animated about something, the way her hands would move in supporting gestures. She also found it somewhat amazing that anyone could talk nonstop for so long.

Sitting together on the train as it departed, Megan turned to Tony and asked, "I'm not boring you, am I? I just thought you might like to know a little about Cleveland."

Tony wasn't bored at all. "No, please continue." However, she was much more occupied with the nearness of her companion than the conversation.

Megan resumed talking with renewed vigor, giving the history of how apartments and condos had just recently come to the downtown area, pointing out the first set as they passed them. Next, she launched into the story of how the track for the River Front Line was built. They exited the train at the East Bank stop.

Tony followed Megan's lead to Old River Road, which was the main thoroughfare in the Flats. Walking along the sidewalk, Megan turned to Tony. "I'd like to give you an overview of the area before we go to the crime scenes if that's okay with you." She was enjoying herself and wanted to delay the gruesome part of the trip.

"Sure, that's fine." Tony didn't mind a short delay as long as she saw the crime scenes before they left.

Megan pointed out various nightclubs, restaurants, and bars. She gave a short history of each one, what type of

entertainment or dining each specialized in, and what sort
of clientele frequented them. Tony kept an ear tuned to
Megan's commentary, but her predatory instincts were
fully engaged as they walked through the nightclub-laden
district.

Megan finished the running narrative and led Tony to
the first of several alleys with signs posted for a "water
taxi." They followed the alley as it curved first to the left,
then back right, and left again before straightening at the
dock. When they reached the dock, Megan turned until she
was facing south, and showed Tony where the last body
had been found.

Tony had already noted that this would be a perfect
place to commit the crime unseen. Voicing the thought
aloud, Megan disagreed and said, "No. It's not that simple. These alleys are traveled constantly throughout the
evening and night. People are always going back and forth
across the river. To be totally deserted long enough to
strangle someone would be almost impossible."

Tony silently disagreed thinking, *I could do it with no
problem. Obviously so can the killer. Now that I've seen
the location, I can understand how he has gone undetected.
He is good,* she acknowledged. "I'll come down here at
night and look at it then."

"Ok, when do you want to? We could come down Saturday night."

Tony looked at Megan and said, "You were kind
enough to take the time to show me around down here
today. You don't need to come back again."

"I want to come. I don't mind, and it'll make me feel
like I'm contributing something to the case. Besides, you
can't come down here alone at night. It's dangerous. No
women travel alone here after dark, and you'd be noticed if
you were all by yourself."

When Tony didn't immediately respond, Megan put
her hands on her hips, her hazel eyes flashing, and added,
"You're new in town. You don't know this area. There are
muggings, stabbings, and," she looked pointedly at Tony,

"murders."

Tony had lifted an eyebrow at the words as her mind took in the absurdity of this conversation. She didn't know if she should be mad or laugh. She could understand Megan wanting to help. It was the rest of it that confounded Tony. *She's worried about me? I'd probably be the most dangerous person here. If she had any idea what I've done for the last ten years, she'd run as fast as she could the other way.* Megan had shown her nothing but kindness. *Would it really hurt to let her come along?* All she planned to do was come down and absorb the essence of the place when it was in full swing.

Tony couldn't deny she enjoyed Megan's company. Still feeling guilty about the incident at lunch yesterday, she ignored the warnings vying for attention in the back of her mind that insisted this was not a good idea. Tony looked at Megan's petulant pose thinking, *She's so damn cute,* and was suddenly drawn into the gold and green vortex of the flashing eyes looking into hers.

Megan had watched Tony's eyes narrow and turn inward at her words. Holding her breath wondering if she had gone too far, she was startled by the intensity of the dazzling blue eyes as they returned to her. Captured by the baby blues, she was totally unprepared for the sensations that surged through her, and barely heard the tall woman say, "Ok."

Bewildered by her body's physical reaction to the silent exchange, Megan was confused and repeated, "Ok?"

"Ok, we can come down here together Saturday night," Tony replied gazing thoughtfully at the small woman, the turmoil of her own emotions firmly back under control.

"Oh...yeah...right...good." Megan quickly turned away and walked down the alley hoping Tony wouldn't notice how flustered she was. *God, what's going on with me?* Glancing over her shoulder, she said, "Come on. I'll show you the other sites."

Tony silently followed, forcing her attention back to the case and her surroundings.

* * * * * * * * * * * *

Megan had regained her composure and, while showing Tony the crime scenes, she observed her companion's
casual air and decided that she hadn't noticed after all.
Thank God.

Tony had not missed anything, but her interpretation
was vastly different from Megan's. She fully expected
Megan to cancel her offer for Saturday. *But that's ok. It's
no big deal. It doesn't matter. I wasn't planning on company anyway,* she rationalized.

They finished visiting the crime scenes and headed
back to the train stop. Megan pointed out the few places
she had missed on the way down and then asked Tony,
"Well, what do you think of Cleveland so far?"

"It's ok, I guess," Tony answered not really knowing
what to say. As far as she was concerned it was like any
other city.

"It grows on ya. You'll see. There's a lot to do here.
We have The Rock and Roll Hall of Fame, the new Science
Center and we've got all the major sports covered. The
Indians are great, but it's really hard to get tickets and
we've got a women's basketball team, The Rockers. The
Cleveland Orchestra is one of the best in the world. When
they're in town, I always go see them." Megan stopped,
momentarily out of words.

Walking beside Megan listening to her, Tony had a
small grin on her face as she thought about how multifac-
eted the small woman was.

Megan glanced up at her tall companion. "Do you
ever talk?"

"Huh...yeah...sometimes," Tony responded, caught off
guard by the frank question. She was actually quite a good
conversationalist when she needed to be. However, since
Megan obviously liked to talk, she was quite content to listen.

"Well then, did you find a place to live yet? Have you
even had time to look? Are you looking for a house or an

apartment? I could suggest some nice places." Megan finished, quite satisfied with herself for asking enough questions that Tony would have to talk for a while.

Tony thought through the questions carefully, and then
answered, "No to the first two, not sure on the third, and
thanks, that would be nice."

Megan's mouth dropped open, and totally exasperated
she complained, "I don't believe you! What kind of
answers are those?"

The tall woman couldn't help herself and started
laughing. She had answered that way purposely just to see
what Megan's reaction would be. Megan was so surprised
to hear the deep rich sound coming from her companion,
that she quickly forgot her exasperation and joined in the
laughter. Taking the train downtown, they walked companionably back toward the Marriott, the smaller woman
continuing to do most of the talking.

* * * * * * * * * * * *

Tony walked Megan to her car, and then thanked her
for her help. "See you Saturday," she said nonchalantly.

"Right. How about I meet you here at nine?" Megan
answered.

"Okay, see ya then." *Well at least she didn't cancel.*

Megan drove home with thoughts rolling around
wildly in her mind. She knew she had some serious thinking to do. Parking the car, along with several other tenants
just getting home from work, she was unaware of the hos-
tile eyes following her moves.

After starting dinner, Megan got a glass of iced tea and
settled into the recliner in the living room. Her thoughts
flickered back over the afternoon, coming to rest on the
moment she had been drawn in by Tony's eyes. Megan
didn't consider herself naive. She realized had she been
with a man, there would have been no doubt in her mind
regarding her body's reaction. Her mind fathomed just as
quickly that no man had ever engaged her senses like that

either. Megan understood for the first time what the words 'animal attraction' meant.

She had taken her share of psychology and sociology courses, so the thoughts running through her mind were certainly not alien to her. What she couldn't understand was that she had never experienced any attraction to women before. She remembered her hero worship of some of her female teachers, but that was considered normal. *But what was normal?* Could the way she felt be normal for her?

Megan thought about her limited sexual experience and realized it couldn't even begin to compare with what she had felt just gazing into Tony's eyes. But it was more than that. She was interested in everything about the woman. She was attracted to her, plain and simple. Megan surprised herself with this candid self-revelation, but what surprised her even more was that it didn't bother her like she might have expected it to.

She sighed with frustration. Maybe she was wrong. Maybe she was reading too much into her reaction to Tony. She had known a few lesbian women in college, and they had been very aware of their sexuality. If that were her niche, how could she not know? She was a grown woman.

Playing devil's advocate in her mind she thought what difference did it make anyway? Tony would never be interested in her that way. Just look at the woman, she was gorgeous. She could obviously have anyone she wanted. Megan tentatively tried to come to terms with her feelings and simultaneously realized she would have to take care not to let her feelings show when around Tony.

Megan wished there was someone she could talk over her feelings with. Her thoughts flickered to David, but no, that was different. He was a guy. More frustrated than ever, she went to check on her dinner.

* * * * * * * * * * *

The next morning Tony decided to develop her own

dress code for the office. She had spent the last several years dressing whatever part she was playing. For the most part it had been anti-establishment and militant groups. So her normal attire had been anything from jeans to camouflage fatigues. Tony liked dressing for whatever the occasion called for, but in her mind sitting in an office or doing street work did not warrant a suit. She decided on a pair of navy blue slacks, a long white shirt, and finishing the ensemble, a pair of comfortable walking shoes.

Tony was so bored she thought she was going to go crazy. If one more person she called told her about a vision of the killer, she was going to throw the phone across the room. *Damn Davies anyway.* All day, she had worked through the hot line tips, and she had about reached her limit. A sudden thought brought a smile to her face, and Tony pulled a number out of her wallet.

* * * * * * * * * * *

When Megan arrived at work, she found two cases waiting for her. One was particularly gruesome and took a long time to complete. The city had been particularly brutal the night before, and Jerry and Dwayne had also been busy. It wasn't often all four were in the autopsy suite together because Jerry had made it clear he didn't like her and did his cases separately. She and David were finishing up when the phone rang.

"David, would you please get that?"

"Sure." David depressed the button for Megan's extension on the phone and answered, "Dr. Donnovan's office."

"Is she there?" drawled Tony who had all of a sudden decided she just had to know if the test results were in.

After asking Tony to hold on, he covered the receiver, winked at his boss, and said, "Megan, there's some lady with an incredibly sexy voice asking for you on the phone." David had never been shy about his sexual preference and loved to tease Megan.

"David, you are so crazy. Give me that phone." Putting the phone to her ear, she answered, "Dr. Donnovan."

"Hi, Megan, it's Tony. I was just wondering if you got the lab results back yet."

Megan smiled at the sound of the voice. "Hi, Tony. Yes. I faxed the toxicology results over to Sgt Davies yesterday. They were negative, but the GMCS showed some slightly abnormal chemical elements. Unfortunately that could take anywhere from a week to a month for the chemist to figure out exactly what the chemical strands mean."

Tony wasn't even particularly angry that Davies had not told her the toxicology was negative. She had just felt like talking with someone normal. *Yeah, right,* her mind supplied.

"Ok, well thanks. I was just curious." Tony tried to think of some other business to talk about. "Do you still want to go tomorrow? You don't have to, you know."

"Of course I want to go tomorrow. I told you, the Flats will be rocking. It's the best time to go. I'll be there at nine." *I wonder why that came up again?*

The conversation had been monitored very closely by one of the men in the room, and a diabolic idea was born.

Chapter 6

Saturday morning, no longer able to stand the confines of the hotel room for another minute, Tony grabbed the phone book, and made a few calls. She left after pulling on her heaviest jeans, a T-shirt, jean jacket, and a pair of well-worn black boots.

* * * * * * * * * * *

Enjoying the feel of the wind against her face, Tony maneuvered the bike haphazardly up the hill, the rear wheel skidding back and forth when she goosed the gas. She reached the top of the hill, looked at the cratered track heading almost straight down, with turns meandering throughout the area, and felt a moment of pure joy at the challenging track. Building her speed down the hill, Tony laid the bike almost flat on a sharp curve, it's weight supported by only one strong leg. She then negotiated a hairpin curve at a speed never intended, sending dirt and dust flying. Seeking greater challenges, Tony entered an S-curve pushing the speed. Rider and bike became as one, navigating the dangerous trail, each responding to the strains put upon it by the terrain.

Careening out of the turn into a swell of hills, adrenaline racing through her body and heady with the excitement, Tony's wild grin was at odds with the dirt covered, sweaty face. She leaned forward to gather momentum, automatically increasing the speed before forcefully throwing her body back and rotating the bike up. She crested the hill, rider and bike leaving the ground effortlessly. Tony shifted her weight forward for maximum extension and guided the bike to the next hill and the next.

A few hours later, her excess energy finally expended, Tony removed her helmet and returned the rented bike. She drove back to the hotel looking forward to a shower.

* * * * * * * * * * * *

Megan decided to go work out. She usually stopped at the health club three to four times a week. Not only did she take pride in staying in shape, but it allowed her mind a break from the pressures of her job. Today, she needed a distraction before she drove herself crazy with self-analysis.

Debating on whether to warm up on the stationary bike or the murderous stair stepper, she decided to go for the physical challenge of the latter. She completed her warm up and worked through an exercise regimen designed specifically for her. After she finished, Megan climbed the stairs to the second floor where the track was located and began lazily jogging around the track.

Megan heard footsteps moving up quickly behind her and moved to the side of the track.

The runner pulled even with her. "Hi, Doc, you aren't going very fast."

"Hi, Mark," Megan replied ignoring his standard greeting.

"Have you eaten yet? Want to go get a bite when you're finished?"

Megan was not ready to go home to her empty apartment yet. *Why not?* "Ok, but give me half an hour to shower and change."

"No problem." Mark smiled, pleased that she had agreed.

* * * * * * * * * * *

After being seated and ordering, Mark asked, "Anything new on the case?"

Megan was in no mood to discuss the case. "I'm surprised you're not over at the station asking around. You'd find out a lot more over there. Is that why you wanted to go to lunch?"

"Megan, you know better than that." Mark was surprised by her reaction. She had always been willing to discuss cases with him. "You seem preoccupied. What's wrong?"

"I'm sorry Mark. I just don't want to discuss the case right now," she answered honestly.

Mark decided to change the subject. "Did you see the game last night?" Megan and Mark finished lunch discussing the Indians and whether or not they would make a return trip to the World Series.

Much later, Megan looked through her clothes trying to decide what to wear. She skimmed through skirts, slacks, and dresses, looking at each, and still remaining undecided. The attire of the Flats was anything from cutoffs to dressy. Pulling a pair of peach colored slacks out of the closet, she added an off-white blouse and decided that it would do.

After showering and blowing her hair dry, Megan looked at her choice of clothes and decided she didn't want to wear that tonight. Going through her closet again, she finally pulled out a simple sleeveless teal dress, whose only ornament was a belt around the waist. Holding it up against her in front of the mirror, she liked the way it set off her eyes. A thought danced through her mind, *You'd think you were going on a hot date or something.* Megan banished the idea. *This is just business, and there is nothing wrong with wanting to look nice.* Megan took more time than usual with her make-up and hair until she decided it was just right before departing.

* * * * * * * * * * * *

Tony took much less time with her attire, choosing black, lightweight slacks and a long blue shirt. Checking her appearance carefully one last time, she went down to wait for Megan.

* * * * * * * * * * * *

Seeing Megan walking toward her, Tony flashed a grin, her eyes slowly soaking in the sight with appreciation. She shoved her overzealous libido down, warning herself, *No more mistakes.* "Hi, there."

"Hi." Megan smiled back as she discretely took in the image before her. *She is so beautiful.*

"Are we going to take the train down again?"

"Yeah, I think it's better than driving down there."

They walked toward the station, and all of a sudden Megan found herself tongue-tied. She realized she was nervous and couldn't think of a thing to say.

Tony noticed her nervousness and was not surprised. *Who could blame her? I have to be more careful about showing my feelings around her. Ok, what's a good neutral subject?* "Have you lived in Cleveland long?" Tony knew the answer but wanted to relax her companion.

Megan, finding her voice, smiled in appreciation, "Yes, I was born here and have lived here ever since. I thought about leaving once, but my sister talked me out of it. We're pretty close and I realized I would really miss her. How about you? Where were you born?" Megan inquired.

"Boston." Anticipating the next question, Tony added,

"I left there when I entered the Bureau and have just traveled around to the places they've sent me since then."

"You don't have a Boston accent."

"I know. In my line of work you have to be able to adapt. You can't adapt with a regional accent." Both women relaxed and conversed easily with each other as they rode the train to the Flats.

Arriving there, Megan and Tony began a slow, leisurely walk past the clubs, bars, and diners just taking in the sights around them. Tony noticed that most of the nightclubs were so crowded, people were standing out on the sidewalk in front of them holding drinks and socializing on the streets. This was definitely not her type of place. It was much too crowded.

Megan had been a regular visitor to the Flats when she was engaged to Ray, and, although she hadn't been down at night for quite a while, nothing had changed. After they had walked the entire area, Megan asked, "Do you want to go in some of the places now?"

"Yeah, that would be good. But we'll be lucky to find anyplace to sit," Tony commented.

"Oh, I know some places we can try. That place over there plays jazz and they're usually not too crowded." Megan turned toward the nightclub leading the way.

Tony had been using her senses to assess the area as they had walked and had so far felt absolutely no threat of any kind other than that usually associated with a very busy, drink catering, night life area. Following Megan, she relaxed slightly. She knew the biggest threat in an area like this was probably muggings and drunks.

Entering the nightclub, Tony noticed an empty table near the back of the room. Turning to Megan, she said, "Let's go sit over there."

Megan seeing a closer table near the band stopped and asked, "What's wrong with this table?"

"I can't see everyone from that table," Tony answered succinctly.

"Oh, yeah, right." Megan had been enjoying herself

so much, she had almost forgot the reason they had come in the first place.

Tony ordered a Coke, knowing the night was going to be a long one, and she wanted to be totally alert. Megan had every intention of ordering a drink, but changed her mind when she heard Tony's order, and settled on a Pepsi.

"What do you think so far?" Megan asked, figuring Tony had plenty of time to get a sense of the place.

"Well, it's certainly a thriving area," Tony replied, thinking of all the people out on the sidewalks.

"I used to come down here quite a bit, but this is the first time I've been here in a few years. It's still the same though. I remember, before my sister got married, we'd come down and bar hop. We used to have fun. We were always careful to stay together though, just as a precaution." Megan saw no reason to add that she and Ray had been regulars.

Just then an attractive man approached the table, looking at Tony he asked, "Mind if I join you?"

Tony looked at him, her eyes hooded, and smiled brazenly. "Yeah, I mind. We're having a private conversation," she drawled. Tony almost laughed at the effect she had on him. *Nothing wrong with having a little fun.*

"Yeah, right. Some other time." He backed away blushing, lewd thoughts running rampant through his mind, as he was bombarded by the sexual aura rolling off Tony in waves.

Megan's heart fluttered at the look Tony had flashed the guy. *God is she sexy.* Tony turned back toward Megan, shrugged a shoulder, and said, "I didn't feel like entertaining tonight."

Megan decided to change the subject. This woman was having an unsettling effect on her. They left the club a short time later.

* * * * * * * * * * *

As the evening wore on, it became harder and harder

to move amidst the inebriated, partying sidewalk dwellers. Megan was having trouble staying up with Tony. Her small stature commanded no respect, and she was jostled about mercilessly. Tony, seeing Megan's plight, gently took her arm, pulled her closer, and cleared a path for them. The tall woman enjoyed the feel of the soft skin beneath her hand and grudgingly relinquished her hold once they cleared the more crowded area.

When Megan felt the warm, strong hand pull her close, she became so distracted she would have walked into a light pole if Tony hadn't guided her around it. After that she figured she'd better concentrate on where she was going. When Tony removed her hand, she almost sighed audibly with disappointment.

With the wildly beating tempo of music and people throbbing around them, talking was impossible. Arriving at a part of the Flats where the noise was more bearable, Tony asked Megan, "Do you want to stop in someplace and sit down for a while?"

"That would be great. These crowds are getting a little to boisterous for me," replied Megan as she thought about getting Tony away from the crowds, into a one on one situation. *Yeah, that would be real good.* What good it would do her was another matter, but she figured she'd worry about one thing at a time. She just wanted Tony all to herself.

"Let's go in here." Megan grabbed Tony's arm and pulled her toward the open door. Tony almost grabbed her arm back and then decided, *What the hell?,* and followed behind the smaller woman. *It is Megan's neck of the woods.*

Tony thought they must have stopped in every nightclub and bar along the whole strip. She also thought about her impressions. While she was sure Megan had not exaggerated the crime, it seemed relatively peaceful tonight.

It was late, and Tony unconsciously relaxed. The evening had been enjoyable. Megan was absolutely engaging, and Tony was unaware of being inexorably drawn

toward her. Entering a nightclub, the two women found a
table with a good view and took seats. Tony decided she
was done working for the night and ordered bourbon and
Coke. Megan followed suit and ordered a Screwdriver.

Engaging in the comfortable conversation that had
marked most of the evening, Megan told Tony some of the
humorous aspects of growing up in a house with an attorney for a father, and his unique way of solving disputes
between his children. She purposely avoided mentioning
her personal relationship with her father. Megan found
that she loved talking to Tony and watching the small
smile that would appear on her face from time to time. She
was glad that Tony seemed more relaxed than she had earlier when they were roaming the streets and other clubs.

Tony was totally captivated by the small woman and
the delightful way she had of expressing herself. They
were mostly through their second drink when a tall, blond-
haired man approached their table. Tony silently assessed
him as he approached, but the focus of her attention was on
Megan.

"Hi, Megan. It's been a long time."

Megan looked up surprised to hear the familiar voice.
She hadn't been paying attention to anyone, except Tony,
and hadn't seen him approach. She had always felt bad
about hurting Ray, but they had parted amicably. Smiling
at him, Megan said, "Hi."

Ray pulled out a chair and joined them. Leaning over
and giving Megan a kiss on the cheek, he said, "You're
even more beautiful than I remember."

Megan blushed. "Thanks. Ray, this is Tony. She's an
FBI agent working on the Shadow case. Tony this is Ray,
an old friend of mine."

Ray looked over at Tony and exchanged greetings with
the tall woman. He noted that she was very attractive, but
he felt intimidated, although she was very polite.

Megan had been caught totally off guard by Ray's
appearance and didn't notice the slight narrowing of
Tony's eyes. Pleased to see Megan again, Ray launched

into a discussion of the good old days and their escapades in the Flats, quickly drawing Megan into the discussion with him.

Tony watched the relaxed interaction between the two for about fifteen minutes before an unfamiliar emotion raced through her. Recognizing it, she knew she needed some space, and fast. Standing up, she said, "I'm going to take a look around. I'll be back shortly." She was gone before either could utter a word.

* * * * * * * * * * * *

The tall woman quickly exited the club and, for the first time in years, was totally oblivious to her surroundings. Forcefully trying to gain the upper hand on her rolling emotions, she moved rapidly down the length of the Flats turning into the last alley. She stopped and, finally, put a name to the emotion assaulting her. It was jealousy.

But that makes no sense. There is nothing to be jealous of. Her mind began waging a battle, the force of her will against emotions held in check for way too long. Tony had mastered the practice of deceit and deception, keeping her emotions firmly under control. Now, finally turned loose, they were wrecking havoc in her mind.

Tony felt betrayed. She had always relied on her mind to provide her with a part to play, and it had always complied. What Tony hadn't acknowledged was that her mind had not failed her. There was no part to play.

Unable to fight the onslaught of emotions any longer, a calmness pervaded her. Tony thought of the way Megan smiled, the gentle curve of her lips that lit up her whole face. Her gorgeous green eyes with gold specks that swirled around, vying for dominance when she was angry. The sharp mind that pretty little head contained, and the gentle curves of her body. She pictured Megan's strong shapely legs, and the gentle roll of her walk. She was so fresh and untainted, and so far removed from Tony's world.

The agent sighed, realizing what she was going to have to do. Her mind returned to the afternoon she and Megan had come to the Flats to look at the crime scenes. She remembered the effect Megan had on her, and when she thought she had felt a connection, Tony sadly remembered all too clearly the way Megan had practically run away from her down the alley. She would return to Megan and Ray in the club, and enjoy what was left of the evening. After tonight, she would step out of the other woman's life, just as quickly as she had stepped into it.

Tony's senses registered a sound, and she left her thoughts behind as her body automatically responded by turning towards the noise. An agonizing blow to her back staggered her before she had time to complete the turn. She saw a dark figure rush by and grabbed her gun from the small of her back. Tony raced after the man running down the alley, her only thought being that of pursuit. By the time they neared the end of the alley, Tony had almost caught her target, when a sudden wave of dizziness surged through her. She felt herself stumble and came to a stop fighting to maintain her balance.

Chapter 7

Megan was caught totally off guard by Tony's abrupt departure. After deliberating for about thirty seconds, she decided to follow. "Ray, it's not safe for her to be by herself out there. I'm going to go with her."

"Come on. I'll help you find her. It's bad enough she's walking around alone, you don't need to be, too."

Megan, glad to have help finding Tony, reached the door and looked both ways. Not seeing the agent, she started down the sidewalk. They quickly looked in the door of each nightclub and glanced down every alley. Megan was beginning to worry even though no more than five minutes could have passed. There was only one alley left.

Looking down the alley, Megan saw the tall woman stagger and sway. She tore down the alley, reaching Tony in seconds, gently placing her arms around her, and, with Ray's help, eased her to the ground.

Megan's trained eyes quickly assessed the large amount of blood coming from Tony's back, and she ordered Ray, "Go get some towels from that bar over there and call an ambulance. Hurry!"

Megan knew Tony had passed out when they lowered her to the ground. She grabbed the bottom of Tony's shirt, wadded it up, and placed it over the wound. She simultaneously applied pressure and checked Tony over with her other hand, to make sure there were no other wounds. Megan noted the weak, rapid pulse, the fast, shallow breathing, and the cool, clammy skin. She knew how dangerous shock was, silently prayed for the quick arrival of an ambulance.

After she finished the quick examination and was satisfied that Tony had no other wounds, she noticed the agent's fingers were still curled around a gun. Megan eased it out of Tony's hand and placed it in her purse. She didn't like guns, but it didn't seem right to leave it there, either. Realizing there was nothing more she could do except wait for the ambulance, a feeling of total helplessness washed over her.

Ray returned with the towels to the sound of sirens in the distance. Megan took the towels, folded them in thick squares, and placed them against Tony's wound. Ray watched, unsure what to do.

Minutes later, although it seemed like hours to Megan, the ambulance arrived. The paramedics came running up with the portable gurney. Megan moved out of the way knowing they were much more adept at starting an IV than she would be. She gave them a report on the patient, indicating her findings. Megan followed behind when the paramedics transported Tony to the waiting ambulance.

Megan moved to the back of the ambulance to climb into the vehicle. One of the paramedics told her, "I'm sorry, Miss, you can't ride in back."

Turning to the paramedic, almost withering him with a glare, she stated with barely controlled anger, "I am DOCTOR Donnovan, and this is MY patient, and I am riding WITH HER to the hospital." She glared at him for a moment waiting for his answer, daring him to defy her. Megan wasn't about to leave Tony's side.

"Ok, sorry. I didn't know you were a doctor." The

paramedic helped her into the back of the ambulance and started to close the doors.

Ray, watching the exchange in silence, was amazed. In all the time he had known Megan, he had never seen such a display of anger from her. "Megan, I'll meet you at the hospital."

"Ok, Ray, thanks." Megan turned her attention back to Tony.

* * * * * * * * * * * *

Megan and the paramedic worked together, giving oxygen, while attaching the equipment that would electronically convey her vital signs to the hospital. When they arrived, the trauma team met them at the doors and took charge of the gurney, wheeling it into a trauma room.

Megan entered the waiting room and paced. She knew this was the best trauma center in the city. What she couldn't understand was why Tony had gone out by herself in the first place. *I told her it was dangerous.* Everything had just happened too quickly, she hadn't been gone five minutes. It was almost like someone had targeted the agent. Megan knew that was impossible because Tony was brand new to Cleveland. What would be the point? She didn't like the way it added up though. She had noticed the trail of blood down the length of the alley stopping at Tony. The damn woman had chased her assailant without regard to her injury. Talk about dumb. But Megan's concern far outweighed any anger at Tony for doing something so foolish.

Looking up when Ray entered the room, she said, "Hi, Ray. Thanks for coming."

"It's no problem, Megan. You know that." Ray looked at her blood covered clothes. "Megan you're a mess. Let me see if I can talk someone out of some scrubs for you."

Megan hadn't even noticed. She was too concerned about Tony. Knowing what a good lawyer Ray was, she

didn't doubt he'd convince them to part with a pair.
Returning a few minutes later, he handed the scrubs to her
and showed her where the women's restroom was. When
she came back, he told her they had taken Tony to surgery.

Walking over to the surgery waiting room, Megan told
Ray, "There's no need for you to stay any longer. I know
you're probably getting cases ready for Monday, and it's
already after three. Why don't you go home?"

"You're right. I do have a couple of cases I'm working on.' Be sure and let me know how she is. My phone
number's on my card," he replied, handing it to her before
departing.

Megan was exhausted. She continued to pace around
the small room, wondering if she could have somehow prevented this from happening, but she couldn't think of anything she could have done. There hadn't been time.

"Dr. Donnovan?"

Megan, startled out of her thoughts, asked anxiously,
"Yes, how is she?"

"She's going to be fine. I have to admit I was worried
there for a while. Her crit was only ten going in, and we
almost lost the BP. She is incredibly lucky. Somehow, the
knife missed her stomach, and kidney hitting only her
spleen. The CT scan showed she was eligible for the
non-invasive spleen trauma protocol. She lost of lot of
blood, but she's in great shape and should be out of here in
a couple of days. She's over in recovery. We're waking
her up now. You can go on over there, but she probably
won't remember it tomorrow anyway. So why don't you
just go home and get some rest and come back later on?"

"Thanks, but I think I'd rather see her for a minute."
Even though the surgeon had been very reassuring, she
needed to see Tony for herself, just to make sure.

Megan walked with the surgeon over to the recovery
room. The nurse who was at the bed asked her, "You want
to wake her up?" She nodded, and the nurse left. Megan
looked down at the vulnerable face sleeping so peaceably.
She placed her hand on Tony's cheek briefly, needing to

touch her, to know she was all right. Gently grasping
Tony's hand, she said firmly, "Tony, it's time to wake up."
When she didn't get a response, she said, "Come on, Tony,
wake up. You've had a long enough nap." She felt the
slight movement of the hand she was holding and watched
the eyes slowly flicker open.

Tony could hear someone calling her. She was so
tired, she wanted to ignore the voice and sleep, but she
couldn't. It was such a beautiful voice. Fighting sleep off,
she followed the voice as it led her to awareness. Opening
her eyes, everything was fuzzy, and she tried to focus on
the face talking to her. "Megan?" Tony's voice was no
more than a whisper.

When Tony uttered her name, Megan's heart lurched.
Taking a deep breath to steady herself, she said, "Yeah,
Tony, it's Megan. You with us again?" She smiled at the
prone figure.

Tony's eyes finally focused on the face smiling down
at her, but her mind was having trouble catching up. She
answered by tightening her hand around the one holding
hers.

"What's your name?" Megan knew the recovery room
protocol from her residency days.

The tall woman forced her answer through her dry
throat. "Tony."

"Tony, what's your last name?" Megan persisted,
knowing it was necessary for her to attain a certain level of
awareness.

"Viglioni." Tony fought her tired mind and tried to
stay awake as she listened to Megan's sweet voice talking
to her.

"That's good. That's real good Tony. It's okay to go
back to sleep now." She watched the eyes flutter close.
Remaining at the agent's side for a few more minutes,
Megan gently removed her hand from Tony's, taking one
last look at the beautiful woman before willing herself to
leave.

* * * * * * * * * * *

Megan took a cab to her car at the Marriott and drove home. She was overtired and couldn't sleep. The events of the evening played themselves over and over again in her mind, and her thoughts focused on the events of the past week.

A week that had started normally had turned into a real roller coaster ride. Getting assigned the Shadow case, meeting Tony, lunch, an afternoon in the Flats, and a wonderful evening ending in near tragedy. The fact that Tony almost died, finally hit Megan's exhausted mind, and tears rolled down her cheeks.

She could no longer kid herself. It didn't matter if she was lesbian, gay, queer, or whatever the politically correct phrase was. What mattered was one tall, dark woman who had wandered into her life and stolen her heart in a matter of days. She knew her body had been screaming hints for days as her mind cried out to know more about the woman.

Tears fell anew when she thought about how unfair it was. She had finally met someone who had literally swept her off her feet, and she couldn't do anything about it. She could never let Tony know how she felt, but at least, maybe, she could have her for a friend. That was better than nothing. She could deal with that. The tears continued until sleep claimed her.

* * * * * * * * * * *

Dwayne arrived home smiling. He had heard Megan talking on the phone with the FBI agent and decided he would remove her from the picture. He needed to catch Megan alone, and he couldn't do it if she was escorting an agent around. The fact that they had decided to visit the Flats had been perfect. That was an area he was very familiar with.

Dwayne had been in a quiet rage for two days after he arrived home and found his wife gone. He had checked everyplace he could think of, and she had just literally disappeared. He'd take care of her when he found her, too. In the meantime, he could fully engage himself with the cause of all his problems, including his wife leaving in the first place, Megan, the bitch.

His plan had been perfect. He arrived early and seated himself inside one of the nightclub's that had windows overlooking the sidewalk. He had simply waited for them to go by knowing they would have to because of the layout of the district. When he spotted them, he followed, blending in with the crowds, staying only close enough to keep them in sight. When they entered the last club, he had waited outside. He knew he couldn't take both of them on and had been getting worried. But good fortune had smiled on him when the FBI agent exited alone.

Following her had been so easy, but it's what he had expected. After all, here was another woman trying to do a man's job. She never even heard him until the last second. His only regret was that whatever instinct had caused her to start turning had probably saved her life.

What he couldn't believe was how she had tried to catch him. Didn't she know she'd been stabbed? At least she never saw his face. Feeling quite pleased with himself he went to bed.

Chapter
8

Megan slept fitfully for several hours. Awakening, the events of the past evening swept through her mind, and she quickly got up and showered. On the way to the hospital she stopped at McDonald's to get some coffee and a Danish.

She checked with information to find out Tony's room number. Pleased to see Tony was in a room by herself, Megan pulled a chair over to the bed and sat quietly, just watching the tall woman sleep.

Tony began to rise toward consciousness. The only change was a slight quickening of the heart rate. Megan, who had been watching the monitors, noticed immediately. Returning her gaze to Tony's face, she watched her beautiful blue eyes slowly open. Tony lay quietly, not having any idea where she was.

"Hi, Tony," Megan said softly, smiling at her.

Tony saw Megan sitting next to her and tried to respond, but her mouth was dry, and she was barely able to say, "Hi." Her mind finally grasped she was in a hospital, and suddenly the events of the past evening came flooding over her. She was mortified. How could she have been so stupid? She had been caught unawares. She remembered chasing someone down the alley and then...nothing. She watched Megan fill a cup with water and place a straw in it. The younger woman said, "Come on, I'll hold it while you drink."

"I can hold it myself." Tony began to sit up, quickly slipping back down again when her body refused to cooperate, and let its pain be felt.

Megan watched Tony's face turn white at the effort and simply put her arm behind the agent's head and lifted the straw to her mouth.

"Thanks." Tony felt utterly embarrassed at having to be helped.

Megan sat back down in the chair at the side of the bed. "How do you feel?"

"Ok," Tony lied. Actually she felt like shit. Her back wouldn't quit throbbing, and it didn't help that the one person she would have liked to impress had to see her like this. Oh, she'd been injured before but always against overwhelming odds, and she'd always managed to get to safety herself.

Megan asked, "Do you remember what happened?"

Tony looked over at Megan, and seeing the concerned look on her face realized she was being selfish and thinking only of herself. Fighting to overcome her embarrassment, she answered, "I remember getting hit in the back and chasing some guy down the alley. I don't remember anything after that."

"What happened after that is you passed out," Megan supplied. "You went into shock, so your body started shutting down."

Tony decided to go for broke, and asked, "So, what's the damage?"

Megan answered bluntly, "You were very lucky. Somehow the knife only hit your spleen. Usually in trauma cases, the spleen is automatically removed. But this is a level 1 trauma center, and they've got a new non-invasive spleen trauma protocol, which basically means all your body parts are still intact."

Tony thought about what Megan had just told her and decided things could be a lot worse considering how careless she'd been.

"You up to answering a question?" Tony nodded, so Megan continued, "What on earth were you doing chasing the guy that stabbed you? Didn't you know you were bleeding?"

"It didn't hurt that much."

Megan mulled that over and realized that was probably the truth. Many people had died of ruptured spleens because they didn't go to the hospital until it was too late, but Megan still had to get something off her chest. "You know you did more damage to yourself than the guy with the knife did. The spleen holds about a liter of blood. That wouldn't be so bad because it's mostly recycled, but when you started running your body was trying to refill it with blood as fast as you were losing it. That was really dumb you know."

Tony's eyes narrowed at Megan's words, but her tired mind acknowledged the small woman was right. What Megan said did make sense, but there was no way she was going to tell her she agreed with her. "Ya gotta do what ya gotta do," Tony replied. "Do you know what happened to my gun?"

Wouldn't you know that would be one of the first things she wants to know? "I picked it up. It's at my place."

"Thanks. You look really tired. Why don't you go home?"

"Later," Megan answered, settling more comfortably in the chair.

The day passed slowly with Tony drifting in and out of sleep with Megan right at her side, refusing to leave even when Tony insisted. Sgt. Davies stopped by and Megan intercepted him at the door. After telling him what she knew, Megan advised him he'd have to come back tomorrow if he wanted to talk to Tony.

Later that evening when the nurses got Tony out of

bed, Megan could not believe how stubborn the woman was when she insisted she could walk without any assistance. Obviously that little idea didn't last long. Megan knew it would be the next day before Tony would be able to move around on her own.

Megan's tired body called it quits late Sunday evening. Whispering to the sleeping woman, "I'll be back tomorrow," she left and went home.

* * * * * * * * * * * *

The next morning, Tony felt decidedly more human. Looking around the room, she noticed Megan was gone. She had looked so tired. Tony was glad she finally went home, but at the same time she missed her comfortable presence. Every time she woke up yesterday, Megan had been right there, putting up with her moodiness, and her anger at herself. The small woman had helped her, even when Tony insisted she could do things herself, which of course she couldn't, but refused to admit.

Tony thought about the events leading to her attack. She acknowledged to herself that Megan was having a very unsettling effect on her. Her life seemed to be spinning out of control, and it was not a feeling she liked. Maybe she should call Huey and request a transfer back to his section. She quickly discarded the idea, rationalizing her decision with the thought that she still had a case to solve. *And I am not doing a very good job of it so far. Besides, if I call him, I won't have time for my personal agenda.* Tony knew her decision to step out of Megan's life was a sound one, but why did that logic fill her with such trepidation? Maybe there was another way, but it would require her getting some measure of control back when she was around Megan.

* * * * * * * * * * * *

Megan knew she had to go in to work. It was Monday

and that was always a busy day. She was going to talk to Dr. Whitehouse and request a few days off, though. Tony would need her. The serial killer had been quiet, so it shouldn't be a problem. Once she was ready for work, Megan placed a call to the surgical ward to talk with the nurses. After ascertaining that Tony was doing very well, she asked the nurse to tell her she would be in later, not wanting to wake the agent if she was sleeping.

Arriving at work, she found David waiting for her in her office. "Hey guy, how's it going?"

Returning her warm smile, he answered, "Great." David studied her closely. "Are you okay? You look exhausted." His eyes were clouded with concern.

Megan smiled at her friend. "It's been a long weekend; I'll tell you about it later. How many cases do we have today?"

"Just two, cause of death unknowns," he answered, silently vowing to himself not to leave today until he talked to her. David had never seen her look so worn out.

* * * * * * * * * * *

Tony looked up as Sgt. Davies entered the room. Mentally groaning, she looked at him and growled, "Don't even start," shifting into a persona that warned, don't fuck with me.

Brian watched the change come over the woman glaring at him. It was enough to intimidate the hell out of anyone. He began to feel a grudging respect for Tony. It was obvious she wasn't a quitter. "Don't sweat it. I just stopped by to ask a few questions and see how you're doing. I stopped by yesterday, but it seems the Assistant Coroner has taken a personal interest in your care, and she wouldn't let anyone in."

Brian noticed the surprise that quickly crossed the agent's face before the mask returned. Tony said, "Sorry about that. I didn't know you were here yesterday. I was still pretty out of it."

"How ya feeling?" Brian asked, concern in his voice.

"Just fine. It's no big deal. What do you want to know?"

"Did you see the guy who attacked you?"

"No. It was dark and he approached from the rear. Obviously I didn't hear him soon enough, because when I started to turn he struck. So there's not much to tell. He was dressed in dark clothes, had an athletic build, was probably 5'10" or 11", about 185 pounds, and that probably describes half the male population of Cleveland," she summed up disgustedly.

"Don't be so hard on yourself. Shit happens," Brian stated gruffly, knowing she would resent any sympathy from him. He looked at her pointedly and continued, "Why were ya down there in the first place? I don't think it's a coincidence that you happened to be in the general area that all the murders took place. I thought we were working on this case together."

"We *are* working on it together, but I can't get a feel for the case stuck on the phone talking to crazies all day. Dr. Donnovan offered to show me around down there, and I accepted. It's that simple. If I wanted to undermine your authority, I'd have never come to you in the first place," she retorted.

Brian believed her. "Ok, just checking. If you need anything..."

"Yeah, I do," Tony interrupted and then paused, trying to decided how to phrase her question. "Did the FBI get notified...I mean...since I'm an agent?" she trailed off.

Sensing where she was going, Brian said with empathy, "No, I haven't sent the report over yet. I was waiting to talk to you first." He quickly made a decision and continued, "Sometimes things get lost."

Tony sighed with relief, gave him a full smile, and said, "Thanks, I owe ya."

Grinning at the unexpected smile, he said, "No, you don't. Just get on your feet so we can get this case solved. Brian turned to leaved and paused at the door. "Now get some rest. I'll keep you up to date."

"Later," Tony responded.

****

Megan had finished up her cases and was completing her preliminary reports when David walked in and sat down. Looking up, she smiled and said, "You're gonna call me to task, aren't you?"

"Yep," he said, flashing a warm grin at her.

Megan gathered her thoughts and started, "You remember when I left early to show the FBI Agent assigned to the Shadow case the Flats?" David nodded. "Well, we decided to go back down there Saturday night. Tony wanted to get a feel for the place when it was in full swing." Megan told him exactly what had transpired, leaving out only her feelings for Tony.

David studied Megan carefully as she related the events of the weekend to him. Her face subtly changed every time she mentioned the agent. A puzzled expression crossed her face when she told him about Tony suddenly leaving. An idea began to work its way into David's mind. By the time Megan finished her story, he felt sure there was more to this than met the eye. He decided he would like to meet the agent.

"God, Megan, that really sucks," David commented. "No wonder you look so tired. What can I do to help?"

"I asked Dr. Whitehouse for the next couple of days off. He complained but gave it to me. If you'd just kind of keep an eye on things here and call me if anything unusual happens, it would really help."

"Consider it done," David assured her. "You going back over to the hospital now?"

Megan nonchalantly shrugged her shoulders. "Yeah. I just want to make sure everything's okay."

"You take care of yourself. I mean it." David gave her a stern look.

"I will. Thanks David. I'll see you Thursday."

"Take care."

* * * * * * * * * * * *

Tony had been examined by the surgeon and was told she could leave that afternoon provided she took it easy. He told her unless there were any problems she could return to work on limited duty in a week. She was to call his office and schedule a follow-up appointment. Tony was ecstatic. She hated hospitals.

When Megan arrived, Tony greeted her with a grin. "Hi."

Megan, surprised at the warm greeting, responded, "Hi, yourself," and answered the infectious grin with one of her own.

"I'm out of here today."

"That's great, but of course you're staying at my place. I've got an extra bedroom," Megan replied, waiting for the inevitable explosion.

"Oh, no, I'm not," Tony countered. "I've already inconvenienced you enough. The surgeon told me you saved my life. Don't you think you've done enough? I am perfectly capable of taking care of myself." Softening her tone, she added, "I just really can't impose on you any-more."

At her words, the hazel eyes flashed, and Tony actu-ally had time to think, *Oh shit*, before Megan said, "Are you done?" The calm voice contradicted her body lan-guage.

"Yeah."

Megan continued, "First of all, you are not capable of taking care of yourself, yet. I happen to be a doctor by profession and a pathologist by specialty. I'd say I'm in a much better position than you to determine what care you need right now. Second, how about if *I* am the one who decides when and if someone is inconveniencing me or imposing on me? I really think that should be my decision. Lastly, you have a friend who happens to care what happens to you, so get used to it."

How do you argue that? Tony's mind sped through a variety of responses, discarding each. Megan had logically and calmly picked apart all her possible arguments.

Taking advantage of the agent's silence, Megan asked, "How about giving me the key to your hotel room so I can get you something to wear out of here?"

Tony pointed to the nightstand drawer and said, "The key's in there," capitulating with those words.

* * * * * * * * * * *

"No," Tony growled.

"You have to," Megan stated firmly.

Irritated, Tony said, "No, I don't."

"Fine. Then you can stay here for a few more days, because you aren't leaving any other way. It is hospital policy and, besides, you can't walk that far." An exasperated Megan threw her hands into the air. This had to be the most stubborn woman she had ever met. *What was the big deal? It must be some silly ego thing.* The argument had been going on ever since the nurse brought the offending item into the room. Maybe a different approach would work.

Tony was sitting on the side of the bed glaring at the wheelchair, willing it to disappear. Megan walked over and bent down until she was at eye level with the sitting woman. "Tony, come on. Please? I'm tired. Let's get out of here."

The disarming entreaty from Megan broke through her irritation. Realizing just how much the small woman had done for her, Tony sighed and said, "Ok, let's just get it over with."

* * * * * * * * * * *

After parking the car, Megan moved around to the passenger side to help Tony get out. She knew, regardless of

Tony's declarations otherwise, that the woman was hurting. Offering her arm, she helped Tony ease herself from the car, the agent's pale face and clenched jaw attesting to the difficulty of the maneuver. Silently cursing her body for its weakness, Tony was grateful for Megan's help on the way to the apartment.

Looking around when they entered, Tony felt some of her tension melt away in the warm, appealing decor. The apartment was huge, and the late afternoon sunlight spilled through the windows, adding to the cheery atmosphere. The living room was tastefully done in soft mauve tones offset by overstuffed furniture designed for comfort. Walking down the hall toward the guest bedroom, Megan pointed out the bathroom, and her bedroom. Tony noticed both bedrooms were identically decorated in light blue offset by ivory. The apartment reflected the owner's personality perfectly.

Tony sat on the bed, and Megan said, "Why don't you lay down? I've got to get some things out of the car. I'll be right back." After Megan left the bedroom, Tony gladly complied. The short trip had depleted what little energy she'd had, and, laying back on the bed, she immediately dropped off into the healing sleep her body needed.

When Megan had gone to Tony's hotel room, she had chosen a lightweight set of sweats for her to wear home from the hospital. She had also picked up some extra clothes and personal items she felt Tony might want. Fetching them now, she hurried back up to the apartment wanting to make sure her guest was comfortable.

Quickly returning to the guest bedroom, Megan realized Tony had already fallen asleep. Standing in the doorway gazing at Tony, Megan felt an almost overwhelming urge for some kind of contact, but afraid she might wake the tall woman up, she just quietly entered the room and placed Tony's things on the dresser before departing. After changing into a T-shirt and shorts, Megan picked up her book before collapsing into the recliner and tilting it back. She began reading and promptly fell into an exhausted sleep.

* * * * * * * * * * *

Tony woke up in a strange room softly lit by moon-light. Disoriented for a moment, she glanced around and remembered where she was. Easing up into a sitting position, she noticed the pain in her back had receded some. Tony turned on a small lamp next to the bed and saw some of her things on the dresser. She slowly stood up and walked over to inspect the items. The agent shook her head as she examined her things on the dresser. She couldn't believe Megan had even taken the time to include some of her CDs and her book. Tony was perplexed by the actions of the compassionate, caring woman. *I've spent so much time fighting for control of my emotions around her, all I've done is give her a hard time the last couple of days, and yet she bends over backwards to do things for me. I really don't deserve this.* Tony vowed to be more considerate to the beautiful woman and went looking for something to drink.

The rest of the apartment was dark except for where light filtered in from the street. Tony walked through the moonlit apartment to the kitchen and turned on the light. Perusing the contents of the refrigerator, she selected a bottle of cranberry juice, before closing the door and looking for a glass. Locating one in a cupboard, she replaced the cranberry juice after filling the glass and turned off the light. She quietly made her way through the apartment to the living room. Tony wanted to sit up for a while and figured that was a good place to do so.

The agent was slightly startled by the sleeping form in the chair. Setting her glass on the end table, she walked over to the recliner. Looking down at Megan, Tony realized the toll the last few days had taken on her. Knowing she'd be more comfortable in her bed, she softly called Megan's name not wanting to frighten her. When she didn't get any reaction, Tony called the small woman's name a little louder. Megan just shifted her body in the chair. She placed her hand on Megan's shoulder and shook it very gently. "Megan, wake up. You need to go to bed."

Megan's eyes came open and, recognizing Tony, she said, "What's wrong? I'm sorry. I fell asleep. What do you need?"

"Stop, already. I don't need anything. It seems you've already taken care of everything. I just saw you sleeping here and thought you'd be a lot more comfortable in your bed," Tony explained, reluctantly moving her hand from Megan's shoulder.

"Thanks, but what are you doing up? You should be in bed. You're supposed to be taking it easy."

"I am taking it easy, but I can't stay in bed 24 hours a day. I'm going to sit up for a bit." Seeing Megan's worried expression, Tony added, "For just a little while. Now, why don't you go to bed?"

Megan realized Tony was right. She was still tired, and her bed sounded really good right about now. "Ok, see you tomorrow."

"G'night."

Tony sat quietly for a while thinking, *I'm in serious trouble here,* and wondering what in the hell she was going to do about it. True to her word, she went to bed a short time later.

* * * * * * * * * * * *

The man walked confidently down the street toward the designated meeting place. He didn't expect to encounter any trouble but was carrying a piece just in case. The man eased around the corner of a darkened warehouse building and stepped into a doorway to wait. He always arrived at least thirty minutes early to check out the area. The precaution probably wasn't necessary, but it was better not to take chances. After all, those who made mistakes paid, and he didn't intend to pay any time soon. That was why he wore his disguise, even to these meetings. No one would ever be able to identify him, not even a low-life drug dealer.

A short time later, he saw his contact make his way across the parking lot in front of the warehouse. Once the drug dealer had passed the doorway he was hidden in, the man stepped out behind him and said, "You got it?"

"Fuck you!" The dealer whirled around angrily.

"No, I don't think so." The man sneered. "Now do you have the stuff?"

The dealer glared and held out his hand. "The money." After counting it, he pulled five small vials out of his pocket. Once the exchange was made, the dealer departed first. The man waited for twenty minutes and then made his way back to his car.

Chapter
9

"Morning." Megan smiled at the tall woman entering the kitchen, thinking, *She is so beautiful.* "How ya feeling?"

"Kinda sore." Tony surprised herself with the honest answer. "But could be worse." She placed her hand on the back of one of the kitchen chairs.

"Did you take your pills?" Megan knew the threat of sepsis was very high in spleen injury cases, and Tony was on heavy doses of antibiotics and a painkiller.

"No, I was going to get some juice first."

"What would you like for breakfast? Let's see, there's eggs, cereal, bagels, English muffins, bananas..."

"Wait," Tony interrupted Megan, quirking a small grin. "How about just the cranberry juice? I'm really not hungry."

"You have to eat something. You're not supposed to take those pills on an empty stomach. How about just eating a bagel?" Megan urged.

"Ok, but I'd like to take a shower first."

"The towels and washcloths are in the hall cupboard next to the bathroom, but you're gonna have to settle for a bath and watch how much water you put in the tub. You can't get the adhesive wet and, when you're done, I want to take a look at your back," Megan said, expecting some sort of argument.

Tony was silent for a minute, waging an internal battle against being told what to do. Remembering the promise she'd made the night before, she simply said, "Ok," to a surprised Megan.

Taking her bath she found out just how much the wound in her back impeded her range of motion and exited the tub in considerable pain. Donning a loose nightshirt, she wanted only to lie down until the pain let up.

Megan heard Tony leave the bathroom and walk down the hallway towards the guestroom. She picked up the bagel and juice and followed. She saw Tony had already laid down. "I brought you some breakfast. Come on, sit up."

"I will. In a little while. I just need to lay down right now." Tony squinted her eyes against the pain.

"What you need is something for the pain, so you've got to eat something. Now come on, sit up." Megan put the bagel and juice down to help Tony if she needed it.

Tony complied, and after Megan saw the pain reflected in her face, she handed Tony the juice and told her she'd be right back.

Grabbing a banana from the fruit bowl in the kitchen, Megan went back to the bedroom and handed it to Tony. "Have this instead." She knew the agent would never get a bagel down.

When Tony finished eating the banana, she looked at Megan and said, "Thanks." She washed the pills down with the juice and laid back down.

Megan sat on the bed next to Tony. "I'm going to check your wound before you fall asleep, okay?" Tony agreed, and she raised the nightshirt to check the wound and was pleased to see that it was healing nicely.

Observing the tightly clenched muscles in Tony's back, she said, "You gotta relax." Megan started kneading the older woman's knotted muscles working her way from the shoulders down, and then from one side to the other in a soothing, relaxing rhythm, while staying well away from the wound.

Tony relaxed under the soothing onslaught and soon fell asleep. Megan pulled her shirt down and gently brushed the hair out of Tony's face with her hand. She then bent over and lightly brushed her lips across the sleeping woman's forehead before leaving the bedroom. Megan knew it would be a few hours before Tony woke, because the painkiller was also a light sedative.

Megan removed a pot roast from the refrigerator, put it in her crock pot, added carrots, and set the control knob to low. The apartment had been neglected, and she went from room to room picking up and dusting. Her thoughts were occupied with ways to convince Tony to give up the hotel room and stay with her until she could find a place of her own.

When Tony woke up, she noted the pain had receded to a dull discomfort. She laid on the bed thinking of the back rub Megan had given her. The pain had taken a back seat to the soothing, soft, small hands. Tony imagined how those hands might feel on other parts of her anatomy. *Oh yeah, you're definitely feeling better. Now get your mind out of the gutter, she was just being nice.* Reluctantly leaving the thoughts behind, the agent got up.

"How ya feeling?" Megan asked, watching Tony closely as the tall woman entered the living room.

"Better than I did. What are you doing?" she asked Megan, who was sitting at her computer desk.

"Just surfing the Internet. I like to do that sometimes. Helps me relax."

Tony walked over and gingerly sat down on the couch, trying to decide how to start. "Um, Megan." She paused, gathering her thoughts. "I just wanted you to know I really appreciate everything you've done for me. I never thanked you for saving my life. Thank you."

Megan walked over and sat down next to Tony.

"You're welcome. I'm just glad I was there. But you know, I was wondering about something that night. Why did you leave and take off by yourself?"

Tony considered the question and tried to decide what to say that wasn't an absolute lie. For some reason the idea of lying to Megan really bothered her, but she obviously couldn't tell her the truth either. "I thought you might like some time alone with Ray," she replied, then added honestly, "It seemed like you were pretty good friends...I just kind of felt like a third wheel."

"Oh, Tony, I'm sorry. I didn't mean to leave you out..."

"No, it's ok," Tony interrupted and then asked a question she wasn't sure she wanted to know the answer to. "Is he your boyfriend?"

"He used to be. We were engaged, twice. Once when I was twenty-one and, then again, when I was twenty-four. I broke off the engagement both times. I knew Ray wasn't right for me. That's the first time I've seen him in over two years. He's really a nice guy. He helped me find you and then came to the hospital to see how you were doing."

Tony breathed an inward sigh of relief, but wasn't willing to follow the line of thought any further. She knew, as lovely as Megan was, she was probably seeing someone, and Tony just didn't want to know if she was.

"What about you, are you seeing anyone?" Megan asked casually.

"No. I move around a lot so..." she trailed off. Tony had just realized it was midday and Megan was still home. "Didn't you have to work today?"

"No. I took a couple of days off. I figured you might need some help getting around."

Tony was stunned. *She took time off to take care of me. What did I do to deserve this?* "Megan, you shouldn't have..."

"Stop. I did what I wanted to." Megan quickly changed the subject. "Now how about some lunch? You need to eat."

After lunch, they returned to the living room. Megan insisted Tony use the recliner because it would be easier on her back than sitting on the couch. Flipping aimlessly through the channels with the remote, she asked, "What do you like to watch?"

"Anything action...sci-fi, cops...stuff like that."

"How about Unsolved Mysteries? There's not much on right now."

"Ok," Tony agreed, relaxing in the recliner.

Megan turned on the program and then glanced over at Tony. "I want to talk to you about something."

Tony looked at Megan and thought, *Uh oh, this sounds serious.*

"It seems like a real waste of money for you to keep that hotel room while you're staying here." When Tony started to interrupt, she said, "Wait, let me finish. Why don't you let me go and get your stuff, and then you could just stay here until you find a place?" she finished in a rush.

Tony hadn't thought about the hotel room. The money wasn't a problem. She had invested very wisely during her years undercover having no real use for her salary since the government paid for everything on covert operations. Actually, she could retire and live quite comfortably on her earnings. But it was really nice here. Could she handle being around Megan for more than a day or two? Or maybe the question should be, could she handle not being around her? Tony sighed inwardly at the dilemma she was in. The situation was obviously hopeless, but the idea of staying here a little longer was really appealing...

Megan studied Tony intently, willing her to say yes. But as the silence lengthened, she prepared to be disappointed, knowing it would be too good to be true.

"Only if I can pay for half of everything while I'm here," Tony responded, adding, "and I go with you to get my things. You shouldn't have to do that."

Tony watched the warm, full smile light up Megan's face and felt an answering one cover her face. *I think I finally did something right.*

* * * * * * * * * * * *

Megan and Tony spent the next couple of hours conversing easily, each opening up to the other slowly, a bud-
ding trust beginning to develop. Megan talked about her
parents, her sisters and brother, and about how it was
growing up in a home that had very high expectations of
each child. She touched on her relationship with her father
vaguely, telling Tony how Ashley had always tried to inter-
vene on her behalf, and how close she was to her sister.

Tony was surprised at how easy it was to talk to
Megan. She shared some of her happy childhood stories,
talking about her brothers, and how they all were in trouble more often than not, admitting she was often the insti-
gator. Realizing she was talking about her brothers, Tony
was shocked into silence.

Then other memories began coursing through her
mind. *Tony was seventeen, had just graduated, and was
waiting to start college along with her brother, George.
They had started and finished school in the same grade.
There was only nine and a half months between them and,
due to the way his birthday fell, he started school a year
late. Both had won partial scholarships and were working
summer jobs. This weekend was a welcome reprieve from
work for both the teenagers. Joey was the youngest at six-
teen and would enter the eleventh grade that fall.*

*They had been anticipating this weekend for a month.
Vinnie had offered the use of his uncle's cabin up in the
mountains of Massachusetts. Their group consisted of
five. Tony, George, Joey, Vinnie, and Sharon. Vinnie and
Sharon were the same age as Tony. The five had often
spent the weekends camping out; their love of the outdoors
unequaled by any of their classmates.*

*Normally they just went to a wooded resort in the foot-
hills. Sharon's family owned one of the lots, so they had a
trailer to crash in. But the idea of exploring the mountains*

excited all of them. They decided to track each other through the woods. Each of the others, except Tony, had had their turn and, as was the norm, she quickly located each of them. Tony decided to have some fun when it was her turn and had led them on a merry chase. They were at least five miles from the cabin.

* * * * * * * * * * *

Tony forcefully thrust the memory of that painful day away, concentrating so hard, her face was tight with the visible effort.

Megan was at her side in an instant. "Tony, are you ok? What's wrong?"

Tony shrugged it off. "Nothing. I was just thinking." She turned her attention to TV and fell asleep.

* * * * * * * * * * *

While the agent was asleep, Megan decided to pick up Tony's things. *Getting in and out of the car was still too hard for her, and besides she shouldn't be carrying things anyway. Best to do it now and avoid having to argue the point.* She had already learned just how stubborn Tony could be. She needed to stop at the store anyway. Before departing, she left Tony a note saying she'd be back in a couple of hours.

Megan had rushed her errands, wanting to get back before Tony woke up, so she could move her things into the apartment unobtrusively. Accomplishing that, she finished preparing dinner. When Tony walked into the kitchen, Megan smiled and teased, "Oh, Sleeping Beauty's finally up." She watched the blush that crept up Tony's face and chuckled. "What's the matter, I embarrass you?" Megan decided Tony was really cute when she blushed.

"No," Tony said automatically. "What're you making?"

"Pot roast and vegetables. I just have to do the salad.

and it'll be done."

"I'll make the salad. Why don't you relax for a while?"

Megan started to object, but seeing the look the tall woman was giving her, decided not to.

Tony smiled to herself. *Salads I can do. Not much else. though.* Cooking had never really interested her. She just usually ate out.

"This is really good," Tony complimented Megan. "It's really nice to have a home cooked meal for a change."

Megan felt her cheeks redden at the praise. "Thanks."

When Tony saw Megan blush, she decided it was payback time and winked at her. "I didn't embarrass you did I?" she teased. "Turnabout's fair play you know."

Looking at the mirth-filled blue eyes, Megan smiled. *God. she's in a good mood. It's hard to believe that this is the same woman I met last week.* Taking advantage of her companion's good humor, Megan nonchalantly said, "I picked up your stuff and put it in the bedroom. Most of it's in the closet. If you can't find something, let me know."

"I thought we agreed that I would go with you. My stuff is not your responsibility," Tony stated pointedly.

"You were asleep, and I had to go out anyway so it was no problem. You would have only aggravated your back, and I didn't want you to have to go through any more pain than you already have. I'm sorry, but that's the way I feel about it," Megan finished, figuring Tony would be mad at her but knowing she would do the same thing again if she needed to.

Tony sat silently for a minute. So far, she was batting zero. She just couldn't win these arguments with Megan. *How are you supposed to be angry with someone for caring about you?* She said the only thing she could. "Thanks."

Tony spent the rest of the evening in the recliner, wanting to be near Megan, dozing on and off from the effects of the painkillers and her body's effort to repair itself. When she was awake, the two women passed the time conversing companionably, watching TV, and just generally enjoying their newfound friendship.

* * * * * * * * * * * *

The next morning Tony was up early and decided there no way she was going to bathe before she ate breakfast and took a painkiller. *No more repeats of yesterday. Well, the back rub was pretty good. Yeah, you're definitely on the mend.* Shaking her head at her incorrigible mind, she went to the kitchen only to see Megan standing there in a short lightweight nightshirt. *Oh God...*Tony was helpless to stop her eyes from raking the length of Megan's body and was only just able to divert them before Megan turned around.

"Mornin'," Megan said smiling.

Tony managed to return the greeting and then decided maybe she better take a bath first after all.

Megan had only gone to the kitchen to make coffee and hadn't been expecting Tony up so early. "Whatcha want for breakfast?" She noticed Tony seemed a little quiet.

You, mentally slapping herself in the head, Tony said, "I think I'll take a bath first."

"If I remember right, that wasn't such a good idea yesterday," Megan countered.

"Um...well...my back's a little better today," replied Tony, turning to make her escape. Megan was having none of that, remembering only too well the pain Tony had been in yesterday. She went over and gently grasped Tony's arm, leading her toward the chair. "Come on. It'll only take a couple of minutes. I'll make eggs. How do you like em'?"

Tony allowed herself to be led to the chair, fighting to control her lascivious thoughts. The small hand that warmed her arm, along with Megan's proximity made this a very difficult feat. *Whoa...take it easy...you can do this. Oh, but this is agony.*

While they were eating, Tony, who had managed to tame her libido for the time being, asked, "What we gonna do today?"

Megan started laughing. "Oh, you are feeling better." She knew Tony needed to take it easy whether she
realized it or not, and she said, "We can do anything you
want as long as it can be done from your bed or the
recliner."

Unbidden images brought on by the innocent comment
cascaded through Tony's mind, and she choked on her toast
and started coughing. Megan was at her side in an instant,
thunking her expertly on the back. "Are you ok?"

Once Tony got her coughing under control, she muttered, "Yeah," and popped one of the pain pills while
silently cursing her back. She said, "I'm gonna lay down,"
her actions belying her words.

Megan followed her into the bedroom and said, "Let
me take a look at your back. You were coughing pretty
hard. I need to make sure you didn't pull anything loose."

Tony laid down grumbling, "Damn back anyway. All I
did was cough, I can't believe this shit."

Megan listened as she raised her shirt and carefully
checked for any damage to the wound. Satisfied there
wasn't any, she massaged Tony's muscles with sure,
smooth movements. "You know, Tony, the muscles in your
back were severed. Even though they have been repaired,
it's going to take a while for them to heal. When you do
something that involves those muscles, it's gonna hurt,"
she said, expertly avoiding any area that might cause discomfort.

Tony forgot about complaining and enjoyed the soothing feel of the back rub. "Thanks, that feels really good."

"It's supposed to. Now just relax." Megan was thoroughly enjoying her task. She loved the feel of Tony's
muscles responding to the gentle kneading. Her skin was
so soft. Marveling at the strong, broad back, Megan continued her massage after Tony fell asleep. Reluctantly
moving off the bed, she repeated her actions of the day
before, brushing Tony's hair out of her face and kissing her
forehead. She knew it was probably the last time she'd get

the opportunity.

* * * * * * * * * * *

The rest of the day passed uneventfully with Megan ensuring Tony rested, and both women enjoying each other's company. Megan opened up about her relationship with her father, leaving out only the darker memories. She acknowledged that her relationship with him had deteriorated from her early teen years, and that no matter how hard she tried, she had never been able to please him. She told Tony how he had always belittled her interests, only encouraging her when it came to school.

Tony heard the hurt in Megan's voice as she discussed her father and instantly disliked him. She listened silently, knowing it was something Megan needed to talk about. Tony decided that anyone who would hurt Megan, especially her own father, should be shot.

"Dad was pretty upset at me for breaking the engagement to Ray. He's a lawyer and since Ray was going to law school when we met, in his mind it was a perfect match," Megan continued, feeling very comfortable with Tony. "But, I always figured when the right person came along I would know, and I didn't feel that way about Ray." *But I do about you.* "What about you? Don't you think you'll know when you meet the right person?"

"Uh, yeah." Tony had not been expecting the question and was caught off guard. Her mind warned her, *Don't go there.*

Megan noticed Tony's discomfort and thought, *Guess that was a little too personal.* Changing the subject, she asked, "What was your father like?"

"I don't know. Mom divorced him when I was three, and I never saw him again." Tony decided to elaborate. "I asked my mother one time who the tall guy with the mustache was that I remembered coming up the sidewalk carrying a little, black rocker." Tony grinned and looked over at Megan. "We had this small child-sized rocker. Anyway,

Mom was really surprised. She couldn't believe I remembered that. Turned out it was my father. That's the only memory I have of him."

"You mean he never came and saw you and your brothers?"

"No."

"Were you ever curious? I mean haven't you ever wanted to find him, just to see what he's like?"

"Nope. Didn't seem much point to it."

"What about your mom? What's she like?"

Tony remembered the last time she had seen her mother. The pain-filled, grief stricken face had looked at her through tear-filled eyes at the funeral. That picture was permanently burned into the recesses of her mind. Shutting her eyes forcefully, trying to stop the memories, Tony clenched her jaw and said, "Can we talk later? I'm really tired. I'm gonna lay down for awhile."

"Sure," Megan said, not fooled at all by Tony's evasion. *Mom is off limits...Mm.*

The day passed quickly, and Megan realized for only the second time in her short career, she was not looking forward to going to work. The first time had been Monday. Tony refused to do anything but enjoy Megan's company. She was sticking firmly to a 'one day at a time' adage.

Chapter
10

David was glad to see Megan when she arrived and quickly brought her up to date on events in the Coroner's office. He told her about the cases that had come in and who had been assigned what. He related that overall it had been pretty quiet.

"You look a lot better," David began, shifting conversation away from the office.

"Yeah, I feel better, too," Megan said. "I was pretty wrung out Monday."

"How's Tony?"

"Oh, she's doing really good. She's a really interesting person. It's kind of hard sometimes to get her to listen to reason, though. She can be really stubborn. But I'm just glad I met her." Megan stated the last comment with more feeling than she realized.

"Sounds like you two have become pretty good friends. I'd really like to meet her sometime."

"How about you guys come over for dinner tomorrow night?" Megan really wanted David to meet Tony. She knew he'd like her, too.

David mused aloud, "Is she staying with you?"

"Oh, yeah. I forgot you didn't know. Just until she finds her own place," which Megan hoped was never.

David thought, *Well, now that's interesting. Megan does seem happy though. Yes, I definitely want to meet this woman who seems to be making such an impact on my friend.* "Ok, what time?"

"How about seven?"

"We'll be there," David answered with a smile.

* * * * * * * * * * * *

Tony was bored and realized just how quickly she had fallen into a routine, and that routine included Megan. With sudden insight, she thought, *I miss her.* She quickly dismissed the notion as ludicrous.

Her back was still bothering her, but if she was careful about how she did things, it wasn't too bad. She flipped through the TV channels finding nothing that interested her. Megan's collection of videos caught her eye, and she walked over to the video case and looked through them. Tony smiled. Megan had everything from *Gone With the Wind* to *Homeward Bound*. *Talk about a diverse collection.* Still restless, Tony decided she didn't feel like watching a movie and decided to see what she could get into on the computer. *Why not?* She noticed a couple of game disks and picked them up. *Lets see. We've got* Pitfall, *nah, too easy. Oh, good ole* Tomb Raider – *that'll work.*

Placing the disk in the CD Rom, Tony quickly advanced through the different levels when the phone rang. "Hello."

"Hi, what ya doing?" Megan asked.

Without thinking, Tony responded, "Waiting for you to get home," surprising herself with the honest comment.

Megan paused, and then figured Tony just must be pretty bored, so she said, "I'll be there in a couple of hours. Did you eat lunch?"

Adroitly side stepping the question and knowing

Megan liked Chinese, Tony asked, "How about you stop and pick up Chinese on the way home. I'm buying."

Megan glanced over at the fax machine when she heard it come to life. "Sounds good to me. Gotta go. See ya later."

"Bye." Tony's mood perceptibly brightened with the phone call.

* * * * * * * * * * * *

When Megan got home, and they sat down to eat, Tony asked, "How was work?"

"Ok. It was fairly quiet. I only had one case, so I got a lot of paperwork caught up. Did you take it easy?"

"Yeah. I played *Tomb Raider* for a while, but you know, I could never understand why they have whosit killing animals. Seems to me she should be killing the bad guys," Tony quipped with a grin.

"Tony, I'm sure," Megan replied rolling her eyes.

"Well, what did the animals ever do to anyone? At least bad guys deserve it."

"You're hopeless," Megan bantered back.

"Ok, maybe androids," Tony amended, "or evil sci-fi monsters."

Megan just shook her head, smiling at Tony's teasing. "What would you think about company for dinner tomorrow night?"

"It's your place. I can make myself scarce."

"I'd like you to be there, Tony. David wants to meet you. I told him about you, and he's a very good friend of mine."

Feigning nonchalance, Tony asked, "Is he your boyfriend?"

"God, no," said Megan chuckling. "He's coming over with his partner, Mike. They're gay."

An almost imperceptible expression flickered across Tony's face. Megan asked, "You don't have a problem with that do you? I mean...well...I could tell them no. But they're really nice. They're no different than anyone else." She anxiously awaited Tony's answer, hoping she wasn't homophobic.

It was everything Tony could do to keep from choking on her food for the second time in as many days. *Problem with that? Oh, yeah, right. Damn, woman, if you only knew. Swallow now before you choke, dummy. Now say something.* "I'd love to meet them." Tony's mind continued to torment her with the irony of the situation.

* * * * * * * * * * *

Megan was performing her work functions on automatic pilot. Although she would never allow her work to suffer, she found her thoughts frequently on Tony. Not wanting to interfere with the agent's rest, she limited herself to one phone call, looking forward to it as a junkie looks forward to a fix. She worried about the day Tony would start looking for an apartment. She couldn't bear the thought of going home to an empty apartment without Tony. Her mind warned her, *Don't go there. Just take one day at a time.*

David noticed how distracted his friend was and wished she'd come and talk to him. He'd always be there for her, and he knew she knew it. But until she came to him, there was nothing he could do. Even though he had a few suspicions, he wasn't sure. He figured he'd find out if he were right at dinner that night.

* * * * * * * * * * *

Tony was disgusted with her limitations. Even though her back felt better each day, she tired easily and still spent a lot of time sleeping. She had quit taking the pain pills deciding they were no longer necessary and all they did was make her sleep. The ensuing result was that she had more time on her hands.

Tony wasn't used to free time. She willed the phone to

ring, hoping Megan would call. It was the one highpoint of her day. Tony had decided back in the hospital to take things one day at a time, knowing it was senseless to worry about things she couldn't control. She was willing to enjoy being around Megan in anyway she could. It was much better than the alternative, which the agent wouldn't even think about.

The last two mornings, she'd gotten up before Megan, made coffee, and waited for her to appear. Tony relished their time together before the small woman went to work, knowing how long the day would be until she got home. Tony knew if she called Brian one more time to find out if they'd made any progress on the case, he would probably hang up on her.

* * * * * * * * * * *

Megan had prepared dinner the night before, so all she had to do was put it in the oven when she got home. Chatting with Tony the time passed quickly, and David and Mike arrived right on time.

Megan made introductions, and shortly thereafter they sat down to eat. David lost no time in starting the conversation rolling. He had a very charismatic personality and was naturally inquisitive. He immediately focused on Tony and said, "Megan says you're new to Cleveland. Where did you move here from?"

"I was assigned to Washington, D.C.," Tony replied, giving her base of operations.

"What's it like? I've never been there," David asked, a mutual assessment playing out between himself and the tall agent.

"It's actually quite an interesting place. I call DC cement city. It seems like you've got to drive twenty miles in any given direction before you saw anything green. It has some great attractions. Besides all the monuments, there are the Smithsonian Museums. Those are a lot of fun to go through. On the down side, everyone is so tied up in their careers or politics they don't have time for anything else except the nightlife. That's pretty wild. The city itself is very expensive to live in and parts of it have a very high crime rate. Most of the people in the know choose to live in Maryland or Northern Virginia."

Megan was amazed. She had never heard such a long oration from Tony. Megan realized she hadn't even begun to scratch the surface of this eclectic woman.

David turned out to be quite the conversationalist, and all four found themselves enjoying the evening. Tony decided she liked the two men, particularly David. She could tell by his easy bantering with Megan that they were actually quite close.

David had watched the interaction between Tony and Megan all evening. He watched the surreptitious glances each lavished on the other, always taking care to make sure the other didn't notice. They were both so discreet that David realized, had he not been specifically looking for it, he might not have noticed. The one thing neither one could hide was the spark that seemed to flow between them whenever they addressed each other. David decided he'd seen enough, but the question was, what to do about it, if anything?

After David and Mike left, Megan asked, "What did you think of them?" She had already determined by the easy interaction between Tony and David that the tall woman didn't have a problem with his lifestyle.

"They're nice. Mike's a little quiet, but David certainly makes up for it. He's quite a charmer." She smiled at Megan, instinctively knowing her answer was important to her.

* * * * * * * * * * *

When Tony woke up the next morning, her first thought was, *Megan's off today.* which immediately catapulted her into an extraordinarily good mood. She got up and headed for the kitchen to start the coffee. Once she had turned it on, Tony took a bath and got dressed. Today she planned to escape the apartment.

When she went back into the kitchen, she found Megan reading the paper. "Mornin'," she said with a grin.

Megan looked up at the smiling woman, greeted her in kind, and thought, *I could get used to this.*

"Wanna go out to breakfast?"

Tony's good mood was contagious, and Megan was quickly caught up in it, but not wanting to take any chances, she asked, "Are you sure you're up to it?"

"Yep. Besides, I really think I should get my car before they tow it."

"Oh, I forgot..." Megan frowned.

"It's not your responsibility. Anyway, you've always driven, so why would you think about my car?"

Megan smiled. "I guess you're right."

"Course I'm right." Tony smirked. "So, where's a good place to eat?"

"The Diner, unless you want something more like Perkins or Bob Evans."

Tony didn't really care where they went as long as they went somewhere. "The Diner sounds fine."

"Ok, I'll be ready in a few." Megan left the kitchen to go shower and get dressed.

They enjoyed a leisurely breakfast, which Tony insisted on paying. "Let me do something for you for a change." Megan couldn't stop the thought from running through her head, *You already have.*

After picking up Tony's car, they returned to the apartment complex to drop it off. Tony climbed into Megan's car, and they left for a tour of the Cleveland suburbs.

* * * * * * * * * * *

The nightmares had been occurring every night. Someone had to pay. It was time. Tonight. He had already picked three likely candidates. Now it just depended on who accepted first.

He dialed a number and hung up when the answering machine came on. The second call ended the same way. Dialing the third number, he heard a very welcome, "Hello."

Putting on the charm, he invited her out for the evening, feeling his heart rate quicken when she accepted. He made arrangements to pick her up at nine, their destination the Flats. His disguise was ready, and the only thing he had left to do was park his second car down in the Flats. He and his date would travel to the Flats on public transportation. He smiled at the power he held over her. He alone knew she was going to meet her destiny.

* * * * * * * * * * *

"That's not fair," Megan complained.

"What's not fair about it? Just cuz I got it right..."

"You get all those right..."

"So. You get all the science and entertainment right," Tony quipped.

"Well, I know some sports, too, but I get all the hard ones," Megan griped, affecting a pout.

Tony tried to look contrite but was unable to keep her smile hidden. "Oh, poor baby." They both erupted into laughter. The two women had been playing Trivial Pursuit and had found themselves very evenly matched.

Megan, tiring of the game, said, "The X-Files is on at seven. Wanna watch it?"

"What? You don't want to play anymore?" Tony asked innocently. Megan glared at her. "Okay, okay, the X-Files is good."

Tony and Megan had grown quite comfortable around each other. Each had found ways to be near the other, without being too obvious. Tony no longer used the recliner, preferring to sit on the couch near Megan. With her height advantage, she could watch the smaller woman without being observed. She had committed everything about Megan to memory, from every curve to every nuance of expression.

Megan, who had always used her hands expressively, found herself touching Tony more and more frequently to make a point. She figured Tony didn't even notice because she never said anything. Both women wanted more, but neither was willing to take the risk it entailed, and so the charade continued.

****

He spent the evening totally charming his date with witticisms and embracing her in a false shroud of safety. Around midnight, he suggested they cross the river to the other side of the Flats. They left the club and took a slow, leisurely walk toward one of the water taxi landings. He led his date down one of the alleys, casually strolling around the first curve and entering the second. He stopped, pulled her close as if to kiss her, and sprayed her in the face with a small bottle in his hand, taking care to divert his face first.

She pulled back in anger, before her body went limp. He held the small woman up in a lover's embrace, watching the panic in her eyes as her body's muscles shut down. Just before she suffocated, from lungs that no longer worked, he placed his hands around her neck, finishing the macabre death rite. Releasing her, he quickly strode to his car and departed the area. He parked the car in his garage and took off his disguise, leaving it on the front seat. He got in his other car, turned on the police scanner, and began driving around.

Tony was awakened by the ringing of the phone and got up to answer it, but Megan had already picked it up. "Hello."

"Brian here. We got another one. South pier of the Flats again."

"Shit," muttered Megan.

"I hear ya. See ya down there."

"Ok."

Tony raised an eyebrow when Megan uttered the mild expletive. "What?"

"I gotta go. He killed another one."

Megan stood up and began to make her way past Tony before a hand stopped her on her arm. "Wait for me. I'm coming, too."

"Oh, no, you're not," Megan said and knew an argument was brewing when she saw Tony's eyes narrow.

"Megan, listen to me. I'm going back to work in a couple of days. There's no reason for me not to go with you to the crime scene. It's my case, too. I feel fine," Tony patiently explained, holding a rein on her temper.

Megan knew the agent had been an extremely cooperative patient. For the most part, Tony had listened to her advice, even though Megan knew there were times when she walked a very thin line between anger and compliance. It was time for a compromise.

"You are going back to light duty. That means sitting at a desk, not walking a crime scene." Megan paused to make her point before continuing, "But I guess it'd be okay if you promise we'll leave when I want."

Pleased to avoid what would have been a major disagreement, Tony said, "Sure."

Chapter
11

Tony and Megan approached the scene, the disjointed flashing of blue and red lights pierced the darkness, lighting their way. A patrolman guarding the crime scene stood in front of the yellow ribbon blocking off the entrance to the scene of the crime. Both women flashed their respective badges and gained entry.

Megan walked over to the body and asked the closest officer, "Has the crime scene been secured?"

"Yes, the body hasn't been moved. This is exactly how we found it," came the response.

Megan knelt down next to the body, pulling her bag close. She checked for a pulse, knowing already she wouldn't find one. She took out her supplies and began her examination.

Tony talked to Brian and gleaned what information she could from him. A slightly inebriated young man had found the body just after three. The few people still on the streets in the area had been detained for questioning. Most of the clubs closed at 2:30, so not many people were still around.

Tony, Brian, and some of the other task force members

interviewed potential witnesses. Still others combed the area for evidence. But, once again, there was little information to be had. No one had been anywhere near the site of the crime. All those interviewed had traveled in pairs or groups, giving them solid alibis.

Megan had finished her preliminary examination of the victim earlier and had stayed unobtrusively in the background watching Tony work. She watched the agent move from interview to interview, sharing comments and observations with the other task force members. She was surprised at the comfortable interaction between Tony and Brian. Both obviously respected the other. Megan realized Tony was in her element and it was reflected in her every action. Tony seemed to be aware of everyone and everything around her. This was an entirely different woman than the one she had come to know over the past several days.

Her thoughts returned to their first night in the Flats. She wondered how this same woman, who seems to be aware of everything around her, moving with confidence and ease around the area, could have been caught so unawares as to have allowed someone to approach her close enough to stab her in the back? Megan decided it must have been a fluke. *Still doesn't make sense, though.*

Dawn began to light the sky, and Megan decided it was time to leave. She knew Tony was tiring because of the subtle changes in her face and movements. Megan knew, even though she was healing very quickly, Tony's injury still caused her some pain. She also knew the woman would try to ignore her body's limitations.

Walking over to her, she took Tony's arm pulling her aside. "Come on. You've done enough. The police can take it from here."

"I can't leave in the middle of..."

Megan immediately interrupted Tony. "I'm telling you your body has had enough. Come on, we'll go tell Brian we're leaving. Besides you promised," she said softly.

Tony knew she was pushing it. Her body had been

complaining for some time now. Relenting, she said, "Yeah, I did. Ok, let's go."

* * * * * * * * * * * *

Later that morning Tony sat drinking her coffee, her mood very despondent. She had known, when she picked up her car the day before, that she had no reason not to start looking for a place of her own. *Well, actually, I can think of a ton of reasons not to look.* Megan hadn't said anything about it, but she didn't want her to think she was taking advantage of her either. Tony sighed. The last thing in the world she wanted to do was leave, but it was very important to her how Megan viewed her.

Megan entered the kitchen and noticed the far away look on Tony's face. Smiling, she said, "A penny for your thoughts."

Tony looked up at Megan thinking, *I really don't want to do this, but what choice do I have?* "I thought maybe we could look at some places today."

At those words, Megan felt her heart constrict slowly and painfully, one word running through her mind, *No!* Turning away from Tony, her emotions in turmoil, and knowing she had to say something, she forced herself to think. "I should go in and do the autopsy on the victim from last night. Couldn't we look next weekend?" Not waiting for an answer, she left the room.

When Megan abruptly left the room, Tony suspected she had upset her, and that was the last thing she wanted to do. She also knew Megan hadn't planned on doing the autopsy until Monday. They had talked about that last night. A faint glimmer of hope flared in Tony's mind. *Maybe she doesn't want me to leave.* Tony went to see where the smaller woman had gone.

Megan left the kitchen and went to the bathroom, knowing how close she was to losing it. *She can't leave, she just can't. I won't let her.* The thin veneer of control crumbled when she realized there was nothing she could do to stop her.

Tony stood indecisively at the closed bathroom door, wondering if she should disturb Megan or just leave her alone. Following instincts that were screaming at her to knock, she did just that. "Megan?"

Shit. shit. shit. get a grip. You can't let her see you like this. Taking in a deep tremulous breath to steady her voice, she managed to say, "I'll be out in a minute." Fighting to regain control, Megan washed her face with cold water and took another few minutes to decide what to do. Then with a determination born of desperation, she decided to fight for what she wanted.

Tony was pacing back and forth in the living room when Megan walked in. One look at Megan's face confirmed her worse fears. She had upset her. Before she could say anything, Megan asked, "Don't you like it here?"

Tony was startled by the simple question and thought of all the things she wanted to say, but couldn't. "Yeah...I like it here...a lot...but I thought...you know...well I didn't want..." Tony trailed off, not sure how to continue. The glimmer of hope in her mind shined a little brighter, and she willed Megan to ask her to stay. But it had to be Megan's decision.

Megan knew that she wanted Tony to stay more than she had ever wanted anything, but she also realized the agent had to want to stay or...refusing to take the thought any further, Megan asked the hardest question she had ever asked, knowing the answer could devastate her, "Do you *want* to leave?"

"It's not what *I* want..."

"Oh, yes, it *is* what you want. It's your decision." Megan paused and then took a colossal gamble she hoped she wouldn't live to regret. "If you want to leave, fine, I'll help you find a place." She turned around to leave the room.

Tony reached Megan in two swift strides, grabbing her by the arm. "Wait...please. I'm sorry. I didn't want you to think...I just thought...I didn't want to overstay my welcome." Her words tumbled out of her mouth as chaotically as her thoughts.

Megan had turned around when Tony grabbed her arm. She said softly, "You never answered my question."

Tony looked at Megan, her eyes conveying more than she intended, and said, "I don't want to leave."

"Good, because I don't want you to either. So it's settled." Megan paused and then added, "I need to go to the store. I'll be back in a little while." She wanted some time alone to assuage her raw feelings.

Tony had some thinking to do, too. While she hated the idea of moving, she had never expected such a strong reaction from Megan. *If I didn't know better...* Tony thought about the last week. Both of them had become very comfortable around the other and tried to anticipate each other's needs. She understood her need to be near Megan, but she thought about how Megan had more and more frequently found reasons to make contact, often placing her hand on her arm as she explained something. Her thoughts continued to go over the events of the past week, and Tony made a decision. *We need to talk...soon.* She knew what a chance she was taking, but the possible outcome seemed worth the risk. If she was wrong and it cost her Megan's friendship, she'd never forgive herself.

* * * * * * * * * * *

Megan drove aimlessly around for a while. She knew how she felt about Tony, but could the agent feel the same way about her? The way Tony had looked at her was more than just friendship. Or was it just wishful thinking on her part? *No, it was real.* But what could she do about it? Tony had given no indication she might be interested...or had she?

Megan remembered how all of a sudden Tony had insisted the couch was more comfortable than the recliner. She thought about how near to her Tony sat on the couch, and the way she placed her arm along the back of it, and

the light contact when she sat back. Megan remembered
the times she had looked up and thought she saw Tony
avert her gaze. What should she do about it? *For now,
nothing.* If she was wrong, she didn't think she could survive another encounter like this morning. *Maybe I'll talk
to David on Monday. He might have some ideas.*

Megan stopped at the grocery store, picked up what
they needed, and returned home. The rest of the day
passed quietly with both women enjoying each other's
company but spending a lot of the time preoccupied with
their own thoughts. This was a day where minds warred
with hearts, logic versus emotion, decisions were made and
discarded, as the battle continued to find the answer to
friendship or more, risk or status quo.

* * * * * * * * * * *

Megan entered her office and saw some mail in her
in-box. She sat down at her desk, and started going
through the contents, stopping suddenly at the sight of an
envelope from the outside lab they used. Ripping open the
envelope, she scanned the contents and shuddered. *No
wonder the victims had never fought back.* The killer had
used a drug in the paralytic class, which induced total
paralysis of the muscles of the body, including those used
for breathing in 30-60 seconds. The bruise marks and the
broken neck were obviously just a ruse to throw off the
police. This particular drug was used in the operating
room for quick intubation of a patient. The reason the toxicology reports were negative was because the drug is
composed of two naturally occurring chemicals in the
body. What made this particular choice of drug so brutal
was the fact that the victim was awake and conscious as
they slowly suffocated, their muscles unable to respond to
the commands of their brain. Megan shuddered again.
What kind of monster were they dealing with?

Megan called Tony, explained the lab findings, and
left it to her to contact Sgt. Davies. She still had to figure

out how the drug was being administered. The usual route of administration was IV or IM. She was positive there had been no needle marks on the victim she had autopsied. She also wondered where the killer was getting the drug. It certainly was not one of the usual drugs on the street, but she mused, in the black market of drugs, money will buy you anything.

Megan changed into her scrubs to autopsy the latest victim. At least she knew what to look for now. She just had to figure out how it was being introduced into the body.

* * * * * * * * * * * *

Tony called Brian, quickly filling him in on the lab findings. He decided to put his officers out on the streets rounding up informers. He gave Tony the number to reach their database so she could check for any thefts of that particular drug in the last year.

Tony didn't really expect any results. This drug was so uncommon, it was unlikely the killer, who had proven quite clever so far, would be careless enough to leave such an obvious clue.

* * * * * * * * * * * *

Megan performed a slow and methodical examination of the body before proceeding with the autopsy. She checked every possible location for a needle entry point. She knew one of the favorites of junkies was between the fingers and toes. This was unlikely because Megan couldn't imagine anyone standing still while someone injected a needle between her fingers.

Of course, there was the unlikely scenario that the victim had agreed, thinking it was crack or heroin, which was making a big come back on the streets, but there was no evidence to support that. None of the toxicology screens had shown any drugs, and a regular user always had residue in their system.

Finding nothing, she thought of everything she knew about the drug. *If it wasn't injected, what method could the killer have used?* She guessed it could be made into an aerosol. It would be just as effective. She decided to take swabs from the mouth and pay special attention to the esophagus, trachea, and lungs during the autopsy, as well as taking samples from them. Megan figured it was worth a shot.

* * * * * * * * * * * *

Tony checked in with Brian periodically throughout the morning, relating her lack of success and getting updates on the informers they were interrogating. Most of the questioning was being done on the streets, except for the more uncooperative ones.

Her doctor's appointment was that afternoon, and she figured she'd be back at work the next day. *Thank God.* She hated sitting around the apartment by herself. She laughed at herself realizing it was probably the first time she had ever looked forward to a doctor's appointment.

Ending her database search unsuccessfully, her mind turned again to Megan. Tony was charting new territory, and she knew it. In the past her actions had been determined by whatever she hoped to accomplish in the name of the job. So when it came to those relationships, Tony had always held a part of herself back, knowing it was just a part to be played. It wasn't that she hadn't enjoyed herself; she had. She had just emotionally distanced herself. But this was different. This was real. She decided to talk to Megan that night. Not knowing what else to do, she decided to just lay her heart on the line and let Megan do as she chose. If she was wrong, it wouldn't matter anyway. Nothing would.

Chapter
12

Megan was busy the entire day and never got a chance to talk to David. As five o'clock approached, she hurried to finish up her cases so she could get home. Now that it had slowed down, Tony was very much on her mind. She was preparing to leave, when the phone rang. Frowning, she picked it up, and said, "Hello."

"This is Dr. Whitehouse. I need you to stay and autopsy a case on the way in now. Jerry went out, but you're on call."

"It can't wait until morning?" Megan asked, wondering why it needed to be done right now. This was a very unusual request.

"If it could wait until morning, I wouldn't be telling you it needs done now," Dr. Whitehouse answered, angered by the question. The victim was a relative of a friend of a friend. He had been found dead, and his friend had asked him if he could rush the autopsy.

Megan called Tony and told her she probably wouldn't be home much before eight. Tony told her she'd order pizza for dinner.

* * * * * * * * * * *

Later, when the phone rang, Tony got up to answer it, hoping it was Megan. "Hello." A strange woman's voice answered her greeting.

"Hi, is Megan there?" Ashley was surprised to hear an unfamiliar voice answering her sister's phone.

"No. Would you like to leave a message?"

"Yes, this is her sister, Ashley. Who's this?"

"Tony. I'm a friend of hers. She had to work late." Tony recognized the name of the caller and knew this was Megan's favorite sibling.

"Ask her to give me a call," Ashley said.

"Sure."

* * * * * * * * * * *

After hanging up the phone, Ashley wondered who Tony was. She hadn't heard from Megan in over a week, and that was very unusual. The last time she had talked to Megan was when they went to dinner. *Now wait a minute.* She had mentioned an FBI Agent she had been quite impressed with, and it had been a woman. *I wonder?* Ashley decided to have lunch with Megan in the very near future. *Like tomorrow.*

* * * * * * * * * * *

After Tony and Megan ate dinner later that evening, Megan returned the call to her sister. "Hi. What's up?"

"You." Hearing Megan laugh Ashley said, "I haven't heard from you lately and just wondered how you're doing."

"Ok. Just been kind of busy lately. You know how it is," Megan answered vaguely.

Ashley smiled at the answer. Yes, Megan was definitely up to something. "Want to have lunch tomorrow? We could go to that little Italian place right down from your office."

"Sounds good," Megan agreed, looking forward to seeing her sister.

"All right. Is twelve thirty ok?"

"Yeah. See you then." Megan was anxious to get off the phone. It was already eight thirty, and she wanted to spend her time with Tony, not talking on the phone.

Walking over to the couch and sitting down, she looked at the tall woman and asked, "What did the doctor say?"

"He said I can go back to work," Tony answered in her usual succinct manner.

"That's all?" Megan asked, looking at her with raised eyebrows. Megan knew it couldn't be quite that simple.

"Well, he did say light duty for awhile," Tony admitted.

"That's more like it," Megan said grinning at her. "So did you turn up anything on the drug search?"

"No," replied Tony absently. Her mind was not on work. She had spent all evening trying to decide how to approach Megan.

Noticing her distraction, Megan said, "What's wrong? Do you feel ok?"

"Yeah, I feel fine. I need to talk to you about something." Tony paused nervously, once again wondering if she was doing the right thing, so much was at stake. "Megan...I really care about you...a lot...more than a lot." She cleared her throat which had suddenly become very dry, and a thought ran through her mind, *Why don't you just tell her the truth, that you love her?* "I love you." Tony, expecting her whole world to come crashing down on her, looked down at her hands, unable to meet Megan's eyes for fear of what she would see there.

When the meaning of Tony's words sank into her mind, Megan's heart began beating erratically. Realizing she had stopped breathing, she sucked in a breath. Barely able to comprehend the emotions surging through her, she tentatively placed her hand under Tony's chin urging her eyes up. Megan focused the torrents of emotion coursing through her into her eyes, and when the baby blues she had grown to love met hers, she said, "And I love you."

When Tony raised her head and met Megan's eyes, she was caught up in the ever-changing vortex of green and gold. She moved her hand to Megan's face and gently caressed her cheek. Her voice became husky with emotion. "How'd I ever get so lucky?" she asked wonderingly, seeing the unmistakable love radiating out from the hazel orbs.

She bent her head and tentatively brushed her lips across the soft, sensuous mouth she had wanted to taste for so long, ready to stop at any hesitation on Megan's part. She brought her lips down again, lingering, savoring the soft feel of the mouth beneath hers.

Megan responded to the gentle kiss, and time ceased to have meaning for the two women. Parting breathless, every nerve ending in her body alive, Megan looked into eyes dark with passion. She placed her hand against the back of Tony's neck and guided her head back down, greeting the mouth with hers.

Megan heard the phone ring and her heart sank. She was on call and had to answer it. "I have to get it." She very reluctantly moved out of the warm embrace, her body protesting the loss of contact. Tony silently cursed the phone.

"Hello."

"Dr. Donnovan, this is Patrolman Reeves. We've got a drive by. I was told to call you."

All Megan said was, "Where?" She wrote down the address and told the patrolman she was on her way. She walked back over to the couch and sat down next to Tony. She gently caressed Tony's face with her hand and smiled. "Don't go anywhere. I'll be back."

Tony shivered at the inherent promise of those words. She said, "Hurry," and sought out Megan's mouth for a fleeting kiss.

* * * * * * * * * * *

Megan was tired. Between the roller coaster ride of her emotions the last few days and her elation at finding out Tony's love mirrored her own, her mind was on overdrive. By the time she had arrived on the scene, did her preliminary examination, and waited for the body to be removed, it was after eleven. Megan resented the time lost with Tony and was happy to be on her way home. She parked in her assigned space, exited, and began walking quickly toward the elevator.

As Megan approached her destination, she heard the whisper of a shoe on pavement behind her. As she started to turn, her arm was brutally twisted up behind her back, and a gloved hand covered her mouth. Trying to ignore the pain in her arm, she struggled to free herself, drove her free elbow into the body behind her, and heard a grunt when she connected. She immediately stomped her heel down onto the foot behind hers, and simultaneously tried to turn into her attacker.

When her heel connected, the arms holding her loosened slightly, allowing her to jerk free. Using the momentum carrying her around, she faced her attacker. Megan felt a shiver of fear course through her when she saw the knife in his hand, and a deadly dance began.

Headlights suddenly illuminated the garage, and the man bolted toward the exit. Megan shakily made her way to the elevator.

* * * * * * * * * * *

Tony had been watching TV while waiting for Megan to return, or rather trying to watch TV. Her mind refused to concentrate on anything but a small, beautiful, blonde woman. When she heard a key in the lock, Tony glanced toward the door and stood up to greet Megan. When the small woman walked in Tony instantly knew something was wrong, and she covered the distance to the door in long strides, ignoring the pain in her back at the quick movement.

She tried to calm her own reaction to the pale face and trembling body and put her hands on Megan's shoulders. She asked gently, "What's wrong?" Megan looked up at Tony's worried face, and tears filled her eyes. Tony wrapped her arms around the small woman pulling her close, murmuring, "It's ok."

The agent led Megan over to the couch and sat down, gently easing Megan down onto her lap. She kept her wrapped in a protective embrace while Megan fought for control.

Megan spoke haltingly. "There was a man in the garage. I didn't hear him, and he grabbed me." She paused and took several deep steadying breaths before continuing. "I got loose...he had a knife...I was so afraid..." No longer able to stop the tears, she buried her face in Tony's shoulder.

Tony held her tightly, her voice soft and soothing. "It's ok, you're safe now." Her tender actions were at odds with her rolling emotions, and she fought to keep her anger at the perpetrator under control. "No one can hurt you now, it's ok." Tony continued the soft cadence of soothing words until she felt Megan relax.

Megan's tight, tension-filled body slowly relaxed against the supportive, secure embrace of the tall woman and her warm comforting voice. A short time later, she lifted her head from Tony's shoulder and looked up at her with a tear-streaked face. "I'm sorry...I guess I just lost it..."

Tony looked into Megan's eyes and raised a hand, her thumb gently wiping away the tears. "You got nothing to be sorry for." Her own heart was contracting painfully with the realization of just how much this woman meant to her. She continued to offer her support by holding Megan close and gently stroking her head.

Megan was content to stay right where she was, wrapped firmly in Tony's arms. Overcome with exhaustion, she fell asleep in the warm embrace. Tony sat quietly holding her, thinking about the attack and trying to get her emotions under control.

Later, her body complaining from sitting unmoving so long, she kissed Megan on the head and woke her. Megan's eyes opened and Tony smiled at her. "Hey, beautiful, how 'bout going to bed?"

Megan looked up into the captivating deep blue eyes of the woman smiling at her and said, "Only if you come, too."

"I intend to," Tony said with conviction.

While they were getting ready for bed, the events in the parking garage came flooding over Megan, and, shaking, she sat down on the bed. Tony moved onto the bed and gently urged her down. She wrapped her arms around Megan's waist and pulled her close until Megan's back was tucked comfortably against her. She murmured to Megan, over and over, "You're safe now. I won't let anyone hurt you. It's ok," until she felt Megan once again relax into sleep. But sleep proved elusive for Tony, and it was almost dawn before she entered its realm.

****

Dwayne was furious. He had bided his time until Megan was on call, and then it was just a matter of listening to the police scanner. When he heard the homicide call go out, he had been filled with elation. He'd driven to her apartment, secreted himself in the garage, and waited.

He could not believe the bitch had escaped. *Of all the rotten luck.* He had waited so long. It was bad enough she fought like a hell cat. He sported a big ugly bruise on his foot to attest to that, but he'd have had her if that damn car hadn't pulled in.

He knew he was going to have to lay low for a few days. She'd be on guard right now. *Damn it anyway.* He'd have to entertain himself some other way for a few days. No problem, some of his other activities had been neglected.

* * * * * * * * * * * *

When Megan woke up, she found herself held in place by long arms wrapped around her waist. Relishing the contact, she thought, *I could get used to this.* Shifting onto her back, she looked at the beautiful woman sleeping next to her and marveled at her luck. She trailed her hand down one of the strong arms holding her. She noticed the early light of day advancing through the window and sighed, gently disengaging herself from Tony's embrace. Megan leaned over and kissed Tony on the cheek before leaving the room.

She started the coffee and went to take a shower. Megan walked back into the bedroom and quietly rummaged through the closet, looking for something to wear. She took her clothes into the other bedroom not wanting to wake Tony.

When Tony woke up the first thing she realized was Megan was gone. She noticed the rich smell of coffee brewing and followed it to the kitchen. Megan had her back to the door, looking in the refrigerator.

Not wanting to startle her, Tony cleared her throat before saying, "Morning."

Megan closed the refrigerator and turned towards Tony with a smile on her face. She walked over and stood on her tiptoes brushing her lips across the tall woman's, before answering back in kind.

Tony carefully searched her face. "How ya feeling?"

"Better." Still feeling a little embarrassed about her loss of control the night before, she said, " I'm sorry about last night."

Tony met Megan's eyes, the love reflected in her eyes. "Don't be."

Megan was surprised by the intensity of Tony's expression. She knew she didn't have much time before she had to leave for work. So, sitting down at the table,

Megan decided to tell Tony what was really bothering her about the attack last night.

"You know, I've been thinking." Megan paused, trying to decide how to proceed. "I've had the feeling lately that someone's been watching me. I know that sounds crazy, but I've felt really uneasy a couple of times in the garage. You know how the back of your neck prickles? But when I looked, there was never anyone there. I guess what I mean is, I'm not sure this was a random...attack." The thought filled her with trepidation.

Tony had taken a seat opposite her and listened in silence as Megan spoke. She reached across the table and held Megan's hands. "Why didn't you ever say anything?"

"I just thought it was my overactive imagination. Since I never saw anyone..." she trailed off.

"Have you ever felt like that anywhere else?"

"No, I don't think so."

"Can you remember anything at all about the guy that attacked you?"

Megan thought about the masked man she had faced and said, "Well, he was about as tall as you. Kind of medium build, but he had a ski mask on so I couldn't see his face. I don't remember anything else."

"That's ok," Tony reassured her before continuing, "is anyone mad at you for anything?"

Megan looked at the concern on Tony's face and answered, "No. Well except for work."

"What do you mean? What about work?" Tony asked, becoming tense.

"Jerry, he's another pathologist, and Dwayne his assistant don't like me much...ever since I got promoted last year. I think maybe Dwayne might even really hate me, but he would never hurt me," she answered.

"Megan, I want to take you to work and pick you up until we find out what's going on," Tony said hoping Megan wouldn't turn her down. She knew the small woman's will matched her own.

Megan was relieved at the offer and said, "Thanks, I'd

like that."

After quickly showering and dressing, Tony returned to the kitchen and quickly finished a cup of coffee. "Ya ready?" Megan nodded and they departed for the parking garage.

Megan studied Tony as she followed the directions she gave her. The car was like a natural extension of her, and she expertly maneuvered the Buick around the other cars on the interbelt. Megan silently acknowledged that she did drive a little fast though.

Tony glanced over at Megan. "Would you mind showing me around at work and introducing me to the people you work with?"

"Sure," Megan replied, puzzled at the request until she realized Tony was acting on her earlier words.

Tony parked the car, and they entered the small, nondescript building. Tony carefully took in the surroundings. She was quite anxious to meet the people Megan worked with. The idea that one of them might be responsible for the attack on Megan enraged her, and she felt a familiar heat begin to rage through her blood.

Megan glanced over at Tony and stopped walking. The woman beside her bore little resemblance to the woman she loved. Tony's entire essence oozed of danger, from the hardened planes of her face to the clenched chin. Her body moved with barely controlled tension. Megan involuntarily shuddered when the hooded eyes turned her way, and she saw a glacial coldness she had never before witnessed.

Tony noticed the reaction she had caused in Megan, quirked a small smile, and let the warmth she felt for the small woman briefly cross her face. She gently squeezed Megan's shoulder reassuringly before, once again, assuming the intimidating appearance.

Megan took Tony to her office first, put her purse in the desk drawer, and locked it. She then led her to the autopsy suite. David walked up, pleased to see Megan but surprised to see Tony. "Hi, you guys," he said smiling until he took in the expression on Tony's face and, unnerved, asked, "What's wrong?"

Tony motioned for Megan and David to go Megan's office. All three entered and she closed the door. Tony explained what had happened in the garage the night before and asked David if he thought any of their co-workers could be involved.

David said, "I'd like to think not, but I wouldn't put anything past Dwayne. The looks he gives Megan when she isn't looking are so full of hatred it's actually scary." Turning to Megan, he asked, "Are you ok?"

Megan looked up, surprised at the revelation from David. She nodded her head, silently answering his question. She remembered the one time she had seen the look of pure hatred Dwayne had given her. But she'd thought that was just an isolated incident. Thinking about it she shuddered.

Tony didn't miss Megan's reaction and walked over to her. She gently placed her hand on her shoulder and asked, "Have you ever noticed this?"

Megan looked up and said, "Yeah, once."

"Thanks, David." Tony paused and then said, "I think it's about time I met Dwayne."

****

Dwayne had been in the supply room and hadn't seen Megan and Tony enter the suite. Tony was leaning against the wall in a corner of the suite observing, as David and Megan planned out their work for the day. Dwayne glared at Megan, never seeing the agent in the corner. He still couldn't believe the bitch had gotten away. Before he had a chance to turn back to his work, a tall, very angry, barely controlled woman was standing in front of him. He was unnerved by the cold look of fury on her face. "You gotta problem with the Doc?" she growled.

Realizing this was the FBI woman he had stabbed and fleetingly wondering how she could be up and around

already, he said, "Fuck you. It's none of your business."
Dwayne remembered how easily he had gotten the best of
her in the Flats. When she didn't respond, his courage
intensified and he said, "Now get out of my face, bitch."

Tony was simply trying to control the urge to break
this lowlife piece of shit into a thousand pieces. She was
also aware of her new limitations due to her back wound.
Finally, gaining some semblance of control, she grabbed
his scrub top and pulled him to within inches of her face.
"If I ever hear of you giving her a hard time, I'll break
every bone in your body, and it won't be under the aus-
pices of the FBI. It'll just be you and me. Got it?" she
growled ominously pushing him away from her.

For the first time in his life, Dwayne's face paled as he
felt the sharp pang of fear in his belly and realized she
meant every word she said. Tony knew her message had
been received, and turning away from him, she headed
over to where Megan and David were standing.

Watching the incident, David whispered to Megan,
"Remind me never to get on her bad side."

Megan whispered back, "Tell me about it."

Both were unaware Tony's keen ears had picked up the
whispered comments, and she made a mental note to talk to
Megan later. "Could I talk to you in the office for a
minute?" Megan was puzzled by the request but said,
"Sure."

After they entered the office, Tony turned around and
pushed the button, engaging the door lock. Walking over
to Megan, she bent her head down and very softly kissed
the smaller woman. It was a light, fleeting kiss, but it conveyed a depth of feeling that was both an affirmation and a
promise. Megan gave her a hug and, as Tony turned to
leave, she said, "If he gives you any trouble at all, call
me."

* * * * * * * * * * *

Tony arrived at the station and went looking for Brian.

She filled him in on the attack against Megan and also voiced some of her concerns. She thought it rather unusual to have two knife attacks within just over a week, even though they were in different parts of town. Guns were the weapons of choice on the streets, and two attacks, with assailants of a similar build, was a little too much of a coincidence in Tony's mind.

"I hear ya. I'll check it out," Brian answered, before asking, "How's your back?"

"Not bad," Tony answered. "Anything turn up with the informants?"

"No. Seems to be a dead end, but we'll keep trying. There's not much else to go on. We've got all the interview files in the conference room if you want to check them out."

"Okay." Tony walked through the squad room to the conference room. She picked up the phone, and called Mike Braxton. "Mike, it's Tony."

"Where in the hell have you been? No one has seen you or heard from you in a week. Did you ever think about calling in?" he ranted angrily.

Tony listened, rolling her eyes at the tirade. "Seems to me, if I remember right, that you told me to keep you informed of any developments," she said, unable to keep the sarcasm out of her voice.

"There was a new victim Saturday," Mike replied, "wouldn't you consider that a development?"

"I am calling you now to give you an update. Besides, I figured you could read that in the paper. There have been no developments in the progress of the case. In other words, there is still literally no evidence linking the perpetrator to the victim," Tony explained patiently. "But if you want me to call you if the killer strikes again, I'll be most happy to oblige. I'm sure you won't mind being called in the middle of the night, right?" Tony finished, smirking to herself.

"I don't think that will be necessary," Mike backed down, "just keep me informed if anything does come up."

"Will do," Tony answered before hanging up the phone. Turning to look at the wall where the crime scene photos were posted, she compared the photos of the newest victim to the other photos looking for any differences. All of a sudden Tony felt like she'd been punched in the chest. What had eluded her about the pictures on her first day on the job just about staggered her now. All the victims bore a strong resemblance to Megan.

Could the attack be related? No. it didn't make sense. The victims had no marks on them except for bruising around the neck. No knife had been used. But could the killer have used a knife to force the victims to do what he wanted? Tony shook her head frustrated. *Too many questions. Not enough answers.* She now had a very personal stake in this case. Picking up the files containing the interviews with the informants, Tony began to read.

* * * * * * * * * * *

Once Megan and David finished up their cases, it was close to lunchtime and Megan remembered she had a date with her sister. She got her purse out of the drawer and turned. "I'm going to lunch with my sister. I may be gone a little longer than usual. Could you keep an eye on things here?" The unspoken question, of course, was would he cover for her if necessary.

David smiled over at her and said, "Of course."

Megan arrived at the restaurant and greeted her sister. Once they sat down and ordered, Ashley asked, "So what have you been up to?"

Megan quickly related the events of the night before. She found she was able to think about it a little more objectively today and left off the part about how, in her mind, she lost it afterwards.

Ashley was very upset. "Are you ok? I mean, really ok?"

"Yeah, I'm fine. It was pretty scary though."

"Pretty scary? I'd have been terrified. Do you want to

stay with us for a while? You know we've got room, and we'd love to have you."

"No." Megan paused, trying to decide how much to tell her sister. "I've got someone staying with me. I'll be fine."

"Is it the woman who answered the phone when I called, Tony?"

"Yeah." Megan smiled at her sister. "She's really fantastic. I think you'd like her."

Ashley looked at her sister and thought, *uh huh.* "Is this that FBI agent you told me about?"

"Yeah." Megan couldn't stop the smile that overtook her face just thinking about Tony.

Ashley looked at Megan and decided she was going to have to do some pumping here. Her sister was not offering much information. "You really like her, don't you?"

Megan glanced at her sister. She was her friend and confidante, both when they were children and now as adults. Taking a deep breath and hoping her sister would understand, she looked straight into Ashley's eyes and said, "I love her."

Even though Ashley had suspected as much, she was surprised at the intensity of Megan's revelation. Reaching over the table and taking her sister's hand, she replied, "That's wonderful. I'm so glad you found someone. I'm really happy for you."

Once again, Megan's face lit up with a beautiful smile. "Thanks. That means a lot to me."

Ashley and Megan finished their lunch, the conversation dominated by Megan as she told her sister all about her wonderful new love.

"I'd really like to meet her. Do you think you could arrange that?" Ashley teased when they were getting ready to leave.

Slapping her sister playfully on the arm, Megan said, "Of course. Let me know next time you have any free time. It's your schedule we'll have to work around, you know."

Ashley, deciding to make sure that was real soon, said, "I'll let you know," and looking at Megan, she continued, "you be careful."

"I will. See ya later."

When Megan returned to her office, David was lounging in the guest chair. "So, what's your sister up to?"

"Oh, you know, same ole," Megan responded.

David hadn't really had a chance to talk to Megan, and he was very concerned about the attack on her. "Are you sure you're all right?" David asked, his face etched with worry.

"I'm ok, really," Megan answered, smiling at her friend. "Besides Tony's going to be escorting me back and forth to work for awhile."

Taking in the dreamy look on her face, he said, "She's pretty special, isn't she?"

"She's more than special. She's..." Megan paused hunting for words that could describe Tony, and coming up blank. "I love her," she said instead, surprised at how the words just popped out of her mouth.

David was around the desk in an instant and wrapped Megan in a big hug. "That's great. I knew it, I just knew it."

Megan looked at him surprised. "What do you mean, you knew it?"

David started chuckling and said, "If it wasn't for the fact that you give it away every time you talk about her, there was dinner Friday night." At the questioning look on Megan's face, he continued, "Every time you mention her name your whole face lights up, Megan. I watched you both at dinner Friday night and it was pretty obvious, no matter how hard you both tried to hide it. Does she know?"

"Oh, yeah." Megan knew that silly grin was on her face again. She just couldn't stop it. "But I really didn't think it was that obvious," she said, a little embarrassed that she could be read so easily.

"I'm your friend, remember. I make it a point to

notice things," David said letting Megan out of the bear hug he had wrapped her in. "I'm soooo happy for you," he said, grinning at her.

Megan smiled back and said, "Thanks."

Chapter
13

Tony pulled into the parking lot fifteen minutes early. She parked the car, entered the building, and headed for Megan's office. She stopped in the doorway when she saw David and Megan chatting. "I'm a little early. I can wait outside."

David and Megan both got up, and each took hold of one of Tony's arms, leading her further into the office. Tony was so shocked, she allowed herself to be led into the office, before getting her voice back. "What's going on?" One of her eyebrows was raised so high it was lost under the cover of her bangs.

David closed the door and wrapped his arms around Tony giving her a big hug. "I'm glad you two figured it out," he said, releasing a very stunned Tony before she had a chance to protest. "See you two later." David left the office grinning.

"What was that all about?" Tony asked, still surprised by the show of affection from David.

Megan smiled up at the tall woman. "Oh, he's just happy for us." She reached up and gave Tony a quick kiss.

Even though the contact had been brief, Tony felt a warmth spread throughout her body. She looked down at

Megan and asked, "You ready?"

"Yeah, let's go." Megan was anxious to leave work and spend time with Tony.

During the drive home, Tony asked, "Want to stop and get something to eat?"

Seeing the affirmative nod from Megan, she continued, "What sounds good?"

"How about Linda's?" Megan asked, smiling over at Tony and placing her hand on her thigh.

Tony covered Megan's hand with her own and said, "Ok, lead on."

They rode along in comfortable silence, broken occasionally by directions being given.

When they finished dinner, Tony asked, "Ready to go home?" She suddenly realized that the word had taken on a new meaning for her. She had a home to go to. *A real home. A home with Megan.*

Megan took in the surprised look on Tony's face and watched her eyes turned inward. Wondering what was going through her mind, she asked, "What are you thinking?"

Tony looked at Megan and smiled, "It's just that I..." She paused, wondering how to explain it. It was such a simple word. But for Tony it was so much more. "It's been a long time since I've had a place to call home." Noticing Megan's puzzled look, she continued, "Before I came here, I always worked undercover. I was never in one place long enough to really have a place to call home." She shrugged her shoulders.

Megan gazed into the deep blue orbs, and said with conviction, "You do now." A smile lit up Tony's face.

* * * * * * * * * * *

Tony flipped through the channels on the radio, looking for a song she knew. Unwittingly stopping on one of Cleveland's most popular station and recognizing an oldie, her voice smoothly joined the country music diva's in her rendition of "The Night the Lights Went Out in Georgia."

Megan felt her mouth fall open. She wasn't sure what surprised her more: Tony's captivating voice, or the fact that she was belting out a country song in perfect harmony with the artist.

When the song ended, Tony felt Megan's eyes on her, and she quirked a smile. "What?"

"That was beautiful, Tony, but I just never figured you for country."

The agent grinned at her companion. "My assignments have exposed me to all kinds of music." Indicating the console, she said, "Take a look." Inside the console, Megan found a variety of tapes containing soft rock, jazz, classical, easy listening, country, and a few genres she didn't recognize. "I see what you mean."

* * * * * * * * * * * *

Arriving home, both women changed into something more comfortable and joined each other in the living room. Turning on the TV and watching the news had developed into a routine for them during the short time they had lived together. That didn't change today. Tony put her arm around Megan urging her closer. Megan complied and captured Tony's mouth with her own for a kiss that quickly lengthened, and the news soon ceased to have any importance.

Megan stood up and reached for Tony's hand urging her up. She led the tall woman to the bedroom and turned to face her once they entered the room. Placing her hands on Tony's face, she looked into her eyes and said, "Kiss me, Tony."

Tony's desire spiraled with Megan's words. She put her hands behind Megan's head and lowered her lips to meet the warm, moist mouth. The gentle meeting of lips became more urgent, and the kiss deepened. Tony raised her head and looked into Megan's eyes. "I want you so much." She wrapped her arms around the smaller woman,

148 C. Paradee

hugging her.

Megan relaxed against the soft cushion of Tony's breasts, relishing the sensations coursing through her body. She lightly ran the back of her fingers over one of Tony's breasts. Feeling her shiver, Megan's voice became deep with desire. "These clothes gotta go."

Tony kissed the top of her head and said, "Yeah," reluctant to release her hold on the gorgeous woman who fit so comfortably against her.

Megan pulled Tony's head down and met her lips while lightly caressing one of Tony's breasts through the thin shirt. Tony moved her hands down Megan's back, cupping her buttocks and pulling her closer. Their kiss deepened, becoming an exploration, and tongue met tongue, thrusting, vying, and urgent.

They ended the kiss breathless, and Tony began unbuttoning her shirt but was stopped when Megan laid her hand on top of hers. "No, let me," Megan said in a quiet, but commanding voice. Tony felt a jolt to her core at Megan's words. She dropped her hands and watched Megan unbutton her shirt.

Slowly unbuttoning her partner's shirt, Megan looked up at Tony and ran her tongue over her top lip. Tony shuddered and wondered how long she was going to be able to stand there before her knees gave out. Megan pulled the unbuttoned shirt open and eased it over Tony's shoulders letting it fall to the floor. She reached around the taller woman and unhooked her bra, pulling it forward over Tony's arms and letting it fall. Megan sucked in her breath at the sight of the firm, full breasts. She was unable to resist running her tongue lightly over the erect nipples.

Tony moaned at the attention her breasts were receiving from Megan. She reached out to pull Megan into an embrace, but the small woman danced out of reach and said, "Wait...I'm not done." She ran a finger lightly on the inside of the waistband of Tony's pants and purred, "You do want me to undress you, don't you?"

Tony's breath quickened, and she shivered. "Yes,

please...hurry."

Megan unbuttoned Tony's pants, pulling them down along with her underwear, letting Tony step out of them. Looking at the naked woman standing before her, Megan said, "You are so beautiful." Running her fingertips lightly down Tony's abdomen, she grazed the dark curls, her breath quickening with desire for the woman standing before her.

Tony took a deep breath trying to steady herself. Looking into Megan's eyes, she purred seductively, "It's my turn, woman." Megan thought she'd melt at the sound of Tony's sexy voice.

Taking hold of the bottom of Megan's top, she pulled it up over her partner's arms and head. She leaned down and placed a warm, moist kiss between Megan's breasts as her hands reached around to unfasten her bra. Drawing it forward, she let it fall to the floor. Placing her hands on the breasts in front of her, she gently caressed them lightly rolling the nipple between her thumb and forefinger. Megan gasped at the sensations flowing through her. "Please..."

Tony saw that the passion in Megan's eyes matched her own, and she dropped her hands to Megan's shorts quickly removing them with her underwear. When Megan stepped out of them, Tony appreciatively took in the sight before her, lowering her gaze from Megan's face to the full breasts, down to the light curly hair, and the wonderfully shaped, firm legs. She husked, "I want to make love to you, Megan."

Megan leaned against Tony, unable to support her own weight anymore. "Yes, now, please." Tony made her way to the bed, never letting go of Megan, pulling her down with her. The outside world ceased to exist for the two lovers.

* * * * * * * * * * *

Tony woke to the soft light of day entering the bedroom. Looking at the woman sprawled across her almost took her breath away. *She is so beautiful...how did I ever get so lucky?* She smiled as the memories of the past night filtered through her mind. For the first time in her adult life, she was happy. And it was all because of this wonderful, small woman who had given her the gift of love.

Since they both had to go to work, she softly called Megan's name and ran her hand through her hair. When she didn't respond, Tony decided to try another tactic. She tickled the smaller woman. Megan woke very quickly and decided to return the favor. A short time and a lot of laugher later, both left the confines of the bed, deciding they had better take showers separately or they'd never get to work.

Megan took hers first, and Tony made her way to the kitchen to start the coffee. She glanced at the clock and saw it was already eight. *Well, that still leaves an hour before Megan is due at the office.* Tony's hours were whatever she chose. Deciding she was hungry, she opened the refrigerator. Grabbing some juice and a couple of bananas, she made short work of them. When Tony heard the bathroom door open, she made her way down the hall.

Megan stepped out into the hall after donning a robe and felt her breath catch in her throat as her new lover padded down the hall naked. Even though she appreciated the sight, she did have to go to work. "Uh, Tony?" she began.

"What?"

"Do you have to go wandering around the house naked?" Megan was unable to take her eyes off the tall, muscular woman moving so gracefully toward her.

"Sorry," she said, lowering her head and giving Megan a quick kiss. She was unable to stop a teasing comment, "Naked's not good?"

Megan grumbled, "You are so bad," but she had trouble maintaining a serious expression.

Laughing, Tony said, "I gotta take a shower, we're running behind."

Megan patted Tony's shapely rear as she passed her

and muttered, "I wonder why?" Tony smiled and continued into the bathroom.

* * * * * * * * * * *

After parking the car, Tony walked Megan to her office. She looked around for Dwayne but didn't see him. "Did Dwayne cause you any problems yesterday?"

"No. I don't even think I saw him after you left." Megan had noticed a subtle change come over Tony when they exited the car, but it was nothing like what she had witnessed yesterday.

After Tony left, Megan went to join David in the autopsy suite, and they started on the cases for the day. Neither saw Dwayne when he entered the room or the look of pure rage directed at Megan.

Dwayne was furious. He still couldn't believe that bitch he had stabbed had had the nerve to face him down. *No woman does that to me and gets away with it.* He'd take care of her, but first he'd see to Megan. Dwayne had forgotten about how intimidated he'd been by Tony.

* * * * * * * * * * *

"Hey, Brian, anything turn up?" Tony asked, figuring he'd know what she meant.

"Well, that depends. If you're talking about the Shadow case, no. If you're talking about assaults with a knife, yes."

Tony's whole demeanor subtly changed. "Well?" she asked with a raised eyebrow.

Brian knew she wasn't going to like what he had to say, but she needed to know. "Since I'm in homicide and the leader of this task force, I haven't been able to keep abreast of what's going on elsewhere in the city." Noticing Tony's impatient look, he continued, "Seems there's a rapist operating on the near West Side. A knife seems to be his weapon of choice. However, he hasn't actually stabbed anyone, so it may be entirely unrelated." Brian was not really surprised to see no visible reaction. Tony had to be the most controlled person he had ever met.

The agent's mind was actually racing ahead. While the chance of either her or Megan's attack being related to each other were slim, she could not ignore the possibility either. She knew her attack could not have been related to a rapist. Rapists did not slash and run, but Megan's attack had been different. Coincidences tended to bother Tony, and she still felt there were too many similarities in the two attacks. There really wasn't much she could do about it though.

"What's on the agenda today?" she asked, quickly shifting gears.

"We got a few more informants to interview. The guys are out rounding them up now. Want to sit in on the interviews?"

Giving Brian an appreciative grin, Tony knew she'd finally made the inner team. She preferred to work alone, but this was the locals' case and trust was important. The stakes had become very high.

* * * * * * * * * * *

Megan finished her cases and returned to her office to do the preliminary reports. She was hoping to get something back from the lab today, but figured it would be at least tomorrow before they had a chance to process the samples. She looked up when someone rapped lightly on the doorframe. She smiled at Mark and said, "Hi."

"Hi. I just thought I'd stop by and see if you have anything you can release on the latest victim. The news has been kind of slow lately."

"No. I still can't release any information yet. The police might be able to tell you more than I can," Megan said kindly.

"I don't suppose you'd want to go to lunch?" Mark asked hopefully. "I stopped by yesterday, but you were already at lunch."

"I think I'll pass this time. Maybe some other time." Megan had begun to feel quite comfortable with her life, and she didn't feel the need to be bothered with things she really didn't want to do.

Mark nodded, not really surprised. "Ok, see you later."

"Bye."

The fax machine came to life, and Megan walked over to see what was being transmitted. Seeing the familiar letterhead of the outside laboratory, her mind began racing with anticipation. She pulled the paper from the tray. *Yes...the drug had been ingested orally.* They were obviously dealing with someone who had a good working knowledge of drugs.

* * * * * * * * * * *

Brian smiled to himself and shook his head. Since Tony had begun assisting with the interviewing, things were moving along very quickly. She simply intimidated the hell out of whoever they were interviewing, and the punks quickly spilled their guts about anything and everything just to get out of the same room with her. They hadn't gotten any new leads on the Shadow case, but they now had tips on one armed robbery, two new drug dealers, and four corner store robberies. The woman was amazing.

* * * * * * * * * * *

Tony walked into the autopsy suite and glanced around. She had already gone to Megan's office, but it had been empty. She saw David and approached him. "Hi. Know where Megan's at?"

David looked at Tony and smiled. "Yes. She got summoned to our fearless leader's office. She should be back soon. She's been gone for a half hour already."

"David, has Dwayne been a problem?"

"Not that I've noticed. He mostly seems to avoid us both, which is fine with me. I really don't like the guy," David said.

"I know exactly what you mean." Tony saw Megan enter the room, and her smile quickly disappeared when she saw the expression on her partner's face. "What's wrong?"

"I'll tell you on the way home. I need to get out of here," Megan said in a very controlled voice. "David, I'll see you tomorrow," as she turned and walked out with Tony, her tense body belying her calm voice.

Tony pulled out into traffic and then asked, the concern evident in her voice, "What's the matter?"

"He is such a jerk. I can't believe it," Megan said, trying to control her anger. "Would you believe he wants to go public with the results of the GCMS test. That'll tip our hand. We can't let that get out yet. All he's worried about is his public image. After all HIS office discovered it. Look how good that would sound in the newspapers." Megan paused, still angry. "He is such an arrogant, egotistical, condescending..."

"Bastard," Tony filled in for her when she ran out of words. "I'll talk to him. I'm quite sure I can convince him that wouldn't be a good idea." Tony reassured Megan. Inwardly, she was angry. *Who did this idiot think he was anyway?* He dumps the case on Megan, and then when she discovers the method of death, he wants to go to the papers without regard to their case simply to bask in the glory. *I'm going to enjoy explaining some things to him.* "I'll talk to him tomorrow, ok?"

"He can be really stubborn. I don't know if he'll listen," Megan said looking over at Tony.

Her partner smiled grimly. "Don't worry, he'll listen." After seeing the expression on Tony's face, Megan believed her.

* * * * * * * * * * *

They decided to stop and work out on the way home.

"Now remember, don't overdo it," Megan cautioned.

Tony rolled her eyes. "I'm fine, really."

They both moved to the stationary bikes and began to warm up.

"How often have you been coming here?" Tony asked.

"Used to be three to four times a week." Grinning over at her companion, Megan added, "I've been a little negligent lately. Can't imagine why."

Tony smirked over at her and said, "Oh, really? Guess I'll have to work on that then." As they slowly increased their speed, Tony couldn't keep her eyes off Megan. Watching the supple muscles rippling in her partner's legs and thighs, and her fair face flushed with exertion, Tony slowed down, distracted.

"Tony...you're staring," Megan teased, not minding the attention at all. Tony just grinned and winked at her. *God, I love when she does that. She is so sexy. Pay attention, Megan. You're supposed to be working out. Yeah, right, like I could really pay attention with her sitting over there grinning at me, and those long perfect legs and...*

"Uh, Megan...come back." Tony smirked at her.

Megan colored slightly, when she realized she was doing the same thing she teased Tony about. "Let's go do the machines. I'm warmed up enough." *More than enough, actually.*

They took turns on the machines, and Tony was pleased to find out that even though her back placed some limitations on her, overall her body was quite well tuned considering the events of the past week. If she pushed it, she should be back to full form very soon. When they finished the leg weight lifts Tony asked, "Want to go do a few laps before we leave?" Megan nodded affirmatively.

Megan set a leisurely pace enjoying the workout. After several laps, Tony picked up the pace. "This isn't too fast, is it?"

"No. But I think I've tormented my body enough. What about you?" Megan knew her partner was pushing things just a little.

"Whatever you want to do," answered Tony, not willing to admit that she'd had enough.

Megan smiled to herself. She was finding it easier to read the subtle changes in her partner and knew Tony's ego would never allow her to admit what she considered a weakness, so she said, "Ok, let's go."

"I get the shower first," Megan quipped when they entered the apartment. Tony watched her walk towards the bathroom. Grinning wolfishly, she thought, *I think not.* She quickly, but quietly, closed the distance between them and walked in the bathroom right behind the smaller woman.

Tony placed her arms around Megan, whispering in her ear, "Sure ya don't want some company?" and nibbled on Megan's ear.

Megan started at the sudden contact, before quickly relaxing against Tony, and said, "I think I could be convinced." Tony placed soft, moist kisses along her neck and moved her hands up under Megan's tank top, lightly caressing the soft skin. Megan felt like all her nerve endings had come alive. Still leaning against Tony, she said, "If you don't stop, we'll never get a shower."

Tony smiled, moving her hands to Megan's waist, letting her gain her balance. Her mouth moved to Megan's ear and her voice dropped seductively, "Are you convinced yet?" Megan turned around and answered her with a kiss.

Chapter
14

Dwayne knew he needed to calm down. He was finding it harder and harder to control his rage. Everything was going wrong. He had not been able to uncover even one clue as to his wife's whereabouts, and Megan, the bitch, had been riding back and forth to work with that crazy FBI Agent. He had stayed away from her at work, not because he was afraid of the tall woman, but to wait for any attention on him to abate. He left the house deciding to take out his frustration in other ways.

* * * * * * * * * * *

Tony walked with Megan to her office and then asked where Dr. Whitehouse's office was. Megan directed her, knowing it was better if she did not go with her. Tony walked along the short hallway and saw the office on the left. She walked in and told the secretary she wanted to see Dr. Whitehouse.

"Do you have an appointment?"

Tony pulled out her FBI identification and said, "I really don't think I need one. This will only take a few minutes." The secretary got up and walked into Dr. Whitehouse's office, leaving Tony standing in front of her desk.

A couple of minutes later, she returned and said, "He can't see you right now. He suggested you make an appointment. He has an opening for next Friday, a week from tomorrow, at ten."

Tony waited until the secretary sat down then walked past her to the Doctor's office. Ignoring the flustered woman who was insisting she couldn't go in there, Tony did just that. Stalking over to the desk, she stopped in front of it and growled, "I need to talk to you, now." She folded her arms across her chest and glared at him.

"You have no jurisdiction here, and I am asking you to leave. When you have properly scheduled an appointment, I'll be happy to see you," replied Dr. Whitehouse, who was very intimidated, but this was his office, and he was the one in charge here.

Tony thought quickly. She knew he was within his rights to ask her to leave. She also knew she had a message she had to get across to him. "Fine, I'll set up an appointment, but don't be surprised when you see the article in the paper tomorrow about how the most junior pathologist on your staff discovered the method the Shadow killer is using on the very first victim she autopsied. Since that happened to be the third victim..." She left the sentence hanging, knowing he would understand her point.

"You can't threaten me," he retorted.

"I'm not. It's a matter of public record that you did the first two autopsies."

"What do you want?" he asked, knowing he had underestimated this woman.

"I don't want the discovery of the drug to be released yet. That will damage our case more than help it at this point."

"I've already scheduled a press conference for tomorrow."

"Well, I guess you'll just have to cancel it or find something else to talk about," Tony advised him.

Dr. Whitehouse knew he was beaten. If he went ahead

with the press conference, he had no doubt the FBI Agent would release a contradictory statement, and her story would be backed up by facts. That could prove to be very embarrassing. "Ok, I see your point. I wouldn't want to do anything to hurt the case," he lied.

Tony smiled to herself and said, "Thanks for your cooperation," before leaving the office. She stopped by to see Megan and told her there would be no press release.

The day passed slowly for Megan, and she waited impatiently for five o'clock to arrive. She was looking forward to going home. *Well,* she mused, *she looked forward to going home every night now.* Smiling, she thought about how everything was so different now. It was hard to believe that all the things she'd always heard about love, and never thought she'd experience, were true. *Well, no, not exactly. This was better than what she'd heard.* She shook her head, deciding she was hopeless.

****

Tony called over to Brian, "See ya tomorrow," and made her way around the desks toward the door to the street. It had been another day of interviewing informants. There had been no new developments, and she was tired of interviewing lowlife punks. Maneuvering through the traffic toward the Coroner's office, she had one thing on her mind, Megan. She just wanted to be with her. It was comfortable. It was nice.

Megan watched her tall lover walk down the hall toward her. She could watch her all day. She moved so fluidly, her walk so perfect, her muscles moving in perfect synchrony with that magnificent body. *She is gorgeous.*

Megan stood waiting in the doorway of her office. Tony was early. "Hi ya." Megan gave her a big grin, "I missed you."

Tony walked into the office and hugged her. She returned her partner's smile and said, "Right back at ya."

* * * * * * * * * * * *

"What is this?" Tony asked looking in the crock pot. "It looks interesting," she said dubiously.

Megan chuckled. "Interesting? That's original."

Tony glanced at Megan and raised an eyebrow, still trying to figure out what was in the crock pot. "Well?"

"It doesn't have a name. My mother used to make it." Megan laughed at Tony's expression and patted her on the stomach. "I haven't poisoned you yet, have I?"

"No, but..."

"Tony, expand your horizons a little," Megan teased. "It's sort of like a goulash."

"Must taste ok, huh?" Megan chuckled when Tony filled her plate a second time.

"Yep. It's really good," Tony said, looking slightly embarrassed. "What time is that guy coming over?"

"He should be here at seven. I never knew they actually came to your house to demonstrate."

"Why not? It's money in his pocket," Tony answered. She had suggested to Megan that getting a cellular phone would probably be a good idea. Tony knew that, even though she wanted to, she couldn't go everyplace with Megan but, for now, she sure intended to try.

"You know, Tony, I was thinking. Did you ever see any of those movies or read any murder mysteries where they tell the reporter a lot of provocative stuff to put in the newspaper trying to lure the killer into the open? You know, stuff like being unable to interact normally with women, so he gets his kicks by killing them because it's the only way he feels he has any control over them, and stuff like that."

Tony nodded her head. "Yeah. But most of the stuff that works on TV and in books, doesn't in real life. It might not be a bad idea, though. We certainly aren't making any progress on the case." Tony mused aloud, "The killer is very cool. Almost too cool. It's really kind of weird. Something should have broken by now. All we've got is a description of someone buying drugs that is so vague it'll never do us any good. Tell you what, let me talk to Brian tomorrow. I think it might be worth a shot."

* * * * * * * * * * * *

Megan sat on the couch looking at the cellular phone. It was very small and would easily fit in her purse. "Don't you think it's kind of cute?"

"It's just a phone," Tony answered, watching Megan play with it. "Here, let me have it. I'll go plug it in."

"I still think it's cute. Look how little it is," Megan said, handing over the phone. Tony shook her head wondering what could be cute about a phone and went to plug it in.

Tony sat down on the couch and stretched her long legs out. Megan settled in next to her comfortably. Tony looked at her and said, "Let's go out to some place nice for dinner tomorrow night."

Megan smiled, liking the idea. "Ok. Want to go to the Ship's Beacon? It's really nice there and the food is good."

"Sure." Tony didn't particularly care where they went as long as she was with the small woman who was relaxed comfortably against her. Tony kissed the top of Megan's head and draped an arm around her shoulders.

"Could I ask you something?" Megan's face had turned serious with a small crease on her brow. She had noticed the past several days, that whenever they were not at home Tony had a completely different air about her. She seemed incredibly in tune with everything around them. Her eyes never stopped scanning any area they walked. It was a predatory alertness. It was like she was in a perpetual state of awareness.

Tony took in the expression on Megan's face as she asked the question and sensed this was not going to be something simple. Guardedly she answered, "Sure."

"There is just something I can't figure out about that

night in the Flats." She paused, watching Tony carefully.
"How did that guy ever get close enough to stab you?"

Tony's expression turned introspective. Her mind
journeyed back to that time and she remembered exactly
why she had been taken off guard. Caught up in the mael-
strom of emotions she felt that night, Tony captured
Megan's eyes with a penetrating gaze. "You see, there was
this beautiful, intelligent woman wearing a teal colored
dress, with absolutely mesmerizing eyes, a body to die for,
and a smile that lit up her whole face who I just couldn't
get out of my mind." Megan's eyes widen in surprise. "I
love you," she leaned over gently capturing Megan's lips
with her own. Words couldn't have explained Megan's
feelings just then, but her response to the gentle kiss did.

* * * * * * * * * * * *

"Hey," Tony responded to Brian's greeting the next
morning. Grabbing a cup of coffee from the never-ending
pot in the squad room, she walked over to his desk and sat
down.

Brian looked at her expectantly. He knew she had to
want something to come and plant herself at his desk.
"Well?"

Grinning companionably, she said, "Dr. Donnovan
came up with an interesting idea. She suggested using the
newspaper as a medium to lure out the killer. What do you
think?"

"I don't know. Might work, ya never know, but I
wouldn't hold my breath." Brian picked up his coffee and
took a sip. "I think I saw Mark in the Lieutenant's office.
He's been covering the story. He'd probably be the best
one to talk to."

"You want to do the release?"

"Oh, no. The brass would never approve it. They're
much too conservative. Besides, the FBI is better at this
type of thing. You don't have to worry about local reaction."

Tony smiled at him. "Laying it on me, huh?"

"Well, as much as I hate to admit it, the public is much more in awe of the FBI than the police." Brian smirked.

"Ok. But I'm going to play the reporter, too. I think his story will be much more believable if he doesn't know it's a ruse. You okay with that?"

Brian shrugged his shoulders. "Yeah. It's your call."

"Good. I'll clear it with Mike." Tony stood up and made her way to the task force room. She dialed Braxton's number and waited for him to answer.

"Braxton." Tony was surprised the Director had answered and not his secretary. "Hi, Mike. It's Tony. I want to make a bogus press release today ridiculing the Shadow killer in an attempt to draw him out a little," Tony said.

"Isn't that a little risky?" Mike asked. "He could go off the deep end."

"Yep. It's a big risk. But since he hasn't left any clues, and doesn't seem inclined to stop killing innocent women, it might be worth it. No guarantees though. I know it's a long shot."

Mike thought about it. It really wasn't any skin off his back. If it backfired, the blame would fall directly on Tony. If it worked, it would make him look good. "What do the locals think?"

"They're okay with it if we take responsibility for the announcement."

"If you think the risk is worth it, go for it," he replied, wanting to make absolutely sure she understood this one was on her.

Tony smiled to herself. He was setting the stage for deniability on his part. No problem, she could deal with that. "Ok. Later." Tony hung up the phone and went to find the reporter.

"Interested in a story?" Tony asked, knowing he'd be unable to refuse.

Mark's eyes brightened. "Did you get a break? The killer finally made a mistake?"

"No, nothing like that. We just want to send him a message." She led him to the conference room, and motioned for him to have a seat. Tony painted a picture of an antisocial, dysfunctional sociopath who preyed on women because he couldn't face his own shortcomings, and it was the only way he could exert control in his otherwise miserable little world. Tony was very careful to lend credence to the statement by pointing out correlations between some of the other known serial killers.

Mark took down all the information provided and, when she finished, he asked, "Do you really think the killer is a sociopath?"

"Of course. He is obviously a pathetic individual with absolutely no conscience." Tony wanted to make sure he was convinced. His delivery of the story would be very important. Tony knew that most sociopaths had methodical, cunning minds and were usually very intelligent. The ones that chose to kill were always difficult to apprehend.

Mark stood and said, "Thanks. I really appreciate the scoop. I'll get right to work on it. I should have it ready for tomorrow's morning edition."

* * * * * * * * * * *

Once Megan and David finished their caseload, they adjourned to Megan's office. "So what's the big news you have to tell me?" Megan asked, smiling at her good friend.

"You know we've been looking for a house." Megan nodded. "Well, we finally found one, and it's right on the lake. You should see it Megan. It's one of the older colonial style houses, and it's in great condition. The roof was just done last year, and the basement is completely dry. The hard wood floors were just refinished, and they look great! It has a completely modernized kitchen and three bedrooms. I've always wanted an extra room for an office, and Mike needs a place to work on his blue prints. We both love it. The loan is already approved, but I didn't want to say anything until I knew for sure. We just have to wait for the closing," David finished beaming with pride.

Megan walked over and hugged her friend. "That's just great. You've waited so long to find a place over there."

"Boy, don't I know it." David grinned back. "You guys will come to our house warming, right?"

"We wouldn't miss it. How long before you close?"

"I'm not sure. Maybe a month," David answered, a wide smile covering his face. "I better go clean up," he said, turning to go back to the autopsy suite.

Megan was working on the preliminary reports of the two autopsies she had done that morning, when the teasing, "Hey, Doc," drifted to her ears.

Looking up at Mark, she said, "Hi. What's up?"

"I just met with the FBI agent assigned to the Shadow case. The FBI is releasing a statement, sort of like a message to the Shadow killer. They believe the killer is some kind of deranged control freak, a bonafide sociopath who can't exist normally in society. Do you have any comments you'd like to add? Is that what you think, too? Or is this just maybe a ruse by the FBI to get the killer to make a mistake?"

Megan thought quickly. Tony obviously hadn't wasted any time on acting on her suggestion. She also had not clued Mark in. *Well that did make sense. The less people that knew, the better.*

"Yes, I think I'd have to agree with their assessment." Megan figured it wasn't really a lie because she actually thought whoever was doing it had to be a monster.

"Do you mind if I quote you as agreeing with them?" Mark asked.

"I don't mind, but I think my boss would probably have a coronary. So let's keep my comments off the record, okay?"

"Sure, no problem. I've got plenty for the story anyway. I better get to work on it. See you later."

"See you, Mark."

Chapter 15

Megan sat in the car next to Tony, her thoughts on their upcoming evening out. It was the first time they were really going on a date. Megan smiled at the thought. No matter that she had tried to deny it, she finally acknowledged that she had treated their night in the Flats as a date, privately, in her own mind. "I'd sure like to hear a song," she hinted.

Tony smiled, quickly glancing at her partner before turning back to the traffic. "See if you can find something on the radio you like."

Megan flipped through the channels stopping on the soft rock oldies channel. Tony knew the song and joined in. When she finished, Megan said, "I love listening to you. How did you ever learn to sing like that?"

"I don't know. I just always could," Tony replied self-consciously.

* * * * * * * * * * *

Megan had made reservations for seven. She took a shower while Tony rummaged through the closet in the spare bedroom and pulled out her favorite dress. It was a

simple black dress with spaghetti straps, moderately low
cut, designed to tastefully outline the curves it covered
before gaining width and ending above the knees. She got
the accessories she wanted out and waited for Megan to
finish showering.

Megan looked through her dresses. Her choice was
somewhat limited because she had steered away from more
than casual dates and hadn't felt the need to waste money
on clothes she wouldn't be wearing. Smiling, she decided
she just might have to do some clothes shopping soon. She
pulled out a white dress with thin straps, the top stylishly
suggestive, fitting snugly at the waist before gradually
becoming full and ending above the knee.

Tony finished in the shower and noticed Megan had
closed the bedroom door. *I guess we're dressing separately today.* She walked down the hall to the guest room.

Unknowingly, each woman's actions mirrored the
other. Both dressed with care, expertly applying makeup,
taking the extra time required to make sure their hair was
perfect, adding jewelry, and taking that last look in the
mirror, satisfied with their appearance.

Tony finished first and went to the living room to wait
for Megan. A short time later the smaller woman
appeared. Their eyes widened simultaneously, each taking
in the other's appearance. Both started to talk at the same
time and they ended up laughing. Tony said, "You are so
beautiful."

Megan blushed at the intensity of Tony's words and
smiled. "Thanks. But you know, since you took the words
right out of my mouth, I guess I'll have to settle for telling
you how gorgeous you are," she said playfully but meaning
every word of the compliment. She watched the red creep
up on Tony's face as she voiced her thanks for the compliment. Tony decided she had blushed more in the past two
weeks than she had in her whole life. She knew the reason
was because it had never mattered before what anyone
thought; but now, the plain truth was, it mattered very
much what the small woman standing in front of her

thought.

Megan and Tony were led to their seats out on the balcony overlooking the lake. Following the waiter, they were both aware of the appreciative looks cast their way by other patrons in the crowded restaurant. Tony was used to it. Megan was not.

"Everyone's looking at us," Megan said, quietly, once they were seated.

Tony smiled sassily, winked, and said, "That's cuz you look so good."

"I don't think I'm the only one they're looking at," she said answering Tony with an equally alluring smile, deciding two could play this game.

Tony looked at Megan and her pulse quickened. If they were going to stay for dinner, she had better change the subject because the way the woman she loved, who just happened to be dressed to kill, was sitting across the table smiling at her was quickly flaming a different appetite. "What are you going to have?" she asked, conceding to Megan.

Megan never missed a beat and said, "They've got really good salmon here. I think I'll have that." She was unable to keep a teasing smile from appearing on her face.

Tony just raised an eyebrow and smirked. "I think I'll have the same."

Megan and Tony enjoyed a leisurely dinner. They were constantly learning things about each other and, with each new discovery there came a greater understanding of and insight into the inner self of the other. They returned home tired but relaxed.

* * * * * * * * * * * *

Tony had always been an early riser, but that had taken on a new attraction lately. The past few mornings, she woke up enveloped in a sense of well being with the weight of her partner resting across her. She relished the comfort she found in their closeness and would wait for her lover to wake up. She loved to watch Megan open her eyes and smile lazily up at her.

Megan woke to the sound of Tony's heart beating a steady rhythm in her ear. She knew the blue orbs were watching her and knew the love she felt was reflected back in them. She slowly lifted her head to meet the eyes watching her. With a sultry smile, she traced her finger slowly along Tony's cheek and down her neck, feeling the quickening of her partner's pulse. Meeting Tony's eyes she began a languid exploration, feeling Tony's quick intake of breath. Tony kissed her, and Megan knew her not so subtle invitation was being enthusiastically accepted.

* * * * * * * * * * * *

Tony was nervous. Ever since Megan had told her Ashley wanted to meet her and was coming over for dinner, she had been uneasy. This was Megan's sister. Her favorite sister. What if she didn't like her? She knew Megan had told Ashley about them, but she didn't want their relationship to make things difficult for Megan. She wryly laughed at herself. Normally Tony didn't give a damn about what people thought of her.

Megan walked over and sat down beside Tony. She could tell her partner was uncomfortable and knew she was worried about meeting Ashley. "Hey, relax," she said putting her hand on Tony's thigh. "You'll like her, and I know she'll like you." Grinning mischievously, Megan said, "She knows I have good taste." The last prompted a smile from Tony.

"You need any more help?"

"You know everything's done," Megan said. "Come here." She urged Tony's head down for a kiss. Megan tucked herself up against Tony's side while they waited for Ashley to arrive. Tony relaxed, comforted by the small woman leaning against her side.

When Megan answered the door, she drew her sister into a quick hug. Taking her hand, Megan led her into the apartment and introduced her to Tony. Ashley had the usual reaction of people meeting Tony for the first time, awe, surprise, and an awareness of a dangerous, yet sensuous, aura surrounding the tall woman.

Smiling to herself, she could certainly understand why her sister was so taken with this tall, appealing woman. "So, Tony, Megan tells me you're an FBI agent. What's it like?"

"It's really just like any other job. You spend a great deal of time behind a desk, or doing legwork researching leads which usually don't pan out. It's not nearly as glamorous as TV portrays it to be."

Megan changed the direction of the conversation at this point, knowing how much Tony hated to be the topic of conversation. "Ashley, did you guys go the Grand Prix today?"

"No, John took the kids to his mom's house for the day. I had to finish up a project for work, so I decided to let them go on alone."

Tony quietly studied Megan's sister. Ashley was taller than Megan, about 5'6", and had golden brown hair and brown eyes. She seemed to be very easy going and smiled a lot. The rapport between the two was obvious by their easy bantering back and forth. Megan and Ashley were both very gregarious, and it wasn't long before Tony's uneasiness subsided and she was drawn into the conversation.

Ashley decided she liked the tall, dark woman. She seemed rather quiet, but Ashley had not missed how her eyes followed every move Megan made and the love they projected. It was very obvious to her this woman was devoted to Megan. She also sensed they shared something very special and was happy with that knowledge.

Later that night, a memory wove its way through Tony's mind. Wistfully, she examined it. A happy time, so long ago. She brutally forced it away, knowing she didn't deserve it, and that it had only been brought on by the interaction she'd seen between Megan and her sister.

Megan looked over at Tony and saw a distant expression on her face. "What are you thinking about?"

Tony left her ruminations and said, "You really don't want to know."

"Tony, I really do," Megan said meaningfully and patted the spot on the bed next to her. "Please?"

Tony looked at Megan and realized the simple word was more than a quest for knowledge; it was a plea for trust. Apprehensively, she acquiesced to Megan's request hoping she wasn't about to lose her partner's respect.

"Ok, but don't say I didn't warn you." She joined Megan on the bed, her blue eyes glittering darkly. Megan just took Tony's hand and held it.

"You wanted to know what my mother was like," Tony began, her thoughts going far back in time. As the memories filtered out, she voiced her thoughts aloud.

"My mother ran the family with an iron hand, but we were a close-knit family, and there was always plenty of love to go around. We didn't have a lot, but there was always food on the table and a roof over our heads. Mom worked two jobs to keep us in clothes and other necessities. She worked really hard. You gotta give her a lot of credit, raising three children alone, and she refused to accept government aid."

"She sounds pretty special," Megan commented.

"Yeah. She is. I think I was probably her biggest trial. I was always in trouble. I had an almost unerring ability to find it, usually dragging my brothers along. Mom always had to come to school to pick me up. She tried her best, but most of our clothes were from Goodwill or the Salvation Army. The kids were pretty cruel. They were always making fun of us. So I retaliated. It didn't matter whether they targeted my brothers or me. I made them pay. So she got called - a lot. She used to tell me, 'Tony, just ignore them. Words can't hurt you.' But, the one thing I had learned from her already was pride. She was proud of us. She never let anyone talk down to her, and I guess that's why I just refused to be looked down on."

Megan saw several emotions cross Tony's face as she related the story of a happy family and a home full of love. "Do you get to see her very often with all the traveling you do?"

Megan saw an expression of pain cover her lover's face. Squeezing her hand gently, she offered her support giving Tony renewed strength to face the haunting memories. She then explained how she, her brothers, and two friends went to the mountains to spend the weekend in a cabin. They were playing around trying to track each other through the woods.

Tony said, "It was my turn."

The figures moved stealthily amidst the trees. The object of their hunt obscured in the branches of a tall tree, watching.

All of a sudden they heard gunfire. As the four on the ground quickly stopped and looked around, Tony exited the tree, landing softly near them. She put up a hand indicating silence and slowly made her way toward the gunfire. The others began to follow, and she stopped and told them to go back to the cabin. At George and Joey's protests, she told them she just wanted to see what was going on, and then she'd meet them back there.

She waited until the others turned back toward the cabin before continuing. On the streets of Boston she had often heard rumors of paramilitary groups operating in the mountains but had never believed them. Tony knew she should just go back to the cabin with the others, but curiosity spurred her on. In the meantime, Joey and George told Vinnie and Sharon that they were going with their sister and they would meet them at the cabin later with Tony. Since George was the oldest, no one questioned his decision.

The boys backtracked; careful to make sure they followed a route different from the one Tony had taken. Her temper was infamous, and neither wanted to incur her wrath. They figured they'd just meet up with her a little further on. and then she'd have to let them come with her.

The gunfire grew louder, and she moved up into the thick trees. From her vantage point, she saw a staggered group of eleven men moving through the woods. They seemed to be chasing something, but she couldn't make out what it was. Watching the group move toward her, a man suddenly came into sight bleeding from wounds to his leg and arm. Her first instinct was to help him, but the group of men chasing him was approaching too quickly. They passed beneath her hiding place closing the gap on the wounded man.

Tony decided it was time to go back to the cabin and get help. There was no telephone, but they did have a ham radio. As she made her way down the tree, there were loud shouts by some of the men, and the staccato clatter of machine guns once again filled the air. Scrambling back up the tree, what she saw froze the blood in her veins. The gunfire had abruptly stopped and the men were standing around two still bodies. The still forms wore the clothes of her brothers. The image burned into her mind as she watched, frozen in horror.

Cursing and bits of conversation could be heard in woods that had suddenly become quiet. "You idiots. Look what you've done. They're nothing but kids." At an unspoken command, the men hauled ass away from the scene of carnage.

Tony never remembered exiting the tree or the mad dash to her brothers. She knelt first next to one and then the other. And as the realization hit her that they were dead and that she'd never hear their voices again, never join them in fun, never laugh with them, never tease them or hug them, never nothing...ever again. When the finality of their death ripped through her, she screamed, so full of hurt and anguish that it rocked her back on her heels. Her heart breaking, she choked out one last desperate plea. "No. God...please, God...no."

She lifted each brother's head into her lap, caressing their faces, tears rolling down her face. The enormity of *her role in this tragedy unfolded in her mind draping a mantle of guilt over her shoulders. Numbness soon followed. This was her fault. She should have just gone back to the cabin with them. She hardly felt the hand that grasped her shoulder, not caring that she might be in danger, knowing she deserved any fate that came her way.*

"Kid, come on," said a man's voice. "We gotta get out of here. They could come back."

She never acknowledged the man and couldn't have cared less if they came back. She deserved it. She had led her brothers to their death.

Desperate, the man walked around, leaned over the still forms cradled in front of her, grasped her shoulders in his hands and shook her. "Come on, kid. Now."

"I'm not leaving them," she said quietly, daring him to defy her.

The man sat down near her, his left trouser leg covered with blood, stanched by a tourniquet. "You can't help them now. The only thing we can do is try to get who was responsible for this. If they come back and we don't get out of here, the same thing may happen to someone else. Please."

At his words, anger built inside her. Her mind had grasped the words, 'get who was responsible for this.' She gently moved each brother's head from her lap and stood. Looking at the man whose arm was still dripping blood, she unsnapped the first aid pack at her waist, and field dressed the wound. Never saying a word, she walked toward the cabin.

The man was Chuck Parker. He was an FBI agent who had infiltrated the paramilitary group that had killed Tony's brothers. He had been betrayed. Once they arrived back at the cabin, he called for help and it came in the way of an FBI team. Tony was airlifted out along with her brothers' remains.

Tony couldn't bear to see the pain in her mother's eyes. She had caused it. She had led her brothers into danger. Her mother turned away from her in her grief and, knowing she was responsible, she turned away from her mother. She accepted the blame for her mother's pain, shouldering it along with the already enormous burden she had taken on. When the double funeral was over, she left home.

The only lifeline offered was from Chuck Parker. As he befriended her, she learned all she could about the FBI and what she had to do to become an agent. With a focus that was to become legendary, she threw herself into her college work. Working part time to support herself and taking courses full time, she had no time left for the mind-numbing grief. She buried it deep inside, her only thoughts were those of revenge.

* * * * * * * * * * * *

Megan had pulled Tony's head against her when the telling of the story had lent silent tears to her lover's face. Her heart cried out at the palpable pain emanating from her partner, and she offered her support through the comfort of her contact. As the tortured eyes met hers, Megan listened to words so filled with self-loathing she almost shuddered at the intensity of them. "So what do you think of me now? I led my brothers to their death."

Megan blinked to clear her eyes. "You didn't kill your brothers. They were killed in a random act of violence because they were in the wrong place at the wrong time." As Tony began to interrupt, Megan placed her fingers against her mouth saying, "Ssh. You need to listen to what I have to say." Tightening her hold on Tony, she continued, "You cannot blame yourself for something you had no control over. You didn't know your brothers hadn't gone back to the cabin," she paused, softening her voice, "no matter how much we may want to, we can't control fate. You never led your brothers to danger. It found them." Megan captured her partner's eyes and looked deeply into them. "Nothing can change what happened." Megan's voice was filled with a quiet certainty. "But it wasn't your fault. Quit blaming yourself. Just let it go."

Maybe it was what the woman-child that had been buried along with the memories in Tony's mind for so long needed to hear and never had, or maybe it was just the conviction she heard in her partner's voice, but as the words caressed her troubled mind, Tony wanted to believe them. Tears are often a catharsis, and Tony's fell freely. She finally mourned her brothers and her lost innocence and took the first tentative steps out of a cloud of darkness that night. It would be a slow process, especially in so troubled a soul, but with love guiding her the healing could begin. Cradled in Megan's arms, the emotionally drained woman fell into an exhausted sleep.

Megan thought about what Tony had told her. She could understand what had happened between her and her mother. Perhaps the worst fate a mother can suffer is to outlive her children. And to lose two children so violently would have been devastating to any parent. Tony's mother had been unable to see the grief shared by her daughter because of her own. Thirty seconds of mindless violence on a warm summer afternoon had destroyed a family. Megan knew there would be no closure for Tony until she saw her mother. But until she was ready to, Megan would be there for her to help guide her out of the dark shroud of guilt she had carried for far too long. Megan also understood the deep level of trust Tony had placed in her to have bared her soul, and she would guard it and protect it at any cost.

Tony woke up the next morning feeling more at peace than she had known in a long time. Looking at Megan, she became so aware of her love for the smaller woman that it almost overwhelmed her. She also realized something else. *I need her. I REALLY need her.* It was a startling revelation for someone who had decided, years before, to never love or need anyone. She didn't know when or how the change had come about, but she couldn't even begin to imagine life without Megan now.

Tony and Megan walked along the shores of Lake Erie, their hands intertwined, watching the waves crash over the breakers.

"It's really nice here," Tony said, loving the sound of the crashing waves.

"Yeah. I've always liked to come to the beach. Sometimes when I was going to college and I needed a quiet place to come just to get away from all the pressure, this is where I came. I guess that's the reason I moved so close to it."

"I'm glad you did. It's kind of interesting that you picked such a friendly place." Megan knew Tony was referring to the large population of people in this particular suburb, who, like themselves, enjoyed alternative lifestyles. Tony had never cared one way or the other what people thought of her, *well except for Megan,* but she didn't want Megan to be uncomfortable, and it was nice to blend in once in a while.

"Well, that part was unintentional," Megan replied. "I just liked the apartment, and it was close to the lake. The other part is just kind of coincidence. But a good coincidence, I think," she said, smiling at Tony.

Relaxing after returning from the beach, Tony and Megan watched a National Geographic special on TV. "Aw, isn't that one cute? Look at those big eyes," Megan said.

"Yeah. It is kind of cute. I wonder what it is?"

The announcer answered the question for them calling the tiny dog a Brussels Griffon.

"Did you ever have a dog when you were a kid?" asked Megan, looking up at Tony.

"Yeah. We had a part Lab dog called Vido. We had a lot of fun with him," Tony responded, "What about you?"

"No. Dad wouldn't let us have pets. He said they were too unsanitary. We always wanted one, though. Every time I rescued a puppy or kitten off the street, he took it down to the shelter. So I finally gave up," Megan replied.

"You rescued puppies and kittens, too? I thought Mom was going to kill me for bringing home all the critters I did. Baby birds, kittens, and even a skunk one time. She was pretty mad about that one. But it was only a baby. If you could have had any kind of dog you wanted, what would you have picked?"

"Oh, I think...um...maybe a cocker spaniel. They're kind of cute. What about you?"

"Definitely a Rottweiler," Tony responded.

"Tony! Aren't they mean?"

"Nope. That's a common misconception because of what some of the idiot owners do to them. If you treat them right, they're just big loveable teddy bears."

"Oh, kinda like you," Megan said, watching her partner closely.

"MEGAN! I am NOT a big, lovable teddy bear! Give me a break!" Tony sputtered with an incredulous look on her face, the image of a brown and white bear with a goofy smile and button eyes floating through her mind.

Megan smiled to herself and thought, *Gotcha.* "I don't know...I think you're pretty lovable." Megan watched Tony's face turn a pretty shade of red before leaning over and rescuing her with a kiss.

Chapter
16

They had finally caught a break in the Shadow case. One of the informants Tony interviewed provided information on a drug dealer that specialized in "unusual" products on the street. His claim to fame was that he could get anything anyone wanted. Brian shook his head, bemused. Tony's unusual interrogation technique had paid off once again. He had the fleeting thought of how nice it would be to have her as a permanent part of the team.

He sent two of the task force members out to try to locate the drug dealer who operated on the East Side. Brian walked over to the cold drink machine and bought two Coke's, taking one back to Tony. "Hey, Tony, if you ever consider leaving the FBI, you got a job here if ya want it," he said, handing her the Coke.

Smiling at Brian, Tony said, "Thanks Brian. I'll keep that in mind, but I think I'm a little too old for the police academy."

"Not too old, just too advanced. You'd probably just embarrass the instructors," Brian said, grinning.

"The man has a sense of humor," she jibed back. "I just hope this pans out. We could use a break."

"Yeah, I know what you mean. The brass have been on

my ass since the last victim."

Several hours later, the two task force members returned with the drug dealer handcuffed between them. The information provided had been solid, and the drug dealer was actually at a meet when accosted by the police officers. They took him to one of the interview rooms.

Brian looked at Tony. "He's all yours."

"Let him sit for a while and worry. Since we got him on a legit bust, it'll soften him up. Besides, he has no idea why we really want to talk to him. Do we offer him a deal if it's worth our while?"

"Yeah. That coke he was selling was small time stuff," Brian said. "If it'll give us a break on the Shadow case, it'd be worth it."

An hour later, Tony made her way to the interview room while Brian ensconced himself behind the two-way glass. Brian watched the tall woman with interest. She walked into the room and looked at the lowlife sitting in the chair. Moving to the chair across the table from him, she sat down. With an even expression, she just sat there watching him.

As he grew increasingly uncomfortable, he shifted around in his chair. He sneered, unable to tolerate the implacable woman sitting across from him. "If you got nothing to say, why don't you get out of here? I ain't gonna tell ya nothing anyway. I want a lawyer."

Tony's expression changed and a feral smile appeared. "Let's see, possession, selling, plus your priors...um...what's that good for, ten to fifteen? I can call you a lawyer, no problem. It's a done deal, you got a ticket straight back to the joint. Got your things packed?" Tony paused, watching the man across from her. His bravado was rapidly unraveling. "A lawyer can't do anything for you, but I might be able to. Now, do you still want a lawyer?"

Looking at her suspiciously, he asked, "What do you want?"

"I heard you been selling some little vials on the

street. I want to know where you've been getting them
from and who you've been selling them to," Tony
demanded, her expression callous.

Tony noticed a slight change in the demeanor of the
dealer sitting across from her. "I don't know what you're
talking about."

Tony mused, *So we do have the right guy. Ok, lets
play.* "Ya know Reg, I don't believe you. I think you
know exactly what I'm talking about. Now we can stop
playing games, or I will call that lawyer for you."

"What's in it for me?" the dealer parleyed back.

"It depends. If you give up the buyer and who you're
getting it from, I'll put in a good word with the prosecutor
for you."

"Fuck that. That ain't good enough." He crossed his
arms and stared defiantly at her.

"Oh, I think it's better than you deserve," Tony said,
pale blue eyes glaring and her smile feral. Walking around
the table, she leaned over and whispered a few words into
his ear and then walked away and leaned against the wall.

From the observation room, Brian watched in amazement. Whatever she had said to the dealer had caused him
to become very pale, and he started spilling his guts.

"I been getting it from some doctor at City Hospital.
He needs money. So he gets me what I ask for. The dude
been buying it, I don't know who he is. We meet in the
warehouse district by the Flats. I only sold to him twice,"
Reg spit out.

"What's he look like?"

"Like any guy. About tall as you. Got brown hair and
a beard and mustache."

"Reg, you going to make me ask you every single
thing? Now tell me about him," Tony growled back.

"He was wearing jeans and a sports shirt both times.
He sets up the meets for midnight and then he always gets
there early before me. He don't talk street. He bought
three the first time and five the second time. Ain't nothing
else to tell."

"Now tell me about the doctor you've been getting the stuff from," Tony said, still leaning against the wall. Once Tony had all the information she felt she could get from Reg, she left the interview room.

Brian grinned at her and said, "You're good. But I really wanna know what you whispered to him?"

Tony just shrugged, quirked a smile at him, and said, "Sorry, trade secret." Brian rolled his eyes.

* * * * * * * * * * *

Megan felt restless. All her autopsy reports were pending until the lab results returned and the city had been quiet. She was glad the Shadow killer had also taken a break. She wondered if it was because of the newspaper article Mark had written. He had done an excellent job of portraying the killer as a bona fide madman. If that article didn't lure him out, nothing would.

Megan's thoughts turned to Dwayne. She hardly ever saw him anymore. Not that she minded, but it seemed a little strange. At one time she just thought he had a temper and would never resort to violence, but now she wasn't so sure. She had seen the look he'd given her yesterday when he thought she wasn't looking. Megan had not told Tony. She was afraid of what Tony might do. Megan still wanted to believe he just had a bad temper and would not resort to anything more than the looks of hatred he seemed especially fond of giving her.

* * * * * * * * * * *

The next couple of days passed quietly with no new developments in the case. Tony and Megan had settled into a comfortable routine. Tony continued driving Megan to work, so Megan took the opportunity to get some warranty work done on her car. In this case it was a toggle switch for switching the air bags on or off. Since she was on call, Tony had told her she could just take her car if she got called out at night.

* * * * * * * * * * *

"Will you just take it easy? You know I'm on call."
Megan said, her hands on Tony's arms. "You can't go
every single place I do. That's why I got the cellular
phone."

Tony knew Megan was right, but that didn't stop her
from worrying about her partner going out alone at night.
"It would make me feel a lot better if I went with you,"
Tony said. "I'll just sit here and worry about you."

Megan hugged Tony. "You don't need to worry. There
will be cops all over the place. Who could possibly bother
me there? Besides you can't enter the crime scene anyway,
so what are you going to do, sit in the car?"

"I don't mind waiting in the car."

Megan looked up at the tall woman's worry-etched
face. She was so over protective. There had been no problems for the last week, and Megan felt perhaps the attack
against her had been random after all. Going out at night
was part of her job. Tony was just going to have to understand that. "Tony..."

"Okay, but I want you to call me before you leave the
crime scene so I can wait for you downstairs." Tony was
not at all happy with the outcome of this conversation.

Megan pulled her head down for a kiss. "I will, and
don't worry. It's okay, really, and besides, the sooner I
leave the sooner I can get back," Megan said, smiling.

"I know." Tony walked with Megan to the car. She
opened the door, reached in and switched on the kill switch
under the dash, and then handed Megan her car keys.
"Don't forget to call before you leave."

"Ok. I'll be back as soon as I can."

Megan drove to the crime scene going over what little
she knew. The victim had been found on the near west side
stabbed to death. Apparently the police were also questioning the possibility of a rape attempt.

Megan got out of the car and followed the flashing lights cutting a path through the darkness as she approached the crime scene. After flashing her badge, she was led to the victim. Megan looked at the body and then quickly turned away. She took a deep breath and forced her mind to find the clinical detachment she had to have in order to proceed with her examination. Megan was having difficulty with that tonight. This was so brutal. *How could anyone do this?* This wasn't just the result of cold-blooded killing; it was the result of insane rage. Finally, corralling her revulsion and swallowing down the nausea this act of atrocity had sparked, she began her preliminary examination.

* * * * * * * * * * * *

Tony waited impatiently for Megan to call. She had been gone for over an hour. Tony knew an hour wasn't very long, but she just couldn't stop worrying. She wished for an end to the Shadow case. The idea that the victims were remarkably similar in appearance to Megan was one she had not shared with her partner, but she hadn't planned on Megan taking off by herself either.

Tony turned on the TV and flipped through the channels before turning it off again. Walking over to the stereo, she turned it on. Music usually relaxed her. Not tonight, though. She had a bad feeling she couldn't shake. Tony trusted her instincts, but she also realized she was very over-protective of Megan and wondered if she was just over-reacting. Starting as the phone rang, Tony quickly answered, "Hello."

"Hi," Megan said. "We should be done here in a few minutes, so I should be home in around twenty minutes or so."

"You be careful. I'll wait by the elevator," Tony said, relieved to hear Megan's voice.

Tony still couldn't shake the sense of foreboding that had come over her, and she decided to go down to the

garage now instead of waiting for Megan to call. Stepping
out of the elevator she moved to a dark area and leaned
casually against the wall. Most of the tenants were already
home, so she didn't expect to see anyone. For ten minutes
she casually scanned the garage looking for anything out
of place.

As her eyes turned toward the garage entrance, Tony
glimpsed a quickly moving shadow near the row of cars by
the door. All her senses were engaged as she felt rather
than saw the other presence. Knowing she wasn't visible
unless someone was within three feet of her, she slowly
scrutinized the rows of cars near the entrance. Her eyes
moved over each car and then down each row. In the third
row, fifth car over, she identified an unnatural shadow.
She riveted her eyes to the spot, her whole body tensing as
she waited for the shadow to move. Tony didn't have to
wait long. The shadowed figure moved stealthily from row
to row, ever closer to the elevator entrance.

Moving deeper in the shadows, she watched the figure
approach. She was now able to make out the shape of a
man, roughly her height, with a medium build. He stopped
and bent down, hidden from view one row over from the
elevator, which Tony wryly noted, was also one row over
from Megan's parking spot.

Tony thought over her options. Megan was due back
any minute now. Obviously the man wasn't here for a
social visit. She had been unable to get a good look at
him, but he loosely fit the description of the man who had
attacked Megan. Yet to roust him now would prove nothing because no crime had been committed. Cursing the
lack of foresight that had caused her to leave her gun
upstairs she moved very slowly along the wall, intending
to be within striking distance once his intentions became
clear.

Headlights illuminated the walls of the garage as the
familiar Buick pulled in and rolled into the parking place
near the elevator. Megan got out of the car, locked it with
the keypad, and quickly looked around before making her

way to the elevator. Tony was supposed to be waiting for her and, even though she didn't like to admit it, she was a little nervous. Her nervousness quickly gave way to concern. It wasn't like Tony not to be here waiting for her. *Well maybe she fell asleep.* That thought didn't bring her much comfort, though, because she had talked to her not even twenty minutes ago.

Megan's mind barely had time to register a body hurtling toward her while simultaneously recognizing it as Tony's when she was practically knocked over by a forceful shove. Struggling to maintain her balance, her heart almost stopped at the sight before her.

Tony saw the man pop up from behind the car and sprinted toward Megan. Without conscious thought she propelled her body forward shoving Megan back placing herself between them. Settling comfortably in to the role of predator, every muscle tense, she waited for him to make the next move.

The sudden movement had caused the man to stop and, when he entered the light, Tony recognized Dwayne. The thought flickered through her mind that he looked like something ripped from the screen of a horror movie. He was covered with blood and was standing in front of her waving a knife around. When she saw the maniacal gleam in his eyes, Tony realized Dwayne had gone over the edge.

Megan backed up against the wall and pulled the cellular phone from her purse. Dialing 911, she requested assistance and then, after identifying herself, she asked that Sgt. Davies also be notified. Disconnecting the phone, her eyes stayed focused on the scene in front of her.

Tony and Dwayne moved counterclockwise feinting in and out. Tony was very careful to stay out of his reach and tried to draw him off balance. When he lunged at her, she sidestepped and attempted to disarm him. His reflexes were quicker than she anticipated and allowed him to escape the movement, her hand only grazing his arm. Lunging in and out, it was a dance of predators, each matching the other's move with a counter move.

Dwayne's gestures were more frenzied and he taunted, "You got lucky last time bitch. You're mine now."

Tony absorbed the words and realized this was the bastard who had stabbed her. Deciding to put an end to this quickly, she thrust her leg up and out in a lightening quick move dislodging the knife from his hand. She moved forward quickly kicking the knife across the floor. Dwayne countered with a spinning sidekick that she partially deflected with her arm while simultaneously leaping away in an attempt to minimize the impact of his blow.

Taking advantage of Dwayne's forward momentum, she threw the weight of her body behind her fist and aimed for his solar plexus. Dwayne's face reflected surprise as he grunted in pain. As he struggled for breath, she followed up by sweeping his legs out from under him, knocking him to the floor.

Tony reached down, grabbing Dwayne by the shirt with every intention of slamming his head into the floor when she heard, "Tony," and felt Megan's hand on her shoulder. For a long second she was frozen before releasing some of the tension from her body letting Dwayne slump to the floor. Keeping the prone figure in sight, Tony turned to Megan.

Megan watched the two face off, praying for the cops to arrive. Tony had put herself in danger to protect her, and there was nothing she could do to help. Megan asked, "You ok?"

Tony quirked a half-smile and nodded her head. "I'm fine. What about you? I didn't mean to push you so hard." Her attention was drawn to Dwayne who had struggled to a sitting position. "That's about as far as you need to go," Tony growled at him.

His retort was lost in the commotion of the arriving police cars, as patrol officers with guns drawn moved quickly toward them. Shouting obscenities at Tony, Dwayne was handcuffed and led to a patrol car.

Tony was giving a patrolman her statement when Brian arrived. He walked over to the patrolman and said, "I'll take it from here."

Brian looked at Tony and Megan. "You two all right?"
Tony nodded her head and Megan answered, "Yes."

"Tony, would you mind coming down to the station to
give your statement? From the looks of him, he's going to
be nailed for more than just attempted assault, and I want
an ironclad case. So let's do everything by the book."

"Ok," Tony said. "I'll meet you down there." She
looked at Megan and said, "I forgot something upstairs."

On the elevator ride, Tony asked again, "Are you ok?"

Megan smiled at her. "Yeah, I'm fine. What did you
forget?"

Tony cocked her head raising her eyebrow slightly and
said, "My gun." She knew Megan was not fond of them.

"Oh," said Megan.

Entering the apartment, Tony headed for the bedroom
to get her weapon. She stopped when she felt Megan's
hand on her arm and turned around. Megan threw both
arms around Tony and drew her into a fierce hug. Returning the hug, Tony asked, "What's this for?"

Megan rested her head against Tony's chest, the whole
scene playing over in her mind, and she knew she would be
lost without this tall, dark woman standing here holding
her. She could never go back to the way her life had been
before. The thought flickered though her mind, *What life?*
"I was so worried about you. He could have really hurt
you. He had a knife. I never want to go through that
again."

Tony rested her chin on Megan's head. "I'll do my
best to make sure you never do," she said, unhappy that
she had worried her lover. "But Megan," she paused, lifting her head and gazing into the hazel eyes, "he wanted to
hurt you, and I'm going to do my level best to make damn
sure no one ever does that, no matter what it takes."

Megan found herself captivated by the deep blue eyes
radiating a love she never thought she'd find. "I love you
so much," she murmured, placing her hands in the long
dark hair covering Tony's neck, gently urging her head

down, and meeting the soft lips with her own.

Tony held her for a few minutes before saying, "I have to go." Reluctantly releasing her partner, she went to get her gun and slipped it into place before going back to the living room. "Why don't you go to bed? I don't know how long I'll be."

Megan looked at Tony and smiled. "I think I'll wait up." She raised her fingers to Tony's mouth to stop the rebuttal. "Just humor me, ok?"

Tony placed her hand on Megan's face, gently caressing it, and said, "Ok."

* * * * * * * * * * *

Tony's beauty wasn't lost on Brian as he watched her walk gracefully across the squad room toward him. He was very fond of the tall FBI agent and impressed with her skill. He had no idea how she had managed to disarm that lowlife tonight, but he intended to find out.

He nodded his head in greeting. "Want to fill me in?"

When Tony finished relating the events to Brian, she noticed a quizzical expression on his face. "What?"

Taking a calculated risk, he asked, "You two stay together?"

Tony was overcome with anger. "I don't see how that's any of your business."

Brian was not fazed. He had expected the reaction. "Tony, I asked you as a friend not a cop. I happen to like you, and I care about people I like. So if you don't want to answer, fine. Don't. It's no big deal anyway."

Tony willed herself to calm down. "Sorry. There's just been so much going on lately. The attack on Megan last week and then the one tonight. If that's not bad enough, all the Shadow killer's victims look like her." Tony's piercing blue eyes met Brian's. "But to answer your question, yeah, we stay together." She paused, briefly, and continued, "And I just happen to be in love with her. So if you don't like that..."

Brian interrupted. "Good. I thought so. So when are
you two coming over to meet my wife and kids?"

Tony was so surprised her jaw dropped open causing
Brian to laugh. Snapping her mouth closed and clearing
her throat, she asked, "You thought so?"

"Hell, Tony, your face gives it away every time you
look at her."

Tony felt her face redden and said, "Um, maybe we
could have a raincheck for after we solve this case."

Brian agreed that sounded like a good idea. "You
ready to interrogate that dirt ball?"

"What, are you crazy? He'll never talk to me. He did
nothing but cus me out the whole time he was being led to
the patrol car."

"It seems he's had a change of heart. Now he's asking
for you."

Tony rolled her eyes. Just what she needed. So much
for getting home anytime soon. "Did he ask for a lawyer?"

"No. He waived his rights. Said he'd only talk to you,
though."

Dwayne had been most cooperative. He drifted from
cursing Tony out for taking a man's job to bragging about
what he did to women who didn't know their place. He
spent the remaining time confessing to a multitude of
crimes, including all of the rapes on the near west side, and
the Shadow killings. He delighted in telling Tony in
graphic detail exactly how he had perpetrated the crimes,
including his attack on her. He was relating each rape case
in excruciating detail and they had already been at it for
two hours.

Tony was repulsed by his graphic depiction of the
crimes he committed and thought about all the irreparable
harm he had caused to the victims that were still alive.
She decided to take a break, more for her sanity than anything. She walked out of the interrogation room and
decided to call Megan to tell her not to wait up. This was
going to be an all nighter.

"Hi," she said smiling into the phone when Megan

answered.

"Hi yourself. When you coming home?"

"I got stuck interrogating Dwayne. He wouldn't talk to anyone else. So why don't you go to bed? It's going to be a long night."

"How about I come down there? I'm really not tired, and I've got to give a statement sometime anyway."

"There's no reason for you to come down here. Your statement can wait until tomorrow and, besides, you'll just be bored."

"I'm bored here. Besides you're down there and that happens to be reason enough for me. I can take a cab down."

"No. I'll have Brian send someone for you, if you really want to come down here."

"I really want to. See you soon." Megan hung up the phone, effectively ending the conversation before Tony could argue the point.

"Hey, Brian," Tony said, walking over to the big man, "Megan wants to come down and give her statement tonight. Her car's in the shop. Is there anyone that can pick her up? Otherwise I'll go get her. It wouldn't take long."

"I'll find someone. There is no way you can leave now. Not with Dwayne singing like a bird. You've only been out of there for five minutes and he's already asking for you."

Tony groaned, her eyes darkening. "You know what I'd like to do with him?"

"Somehow I don't think I want to know," Brian said. "Go ahead and get it over with. I'll find someone to pick up Megan."

"Thanks," she said and walked back toward the interrogation room.

Chapter 17

Megan hung up quickly before Tony could change her mind. There was no way she was sitting in the apartment by herself as keyed up as she was. Even if Tony was busy, there would be cops to talk to, and that was much more appealing than staying at home. The fact it was close to midnight was no big deal. She put on a pair of jeans and a pullover top and waited for her escort.

A short time later the doorbell chimed. Megan depressed the button on the speaker near the door and asked, "Yes?"

"I was sent to pick you up," came the distorted voice through the speaker.

"Ok." Megan pushed the button to disengage the lock on the downstairs door. A few minutes later, a knock sounded on the door. Megan looked through the peephole and opened it, smiling at the familiar figure. "How'd you get elected?"

Mark lazily smiled and said, "I heard what happened on the scanner so I went over to the station and waited for them to arrive. Tony's been tied up in the interrogation room, and a semi turned over on dead man's curve again. All the patrol units are tied up over there because it happened at the same time the circus let out. So Brian asked me to come and get you."

"Thanks. I really appreciate it."

"No problem, I'm just glad I'm not stuck in that traffic. You ready?"

"Yeah. Let's go."

* * * * * * * * * * *

Tony took another break. Her mood was very dark after spending another hour in the interrogation room. Dwayne had started describing the murders, but for some reason he refused to go into detail like he had on the rapes. He was toying with her, and she could think of some very creative ways to make him talk. Unfortunately, she couldn't do that here.

Her thoughts quickly brightened at the thought of seeing Megan. She should be here now. Even though she had tried to discourage her from coming down, there was no one Tony wanted to see more right now.

Tony walked through the squad room and then to the conference room. Not seeing Megan, she asked Brian, "Do you know where Megan's at?"

"She'll be here any minute. There's a big accident on the innerbelt, and they got tied up in all the circus traffic. Mark just called in and told me why it was taking so long."

"Mark, as in the reporter?" Seeing Brian shake his head affirmatively, she asked, "Why did you send him?"

"The patrol cars are all tied up on the accident and, besides, he and Megan know each other."

"Oh, that's right." Tony turned away and walked into the task force room. She wanted to focus her attention away from Dwayne and looked around the room. She saw an envelope with the familiar FBI logo on the corner resting in her in-box. Walking over, she picked it up and opened it. She sat down at the table to read. Tony had requested this background check over a week ago, but had had to call in a few markers to get the military file. St.

Louis wasn't real fond of releasing information, even if it was to other government agencies.

****

Megan looked over at Mark and asked, "Why are we going this way? It'd be shorter to just cut through on West Third."

"We should miss all the traffic this way. A lot of other people are probably using that cut through," Mark said, steering the car down the hill leading into the Flats.

Megan was still puzzled at the route Mark had chosen. If they followed the Flats straight through they would exit right into downtown Cleveland and, if the circus had just let out, they would be right in the middle of all the traffic.

"Anything new on the case? Did the newspaper article help? Do you think the killer got the message?" Mark asked amiably.

"Nothing new that I know of. But you really did a good job on the newspaper article. If it doesn't send a message to the killer nothing will," Megan said.

After exiting the West Side of the Flats into downtown, they became embroiled in traffic. While they were sitting in the standstill traffic, Mark picked up the cellular phone mounted on the dash and called Brian. "Hi, Brian, it's Mark. We're stuck in the traffic downtown, but we should be there shortly. I figure another twenty minutes or so."

Mark muttered, "Damn," when he missed a turn and was unable to get into the right lane. He tried to maneuver through the traffic to the left lane so he could turn and go back, but ended up being forced to make a turn, putting them on the road leading to the East Side of the Flats.

"Looks like we get to tour the other side now," Megan quipped, amused at his uncharacteristic slip of the mild curse. She had never heard him utter anything worse than darn. Just then her cellular phone rang. Pulling it out of her purse, she answered, "Hello."

The words of the file burned themselves in to Tony's mind, and she was momentarily stunned. Panic reared its ugly head when the ramifications of what she had just read settled to the forefront of her brain. She stood up and took a deep breath, forcing herself to focus. A familiar coldness washed over her. A very capable FBI agent had entered the room. One of the best, and most deadly, FBI operatives left the room a short time later.

Adrenaline raced through her body as Tony walked around to the side of Brian's desk. She grabbed his shirt near the collar and literally pulled the large man to his feet. "You bastard. If anything happens to her, I'll kill you."

Brian was shocked as he was lifted to his feet. No one was that strong. He hardly recognized Tony. He had watched her intimidate the hell out of the informants when she interrogated them, but that image paled in comparison to the woman standing before him. Looking in to the dark, hooded eyes glaring at him, Brian had no doubt she meant exactly what she said.

"Tony, calm down. What the hell's going on? I'm on your side, remember," Brian said with a forced calmness he did not feel.

Tony let go and, in a voice so cold it was devoid of emotion, she said, "Mark is most probably the Shadow killer, and YOU sent him to pick Megan up. Get some men down in to the East side of the Flats now. Make sure they understand to use the landline only. No radios. You make it damn clear no one plays hero. I don't want anyone approaching him," she growled. "While you're contacting them and waiting for the call backs, I'm going to try to reach Megan by cellular phone and warn her."

Tony was so relieved to hear Megan answer the phone she had to sit down. "It's Tony. Just listen and don't say anything. I think Mark may be the Shadow killer. If you get any opportunity to get away from him, take it. Now just act like I'm asking you when you'll get here."

Megan was surprised at Tony's words. Answering

nonchalantly, she said, "We'll be there shortly. We got forced into a wrong turn downtown and ended up in the East Side of the Flats. We should be there in another ten minutes or so," Megan said.

"Ok. We're on our way," Tony said.

Putting the phone back in her purse, Megan thought about what Tony had said. She was having a hard time thinking of Mark as a killer. She had been out to dinner with him several times, and he had been nothing but a perfect gentleman. Even tonight, although they were taking a round about way to get to the station, he had made no threatening overtures. But she knew Tony would not unnecessarily alarm her either. Maybe she could draw him out a little.

She needn't have worried; Mark was ready to talk. "Who was that?"

"Tony. She was just wondering when we were going to get there."

Mark pulled into the one large parking lot in the Flats. Megan became alarmed. She looked around and saw the Flats were still busy. "Mark, why are we stopping here?"

"I wanted to talk to you. I knew once we got to the station I wouldn't get the chance," he said, smiling over at her. Mark watched Megan closely as he talked. "You look a lot like my aunt did when she was younger. I lived with her after my parents died. She took me in out of a sense of responsibility. You know, family and all that. She didn't like me though. She blamed me for my parent's deaths. She was right, too, but she couldn't prove it. After all, I was only ten when they died."

Megan felt a chill at Mark's words and slipped her hand toward the door handle. To keep Mark from noticing what she was doing, she asked, "Why are you telling me this?"

"I just want you to understand why I'm going to kill you," he said, with the pleasant smile still firmly in place on his face.

Megan forgot all about stealth. The cold reality that

she was sitting next to the Shadow killer sank into her mind, and she grabbed the door handle lifting it. The door did not open. Mark said, "Oh, you can't get out. The door has safety locks. Only I can control them. Now how about just sitting there quietly. It wouldn't do to have someone notice you struggling to get out of the car."

"Why are you doing this? What's it going to accomplish?" Megan asked, deciding her only option at this point was to keep him talking. Help would be arriving soon, if she could just keep him occupied until then. "I thought we were friends."

"So did I. I really thought you were different. But I was wrong."

"Mark, what are you talking about? I've haven't done anything to you."

"Oh, but you did. Remember when I asked you if you agreed with the statement your FBI friend issued? When you said you did, that kind of put everything into perspective for me," Mark paused and chuckled. "You almost fooled me. Gotta give you a lot of credit for that."

If Megan had any doubt she was dealing with a cold-blooded sociopath, the eerie chuckling completely dispelled the notion.

****

Tony hung up the phone and moved quickly through the squad room dodging desks. "Brian, come on," she said, passing his desk en route to the front doors of the station.

Brain had finished notifying the patrol officers and task force members, and forward momentum was moving his large frame the instant he cleared the chair. Running after Tony, he gained the street seconds after she did and yelled over at her, "My car. I've got a light." The car was moving before either door was closed. Brian slapped the light on top of the car and then turned to Tony. "Fill me in."

"We should've had all this before, but because he was in the Army, and you know how St. Louis is about letting loose of those records, everything was being held pending the arrival of the Army file. First off, his parents mysteriously died in a house fire in which the firemen found Mark standing outside the house watching it burn. It was determined the fire was caused by arson, but the case was never solved. No one ever understood how he got out. He was only ten years old.

"From there he went to live with an aunt. She died mysteriously when he was seventeen. The brake line on her car had been cut. Shortly thereafter, he joined the Army. He was an Operating Room Technician. At each of his three assignments, there were some mysterious deaths. Patients who had routine surgeries like appendectomies died of unknown causes. When he was reassigned, the mysterious deaths would stop.

"He was under investigation by the Army when he got out in 1996. They never had anything on him except suspicions. So after his discharge they coded his file to preclude him ever from re-enlisting. Since it was coded, it took longer to get the file and find out why he was barred from re-enlistment."

"That doesn't really prove anything," Brian said, weighing the evidence she provided.

"No, it doesn't. But since death seems to follow him around, are you willing to gamble with Megan's life?" Tony ominously growled at him. "Because I'm not. Now will you step on it? I'd like to get there before daylight."

"Take it easy, all right? What good is it going to do us if we get in an accident on the way there?" Brian asked, trying to calm the agent sitting next to him. "Everyone is supposed to meet at the entrance to the Flats. We'll rendezvous with them there. If you don't have any better ideas, the best bet seems to be having everyone on foot covering different sectors."

"Fine," Tony said, forcing herself to stay focused and not think about the possible outcomes of the night.

Chapter
18

Tony was becoming frantic. They had been looking for fifteen minutes, and no one had seen any sign of Megan or Mark. The Flats just weren't that big. All the radios had been switched to an alternate channel that couldn't be picked up by anyone listening to the police bands. Tony began loping easily through the Flats. Too much time had passed; she had to find her soon.

Tony turned down the first alley, her long stride quickly covering the distance to the pier. She turned left along the pier heading for the next alley that would take her back up toward the streets of the Flats. Relentlessly, she covered the ground, the only thoughts in her head, *No, not again. I've got to find her. Not again. I won't let it happen. Not again. Not again. Not again.* The words echoed an eerie cadence in her mind coinciding with her footsteps. The only sound was that of her soft-soled shoes hitting the pavement.

Not finding them in the second alley, Tony ran along the street, dodging people, increasing her speed en route to the next alley. She came up on it fast, made the right turn into the alley, and ran toward the sound of the river. She

momentarily paused. *No one. nothing. empty.   Where is
she?* There was only one more alley.

* * * * * * * * * * *

Mark looked out the window of the car and said,
"Looks like we might have company. Better get moving.
Oh, and Megan, don't try anything stupid." Megan found
herself looking down the barrel of a gun.

"Now, this is what we're going to do. You scoot over
to my side of the car when I get out. Then you get out. If
you try to attract attention in any way, you'll just die
sooner. I don't really care whether I kill you here or at the
pier," Mark said, still smiling pleasantly.

Megan was in a panic. He was a monster. Even if
Tony arrived in time, what could she do? Mark had a gun.
She took a deep breath trying to calm her frayed nerves.
She knew if she lost it, she wouldn't have a chance. The
only thing she could do was play along and wait for an
opportunity to present itself.

After making her way across the seat, she stood next
to Mark outside of the car door. He draped an arm across
her and kept the gun pressed against her side under the
cover of his jacket. They made their way through the Flats
staying in the most crowded areas, looking just like every
other couple strolling along.

"Why don't you just let me go? This place is crawling
with cops. Everyone knows I'm with you. You could get
away then," Megan asked, very reasonably.

Mark glanced at her and said, "You just don't give me
any credit do you? Don't you think I planned this? This is
the ultimate thrill Megan. I get to kill you right in front of
their noses, and I still get away. I'm not into suicide.
Everything's been in place for days. I just got lucky
tonight when Brian asked me to pick you up."

"You'll never get away with it. No plan is good
enough to get around all these cops," Megan said, trying to
make him angry enough to reveal what he had in mind. If

she did that, she just might have a chance.

"I know what you're trying to do. But it really doesn't matter, so I guess I'll tell you. We are going down the last alley. You see the cops started searching there first and are now making their way up the street. Once we get down there, you and I are going to take a walk along the pier. That's where it ends for you. I just slip into the water. I already have my papers for my new identity and a disguise hidden in plastic under the pier across the river." Mark looked very pleased with himself as he related his plan to Megan. Mark had timed it perfectly, and they were now on the pier.

Still keeping the gun aimed at her, he pulled a small bottle from his pocket.

Megan shuddered, knowing all too well what the contents held. If he got close enough to the river maybe she could knock him in. She thought about some of the self defense moves she had been taught and wondered if she could pull it off without getting shot in the process. He just wasn't close enough.

* * * * * * * * * * * *

Tony ran down the last alley. As she neared the end, she heard a male voice. Slowing, she merged with the shadows along the walls and stealthily inched her way forward until she could see who was talking. Tony froze at the sight. Mark was standing on the pier holding a gun on Megan with one hand and a small dispenser in his other. He moved the small container toward her, and said, "Goodbye, Megan."

In a smoothly practiced move Tony drew her gun. She scuffed her shoe against the ground, hoping to draw Mark's attention, knowing she would have only one chance to take him out. His gun momentarily moved off of Megan and toward the sound. As he glanced at Tony, Mark depressed the lever spraying Megan in the face with the aerosol contents of the bottle. When Mark's gun moved away from

Megan, Tony fired. Megan and Mark simultaneously fell
to the ground.

Tony was at Megan's side before she hit the ground.
Cradling Megan in her arms, she broke all radio discipline
and yelled into the radio, "Call an ambulance now!"

Tony's mind fought to remember everything Megan
had told her about the drug. *Think. It paralyzes the mus-*
cles. The victim can't breath. I need to breath for her.
Tony began mouth-to-mouth resuscitation, her mind continuing to feed her instructions. *The victim can hear and*
feel and see everything, but their muscles won't respond.
Tony looked into Megan's eyes and saw the panic reflected
back at her. In between measured breaths, she told her,
"Just hang on. Help's coming." *Breath. The drug's effects*
wear off quickly, just keep breathing for her.

As Tony continued the rhythmic breathing, Megan's
eyes began to get glassy. *She's not getting enough air.*
Tony increased the frequency of the breaths, unable to talk
but her mind carried on it's own conversation. *Hang in*
there, please. Just a little longer. Don't give up. I love
you. Don't leave me. Tony was unaware of her free falling
tears as she pushed herself to dizziness trying to get air
into Megan's lungs. *Not again, please God, not again.*
Come on Megan, stay with me. Help's on the way. Tony
didn't know how much time had passed, but becoming
lightheaded with effort, she knew she couldn't keep going
much longer. She ignored the cops when they arrived, her
mind totally focused on keeping her lover alive.

Megan felt her panic rise when the effects of the drug
took hold, and she found herself unable to breath. Then
Tony was there. Megan was never so glad to see anyone in
her life. She felt the air her partner was forcing into her
lungs, and her panic subsided. Tony wouldn't let her die.
But even though air was being forced into her lungs, her
oxygen deprived body needed more.

She felt lightheaded and, as blackness approached, she
thought, *I'm going to die. I love you, Tony. It's not your*
fault; you did your best. Don't blame yourself. Before the

darkness totally engulfed her, she began to feel less light-headed. Her eyes cleared, and she watched Tony work harder forcing more air into her lungs. Her face became wet from the tears falling from Tony's eyes as she worked feverishly to save her.

Frantically keeping up her resuscitation efforts, Tony felt a small trickle of air escape Megan's mouth. This was not the passive outflow of the air she had breathed into her partner's lungs. Not totally sure it wasn't her imagination, she forced more air into Megan, her adrenaline kicking in, as her stamina was giving out. More air rushed out this time. Stopping and placing her hand on Megan's chest, she felt the muscles contracting and rhythmic breathing begin. *She's breathing, oh God, thank you.* The last effects of the drug wore off, and Megan's breathing settled into normal respirations, her muscles responding to her brain's commands. Tony sat down on the ground next to Megan and lifted her head and shoulders into her lap. Waiting for Megan to regain command of all her muscles, she was too overcome with emotion from the close call to say anything and cradled her lover's prone body in her arms.

* * * * * * * * * * *

Tony followed the orderly taking Megan to her room, the ambulance ride and chaotic events in the emergency room playing through her mind. They were keeping Megan overnight for observation. Once her partner was put into bed, she pulled a chair over, sat down, and reached for Megan's hand. Tony's heart had finally returned to normal, but the close call had totally rocked her, and she watched Megan with barely controlled tears.

Megan looked at Tony's red-rimmed eyes and squeezed her hand. "Hey, it's okay. I'm fine, really."

"I thought...I thought I was going to lose you," Tony said, struggling for control. "I don't know what I'd do without you. I was so afraid...I love you so much."

Looking into Tony's eyes, Megan said, "I know you

do, and I love you, too. I was scared, too. I didn't want to leave you...leave what we have. You were pretty amazing. You know you saved my life, don't you?" She impishly smiled, "Does that mean we're even?"

A small smile appeared on Tony's face. "I'm just glad you're ok. I never want to go through that again."

Megan's squeezed Tony's hand. "Don't worry, neither do I."

Tony leaned over and kissed her lover on the forehead. "I should go and let you get some sleep before they kick me out of here."

"Mark's dead, isn't he?"

"Yeah. Brian told me when I was in the waiting room. I didn't have any choice."

"Tony, believe me, I'm not criticizing you. If you hadn't been there..." Megan shuddered. Tony sat on the bed and drew Megan into a hug, murmuring softly, "It's ok. You're safe now."

* * * * * * * * * * *

Tony and Megan took the next few days off, just enjoying each other's company. It was a well-deserved rest for both of them.

"I talked to Brian earlier. Dwayne's been indicted for one murder and for all five rapes on the West Side. Some of the victims agreed to testify against him, so he's looking at the death penalty."

Megan smiled at Tony. "You know, since I've met you there hasn't been a dull moment." Tony put her arm around Megan, pulling her closer.

Looking thoughtful, Megan said, "This case would make a really good book. Just think...a drug that's close to impossible to detect, an organized sociopath..."

"So, why don't you write it?"

"I'm not a writer, I'm a doctor," Megan said.

"You said you once wanted to write. Why can't you do both? There are a lot of authors that are doctors."

"Yeah, I know."

Tony looked at Megan. "What changed your mind about writing? Did you just lose interest?"

"It's kind of a long story."

"If you don't want to talk about it, that's ok."

Megan glanced at Tony and saw the fleeting expression of hurt, before laying her head against her shoulder. It was time to share. "I did want to be a writer once. As a child, I loved stories. I don't remember ever learning how to read. It just seems like I always could. Dad didn't like me reading all the time. He'd take the books. It was a real challenge to keep some of them hidden. Back then, I knew I was going to be a writer. My goal in life was to write fiction." Megan paused to gather her thoughts. "Are you sure you want to hear this? It's really kind of boring."

Tony kissed her on top of the head. "Yeah. I'm sure."

"When I was in junior high, my English teacher put a sentence on the board. I don't even remember what it was anymore. She told us to make up a story one page long using the sentence. Well for some reason something clicked when I saw that sentence, and I wrote a science fiction story. You know how sometimes you can just tell something you did is really good? Well that's the way I felt about that story. I got an A. The teacher wrote 'excellent' on it. I was so proud of myself. I couldn't wait to get home and show it to Mom and Dad."

Megan's thoughts flashed back, and the scene from so long ago played through her mind. She was drawn out of her private reverie when Tony asked, "So, what did they say?" Megan sighed, taking comfort in the closeness of her partner. When she didn't answer, Tony said, "If you don't want to talk about, it's ok."

"No, it's not that. I just haven't thought about it for a long time. For some reason this case just made me think about writing, and how it would make such an interesting story. I never thought I'd feel that way again."

"I take it they didn't like your story," Tony surmised.

Smiling ruefully, Megan said, "Yeah, I guess you

could say that. I got home and Mom wasn't around. I
found Dad in the living room. He didn't believe I wrote
the story. No matter what I said, I couldn't convince him it
was my work."

"Why didn't he believe you?" Tony asked, puzzled.

"He, more or less, said I wasn't capable of writing
something of that quality. He could be a little abusive, so
he convinced me to give up the idea of writing. It worked.
I never wanted to write after that. Kind of lost that creative streak."

Tony waited for Megan to look at her. When the hazel
eyes met hers, she said, "Megan, you never lost your creativity. That's something you can't lose. You can ignore
it, or bury it, but it's still there."

Megan smiled, intertwined her hand with Tony's and
said, "You're so sweet. I know you're just trying to make
me feel better. But I've never even had an idea for another
story again. It's like that part of my brain doesn't work
anymore."

"It works just fine. It shows in everything you do.
Take work for instance. Who else would've thought of
some of the things you've done to find evidence, especially this last case? That takes creativity. It's still there,
love."

Megan looked into Tony's eyes and saw her partner's
belief in her. She was glad she had told Tony. Maybe she
was right. "Ya think?"

Tony never hesitated and, with total conviction, said,
"I know."

* * * * * * * * * * *

Later Tony sat on the couch next to Megan. "I need to
take a trip to DC."

"Why?" Megan snuggled up to Tony.

"Take care of some business. See, I was the top grad-
uate of my class at the academy so I got my choice of
assignments. I picked covert ops because I wanted to go

after groups like the one that killed my brothers. My job was to make sure they were no threat to the government. Brought a lot of them down, too."

Megan smiled. "I'll bet."

"Not for the right reasons, though. I did it for revenge. I treated each group I was assigned to like they were guilty of killing my brothers. I wasn't any better than the men who shot George and Joey. I finally woke up. That's why I asked to be reassigned."

"I'm glad you did."

"Me too." Tony smiled. "Before I left, I found out the leader of a group I had reported as no threat haad mysteriously died. I figured once I finished with this case, I could do some private investigating. Call in some markers and find out what happened."

"I don't like that idea at all. The Bureau should handle that. You told me once you liked your old boss. Turn it over to him. You've spent enough time working covert. Let them handle their own problems."

Tony grinned. "Just so happens I agree with you. That's why I need to go to Washington. There's a slight possibility I could be wrong. I hope I am. But, I still want to review my cases and make sure they haven't been tampered with."

Megan smiled mischeviously. "So when are we going? I want to see the Smithsonian Museums and I heard you can get tours through the White House. That would be fun."

"Yeah, ya can. When do you want to go?" Tony asked, as she kissed Megan's neck.

"Umn...well..."

Tony raised her head and said, "You know Megan, I was thinking about what we were talking about the other day...about you being creative."

"And?"

She draped her arms loosely around Megan's waist and purred, "I can think of some other ways you're very creative."

Megan chuckled and said, "Oh you can, huh?"

"Yep. So when should we leave?"

Megan turned around drawing Tony's head down into a soft, lingering kiss. Breaking contact momentarily, she said, "How about later?"

Dancing With Shadows

Chapter
1

Huey Straton settled his large frame comfortably in the chair, leaned back and propped his feet up on the desk. He had an hour until his next appointment. It was the first one today he was actually looking forward to.

Antonia Viglioni had called him a couple of days ago and asked to see him. Smiling, he knew the reason for the visit. Life in Cleveland had turned out too mundane for her. He'd known all along that she'd never be happy outside the fast life in covert operations. *Maybe I'll tease her a little first. Let her think we don't need any covert agent right now. Yeah. That would work.* Smiling to himself, he picked up the cordless phone and went through his messages, returning calls.

Tony Viglioni walked down the familiar hallway toward Huey's office. Knowing she probably wouldn't have a reason to visit this part of Quantico again, her thoughts flickered back in time to when she had last seen her ex-boss. It had been less than two months ago, yet it seemed a lifetime. Tony remembered the uneasiness and fear she had felt about her decision to transfer. It was going to require a major life change to emerge from the shadows of deep cover assignments and adjust to the ordinary life of a regular FBI agent. She had adjusted to her new lifestyle and was happier than she'd ever been. All the worry had been for nothing. Tony smiled to herself and acknowledged the transition wouldn't be going so smoothly without Megan's help.

The FBI agent focused her thoughts on the upcoming meeting. She was looking forward to seeing Huey again. It would be nice to voice her concerns to him. *I hope I'm wrong. If I'm not, it has to be someone from inside the agency. What would the motivation be? Well, Huey should be able to figure that out. I'll turn it over to him and be done with it.*

Tony didn't know many other covert agents. She had operated out of a small cell in which each agent knew only one other. The tall woman knew this was for their protection. If an agent were compromised, the entire cell wouldn't be exposed.

She stopped in front of a door with a placard attached to it identifying it as the office of the Director of Covert Affairs. Tony walked over to the secretary's desk and smiled fondly at the elderly woman sitting behind it. "Hi, Jean. How are you doing?"

Jean returned the smile. She had always liked this agent. The tall attractive woman was always pleasant and took the time to speak. "Hi, Tony. It's good to see you." The secretary picked up the phone and pressed the intercom button. "Mr. Straton, Agent Viglioni is here to see you." Nodding her head, she said, "Okay," and hung up the phone. "You can go on in."

Tony flashed her a smile. "Thanks."

Huey hung up the phone and walked to the door to greet the special agent. Smiling at her, he was amazed that he had forgotten just how attractive she was. Tony was wearing a mauve suit with a very light, rose-colored blouse accenting her olive complexion. Her thick, black hair flowed loosely over her shoulders with longish bangs almost covering her eyebrows. The tall woman's skirt was

fashionably short ending just above the knee, yet professional in appearance.

"Are you going to stand there and stare, or are you
going to ask me to have a seat?" Tony asked, smirking, her
blue eyes twinkling. She was used to this reaction from
her boss and loved to tease him.

Huey's face warmed at the comment, but not one to be
caught short, he replied, "Hey, you can't blame me for
looking. And, besides, if you didn't come in here looking
so good I might not have noticed."

Tony chuckled and said, "I look the same way I always
look, but thanks for the compliment." She walked over to
the chair in front of his desk and sat down. "Same old
Huey. So did you get the files on my last two cases? I
asked Jean to make sure they were available for this meeting."

"Yeah. I got them. But what do they have to do with
anything? And how are you, Tony?" Huey asked, trying to
keep a smug expression off his face, but wasn't entirely
successful.

"I'm wonderful. And why are you grinning like a
Cheshire cat? Got something up your sleeve? Whatever it
is, it won't work."

Huey's smile lost some of its luster. *Wait a minute.
That didn't sound like someone who was unhappy and
wanted to come back to the fold.* It was time to ask a few
specific questions. He peered intently at Tony. "How do
you like Cleveland?"

Tony smiled at her ex-boss. "I like Cleveland just
fine. You giving me that assignment was the best thing
that ever happened to me."

Years of experience had taught Huey the art of controlling his facial features when meeting with his subordinates. Even so, he was just able to prevent his mouth from
dropping open in surprise. The smile remained plastered
on his face, but it no longer reached his eyes. "Care to fill
me in?" Huey was careful to keep his tone neutral. *Damn.
I can't believe she's content there. What in the hell could*

have happened in Cleveland? I told everyone she was coming back.

"I met someone wonderful." A mental image of Megan filled Tony's mind. "Guess I should thank you for giving me that assignment."

Huey watched the change come over Tony when she spoke. Gone was all the business, sometimes teasing agent he was used to dealing with. She practically glowed. It was obvious that, whomever she had met, this was not just a diversion. This was very surprising. One of the things that had made Tony so effective was her ability to remain detached. *Whoever it is, they must really be something.*

The Director left his position propped against the desk and walked around it to sit down in his chair. He needed to gather his thoughts. Things were definitely not going the way he'd planned.

All of a sudden it dawned on Tony why Huey thought she'd made the appointment. Raising an eyebrow, she asked, "You thought I wanted to come back?" Her voice rose as she finished the query conveying her surprise.

"Well, Tony, think about it. What other reason could you possibly want to see me for? It made sense to me. You're one of my best agents. Couldn't see you rotting away in a desk job."

"Was, Huey. The key word is *was.* I am now just a regular special agent like almost everyone else in the agency. I have a place to call home now, and I'm not going to throw that away. I never knew what I was missing. I do now. I'm not the agent you remember." Tony smiled kindly at her ex-boss, knowing he was disappointed.

"What did you want to see me about then?" Huey was now genuinely curious.

"Could I see the files on the cases I asked for? I just need to verify something first." Tony imperceptibly tensed. This would let her know if her suspicions were correct. *I hope I'm wrong.*

"Technically, since you're no longer assigned to this office, I can't authorize that. Is there something specific you want to know?" Huey asked, picking up one of the reports and flipping through it. He had quickly scanned the files before the meeting and they looked like routine cases.

Tony raised an eyebrow and said, "I'm the one who wrote the reports."

"Well then it seems to me you should know what they say," Huey answered reasonably.

The agent knew Huey was just following procedure, but she'd wanted to look at them first to see if they had been altered and, if they had been, how her signature had been forged at the bottom. Tony sighed. "Would you read me the impressions at the end?"

Huey picked up one of the reports, flipped to the last page, and read the passage in question. "This organization is deemed to be no threat to the security of the United States or to the safety of other citizens."

A sense of relief flooded the tall woman. "What does the other say?"

After flipping to the back of the second report, Huey read the summary. "Based on the irrefutable evidence that this organization is planning a major terrorist activity, I recommend termination at the earliest possible time."

Tony's eyes narrowed and, in a steely voice, she said, "I never wrote that." Her thoughts turned to what she had written and, for Huey's benefit, she added, "My impression was that there was absolutely no threat from that group. They were merely soldier wannabes."

Huey forgot his disappointment and said, "What are you saying? Do you think someone falsified your report? That's a very serious accusation, Tony."

She nodded, looking pointedly at Huey. "Yes, it is. Unfortunately, it happens to be true." Standing up, Tony paced back and forth in front of his desk. "I just can't imagine why someone would do that. You know how rare termination orders are. I recommended further evaluation of most cases I felt were potential threats."

Tony had unconsciously reverted to her most intimidating persona, and she met the Director's look with cold blue eyes.

Huey's mind registered the change in the glaring tall woman standing in front of him before he was even cognizant of it. She was radiating an essence of danger. He felt a chill run through him. "Hey, take it easy." *She certainly hasn't lost her edge. I'd hate to be on the receiving end when she's like this.*

Tony forced herself to relax. *Just turn it over to him. That's what you came here for. You're out of it now.* She took a deep, calming breath. "Sorry. It just infuriates me that some asshole is doing this."

Huey thought quickly. This was very delicate. Tony was one of the best agents in the agency. He had no reason to doubt her. But no matter what he thought, it was going to be difficult to try and investigate something of this magnitude on the word of one agent. One thing was bothering the Director. "Why didn't you say something before now?"

"Because I wasn't sure. I needed some time to think about it. I was going to check it out on my own. I decided it would be better to run it over to you." *With a little encouragement from Megan, of course.*

"Okay. I'll look into it. There is a possibility you could be called back to Washington to testify if evidence is uncovered to support your accusation."

Tony nodded her head. "Yes, I know."

Huey stood, indicating the meeting was over. Tony walked with him to the door. "Good seeing you. Take care of yourself."

"You, too."

* * * * * * * * *

Sunlight suddenly emerged through the clouds, casting its rays upon the hotel's glass balcony door. Megan raised a hand to cover her eyes from the unexpected glare. She was sitting at a small table in the hotel room looking at a pamphlet about tourist attractions. It had been a cloudy, rainy day, and the sun was a welcome reprieve.

Standing up, Megan walked over to the window and opened it. The bright light filtered through the window accenting the red highlights in her hair. Little dust particles danced about, visible in the shaft of sunlight.

Megan smiled at the sight. She remembered trying to catch the elusive flying particles as a child and her disappointment when she couldn't. Laughing at the memory, Megan thought, *The sun always makes you feel so good.* It had been sunny when they'd left Cleveland that morning bound for Washington, D.C. and a bit of trivia popped to the forefront of her mind. Cleveland was a top contender for the fewest days of sunlight per year. Amused, she thought, *What a thing to be known for.* A few minutes later the wayward sun once again disappeared into the clouds.

Megan turned away from the window and glanced around the hotel room. Tony probably wouldn't be back for another hour or two, and she didn't want to watch TV. She remembered seeing an entrance to an indoor swimming pool when they had arrived at the Marriott. *That's what I'll do. It wouldn't hurt to get some exercise. I've been kind of lazy lately.* That thought prompted another of a tall, dark, beautiful woman who had been taking up a large part of her time. Grinning, Megan thought, *Not that I've minded.*

Megan took her black Speedo out of a drawer and looked around for something to wear over it. A white, cotton, button down blouse of Tony's hanging on the clothes rack caught her eye. It was perfect. Megan chuckled, knowing her partner was so much taller than she was, it would probably hang halfway down to her knees.

Last time she had borrowed one her lover's tops, Tony suggested they go shopping since she didn't have anything of her own to wear. Her soulmate's dancing blue eyes and the half-smile that couldn't stay hidden gave her away.

Funny thing is, I have way more clothes than she does. I just like to wear her things. It makes me feel closer to her. Shaking her head and smiling, she thought, *You are just a hopeless romantic.*

After donning her Speedo and white shirt, she grabbed a towel out of the bathroom. Megan shivered in the cool air conditioning and had goose bumps over the exposed parts of her body by the time she reached her destination.

The warm, humid air around the pool was a welcome reprieve. Megan was surprised to be the only visitor. Setting her towel on one of the lounge chairs, she removed Tony's blouse and her thongs and dove into the water.

Megan swam the first length slowly and leisurely wanting to give her muscles a chance to loosen up. Reaching the end of the pool, she kicked off the wall, her well-toned leg muscles propelling her a quarter of the length of the pool. With powerful arm strokes and a forceful kick, she pushed the muscles in her body wanting to give them a good workout. After swimming several laps, Megan slowed her stroke, just enjoying the feel of the warm water against her body. She rolled onto her back and floated, only occasionally propelling herself with a lazy stroke that generated a ripple traveling the length of her body before disappearing.

Megan's thoughts drifted to her relationship with Tony. A warm smile covered her face. *I am so in love.* Chuckling to herself, Megan remembered the first time she had seen Tony. She hadn't even wanted to meet her that day, but Tony had been very persistent. Curiosity, spurned on by a very alluring voice, had finally gotten the best of her, and she'd agreed. Her life hadn't been the same since. It was hard to believe how new their relationship really was. They had reached such a comfort level with each other; it was hard to believe they had only known each other for a few months.

This was a well-deserved vacation for both of them. Megan was looking forward to seeing some of the sights, particularly the Smithsonian museums. From what Tony had told her, most of the other major attractions were in close proximity, and it wouldn't be too hard to see most of the monuments even with the limited time they had.

A half-hour later, her body pleasantly tired, Megan swam to the deep end of the pool and pulled herself out using the bars. After toweling off, she watched the antics of two young children who were playing in the water under the close supervision of a woman. Her identity was revealed when one of the children addressed her as Mom.

Megan smiled over at the busy mother who gave her a grin and shook her head. A short time later Megan decided to head back to the room so she could take a shower and do her hair before Tony got back. They were going to go to dinner and then come back to the room and relax.

It had been a longer day than they expected. Their plane had been delayed for two hours in Cleveland for mechanical reasons. When they finally arrived at the hotel, it was time for Tony to start getting ready for her meeting with Huey. Since most of the day had been spent at the airport or on the plane, they decided to start their sightseeing the next day.

Megan took a leisurely shower washing all the chlorine from her body and hair. After drying off and putting her underwear on, she unwrapped the towel from around her head and began blow-drying her hair. Megan had already decided to wear it loosely around her shoulders.

Tony entered the room and heard the hair dryer. She walked into the bathroom, wrapped her arms around Megan's bare midsection, and pulled her close, kissing an exposed part of her neck.

Megan saw Tony's image in the mirror a fraction of a second before she felt the warm, moist mouth against her neck. Her mind barely had time to register surprise before her body acted of its own accord and leaned into the one behind hers. She smiled at Tony's reflection in the mirror. "Hi. I didn't expect you back yet."

"Weeelll, I could always leave and come back later," Tony drawled, smirking.

"I don't think so." She turned around in Tony's arms, drawing her lover's head down for a lingering kiss. "Umm. I like that."

"Me, too. You hungry?" Tony nuzzled Megan's neck, before releasing her. "You smell so good."

"Come back here." Megan reached out for Tony.

Winking at her soulmate, Tony said, "We're supposed to go eat."

"Yeah, I know." Megan affected a pout. "So how'd it go?"

"Fine. We can talk about it over dinner. You are hungry, aren't you?" Tony asked, glad the business portion of the trip was over

"Yep." Megan grinned, adding, "For more than one thing."

Tony ran her fingers across Megan's cheek. "So am I. So let's go eat now. We'll get back quicker."

Megan smiled, "Okay. I'm starved. I worked up quite an appetite at the pool this afternoon."

"Oh, no. Hope we have enough money."

"Very funny!"

"Well..." Tony grinned when Megan gave her a mock glare. "Okay, okay. Let me find something to wear." Slowly drawing her eyes down Megan's body, she said, "I think maybe you should get dressed, too, or we might not make it to dinner after all."

Megan cocked her head to the side and looked at her partner. "Okay, but keep that thought."

Tony winked. "Count on it."

After a quick discussion, they decided on the Chesapeake Bay Seafood House. Tony explained it wasn't known for atmosphere, but it had great seafood and the dress was casual.

Megan sipped on her coffee eyeing her partner. The room was well lit and had a steady turnover of diners, but the tall, dark woman across the table was the only patron she noticed. "You weren't kidding when you said they had great seafood. I'm stuffed."

"I used to come here a lot when I was in D.C. It's probably my favorite seafood house." Tony smiled. "I thought you might like it."

"You never did tell me how your meeting with Huey went." Over dinner they had talked about what sights to visit on their vacation and had just enjoyed the good food. But Megan wanted to make sure Tony was okay with her meeting and was comfortable with her decision to turn her suspicions over to Huey.

"It went ok. I told Huey what I thought, and he said he'd check it out. He did mention that if anything came of it, I might be required to return and testify."

"Do you think that's likely?" Megan knew that most cases never ran according to schedule, and she was not enthused about the possibility of Tony having to return to Washington.

"It's really hard to say. He only has one case to go on. It's not much. But Huey's quite tenacious and he has access to a lot of resources. Time will tell, I guess," Tony said, shrugging her shoulders. When Megan finished her coffee, Tony asked, "You ready to go? We can start walking until we see a cab. It's nice out tonight."

"Sounds good. I could use a walk after eating all that food."

Tony laughed. "We both ate a lot. It'll do us both good."

The earlier rain had lessened the humidity, and the night was clear and warm. Megan was surprised at the number of people still out and about. "There are a lot of people out tonight."

"D.C. is known for its night life. It wouldn't matter if it was three in the morning, there would still be people on the streets."

"But not us," Megan said, a sultry smile lighting up her face.

Tony looked at Megan and saw the sexy provocative smile. Her heart skipped a beat before quickening, and she agreed, "No. Not us."

Brushing against Tony's body without losing a step, Megan said, "We have other plans."

Tony smirked at her partner. "Yes, we do, so let's find a cab."

* * * * * * * * * *

Both women felt the cab ride back to the hotel lasted forever, prolonged by the teasing touches passed back and forth that held the promise of what was to come. Entering the hotel room they kicked off their shoes and embraced. Tony lowered her head and, when her mouth met Megan's soft, moist, slightly parted lips, she felt a jolt of pleasurable sensations. When the kiss ended, she looked into Megan's eyes and was captivated by the swirling gold flecks in the sea of green. Tony's heart fluttered wildly and, placing a hand on either side of Megan's face, her voice husky with desire, she said, "I want you."

Megan felt shivers run up and down her body at the sound of Tony's low throaty voice. Looking into blue eyes almost black with passion, she placed her hands in the thick, dark hair guiding the taller woman's head down and met her mouth with her own. The lingering kiss quickly became deeper and more urgent as tongues sought and gained entrance thrusting around and against each other in a sensuous dance.

As the passionate kiss ended, Tony moved her arms from around her lover and unbuttoned Megan's blouse. Her eyes never left her lover's, as she eased the blouse down over Megan's arms, her fingertips trailing its path until it fell to the floor. Moving her hands behind her partner she unfastened the bra and, with fingers just grazing skin, she freed it from her lover's arms.

Megan's breathing quickened at Tony's touch, pleasurable sensations running rampant. "Tony...hurry," she murmured and placed her hands under Tony's top slowly moving upward until she reached the full, firm breasts.

Taking one in each hand, she gently kneaded them encouraged by her partner's sharp intake of breath.

Tony leaned into Megan's hands, moaning, as the throbbing between her legs grew in intensity. She moved her hands down to her partner's slacks, unbuttoning and unzipping them. She slid a hand inside, her desire escalating when a shudder coursed through her lover.

"Oh, God, Tony wait..." She dropped her hands from Tony's breasts and pulled her pants and underwear down. Tony quickly drew her top over her head and tossed it across the room. After removing her bra, she undid her slacks and kicked them along with her underwear free of her legs.

Reaching for Megan, she said, "You are so beautiful." Pulling her close, she backed up to the bed, her lips meeting the full sensuous ones of her lover. When they reached the bed, Tony fell onto it pulling her lover with her. Lifting them the rest of the way onto the bed, she turned until she was stopped by Megan's sultry voice, a restraining hand on her shoulder.

"No. I want you here." A shiver ran through Tony's body at the words, and the throbbing between her legs became more insistent, her heart thundering uncontrollably as she relinquished control to her partner. Megan looked into Tony's passion-filled eyes and placed a fleeting kiss on her lips. As she placed soft moist kisses along her lover's neck, she could feel Tony's racing pulse. Megan ran her tongue across her upper lip, slowly lowering her lips to her partner's waiting mouth, and they left the world behind for a lovers' paradise.

Chapter
2

After a short ride on the Metrorail, Tony and Megan exited the train and walked toward the mall. Megan said, "We have to get through the last three today because I still want to see the monuments."

Tony smiled at her partner whose dancing hazel eyes and winning smile was contagious. Anything Megan wanted to see was fine with her. Tony had been through all the museums and wanted her partner to enjoy their brief vacation.

Several hours later, Tony and Megan were sitting in the restaurant area of one of the Smithsonian's eating cold turkey sandwiches and drinking iced tea. Tony nudged Megan under the table with her leg. Megan glanced up, smiling. "And what was that for?"

"What are you thinking about?" Tony had watched Megan drift off and was curious.

"I just can't believe that we've been here all morning and have only been in one museum. Some of those portraits were gorgeous. There's just so much to see."

"We've still got all afternoon. We may have to be a little quicker about going through them though," she teased her partner.

"This is probably really boring for you since you've seen them all before," Megan commented hoping she wasn't boring Tony to death. She knew the tall woman would never complain, and she wanted her to have fun, too. But this was the third day they had visited the mall.

Tony reached across the table, brushing a wisp of hair out of Megan's face. As they gazed into each other's eyes. Tony was overcome with the love she felt for the young woman. Her eyes conveyed the depth of emotion she felt. "Megan, nothing I do with you is boring. If we sat home after work every evening and watched TV, I wouldn't be bored if you were right there with me."

Megan felt a warm glow fill her inside at the softly spoken words. A smile covered her face. Tony always made her feel so special. She felt her cheeks reddened at the compliment. "You are so sweet."

Blushing in return, Tony's grinned and said, "Sshh. Somebody might hear you," grinning to lighten the moment.

Megan chuckled knowing Tony's self image did not necessarily include the word sweet. "I know, I know, we have to keep your image intact."

* * * * * * * * *

Tony walked beside Megan through the American History museum content to follow her partner's lead. She remained attentive to Megan but had donned her public persona with all senses tuned to their surroundings.

Hearing a commotion, Tony quickly located the source. A little boy was expressing his unhappiness vocally while lying in the middle of an adjoining aisle. His small legs were steadily beating a rhythm of their own against the floor.

Her attention momentarily diverted to the child, Tony didn't see the man who came barreling around the corner of the aisle in time to stop him from clipping Megan hard, and almost knocking her into the American flag display she was looking at.

Reflexes automatically took over and she grabbed her partner's arm stopping her momentum into the display. Tony's eyes narrowed as she tracked the path of the rude tourist. Knowing Megan was ok, she said, "I'll be right back," with every intention of explaining some manners to the idiot.

The hard impact against her shoulder had caught Megan unaware and, before she even realized her balance had been disrupted, she felt a strong hand on her arm steadying her. At her partner's words, she quickly placed a hand on Tony's arm. "It's okay. Forget about him." She had seen the look on her partner's face and knew just how overprotective she could be. "He didn't do it on purpose. He never saw me."

In an unforgiving voice Tony growled, "He could have stopped and apologized," but the hand on her arm had dissipated some of her anger and the rest drained away when she looked at the gentle kind face of her lover smiling up at her.

* * * * * * * * *

Megan was enjoying herself. Even though Tony was a little overprotective, it was reassuring to know she was there for her. It made her feel safe and protected.

A short time later as Tony was glancing around, she heard Megan let out a peal of delighted laughter and turned her attention to her partner.

Megan turned to her with a wide smile on her face. "Look. It's Dorothy's shoes from the Wizard of Oz. I can't believe they're in a Smithsonian museum."

Tony smiled warmly at her companion. Megan's enthusiasm was so special. She was such a joy to be around. *I don't know what I did to deserve you, but I'm going to do everything I can to make you always want to stay.* "Kind of cool, huh? I guess someone decided they must be part of the American tradition," Tony said unable to wipe the matching grin off her face when she met the happy sparkling eyes that greeted hers. Chuckling to herself, she thought, *we probably look like two silly teenagers. But right now, I really don't care. When she's happy, I am, too.*

The Natural History museum was less crowded than the American History museum had been, and the two women were able to look at the exhibits in a more leisurely manner. One of the exhibits caught Megan's attention. "Hey, look at this. I didn't think those things still existed. I can't believe there is actually an expedition looking for them right now."

Tony stood next to Megan and looked at the large display. Grinning she asked, "When you were a kid, did you ever watch those *Voyage to the Bottom of the Sea* repeats? The submarine was attacked by one once."

Bumping her partner with a hip, Megan said, "I'm being serious. I thought they died out a long time ago." She turned her attention back to the giant squid display. "I wonder if they'll find one? When we get home I'm going to go online and check for updates."

Tony shook her head amused that Megan found giant squids so interesting. "Come on. Let's go see the dinosaurs."

Megan, feeling the need to get back at her partner, said, "Don't tell me, *Jurassic Park* is your favorite movie."

Tony laughed. "Maybe not favorite, but I liked it. I thought the T-Rex was cool."

"You would. I'm surprised you didn't like the raptors the best," Megan retorted before looking into the mirth-filled, blue eyes watching her and breaking into laughter.

Walking along, trying not to miss anything, Megan looked up when she heard Tony call her name.

When Tony had the smaller woman's attention, she continued in a stage whisper, "Your stomach's growling."

"What do you expect? You walk my legs off all day and all we eat is a sandwich."

Tony gave Megan an affectionate adaptation of her look and said, "Excuse me? And just who was originally going to try to see all the museums in one day?"

"I know you're not talking about me. I'm the tourist, remember? I don't know any better. You're supposed to be the tour guide. Just because you tried to starve me today, don't blame it on me."

Tony rolled her eyes and said with an exaggerated sigh, "Somehow I don't think I'm going to win this one."

"Got that right," Megan said grinning.

"Would the tourist care to join the tour guide for dinner back at the hotel? Room service with all amenities?" Tony asked, bowing her head.

Laughing, Megan said, "The tourist would be delighted to."

* * * * * * * * * *

The wind blew softly bending the blades of grass around the water. Facing the Reflection Pool in front of the Lincoln Memorial, Megan was filled with a sense of peace and well being. Tony stood next to her, their bodies barely touching but both comforted by the contact. It was a quiet moment in an otherwise busy day.

Megan thought about all they had crammed in the last several days and of how considerate Tony had been, making sure she got to see everything she wanted to, culminating in their visit to the monuments today. Tony had been a patient, attentive guide and saved this stop for last.

Her thoughts turned to the remaining stop on their vacation. She wasn't sure what the next few days would bring and, for now, Megan didn't want to think about it. Later would be soon enough. She raised a hand to brush a stray piece of hair out of her face. The breeze felt good after the hot afternoon sun.

The sun was sinking, but the Washington Monument was still mirrored in the clear rippling water. Megan glanced up at her partner and smiled into the blue eyes watching her. "It's really nice here. It's so peaceful."

"I know. I used to come down early in the morning and sit on the steps of the Lincoln Memorial and watch the sun come up." Tony knew a moment of pure contentment just standing there with her lover. A short time later the two women walked back toward the mall entrance to catch the Metrorail back to the hotel.

* * * * * * * * * *

The alley was devoid of light and quiet except for the muted sound of soft-soled shoes striking the pavement at regular intervals. A lone figure moved confidently down the alley, at home in the darkness. He stopped in front of a door that would have been invisible except for the faint hint of light where the door met the frame. His ears were assaulted by a cacophony of sound amplified by the deep bass of musical instruments reverberating off the walls. Walking down the dimly lit hallway, the man stopped at a door with the word 'private' written across it in gold script and entered, leaving the din behind.

The room was designed for comfort with four over-stuffed chairs and two love seats arranged around a large marble top coffee table. The furniture's soft earth tones were accented by plush beige carpeting. Lamps covered with ornately decorated glass shades lit the room creating uneven shadows on the wood grain paneling. On the other side of the room was a table that provided a large wood surface for anything from playing cards to holding a meeting. Tonight it would be used for the latter.

Looking at the five occupants sprawled comfortably around the room he nodded in greeting and received nods and murmurs of, "Hey, Ben," in return.

Ben walked over and set his briefcase on the large table. Turning to the fully stocked bar, he quickly perused the labels. Settling on scotch, he poured two fingers before adding ice. Ben was in his forties with chestnut brown hair that was just beginning to gray. At 5'10" and 180 pounds he was in top physical condition and moved with the grace of a natural athlete. He was dressed casually in black chinos and a blue, button down sports shirt worn open at the neck.

Taking a large swallow of the drink, he said, "Let's get started." He waited for the three men and two women to take seats around the table, cognizant of the puzzled expressions on their faces. Ben had never called all the agents to a single meeting before. It was the first time most of them had seen the others.

"I called this meeting tonight because we have a potential problem. An ex-wet Ops/infiltration agent has filed a complaint that her reports have been tampered with. This could cause us some serious problems. The repercussions from this accusation could close us down permanently. And I don't even want to think about what would happen if the press got a hold of it."

Pausing, he ran a hand through his short-cropped hair. Only one man present knew him well enough to recognize that simple action as extreme agitation. "Our backers are already getting nervous. My sources say an unofficial investigation is being planned. For right now I am going to halt our activities and try to find a way onto the investigating committee."

The group had originally been formed as a means of quality control to check out some of the agents' reports and to ensure the standards of the FBI were being upheld. They were fifty-three members strong, and their official function was to infiltrate random targets a second time and independently report their findings. The Quality Control Division randomly selected targets. Over the course of the last few years, there were several instances where these agents' impressions differed from the original agent's.

Two members of the Quality Control Division, unbeknownst to the others and hiding behind the guise of what
was best for the country, had begun earmarking some of
the files for further action. Subsequently, an unofficial
subgroup was formed consisting only of the agents present
at this meeting. Their sole function was to carry out termination orders.

One of the men, dressed casually in jeans and a
maroon pullover, cleared his throat. Ben looked up at the
sound. "You have a question?"

"Is this investigation being planned because of an
accusation of one agent?" Sherman knew that for an investigation to ensue there had to be strong evidence of foul
play.

"Yes, it is. Her word carries a lot of weight with the
Director."

"Well, seems to me they couldn't very well investigate
if the only complainant wasn't around," Sherman
answered, a cold smile turning up the corners of his mouth.
At thirty-five, he was one of the oldest agents in the room
and the most deadly. He had been recruited into wet Ops
straight out of training based on his psychological profile. Sherman enjoyed killing and felt absolutely no
remorse. The Bureau weeded out recruits with sociopathic
tendencies in the psychological testing. But tests don't
always accurately assess personality traits.

Ben met Sherman's slate gray eyes and smug look with
a smile. "That would probably work in most cases. But
the fact that she is, if not the best, one of the best agents
the Agency has ever produced might make that a little difficult." Looking pointedly at Sherman, he continued,
"Ever hear the name, Viglioni?"

Sherman felt a strange sensation. Identifying it, he
realized it was panic or as close to panic as he had ever
come. Narrowing his eyes, he thought fast. This was a
much more serious situation than Ben could ever imagine.

Viglioni was a legend in her own time. She had the
distinct honor of never failing on a mission regardless of

the danger to herself. She was said to be without fear and heralded throughout the halls of Headquarters as the ideal agent. Sherman always felt those rumors were highly exaggerated and only spread as an incentive to the male agents.

The best way to change Ben's mind would be to get the support of the other agents in the room. "You think she's better than we are collectively?"

"I never said that. But I can guarantee that some of you would die trying to take her down. I've seen her in action. Trust me when I tell you she is not someone to be taken lightly. It's not a good idea anyway, because of her high profile. Now if you have any other suggestions, I'd be happy to entertain them."

"I still think we should just eliminate the problem. There are ways to make it look like an accident. No one would be able to prove anything. We're finished if what we're doing is uncovered. I don't plan on going to prison or dying in the chair," Sherman retorted and added, "I rather take my chances, and if some of us die, so be it."

"Yeah..."

"I'm not going to rot in prison..."

"He's right..."

Ben slammed his empty glass down on the table and raised his voice to regain control of the meeting. "Stop your whining and listen up. The committee may not uncover anything. The Agency does thousands of infiltrations each year. In view of that, the scope of our operation has been quite small. You kill her, and it might be kind of hard to explain the dead agents associated with the 'accident.' For now we lay low and wait."

"I still don't like it," Sherman said and smiled inwardly at the agreeing murmurs around the table.

Ben shoved his chair back and stood up glaring at Sherman. "That's enough. I'm in charge here, not you. Maybe you'd like to be assigned to a desk job. That can be arranged, you know."

Sherman's face reddened and he met the eyes of the man he had considered his friend. Ben was toying with their futures. He was willing to take a chance and compromise all of them instead of just eliminating the problem. The fact that his opinion was influenced by being directly responsible for this development never fazed him. He said, "Okay. We wait." *But I intend to do what I have to.*

Ben's gaze drifted slowly around the table making eye contact with each agent. "If there are no other questions, you're free to leave. I'll be in contact."

The agents left the same way they had arrived, individually and at irregular intervals.

Sherman was the last to leave. Turning to Ben, he smiled and said, "Later."

Ben nodded, and Sherman exited the room. Sighing, he poured himself another drink and took a large swallow. He hadn't expected his authority to be challenged. When the backers had approached him about a way to eliminate potential threats against the government and other citizens, he had agreed to act as liaison and had personally chosen each member of the secret team.

They had also discussed how to administratively handle the cases that were to be acted on. They had a choice of not altering the records and taking the chance that one of the desk jockeys would notice the discrepancy when the termination report was filed or changing the reports. They had opted for the latter. But which one of those two old fools had been stupid enough to target one of Viglioni's cases? Well it didn't really matter now. The damage was done.

* * * * * * * * *

Megan's thoughts had returned to the next stop on their trip. She was worried. Tony tended to internalize things, but this was something they needed to talk about. Maybe her partner was rushing things. It was a major decision and, if Tony wasn't sure about it, she should wait until she was.

Megan moved from the comforting backrest Tony was providing and scooted around on the bed until she was facing her. Looking into the deep blue eyes that were watching her quizzically, she said, "You haven't said a thing all weekend about..."

"I know," Tony said interrupting her. Tony closed her eyes and ran a hand through her hair. Opening her eyes, she said, "I've been thinking about it a lot."

Megan looked into her partner's worried eyes. Raising a hand to Tony's face, she gently stroked her cheek. "You don't have to do this. There's no rush. If you're not ready, Tony, it's ok. Don't push yourself."

Tony saw the concern on Megan's face and the love shining brightly out of the green and gold eyes. A small sigh escaped her mouth. "I have to. It's something I should've done a long time ago." She paused for a moment, trying to verbalize her feelings. "You know all the stories we've told each other...about when we were kids...well...I guess it made me realize how much I miss my mother. Even if it turns out bad...at least I'll know."

Megan leaned over and hugged her partner. Tony relaxed against her lover before pulling away. "I think it might be best if you just go on back to Cleveland, and I'll meet you there in a couple of days. If it doesn't go well, I don't want to put you through that."

She's blocking me out. Megan tried to hide the deep sense of hurt she felt by averting her face. Turning back to face her partner, she said, "We planned this trip together. Not just the fun part, the whole thing. No matter how it goes, I plan on being there for you."

Tony felt a sinking feeling in her stomach when she saw the hurt on Megan's face. *Look what I've done now. I have to make her understand.* Reaching out, she placed her hand around one of Megan's smaller ones. "I'm just thinking of you. I love you, and I don't want to take a

chance and ruin the fun we've had the last couple of days.
It's my problem, not yours."

Tony only had a moment to register the impact her
words had on Megan before the hazel eyes flashed and her
face reflected anger.

"What do you mean it's not my problem? I thought we
were partners. I love you, Tony, and that means sharing.
Not just the good but the bad, too. After all we've been
through I can't believe you said that."

"I didn't mean it like that..."

"Well, just how did you mean it? It certainly sounded
like that to me," Megan retorted, more hurt than angry.

All of a sudden the words she had uttered hit her from
Megan's perspective. Swallowing hard, her mouth dry, she
moved over to Megan wrapping her in her arms. She felt
the stiff, tension-filled body against hers. "I'm sorry, love.
I didn't mean it the way it came out. I thought it was selfish to drag you along with me for moral support. I wasn't
trying to leave you out."

Megan felt some of the tension drain from her body.
"You forgot one thing. I'm here because I want to be. It's
a choice I made when I fell in love with you. It's not up to
you to decide what you think is right for me. Those are the
kind of decisions we make together." Megan hesitated,
and then added, "If you don't want me to go, fine. But
remember one thing. It's not just your problem anymore.
It affects you, so it affects me, too."

Overcome with emotion and unable to speak, Tony
tightened her hold on Megan hoping the increased contact
would convey the depth of her feelings and take away
some of the hurt her words had caused. Finally able to verbalize, she said simply, "I want you to go."

* * * * * * * * *

Charles stood in front of the mirror tightening the knot
in his tie, making sure it was perfectly centered. As one of
the senior partners in the law firm, he felt it was important

to set the standard and this included professional appearance. Satisfied, he left the bedroom and walked down to the kitchen for his usual breakfast of two eggs, toast and coffee.

Barbara looked up when her husband walked into the kitchen. "Morning," she said, setting his breakfast on the table. "How was the trip?"

"Just routine," Charles said. He had been on a business trip for two weeks visiting some of the law firm's more prestigious clients and had returned on an early morning flight. He traveled frequently for this purpose, but this trip had been longer than normal because the corporate agreement the firm had drawn up for one of the clients had been inadequate for their needs.

Smiling, knowing Charles would be pleased, Barbara said, "I saved some papers you might want to see. Megan made the headlines."

Charles looked up, his attention now fully on his wife. "Was it about that serial killer case she was working on?"

"Yes. She and an FBI agent were credited with solving the case."

"Let me see them."

Barbara handed him the two newspapers and sat down to join him for coffee.

Reading quickly, Charles smiled, very proud of his daughter. This reflected very favorably on the family image. He remembered when she defied him and entered medicine instead of following his footsteps and becoming a lawyer. Then, when she had told him she was going to be a pathologist of all things, he almost lost it. It was one of the very few times he had not been able to persuade her to his way of thinking. If she was going to bring honor to the family, then maybe it wasn't such a bad decision.

Charles looked up and said, "Invite her over for dinner. And Barbara...make sure she comes this time." His daughter was a little too independent for her own good.

"I'll invite her. But you should know by now that whether she comes or not will be her decision." Barbara knew exactly why Megan didn't visit more often. The reason was sitting across the table from her. Charles just wouldn't quit hounding her about her job and personal life.

Charles frowned and said, "Make sure she realizes that she has an obligation to us."

Barbara looked at her husband and shook her head. When would he learn that this particular daughter was done bending to his will?

After he finished his breakfast, Charles kissed Barbara goodbye and departed for the office.

Chapter
3

Tony had the cab driver drop her off at the corner to give her more time to go over in her mind, once again, how to approach her mother. She wanted to see her mother, but she had no idea what her reception would be. *What if she doesn't want to see me? What do I do then? I don't even know what to say to her.* Tony had spent the whole flight to Boston going over what she was going to say when her mother opened the door. Megan had simply said, "Tony, you will know what to say when you see her. Trust me on this one."

Hoping Megan was right, Tony sighed as she stood on the sidewalk looking at her childhood home. The small white house with green shutters still looked the same. Her lips turned up in the barest hint of a smile when she saw the red roses around the base of the house and the plant hangers with brightly colored flowers adorning the porch. Her mother had always loved flowers.

Tony's thoughts turned back in time to when she was four years old. Wanting to please her mother, she had picked a bouquet of beautiful little yellow flowers. Her mother had rewarded her with a hug and a kiss, told her

they were the most beautiful flowers she had ever seen,
and put the dandelions in a vase on the kitchen table. They
had remained there until they finally wilted and died.

It's time, her mind nudged her. Tony snorted and
thought, *Yep, here I am- a big, bad, fearless FBI agent and
my stomach is in knots over seeing my mother.* With the
steely determination that had marked her success in the
FBI, Tony pushed her doubts aside and walked up the sidewalk to the front door. Ringing the doorbell, she stood
waiting for her mother to answer, her mind a contrast of
conflicting thoughts.

Rosa finished dusting the coffee table and glanced
around the living room. She was in her late fifties, but had
aged well. A handsome woman, her face was offset by a
pair of deep blue eyes and short, wavy, black hair that was
just beginning to gray. She wore a yellow dress with short
sleeves and full skirt. Rosa was 5'6" and still stood tall.
Over the years she had put on a few pounds, but she wore
them well. One of the pillars of the small community she
lived in, Rosa was a kind woman and well liked by her
neighbors. Her own life had had its share of tragedy, yet
she was always there to listen to their problems and offer
sensible advice.

Her eyes rested on the one shelf she hadn't dusted yet.
She always saved it for last. Walking over and standing it
front of it, Rosa looked at the three pictures. Picking up
one, she wiped the surface of it. Her first born, George,
had been such a handsome boy. He had looked a lot like
his father with his brown hair, brown eyes and Roman
nose.

Setting it down, she picked up the next one. Running
the cloth over it, she looked at the picture of Joey. He had
been her youngest child. He had a heart of gold that
matched his blond hair. The smile on his face was a testa-
ment to his whole personality, sunny. She returned the picture to its place on the shelf.

She picked up the picture she had saved for last. The
picture was of a teenager with dancing blue eyes and

shoulder length black hair. The high cheekbones gave the face a sculpted appearance. White teeth contrasted sharply with the tanned face smiling brightly out at her, and the face held a promise of beauty yet to be fully realized. She walked over to the couch and sat down, the picture in her hands, the dusting forgotten.

Holding the picture out, away from her, she saw dark circles form under eyes that were now red rimmed from crying. The tanned face became pale and looked haunted. The happy, fun loving teenager was gone. That was the way her only daughter had looked the last time she saw her at George and Joey's funeral. She had been so lost in her own grief, she had been unable to share her daughter's. She remembered Tony blaming herself for their deaths. She knew better, but she had been in shock from the cruel turn of fate and been unable to console her.

Rosa reflected on the words of her friend, Joyce, about a week after the funeral. She had said, "Rosa, sometimes there are very special people put on this earth for just a short time. They affect everyone they come in contact with. They spread love. They are a joy to know and a gift to be treasured. Accept the gift you were given and remember the happiness they brought you." The words had struck a chord deep inside her and allowed the healing to begin. She finally accepted their deaths and was able to move on.

Her thoughts returned to the present, and she asked the questions she asked herself every day. *Tony, where are you? Are you ok? Have you found happiness? Do you still blame yourself? Do you ever think about me or miss me as much as I miss you?* She hugged the picture to her breast, the cold hard surface a poor substitute for the living, breathing daughter she knew was out there somewhere.

She had tried to find her. Rosa had contacted all their friends and everyone else she could think of who might know where her daughter was. It was as if she had disappeared into thin air. The police did file a missing person's report, but nothing ever came of it. Rosa doubted they even looked for her since it was obvious she had left by choice when the events of her departure were revealed.

The last attempt she had made was several years ago after finally saving enough money for a private investigator. He told her Tony had graduated from college and then entered the FBI, but there the trail ended. The only consolation Rosa had was knowing that her daughter had to be alive or the FBI would have notified her.

Rosa stood up and walked slowly back to the shelf. She lovingly set the picture in its place between her two sons. *I love you, Tony,* was the thought she turned away from the shelf with.

Walking into the kitchen she took her shopping list off the refrigerator. Adding eggs to the list, she set it on the table and went to get her purse. It was a warm, pleasant day, and Rosa was looking forward to the walk to the market. Her friends, Mary and Gino, owned it. The neighborhood had changed very little from when she first moved in so many years ago. It was full of Italian immigrants, and they took care of each other. It was often referred to as Little Italy.

Rosa picked up the shopping list and put it in her purse. She had just opened the back door when the doorbell rang. Shutting the door, she turned around and made her way to the front of the house.

She opened the front door and said, "Yes?" and a heartbeat later her eyes widened and a look of shock covered her face. A gasp escaped her mouth and she closed her eyes tightly, murmuring, "Mi Dio. Non e' possibile, sto allucinando." She was afraid to open her eyes and afraid to hope until she heard the barely audible, "Mom..."

The door opened and Tony looked into the deep blue eyes that met hers. Everything became surreal. She heard her mother say, "Yes," and then saw her face transform into a look of disbelief. She heard a gasp and her mother's whispered words, "My God. It's not possible, I'm hallucinating," and the eyes tightly closed. Tentatively, she said,

"Mom..." and watched the eyes slowly open revealing a myriad of emotions.

Rosa opened her eyes and looked at the tall woman wearing jeans and a blue pullover top standing in her doorway. The casual clothes did not detract from her natural beauty. Her heart racing out of control, she asked the question she already knew the answer to, but needed to voice. "Tony...is it really you?" Rosa raised a hand to her daughter's face needing to touch her. Finally convinced her mind was not playing a cruel joke on her, she murmured, "Non sono pazza."

Tony's mind and emotions registered several things simultaneously. Her mother was not upset with her. She seemed glad to see her. Could that be true? Had her long, self-imposed exile been unnecessary? It certainly appeared her fears had been groundless. Not knowing what to say and overwhelmed at the enormity of the thoughts churning in her mind, Tony stood there mutely.

Rosa gained a semblance of control and placed her hand on Tony's arm pulling her into the house. Shutting the door, she turned to her long lost child. Walking up to her, sensing her daughter's discomfort, she said, "I have missed you so much, Tony. Would you give your old mother a hug?"

Tony covered the few steps between them, wrapped her long arms around her mother and felt the answering squeeze. During that one moment of contact between mother and daughter, feelers were tentatively sent out touching a bond severed years ago. "You are not old, and I've missed you, too," she said quietly to her mother.

Ending the hug, both women stood there awkwardly. Rosa said, "Can you stay for a while?" She almost laughed at the absurdity of the words. Her prayers had been answered, and now she didn't even know what to say to her own daughter.

"Sure," Tony answered.

Rosa smiled. "Good. Sit down. I'll get us something to drink. What would you like? I can make some coffee. I have orange juice..." She stopped when she realized she was just prattling on.

Tony felt some of the tension drain out of her. Realizing her mother was as nervous as she was, she said, "Coffee would be great."

Sitting on the couch, the rich smell of the freshly brewed coffee permeating the air, the two women looked at each other. Both noticed the changes that had occurred in the other over the years. Tony saw lines she never remembered on her mother's face and a few strands of gray in her hair. She had gained a little weight but had really changed very little in appearance. Rosa was pleased to see that the young gangly teenager she remembered had grown into the beautiful woman she had always known her daughter would become.

Tony asked, "How are you, Mom?" The question was simple, but it was a starting place. Rosa accepted it for what it was and told her daughter about their friends and brought her up to date on the small community she had grown up in.

"What about you? Where do you live? Are you married? Are you still in the FBI?" Rosa stopped when she saw Tony raise an eyebrow and look at her, the question clearly written across her face. Rosa met her daughter's eyes. "I tried to find you. I hired a private investigator. He told me you had entered the FBI, but couldn't find out anything else."

Tony took a deep breath, "I never meant for you to worry. I just thought it was best for me to leave."

The older woman looked at the troubled face of her daughter. She had not been there for Tony when she needed her and had lost her. She was getting a second chance and she intended to make the most of it.

Reaching over, she took one of Tony's hands between hers. "You left because you needed me and I wasn't there for you. I couldn't see past my own grief to share yours. I knew you blamed yourself but I was helpless to act. That was very selfish of me." Rosa paused to gather together the words that should have been spoken so many years before. "It wasn't your fault. I know that now and I knew it then." Looking into Tony's eyes, Rosa continued, "I'm so sorry, Tony. If there was any way I could go back and change things, I would. But I can't. Can you forgive me?"

The words impacted on Tony like a sledgehammer. Disbelief and relief warred with each other. After years of shouldering the blame in her own mind, she had to make sure. In a voice just short of incredulous, she asked, "You didn't blame me?"

Look what I have done to my own child. "No, Tony. I never blamed you." Rosa's voiced hitched and she took a moment to compose herself. "I'm so sorry I never told you that then."

An enormous weight lifted off her shoulders and seeing the tears spilling down her mother's face, she gently squeezed the hand holding hers and said, "It's ok, Mom. Don't cry. You'll make me cry, too." With moist eyes, Tony leaned over and hugged her mother, "It's ok."

"You are still the good person you always were, Tony," Rosa said when she was able.

Tony was a little embarrassed by the compliment and decided to change the subject by answering the questions her mother had asked. "I live in Cleveland now, Mom, and I'm still in the FBI. I worked covert operations for years. That's why the guy you hired couldn't find me."

"Do you like it there?" Rosa asked.

"Yes." Smiling Tony added, "Some great people live there."

"You have such a pretty smile, Tony."

"Mom...!" Tony said rolling her eyes.

Rosa laughed at the familiar action by Tony. "Well, you do. Have you met anyone?"

Tony looked at her mother. *How do I handle this?* With a straightforwardness that was her style, she met her mother's eyes. "Yes, I have. We are not married yet, but we have talked about a commitment ceremony."

"A commitment ceremony? That's a strange thing to call a wedding. Is this something new?" Rosa drew her eyebrows together in question.

Tony said simply, "I am in love with another woman." Seeing the shocked expression cover her mother's face, she continued, "You'd like her, Mom. She's the most wonderful person I have ever known."

"But a woman, Tony. Why?"

Tony looked into her mother's eyes and saw her confusion. Words were inadequate to describe how she felt about Megan, but she had to try to help her mother understand. "She is kind and gentle and smart and beautiful and strong and she loves me." Tony paused and then decided to tell her mother the part Megan had in their reunion.

"Shortly after we met, I was injured. She took care of me and while we got to know each other we shared childhood stories. I told her what happened to George and Joey. She helped me to realize that it wasn't my fault." Tony stopped for a minute and smiled at her mother. "Sooner or later I would have come back, Mom. But it is because of her that I am here now."

The war waging in Rosa's mind came to a screeching halt when the implications of the last thing her daughter said registered. She had watched Tony's face change when she spoke of this woman. She would have to be blind not to see the love Tony obviously felt for her. Rosa wasn't sure how she felt about this new revelation, but she was not going to turn her daughter away again. She appeared to be very happy and, with that thought in mind, Rosa said, "Tell me about her."

Tony sighed inwardly with relief. This was going better than she had hoped considering her mother was a devout Roman Catholic. A large, warm smile covered her face and she told her mother about the woman she loved.

Rosa watched the play of emotions cross Tony's face when she spoke. If a person could glow, her daughter did.

Tony talked for over an hour before saying, "I really should go now. Megan is waiting for me at the hotel."

Rosa had been caught up in Tony's description of Megan and was intensely curious. "I'd like to meet her, Tony. Could you go get her and come back? I'll make lasagna for dinner. Is that still your favorite?"

Tony smiled. "Sure, Mom, and your lasagna sounds great. What time do you want us to come back?"

"How about five o'clock? I need to go to the market and pick up a few things."

"We'll be here," Tony said, standing up and hugging her mother. "I need to use the phone to call a cab."

"There's no need to call a cab. I can take you."

* * * * * * * * *

Paul Lewis followed the hostess to a booth in the rear of the diner. He ordered tea and thought about the call from his friend. Sherman had never requested a personnel file before. Their friendship had developed to a point that each fully trusted the other. But still, this was unusual, and why a file on an agent? Shaking his head, he thought, *It doesn't make sense.*

Sipping the hot tea, Paul thought about the first time he'd met Sherman. It had been three years ago. He was working his first covert assignment. He remembered his excitement when he was able to infiltrate a militia group that no one had been able to penetrate before. He was young and optimistic and wanted to make his mark among the seasoned agents.

He left to make a routine drop and was unaware he'd been followed. Upon his return, the leader of the organization questioned him, and he'd made up an excuse about seeing an old friend, but the leader was clearly suspicious and he came away from the meeting very uneasy. Later that night Paul pulled out the emergency transmitter and sent a message asking to be relieved from the assignment fearing his cover had been blown.

The next day he was advised to return to base. He almost made it, too. The camp was a mile behind before his legs were knocked out from under him and he heard the echo of a high-powered rifle. In excruciating pain, he tied a tourniquet around his damaged leg and sent off an emergency transmission before passing out.

When he regained consciousness, Sherman had put him in the back seat of a car to transport him to a hospital. He now had a five-inch steel pin in his leg and walked with a slight limp. If it hadn't been for Sherman coming along when he had, he would be without that leg. But Paul was no longer physically fit to do covert work and, because of this, he held a deep-seated hatred for all militia groups.

When Sherman told him about what two of the committee members were doing, he requested a transfer to the covert files area. The rogue committee members reviewed all the cases in which the new agent's report deviated from the original agent's report selectively choosing some for further action by Ben's group. The cases they did not target were returned for filing.

Paul reviewed each of the files that had not been selected, and the ones involving militia groups, he copied and gave to Sherman. He altered the reports identically to the ones altered by the two committee members and filed the termination order after Sherman personally eliminated each leader.

Sherman stood near the table for a moment and watched his friend. He was twenty-eight, but still looked like a kid. His red hair and freckles contributed to his youthful appearance. "Hey, Paul..." he said, sliding into the opposite side of the booth.

Paul nodded, leaving his thoughts behind.

"Man, you were a thousand miles away." Sherman looked closely at his friend. "Did you get the file I asked for?"

"Yes. But what do you want an agent's file for?"

Sherman quickly told Paul about the meeting with Ben, finishing up by saying, "That was one of the cases you provided me with. The last thing we can afford is to have Ben uncover what we are doing. If she is eliminated, she can't testify that her report was altered."

"I still don't like it. She's an agent."

Sherman decided to exploit Paul's hatred of militia groups. "If she had done her job in the first place, this would have never happened." When the youthful face aged with bitterness, Sherman pressed on. "If we have to stop now, the militia groups win by default. You're the one who loses. Your career was ruined because of them. Think about it. She is actually protecting them."

What Sherman said made sense. She was the one who was at fault here, but Paul was still not comfortable with targeting an agent. "Okay. But Sherman...I'm not providing any more personnel files."

"Relax. I'm only doing this because it is necessary. I'm not crazy about taking out an agent either," Sherman lied. "Don't worry. She is just going to have an accident. No one else will be hurt. I'll make sure she's alone."

Paul nodded. "Okay. The file is in my trunk."

****

Megan laid her book down and looked at the clock on the dresser. Only ten minutes had passed since the last time she looked at it. Disgusted that she couldn't lose herself in the book, she walked over to the window and looked out. It made sense that the longer Tony was gone, the better the chance things had gone well. But her mind had decided to play devil's advocate and insisted that if her partner were too upset, she might not come straight back to the hotel.

Megan turned around when she heard the door open. Before she had a chance to ask how things had gone, Tony had crossed the room and wrapped her in a big hug, a huge grin on her face. Laughing, Megan said, "I guess things went ok."

"Yep. Mom invited us for dinner," Tony said, finally releasing Megan. "She's making lasagna."

Megan hadn't expected this and she became uneasy. "She did?"

"Well, after I told her about you, she asked to meet you."

Trepidation filling her mind, Megan asked, "Did you tell her?" She paused suddenly at a loss for words.

Tony saw the worried expression on her partner's face. Taking Megan's hand, she led them over to the bed and sat down, guiding her lover onto her lap, her arms loosely draped around her. "Yes, I did." Tony paused searching for the right words. "I know there are times when I forget to think of both of us." *Like last night.* she silently added. "I never had to do that before." Tony looked into Megan's eyes and continued, "But you are more important to me than anyone. You are a part of my life now. She needed to know that."

Megan's mind struggled to grasp the enormity of the chance Tony had taken. She had been willing to risk a renewed relationship with her mother by telling her about them, yet she did anyway. Megan said, "I love you," and drew her partner's head down, meeting her lips with her own.

* * * * * * * * * *

Sherman sat at the table in his room carefully going through the file on Antonia Viglioni. He grudgingly acknowledged that it was quite impressive. She had excelled from the time she entered the academy and with each assignment became more proficient. What a worthy opponent she would have been to take on. Too bad he had to stage an accident.

The only thing he didn't understand was why she had requested a transfer out of covert operations and taken a desk job in Cleveland. It was obvious she had a personal interest in militia groups because of her brothers' deaths. *So why did she transfer? It doesn't make sense.* Abandoning that train of thought, he decided it really didn't matter anyway. It wouldn't change the outcome.

Knowing he couldn't plan what type of accident to stage until he arrived in Cleveland and became familiar with her schedule, Sherman wanted to cover anything that might come up. With that thought in mind, he mentally listed the things he needed to do before departing. *Request leave, rent a car, pack weapons and alternate identities, take pertinent information from the file, put the file in his safety deposit box and see about acquiring some electronic equipment.* He knew the last item might be difficult. The agency usually provided this and he couldn't very well ask for it.

After taking his suitcase out of the closet, he packed enough clothes to last a week, making sure that he included a wide variety. If for some reason he were gone longer than a week, the hotel would have laundry services. Sherman then mentally ticked off the other things he might need as he packed them.

Satisfied he hadn't forgotten anything, he closed the suitcase and departed for the administrative offices to request leave. Ben had actually done him a favor by halting all operations. Since he wasn't assigned to a case right now, he knew the leave would be automatically approved.

* * * * * * * * *

Megan looked in the mirror again, checking her appearance for the third time. Making another minor adjustment to her makeup, she sighed and hoped she would make a good impression on Tony's mother. *I need to relax. I'm a nervous wreck.*

"You ready, yet?" Tony called from the other room.

Looking in the mirror once more, Megan answered, "Yes," and walked out of the bathroom.

"You look nice," Tony said, smiling at her partner.

Megan was wearing a pair of wine colored slacks and an off-white blouse. She had put on a pair of gold earrings with a matching rope style necklace. Tony had donned a pair of white slacks and a teal, V-neck pullover. A silver chain adorned her neck. She would have rather worn jeans, but Megan wanted to wear something a little less casual to meet her mother in and, knowing how nervous she was, Tony had decided to dress in kind.

Megan smiled at the compliment before her thoughts turned once again to the upcoming evening. "Well, I guess we should get going," Megan said after looking at the clock. The last thing she wanted to do was be late.

They arrived promptly at five. Rosa opened the door and invited them in.

"Mom, this is Megan. Megan, this is my mother, Rosa," Tony said smiling, while unobtrusively watching her mother.

"Hi," Megan said smiling. Looking at Tony's mother she could see the family resemblance. Both had blue eyes and black hair, but there the similarity ended. Tony had high cheekbones, fuller lips and a smaller nose. Rosa was quite attractive in her own way, though.

"Hi, Megan." Rosa smiled at her guest. She took in the beautiful woman with blonde hair highlighted with red and soft hazel eyes. She was a little thing, but well proportioned and there was a warm smile on her face. "Why don't you both have a seat? Dinner will be ready in about fifteen minutes."

"Need any help?" Tony asked.

"No. I've got everything under control. Do you two want something to drink while you're waiting?" asked Rosa.

"No, thank you," Megan said followed by "No, thanks," from Tony.

Rosa went back to the kitchen leaving her guests to entertain themselves for a few minutes.

"Your mother's pretty," Megan said.

Tony smiled. "I think so, too, but I may be a little prejudiced." She noticed Megan's hands clasped nervously in her lap and covered the smaller hand with her own. "Hey, relax."

"I'm trying. I'm just a little nervous," Megan said and thought, *Yeah right. Try very nervous.*

"There's no need to be," Tony said, reassuringly. Tony was surprised at how comfortable she was. It just seemed right to be here at her mother's house with her partner. A few months ago if anyone had said there was ever any possibility of this, she would have laughed it off. *Life is strange sometimes,* she acknowledged silently. *But this time in a good way.*

Megan looked around the living room. It was decorated simply, but felt warm and cozy. The furniture was old but well cared for. A shadowbox on the wall contained little knickknacks. On a shelf across the room there were three pictures. Focusing on them, Megan recognized a younger version of Tony and two boys. She knew they had to be Tony's brothers. All three were quite different in appearance, yet the family resemblance was apparent.

Rosa bustled around the kitchen. Taking the lasagna out of the oven, she placed it on the table on a couple of hotplates. She had already set the table and prepared the salad ahead of time. She was looking forward to chatting with her daughter and her friend. Taking out a bottle of salad dressing, she called out, "It's ready," and waited for her guests to join her at the table.

"This is really good," Megan said smiling over at Rosa.

"Sure is," Tony agreed.

"Thank you," Rosa said before directing her attention to Megan. "Tony tells me you're the Assistant Coroner in Cleveland. How did you get interested in that line of work?"

"One of my classmates was murdered when I was in college. That's when I decided that I wanted to do my part to help stop the senseless violence. I felt I could do that in forensic pathology."

Rosa heard the passion in her voice when she spoke about her job. It was obvious she had a good heart. She seemed so young for a job like that. "Do you come from a large family?"

"Well...I have two sisters and one brother. I never thought of our family as large though."

"They must be very impressed to have a sister who is a doctor," Rosa commented.

Megan blushed. "No, not really. Charles is an attorney just like Dad, Ashley is a CPA and Taylor has an MBA."

Tony looked at her partner and said. "I think Megan's being a little modest. She was credited with finding out how a serial killer was murdering his victims. No one else had been able to figure it out."

Megan thought, *I'm gonna kill her.* Looking at Rosa, she said, "Your daughter was credited with solving the case and made the front page of the newspaper."

"So did you," Tony retorted.

Rosa looked from one to the other and chuckled. It had been so long since young people had been around. It felt good.

Tony and Megan looked at Rosa. "What are you laughing at?" Tony asked.

"You two," Rosa said smiling.

Megan and Tony answered a multitude of questions during the meal. Megan found Rosa easy to talk to and had relaxed enjoying the dinner. Her outgoing nature reasserted itself and she often gave elaborate answers to Rosa's delight.

When they were finished eating, Rosa said, "I made cannoli's for dessert. Anyone want one?"

Tony's mouth watered. Not only had her mother made her favorite meal but also her favorite dessert. "I do." Rosa smiled when she saw the delighted look on Tony's face. It was so good to have her daughter back again.

"I'd like one, too, please." Megan had never had a cannoli and had no idea exactly what it was other than a dessert, but judging by Tony's reaction, she was willing to try it. She had a weakness for desserts anyway.

Megan took a bite of the Italian delicacy. It was delicious. The pastry shell was filled with a blend of cheese, chocolate and fruit. She and Tony both consumed two of them before helping Rosa clear the table and retiring to the living room.

Rosa sat in her favorite chair facing Megan and Tony on the couch. She had decided to be blunt. This was a personality trait her daughter shared. "Tony said you took care of her when she was injured. What happened?"

Megan glanced over at Tony who just shrugged her shoulders. *Okay, where to start?* "We were working on a serial murder case together. Tony had only been in Cleveland a few days, and she was stabbed when we were investigating the area the murders occurred in," Megan said, trying to be honest, but not wanting to embarrass Tony.

Rosa turned her attention to her daughter. "You were stabbed?"

"It was just a fluke. The guy got lucky," Tony hedged. "It was no big deal."

"No big deal, huh? Have you been wounded before?" Rosa looked pointedly at her daughter.

Oh, God. How do I get out of this one? "A couple of times, but never anything serious." Tony knew her comment wasn't entirely accurate, but she'd come out ok, so her mother really didn't need to know the details.

Rosa had a feeling Tony was down playing her answer but decided to let it slide for now. Turning to Megan, she said, "Tony tells me she loves you."

Tony's eyes widened, and she had to stop her mouth from dropping open. "Mom," she said, in a cautioning voice.

Meeting her daughter's eyes, Rosa said, "I want to talk to Megan about this. You told me you love her." Directing her attention back to Megan, she asked, "Do you love Tony?"

Megan had become very uncomfortable. It just seemed so strange to be talking to Tony's mother about her feelings, but this was a question she could answer easily. Her words laden with feeling, she said, "Yes, I do. More than I ever believed possible." Glancing at Tony, she continued, "I can't imagine life without her."

Tony smiled at Megan and relaxed a little. Even though she and her mother had already had this conversation, she had not wanted her partner to feel uncomfortable. But it looked like Megan was handling it just fine.

Rosa met Megan's eyes, and what she saw there wiped any doubt about this woman's commitment to Tony from her mind. She was also surprised to find that she liked Megan. She had been prepared not to.

Rosa was a religious woman, but she knew that God would never condemn two people for loving each other. Setting aside years of religious indoctrination, she made a decision. "Well, then I'm happy for both of you. But you do know you have chosen a path that will not be easy."

Megan and Tony both nodded, acknowledging the truth of the words. "We know that and we've talked about it," Tony said to her mother. "But it's the right path for us and that's what really matters."

"Yes, it is," Rosa agreed.

"So, Tony...how about telling me about some of your adventures?"

The rest of the evening passed quickly.

* * * * * * * * * *

Tony had insisted on calling a cab because of the late hour. She looked at her mother and said, "The cab is probably here. We should get going." She paused and then added, "Mom, I want to go to the cemetery while we're here. Would you come with us?"

Rosa looked at her daughter and said warmly, "Of course I will."

"We could meet you here at nine," Tony said.

"How about if I pick you up from the hotel at nine?" Rosa asked. "There's no reason for you to have to take a cab here first."

"Okay. Thanks." They all stood up and walked to the door. Tony turned around and hugged her mom. "Thanks. Dinner was great. We'll see you in the morning."

"It was nice meeting you, Rosa. Thanks for dinner." Before Megan had a chance to turn around, she found herself being hugged by Tony's mother.

"It was nice meeting you, too, Megan. See you both in the morning."

Chapter
4

Barbara was frustrated. Every time she called Megan's number the answering machine picked up. It was ten o'clock, and it didn't make sense that she wasn't home yet. And it didn't help matters that Charles kept insisting she keep trying. Knowing that Megan and Ashley kept in close contact, Barbara decided to call her oldest daughter.

"Hello," Ashley said, placing the phone between her shoulder and her ear while taking the twins' clothes out of the dryer.

Sitting down, Barbara said, "Hi. How are the kids?"

Surprised to hear from her mother this late, Ashley said, "Hi, Mom. They're fine. Let me tell you bedtime didn't come soon enough tonight. I don't know where they get all their energy from."

Barbara laughed and said, "They take after their mother. You were quite a handful yourself."

Ashley snorted. "Yeah, right. Why is it that all mothers love to tell their daughters that?"

Still chuckling, Barbara said, "Because it's true. But the reason I called is because I have been trying to get a hold of Megan all evening and there's no answer."

So that's why she's calling now. "She's on vacation and should be back tomorrow or the next day. I forget which."

"Megan actually took a vacation?" Barbara was surprised. "I can't believe it. She hasn't taken vacation since she started that job."

"I know. It's about time she took some time off," Ashley agreed, preparing herself for the questions that were sure to follow.

"Where'd she go?" Barbara couldn't believe Megan hadn't even mentioned taking a vacation to her.

"She went to D.C. with a friend of hers," Ashley said, still expertly holding the phone while folding clothes.

"What friend? Has she met someone finally? It's about time," Barbara said pleased.

Ashley smiled to herself, thinking, *Oh, yeah. Mom. She sure has. But you're going to go off the deep end when you find out.* "She went with the FBI agent she met while working on that murder case. What did you want her for anyway?" Ashley asked, attempting to redirect the focus of the conversation.

"Your father wants her to come over for dinner. I showed him the articles in the paper. He's really proud of her."

Ashley rolled her eyes. *Yeah, right.* "You mean she finally did something he approves of? I can't believe it."

"Ashley!" Her oldest daughter could be so impertinent.

"Well, it's true." The way Ashley saw it, she was only stating a known fact.

Barbara decided to ignore the last comment. "Well, if you talk to her before I do, tell her I've been trying to reach her."

"Okay, Mom." Once she finished with the clothes, she planned to call and leave a message for Megan so she could give her fair warning.

"Bye."

"Bye," Ashley said before laying down the phone. Her thoughts turned briefly to her younger sister and she smiled remembering how happy Megan had been when she told her they were going on vacation.

* * * * * * * * * *

Sherman walked into the Renaissance Hotel carrying his suitcase and approached the desk in the lobby.

"Can I help you?" the desk clerk asked looking up.

"Yes. I have reservations for Scott O'Malley," Sherman said. He took a Visa card out of his wallet and handed it to the woman assisting him.

Once the paperwork was completed, he took the key he was given and headed for the second floor. After he entered the room, he laid the suitcase on the bed and unpacked his clothes. He then sat down at the table, unfolded the map he had picked up before exiting the turnpike and located the streets he had written down in his notes from Viglioni's file.

After he located the street the hotel was on, Sherman circled it and looked for Edgewater Drive. He found it in a suburb called Lakewood and circled it. Taking a yellow highlighter, he marked the route from his hotel to the newly marked street on the map, carefully noting that it could be reached off the Route 2 expressway.

Next he looked at the downtown area searching for East 9th Street. The Federal Building was located on this street and Sherman knew this housed the local FBI office. He marked the shortest route from the hotel to the Federal Building mentally noting it was within walking distance. Committing the directions to memory, he folded up the map and put it in his rear pocket. It would be handy to keep in the car just in case he needed it.

It was still early and, not wanting to waste time, Sherman decided to check out both places and become familiar with the routes.

* * * * * * * * *

Glancing at the lake while driving down the scenic route, he saw the waves breaking against the shoreline, an indicator that the weather report predicting thunderstorms was probably correct. He loved thunderstorms. The devastating power of lightening had intrigued him since he was a boy. It reminded him of himself. It destroyed what it hit.

Sherman exited the freeway at Edgewater and followed the well-marked route until he located the address he was looking for about a half mile from the highway. After parallel parking on the crowded street, he sat in the car and looked at the apartment building. It was situated between two other apartment buildings and another complex was on the same side of the street he was parked on.

He got out of the car, sauntered across the street, and walked into the middle building. It had a security system that required you to ring the apartment of the tenant you were visiting. Sherman had already ascertained from the apartment number 412, that it should be on the fourth floor.

Sherman pushed two door buzzers and was not surprised when neither was answered since most of the tenants were at work. He arbitrarily rang two others and smiled at his quick success when the door buzzer released. As was the case in most apartment buildings, people often just released the door without checking who it was.

Locating the mailboxes in a room off the lobby, he quickly search for 412, surprised that in addition to the name he had been expected, Megan Donnovan was also listed on it. This was surprising considering Viglioni had been in Cleveland for less than two months. Sherman decided this could actually work to his advantage.

The agent casually walked over to the elevators giving every indication of belonging in the building. He got off the elevator on the fourth floor and walked almost to the end of the hallway before locating 412 on the north side of the hallway. This would be perfect if the apartment complex across the street had any vacancies. Smiling at his luck Sherman walked back to the elevator. This job just might turn out to be much easier than he expected.

He took a detour to the basement. Making sure no one was observing him, he took the electronic pick gun out of his pocket and unlocked the door that gave him access to the telephone and electrical lines. He didn't expect to need to use anything here, but experience had taught him it was better to cover all contingencies. After checking out how the lines were routed to the various apartments, he returned to the lobby and left the building.

****

Tony cleared the table and threw out the empty Chinese food containers. After wiping off the table and putting the dishes in the dishwater, she opened the cupboard. Raising her voice so Megan could hear her, she asked, "Want something to drink?"

"Iced tea would be great." Megan was listening to the messages on the answering machine. So far, three were from her mother and one from Ashley. She depressed the machine to listen to the last message. "If you are a homeowner..." Megan quickly pressed the erase button. *What's the use of having an unlisted number? It never stops the telemarketers.*

Tony opened the freezer and placed several ice cubes in each glass. Getting the iced tea they'd picked up on the way home out of the refrigerator, she filled both glasses and carried them into the living room.

Megan looked up when Tony walked into the room. She unabashedly watched her partner walk across the room with the feline grace that was integral to her. Tony set the two glasses down on the coffee table before joining Megan on the couch. Leaning over she placed a fleeting kiss on Megan's lips. "You shouldn't look at me like that. We'll never get anything done."

"It's your fault for wearing those short shorts and showing off your legs," Megan teased, smiling.

"Well, I guess I could put on some jeans."

Tony started to stand, but Megan grabbed her arm chuckling. "No, you don't." Laying her hand on her lover's thigh, she continued, "I like what you're wearing just fine."

"Well, ok. If you insist," Tony teased. "Who called?"

"Ashley called once and my mother called three times. Ashley said to make sure I call her before calling Mom. Wonder what's up with that?" she mused.

Tony handed her partner the portable phone. "Maybe they want you to visit. You said Ashley mentioned it last time you saw her."

Megan punched in her sister's number. "Yeah. That's probably it."

"Hello."

"Hi. What's up?" Megan asked.

"Hey, Sis, how's it going? Did you have fun on your vacation? Did you see everything you wanted to?" Ashley asked, the questions pouring forth nonstop.

Smiling into the phone Megan said, "It was great. I don't think it's possible to see everything, but I sure tried."

Megan poked Tony in the ribs with her elbow when she heard her partner murmur, "Ain't that the truth."

Ashley laughed and said, "I bet you did. Did you get any pictures?"

"Yep. I got some really good ones. Maybe we can do lunch one day next week. I can show them to you then," Megan said, looking forward to seeing her sister.

"Okay. I'll look at my calendar tomorrow and give you a call. You'll be at work, right?"

"Uh huh. I can't believe how fast our vacation went. It sure doesn't seem like we've been off a week and a half. How are John and the twins?"

"John's fine. Been working long hours though. The kids...now that's another story. I'll fill you in on their latest exploits when I see you." Ashley loved to talk about her children and couldn't wait to tell Megan what they'd been up to lately.

"So why did you want me to call you before calling Mom?" Megan asked, while reaching for the glass of iced tea.

"Dad got back early Monday and Mom showed him the paper with you on the front page." Ashley gave Megan a chance to digest that little nugget of information and then continued, "So of course he's bursting with pride and wants to see you."

Megan sighed. She should have known. He hadn't approved of anything she'd done since she entered medical school. But her picture in the paper would be a big ego boost for him.

When Megan didn't say anything, Ashley said, "You know you haven't been over there for a while. They do miss you."

Megan sighed. "Yeah...I know they do. I'm just not comfortable there. Dad's always got some snide remark to make about my career and it's going to be really hard to take his enthusiasm all of a sudden just because my picture was in the paper."

"It's up to you. But it would probably be best to go and just get it over with. Next time he'll be back to normal anyway," Ashley commented. If nothing else, their father was predictable.

"Yeah, you're right. Guess I better call them now. Thanks for the warning," Megan said.

"No problem. I'll give you a call tomorrow."

"Okay. Bye."

"Bye."

Megan laid the phone down and looked at Tony. "You were right."

Tony had never met Megan's father but already disliked him just from some of the things Megan had told her. "You don't have to go if you don't want to."

"I know. But I haven't seen them for a while, and they are my parents. Dad can be very persistent, and he really doesn't understand why I don't visit much."

Tony met Megan's eyes and said, "How can he not understand? It's not like he supported you in anything you ever wanted to do."

Megan watched the expression harden on her partner's face. She knew Tony had no use for her father. She also acknowledged that what Tony said was true. "He honestly believes he was looking out for my best interests. I'll just go and get it over with."

Tony's thoughts were dark. In her mind he was nothing but a control freak that had used mental and emotional abuse and, on a few occasions, physical abuse to get Megan to conform to his wishes.

Pushing the dark thoughts from her mind, she knew that regardless of her personal feelings, she would support Megan's decision. "You do whatever you think is right." Quirking a half smile, she continued, "It'll be over before you know it."

Megan smiled a silent thanks to Tony. Her partner might not understand, but she was there for her and that was good enough. She picked up the phone and dialed her parents' number.

Barbara heard the phone ring and looked around for it. She found it on the kitchen counter and quickly answered it. "Hello."

"Hi, Mom," Megan said, sitting forward on the couch.

"You're finally back. Did you have fun on vacation? You never even mentioned you were going," Barbara said, wanting Megan to know her feelings were a little hurt about not being told about the vacation.

"Sorry, Mom. It was kind of a spur of the moment decision. But, yeah, it was fun. It ended too soon though," Megan said, standing up and walking over to the balcony.

Placated, Barbara said, "Well, I'm glad you finally took some time for yourself. You spend way too much time at work."

Megan smiled to herself thinking, *Not anymore.* "It was kind of nice for a change."

"Your father and I would like you to come over to dinner Saturday. He's really proud of you," Barbara told her daughter, hoping what she said would convince Megan to accept. The last time she had come to dinner all Charles had done was belittle her job.

"Sorry, Mom. We're going to the game Saturday evening." Megan was glad she already had plans because Saturday was just a little too soon. She wanted more time to mentally prepare herself if her father decided to attack her job again.

Wouldn't you know she'd have other plans? "What about the following Saturday then?"

That would work. "Okay. What time?"

Barbara sighed in relief. Now she wouldn't have to listen to Charles complain about Megan never visiting. "How about six-thirty?"

"Okay. See you then."

"Bye, Megan."

"Bye." Megan disconnected the call and laid the phone down. Scooting closer to Tony, she waited for her partner to move her arm before snuggling up against her.

Chapter
5

Tony sat in her small cubicle in the FBI office going through her inbox. Shortly after arriving, she requested an appointment with Mike Braxton. His secretary told her he wouldn't be available until one o'clock. Tony knew that was a crock of shit. He'd already been out to chat with some of the other agents. He was probably still pissed she refused to take all the credit for solving the case and had credited both the Assistant Coroner and the police department. After her statement, his claims that the FBI single handedly solved the case met deaf ears.

Leaning back in her chair, she picked up a new directive about surveillance techniques and began reading it before quickly discarding it. Other than using more ambiguous language, nothing had really changed.

Bored, Tony decided to go see what the other agents in the office were working on. She glanced around the office, looking for a familiar face, and walked toward the only one she'd actually interacted with. "Hi, John."

John looked at the beautiful woman standing in front of him and smiled warmly. "Hi, Tony. Welcome back."

"Thanks. What're you working on?"

"I'm just finishing up the paperwork on an embezzlement case. Have you met Keith?"

"No, not yet. How many agents do we have?" Tony asked, curious about Cleveland's resources.

John got up and walked with Tony over to Keith's cubicle. "Right now, we have twenty. But we're supposed to have twenty-eight, so we're spread really thin."

"Tony, this is Keith. Keith, Tony."

Keith was short and slender with dark skin and black hair cut close to the scalp. Smiling a greeting, he stood and shook Tony's hand. "Hi. I've heard a lot about you."

"Good, I hope," Tony answered automatically, smiling at the friendly agent.

"Mostly. But I don't think you've made any points with the boss," Keith quipped. He decided he might as well give her fair warning.

"I figured as much." She could care less what Braxton thought of her. He'd just have to get over it.

John took Tony around introducing her to the other agents that were in the office. After meeting everyone, she returned to her office. Sitting down at the desk, she continued going through her inbox. The unimportant paperwork was wadded up and expertly banked off the file cabinet into File 13.

* * * * * * * * * *

David looked up when Megan walked into the office. He was sprawled in a chair waiting for her. He got up, a big smile on his face, and walked over and hugged Megan. Grinning at her, he said, "I'm glad you're back. I missed you. How was the vacation?"

Returning his hug, Megan stood back, smiling warmly at her friend, and said, "Great. I took a bunch of pictures. I'll bring them in tomorrow to show you. How's the new house?"

"We love it. It's so nice to have a place to call your own," David said. "I don't think we'll ever get all the boxes unpacked. But we already set up Mike's office. He loves being able to have a place to work now and his boss loves his new drawings." Concern written clearly across his face, David continued, "But Mike's not been feeling well lately. We think he's got a sinus infection. He's just miserable."

"Sinus infections can be serious. He should go to the doctor," Megan said. She knew that sinus infections left untreated had the potential to cause death.

Sitting back down in the chair, David said, "He has an appointment for tomorrow."

"Good. Tell him I hope he feels better." Megan sat down at her desk and put her purse in the drawer.

"I will." David was very excited about his new house and could hardly wait for Megan and Tony to come and visit. "When he does feel better, we want you both to come over."

Megan smiled warmly at David. "We'd love to." David had told her about their new house and she was looking forward to seeing it. She also knew her friends were planning on having a house warming party once they got the house in order.

David turned mirth-filled eyes toward Megan and grinned, saying, "Oh and we have two new members in our family."

Megan looked at David cocking her head with a puzzled expression on her face.

Chuckling, David said, "Two beautiful kittens. We just love them. One is black and white and we named her Velcro. The other is calico and her name is Huggy."

"Ooh. They sound adorable," Megan said. "I can hardly wait to see them." Megan had a big soft spot for animals. Reluctantly changing the subject, she said, "So how's the case load been? Anything interesting?"

David's face turned serious. "No. Just the regular stuff. Dr. Whitehouse has been on a rampage lately though."

When David's mood changed at the mention of work, Megan thought, *This doesn't sound good.* "What about? I'm surprised he's not still basking in the glory from the Press Conference."

"Yeah, I know what you mean. He sounded like a jerk when he kept telling the press that his office discovered how Mark was killing his victims. I think he's still pissed that you made the front page."

Megan shrugged her shoulders, "I didn't know that would happen. It would have been fine with me if it had been his picture instead of mine on the front page."

"Oh, I don't know. I thought you and Tony looked cute side by side on the front page," David said grinning.

Megan chuckled and said, "Well, I didn't mind that part."

You know, you'll never convince him that it wasn't staged and I think he's already started exacting revenge," David said.

"What do you mean?"

"The two cases he assigned you today are a guy they pulled out the river who's been dead awhile and a suicide that jumped from the 17th story of an apartment building." David looked at Megan sympathetically. *Whitehouse is such an asshole.*

Megan sighed. Just what she wanted to do on her first day back. Resigning herself to her fate, she said, "Might as well get them over with. I'll change and meet you in the suite." Turning back to David she added, "Let's do the drowning first." Megan wanted to get the worst case out of the way.

* * * * * * * * *

Once the autopsies were completed Megan changed into her street clothes and returned to her office. Suddenly, all she wanted to do was hear Tony's voice. Picking up the phone, she dialed her lover's number.

"FBI. Agent Viglioni."

Megan felt some of the tension ease from her body when she heard the familiar, welcome voice of her lover. "Hi. How's it going?"

Tony smiled into the phone. "Hi, yourself. Ok, but kind of boring. I'll be glad to get home today." She was always careful of what she said when at work. She was well aware that the phones could be monitored at any time.

Megan sighed. "Yeah. Me too. It's been a rough morning."

"How so?" Tony asked concerned. Megan loved her job and this was an unusual comment.

"I think the great Dr. Whitehouse didn't like me making the headlines instead of him," Megan said sarcastically.

"That really doesn't surprise me," Tony said, thinking about the time that she had met Megan's boss. "Anything I can do to help?"

Feeling more relaxed, Megan said, "You already have. I'll see you later, ok?"

Tony smiled into the phone. "Okay. Take it easy and don't let him get you down. Just remember, he's a jerk."

"I keep telling myself that. Bye," Megan said already feeling better.

"Bye," Tony said.

* * * * * * * * *

Mike walked into the conference room and handed a file to each of the agents seated at the table. Walking to the head of the table, he began briefing them.

"One of our undercover agents has located the headquarters of a major money laundering operation. We're going to set up surveillance in an apartment over an antique store across the street from the suite they are using. The owner has been quite cooperative and agreed to stay with relatives for the duration of our operation."

Mike looked at his notes and continued, "All the information you need is in the files you have been provided.

There will be two teams of six agents. You will work in pairs covering each shift. You will work rotating shifts. Team 1 will work three days, be off one and then work two on a rotating basis with Team 2."

Tony looked through the file while listening to the briefing. She hated surveillance work. There was nothing more boring. Hopefully they would get the information they needed to nail this group quickly. Shift work sucked.

She looked around the table at the other agents. Keith and John, she'd already met. Carlos, Brandon, and Steve had introduced themselves before Mike started the briefing. Mike had informed them that they made up Team 1 and he would be briefing Team 2 separately because he had not finished contacting all of them. They were being pulled off other cases to work this one.

"I will personally oversee this operation. At the end of each shift I expect a written report detailing the events that occurred. Leave it in my mailbox. Are there any questions?"

Tony almost rolled her eyes at the last announcement. You couldn't oversee an operation from the office. It required an agent in the field or the very minimum a liaison in the field. This guy was a real piece of work. The surveillance would be worthless if they needed to move and had to find Mike. Why should she have expected anything else? It was bad enough the teams were being briefed separately. Any raw recruit learned that if you don't have everything in place, including agents, you didn't start the operation until you did. *Basic Procedure 101.*

"Since there are no questions the operation starts tomorrow. Keith and Tony you take first shift. Carlos and Brandon you're on second shift. John and Steven you get the graveyard shift." Mike looked at the agents. They all had inscrutable expressions on their faces. Uncomfortable, Mike said, "If there are no questions, you can go now."

After Mike left, Tony asked John, "Where did he come from anyway? He doesn't know a thing about field Ops."

"Tell me about it. We've had to put up with him for the last two years. His daddy is a friend of the Director. It's called politics."

"Great. That'll be a real comforting thought next time my life's on the line."

* * * * * * * * * *

Tony unlocked the door and entered the apartment. After the briefing, she had reviewed the case file and agreed to meet Keith tomorrow at the Federal building at six in the morning. They would be traveling in vehicles provided by the agency to and from the surveillance site.

Walking into the bedroom, Tony changed into shorts and a T-shirt. She was home early and decided to make dinner and surprise Megan. Her partner was a better cook, and they had settled into a routine where she cooked and Tony cleaned up afterwards.

Deciding to make a chef salad, she took everything she needed from the refrigerator. Placing a tomato on the cutting board, she cut it into squares, her thoughts on her new assignment. She still couldn't believe Braxton. Shaking her head at the absurdity of the situation, she hoped for a quick conclusion. The shifts required would mean less time with Megan, and that she was not looking forward to. The salad finished, Tony glanced at the clock. Megan was due home any time so she set the table, putting the salad in the refrigerator.

Megan entered the apartment and saw Tony standing in the kitchen. "Hi. You're home early," she said smiling at her partner.

Tony walked over to Megan and said, "Yeah. I got a new case starting tomorrow and the briefing finished up early." Leaning over she kissed her partner. "Are you hungry? I made salad for dinner."

Megan felt the stress of work slip away when Tony's mouth met hers. Smiling, she said, "Sure am. Let me change first."

After eating, Tony sat on the couch next to Megan with her arm around her lover. Megan told her about her day and Tony shook her head in disgust. "At least the idiot can't save any more cases for you."

Megan snuggled closer to Tony. "I just got back to work and I can hardly wait for the weekend to get here."

Smiling ruefully, Tony said, "I've got to work Saturday. We're doing surveillance and we'll be working rotating shifts."

"You do? What about the game?" Megan asked disappointed. She hadn't seen the Indians all season and had really been looking forward to the game.

Tony had forgotten about the game. Seeing the fleeting look of disappointment on Megan's face, she thought, *thank God I pulled days first*. "We can still go. It doesn't start until five after seven. I'm on days for the next three days, and then I'm off Sunday and work evenings Monday and Tuesday."

Megan laid her hand on Tony's thigh. Drawing an invisible design on her partner's bare leg, she said, "Evenings? We won't even get to see each other."

Tony sighed and said, "I know. Hopefully it won't last long."

Megan laid her head against Tony's chest thinking about how long Monday and Tuesday evening were going to be without her partner while aimlessly running the tips of her fingers up and down Tony's thigh. Feeling the muscles beneath her fingers tighten, she looked up and saw deep blue eyes gazing at her.

"Oh," Megan said smiling, lifting her hand only to have Tony grab it.

"Don't stop now." Tony guided her hand back to her leg while capturing Megan's lips with her own.

Megan felt her body responding to the soft, full lips of her partner and she moved her hand up cupping the area between Tony's legs, squeezing lightly through the shorts.

"Oh... Megan," Tony murmured, her desire escalating. "I love you." Capturing an earlobe between her lips, she moved a hand underneath Megan's top working her way up to the breasts, fondling first one and then the other.

Megan loved the effect her touch had on her partner, but that was only a fleeting thought when her body reacted to Tony's hands on her breasts. Tony gently eased Megan onto her back. She wanted to see the full, firm breasts her hands were kneading.

Laying over Megan and supporting her weight on her elbows, she lifted Megan's top and lowered her head running her tongue around the nipple of one of the full breasts. Kissing each nipple, she looked into Megan's passion-filled eyes. Lightly kissing her lover, she said, "This couch is too small," before kissing each of the nipples again.

Megan's nerve endings were sending shivers up and down her body. Not wanting to stop, but her movement limited, she nodded in agreement, letting Tony help her up before they retired to the bedroom.

* * * * * * * * *

David opened the door and walked in. Mike was sitting at the table and looked up despondently. "What's wrong?" He walked over to his partner. "What did the doctor say?"

"I'm allergic to cats," Mike said sadly, knowing how much David loved the two kittens.

David breathed a sigh of relief. "God, Mike. You scared the hell out of me."

"But the doctor said we had to get rid of the kittens."

"I'm just glad that's all it is. I know we'll miss the kittens. But you're much more important to me than they are," David said, hugging his lover.

"I just can't believe that out of all the testing the only thing I'm allergic to is cats. It was nice having them around the house during the day when you're gone."

Wanting to make Mike feel better, he said, "Once we find a good home for Huggy and Velcro, maybe we can get a puppy. Where are the kittens?"

"I had to put them in the den for a while. My eyes were really bothering me. You can let them out now."

"It won't hurt them to stay in the den for a little while. I'll just play with them in there," David said. "You know those pictures we took? I'll take one down to Trading Times tomorrow and run an ad. They're so cute it should be easy to find a home for them."

"Yeah, I guess. I still hate the idea of giving them to strangers."

David looked at Mike. "Don't worry. If we don't both like who wants them, we'll just wait until the right person comes along."

Mike's face brightened a little. "Okay. I guess I'm just a little overprotective of them."

"I think we both are. Why don't we go out and eat tonight? We haven't done that for a while. We could go to Diana's."

Mike smiled. "Sounds good."

* * * * * * * * * *

Sherman was sitting on the balcony in a lawn chair. He had spent parts of the last three evenings here. His surveillance equipment was set up and, based on the information gleaned, he had formulated a couple of different plans.

Walking inside, he picked up the binoculars and trained them on the bay window across the street. It was early and the curtains were still open. He could only see the portion of the living room near the large bay window, but if this had been a regular case, Sherman would already have taken her out with a high-powered telescopic equipped rifle.

Smiling Sherman acknowledged this was fun. This case presented a real challenge because he had to develop the perfect accident. Not only did it have to take out the target, but there could be no suspicion that it was anything but an accident. Everything was going well though. Sherman still couldn't believe his luck at finding an apartment in such close proximity to his target.

He had known the location of the surveillance case she was working on since Thursday. He had simply parked his car on a side street near the Federal Building that gave him an unobstructed view of the garage entrance. When she left in the agency car with the other agent, he followed. This had actually been easier than he thought it would be. The early rush hour allowed him the luxury of blending in with the other drivers.

Sherman never acted until he had enough information. The location of the surveillance site was not of immediate importance, but he wanted to know where his target was at all times. If a contingency plan became necessary, he would be prepared.

When the lights went off in the apartment across the street, Sherman prepared to leave and return to the hotel. Smiling, he thought, *soon*.

****

Tony was getting irritated. They were at the Tower City station of the Rapid Transit and had been unable to board two other trains because of people pushing and shoving in front of them. She could see the headlight of another approaching train and decided she'd make sure they got on this one. She'd had enough of this particular crowd and just wanted to get home.

Megan looked at Tony and saw the hardening of her face. Her partner had been remarkably restrained considering they had literally been shoved away from the doors of two other trains. She wished she had thought about the Garth concert before suggesting they take the train to the Indians game. It was always crowded at the station after a game, but nothing like this.

Placing her hand on Tony's arm, she squeezed it lightly before letting go. She met Tony's eyes and shrugged her shoulders, saying, "Next time we'll drive, ok?"

"It's not your fault these idiots are so damn rude," Tony said, relaxing a little. Quirking a half smile, she added, "But I would rather drive next time."

The train entered the tunnel and the jostling began again. After a particularly hard bump from someone standing behind her, Tony finally had enough. She had just started to turn around and let the asshole know she did not appreciate it when he stumbled forward losing his balance. Unable to stop her forward momentum with the weight of the man pressed against her, they fell from the platform onto the tracks and into the path of the oncoming train.

Chapter
6

Megan watched horrified when her partner and the man fell onto the tracks right in front of the train. Screaming, "Tony..." she was on her knees in a second leaning forward, her upper body protruding over the tracks holding out her hand for Tony to grab.

Before Tony even saw her, Megan was roughly lifted to her feet and jerked back by someone who had grabbed her around the waist. Fighting wildly, her mind imprinted with an image of her partner pinned beneath the man on the tracks, she yelled desperately, "Let me go!" But the screams of people who saw what happened had attracted the attention of the transit police, and her sight was blocked when they pushed people back. All she could hear was the screeching of metal against metal when the brakes were slammed on.

"Stop it," the stranger said harshly. "You could have been killed."

Megan stopped struggling. Turning her head to look at the stranger, her voice conveying a calmness she did not feel, Megan said, "Please, let me go."

The moment he released her, Megan pushed through the crowd, her heart pounding painfully, *Please let her be ok.* but knowing it would be a miracle if she were. Pushing past the transit cop, afraid to look but having to know, she stood at the edge of the platform and forced herself to glance at the tracks.

When Tony felt herself fall, her mind automatically registered that the ground was too close to do anything but ready herself for the impact. Adrenaline and reflexes honed by years of training took over, and the instant Tony landed she wrapped her arms around the man on top of her. Freeing her left leg, she drew it up until her knee was bent at a 45-degree angle. Using it to propel them, Tony shoved off, rolling both of them over the track and out of harm's way. On the far side of the tracks, she watched the train finally come to a stop several feet beyond them.

Tony lifted herself off the man and slowly stood up, her mind assessing the damage to her body. Her right thigh was throbbing, but she could detect nothing serious. Ignoring the stinging of the scrapes along her arm and hands and the pain in her leg, she held out a hand to help the shaken stranger to his feet, asking, "Are you ok?"

Grabbing her hand and heaving himself up, he said, "Yeah. I'm ok. I think," and then added, "thanks."

"Then would you mind telling me why you were shoving so hard? You could have killed us both," Tony said, her voice hard.

The man looked at the woman standing there glaring at him and was suddenly very afraid again. He had just narrowly escaped death and this woman looked like she was ready to kill him herself. "Someone behind me pushed me. That's why I lost my balance. I was trying not to fall into you. I'm really sorry," he sputtered.

Tony looked for any signs of deception and found none. It didn't make sense anyway. He wouldn't have lost his balance if he were just trying to push forward. "Did you see who was behind you?"

"No. First thing I knew I was falling into you," he said, anxious to convince her that he wasn't responsible for their fall.

Just then, transit personnel spotted them and shouted, "Over here! They look ok."

Megan heard shouts but, amidst all the chaos on the platform, she couldn't hear what they were saying. Yanking her arm out of the grasp of the transit cop who had ordered her back, she jumped down onto the tracks. Crossing in front of the train to the opposite side, she saw several people making their way up the far side of the tracks, and one was unmistakably her partner. Megan broke into a run, never noticing the tears of relief that were steadily streaming down her face.

Tony saw Megan come around the front of the train and begin running. Separating from the group, she opened her arms to meet her partner. Megan threw her arms around Tony and felt her partner's arms encircle her. In Tony's comforting embrace it impacted on Megan how close she had come to never knowing this feeling again, and she cried harder unable to say anything. Tony held her tightly saying, "Sshh. It's ok."

The other victim and the transit workers stood around uneasily. Tony looked up, her eyes hard, and asked in a tone that indicated there was only one answer, "Could you give us a minute?"

"Yeah, sure," one answered, and they turned and resumed walking up the side of the track.

Tony continued to hold Megan, both comforted by the contact. Megan gained a semblance of control and looked up at her partner. "I thought you..." She stopped, unable to continue.

Raising her hand to Megan's wet face, Tony wiped some of the tears away with her thumb. "So did I," Tony admitted. Taking hold of the dry bottom of her tear soaked T-shirt, Tony lifted the edge to Megan's face wiping it off. "We better go before they come looking for us."

* * * * * * * * * *

Tony unlocked the door, pushed it open letting Megan enter first, and then followed her. She was tired and her leg was protesting angrily, but she was worried about Megan. Her partner had been uncharacteristically quiet.

The paramedics had checked Tony over when she refused to go to the hospital. Since some of the passengers on the incoming transit train had been jostled when the driver slammed on the brakes, total chaos had reigned. There were no serious injuries, but it took over an hour before the police had completely established order, allowing time for some of the local reporters to appear. When the police finally took her statement, Tony had been questioned for over an hour about the bizarre accident. It was just good to be home.

Megan was exhausted. The emotional anguish she had endured for those few minutes tonight had taken their toll. It had driven home again just how important a part of her life Tony was. Turning and hugging her, Megan's mind was still coming to grips with the fact that her partner was safe; that against incredible odds, she was right here. The familiar feel of Tony's arms around her, as the agent rested her chin on her head, melted some of the tension out of Megan's body.

"You ok?" Tony asked softly.

Looking up at the concerned blue eyes watching her, Megan felt a twinge of guilt. Tony had hurt her leg and her arm was scraped up pretty badly, and yet she was still worried about her. She should be taking care of Tony. Smiling wanly, Megan said, "Yeah. How does your leg feel?"

"It's a little sore," Tony admitted. "Nothing serious though."

"I want to look at it."

Tony kissed her saying, "Okay." She was willing to do anything to make Megan feel better. Removing her jeans, she watched Megan examining the bruises on her legs. The largest was on the outside of her right thigh extending from just below her hip halfway to the knee. Tony knew that was where she took the brunt of the weight of the man when hitting the tracks.

Megan's trained eyes and hands were closely checking over her partner. "Ooh. This is really nasty," Megan said, looking at the angry gray and purple discoloration. The skin was swollen and warm to her touch. Megan stood up and said, "We need to get some ice on that. It'll help with the pain and swelling."

Tony kissed Megan on the forehead and said, "Okay. But I want to take a shower first."

Megan raised her hand to Tony's face and softly stroked her cheek, reaffirming that her lover was indeed safe, before saying, "I'll get the ice ready."

When Tony went to take a shower, Megan got out a bottle of peroxide and some square cotton patches. Getting a zip lock gallon size baggy, she went to the freezer and poured the contents of the ice cube bin into it. Closing the bag, she put it in the freezer along with the ice cube trays she had refilled.

Tony stood under the soothing warm water, an unbidden curse escaping her lips when it hit the raw skin on her arm and leg. Washing the dirt from her body, being particularly careful with her arm and leg, she thought about the unusual accident. It didn't make any sense. The guy that fell into her said he was pushed. But everyone on the platform was pushing and shoving. It would have taken a powerful shove to cause him to lose his balance. Why would anyone be shoving that hard?

When she got out of the shower and dried herself off, she was no closer to making sense of the events of the evening. Shaking her head, she decided it was probably one of those fluky things that sometimes happened.

After donning a sleeping shirt, Tony walked to the kitchen limping slightly. She eased herself down into one of the chairs, taking care not to aggravate her leg.

Megan had put the peroxide and cotton squares on the table and was waiting for her. Picking up a cotton patch, she thoroughly dampened it with peroxide. "Let me see your arm." Looking at the scraped skin, she frowned and said, "You really got your arm good, didn't you?" and started cleaning the wound.

Tony flinched when the peroxide came into contact with the raw area on her arm.

Megan looked up and said, "Sorry...I know it hurts. I'll be done in a minute." Once Megan had applied the peroxide to Tony's arm and hands, she said, "Let's go into the living room. You need to lay down so I can put the ice on the worst of that bruise."

Tony laid down on the couch on her side watching her partner. She grimaced when Megan laid the cold ice against the warm angry bruise. Looking into her partner's sympathetic eyes, Tony wondered for what was probably the millionth time how she had ever gotten so lucky. Taking a hold of Megan's hand she said, "I love you."

Megan bent down, kissing Tony on the cheek. "I love you, too." Standing up, she placed a hand towel over the ice bag and said, "Hold this in place. I'm going to take a shower," pausing a moment, she added, "and keep the ice on, ok?" giving her partner a warning look.

Tony grinned at Megan. "Okay."

Megan insisted she keep the ice on for twenty minutes. Even though her skin was protected from the ice by a thin cloth, after about ten minutes Tony decided her leg hurt more from the ice than the bruise. When Megan returned to the living room, she removed the ice bag. When Tony started to get up, she said, "You might as well stay there. In twenty minutes it goes back on again."

"I think we should just go to bed," Tony suggested, smiling.

Megan returned the smile. "We will after the next time. Tomorrow you'll be glad we did this," she said before taking the ice bag back into the kitchen and putting it in the freezer.

Tony wasn't so sure about that, but Megan sat on the coffee table right next to her the whole time, and when her leg ached from the ice, looking into the caring hazel eyes somehow made it hurt a lot less. But she was still glad when Megan finally removed it, allowing them to go to bed.

Chapter
7

The fresh smell of rain wafted through the window, carried across the room on the cool breeze. Megan's eyes slowly opened, the morning light brightening the room through the curtains. Her head was resting against Tony's chest, the steady heartbeat echoing a soft cadence in her ear. Her arm lay across her partner's midsection, and she could feel Tony's arm resting across her back.

Sensing Tony was still asleep, she slowly lifted her head and looked at her lover. This was a rare opportunity. Her partner was usually awake before she was. *She is so beautiful.* All the tension from the night before was gone and her face was relaxed and peaceful. The corners of her mouth were turned up and Megan smiled at the sudden thought that Tony must be dreaming about something good and she hoped she was in it, too. Very slowly raising herself up so as not to wake her partner, she got up from the bed. Megan looked at Tony one more time before she leaned over and kissed the agent's forehead. "I love you," she whispered.

When Tony woke up, the first thing she noticed was Megan wasn't there. She must have been more exhausted than she thought not to hear her partner get up. Moving, she realized she was also very sore. Sitting up slowly, she eased her legs over the side of the bed favoring the bruised one.

Gingerly standing up, she tested it before putting her full weight on it. It was stiff and complained angrily when she put weight on it. Ignoring it, but compromising a little, she favored it slightly while walking to the bathroom.

Megan was in the kitchen cooking breakfast. "Morning." She smiled at Tony. "How does your leg feel?"

"Not bad. Still a little sore," Tony said, underplaying her discomfort.

Megan looked at Tony pointedly. "Just a little? You have remarkable healing abilities then, because it should hurt more today than it did yesterday."

You'd think I'd know better by now. Tony drew her eyebrows together and with a questioning look on her face, she asked, "What? You didn't know that?"

Chuckling, Megan walked over saying, "You're incorrigible," before reaching up to kiss her. She unobtrusively watched Tony ease herself into the kitchen chair and decided another ice treatment was in order.

After they finished eating, she filled another bag with ice and handed it to Tony saying, "I'll clean up out here. Go put this on your leg."

"Megan, it's fine. I don't need any more ice," Tony said in her most convincing voice.

Looking her partner in the eyes, Megan said emphatically, "No, it's not fine. It shows every time you move." She softened her voice, "It really will help."

Tony was not the least bit happy about the prospect of putting the ice on her leg, but seeing the concern on Megan's face, she took the bag of ice from her partner. Knowing Megan would be watching her, she walked into the living room trying not to favor her leg, grumbling under her breath, "This is really getting old."

Megan shook her head while watching Tony try to walk without limping. She had been through this with her partner before. For some reason, she seemed to think acknowledging pain was a weakness and, if you ignored it, it would just go away. When she was finished in the kitchen, Megan went to the bedroom and changed out of her nightshirt and into a pair of shorts and a pull over top.

Tony had turned on the TV and was flipping channels with the remote. Finally settling on the Discovery Channel, she looked up when Megan walked in. Megan said, "Another five minutes and you can take it off. I'm going to do the laundry."

Oh, no, you don't. "It's my turn to do the laundry," Tony reminded Megan, although she was quite sure Megan didn't need the reminder.

"Yeah, I know. But I'm not doing anything so I figured I'd just do it," Megan said knowing she was pushing it but hoping Tony would agree. She wanted Tony to take it easy.

Tony thought quickly. She knew Megan was only thinking of her, but she had no intentions of being treated like an invalid just because she had a bruise on her leg. "Okay. While you're doing the laundry, I'll go grocery shopping."

Megan almost rolled her eyes. Grocery shopping entailed a lot more walking than doing the laundry. The laundry room was only three doors down from their apartment. Shaking her head and smiling at the innocent look on Tony's face, she said, "You win. Go ahead and do the laundry. I'm going to do the grocery shopping." When Tony smirked, Megan walked over and planted a kiss on her mouth. "Just remember what they say about pay backs."

Tony sat up and took the ice off her leg. Walking with Megan into the kitchen she said, "How about picking up some peaches? Maybe a peach pie, too?"

"Didn't we just have that last week?" Megan teased. One of the reasons she had changed to the peach scented shampoo and bubble bath was because of how much Tony loved peaches.

Tony cocked her head to the side and with a winning smile said, "Please."

Megan walked over and hugged her. "Like I could really say no to that."

Tony kissed Megan. "Thanks."

After Megan left, Tony took the clothes out of the hamper and put them in the laundry basket. Stripping the bed, she added the sheets and a few other loose clothes in the bedroom to the basket and walked into the kitchen to get the laundry detergent from the pantry.

Tony was disgusted to find that she still had to favor her leg walking down the hallway. But on reflection, she decided she really shouldn't be upset. It could have been a lot worse. She vividly remembered being awash in light from the headlight of the train and honestly didn't know how they had managed to escape the wheels of the transit train. *At least Megan seems better today.*

Megan exited the elevator and walked toward her car. Passing another tenant, she stopped and turned to look at him again, but he was walking toward the elevator, his back to her. There was something about him that seemed familiar. Shaking her head, she decided he probably just reminded her of someone she knew.

Megan pushed the shopping cart down the aisles of the small neighborhood grocery store. The prices were a little higher than the larger chains, but it was more convenient, and it was worth it just not to have to deal with the crowded larger store. Stopping in front of the fruit display, Megan looked at the peaches. Selecting a dozen, she thought, *this should last her a while.* Leaving the produce area, Megan headed toward the bakery.

Tony opened the door of the apartment and heard the phone ringing. Picking it up in the kitchen, she said, "Hello."

"What's with you anyway? You're not even back in town a week and you're in the paper again. Just can't stay out of the news, can you?" Brian teased, effectively concealing his concern.

Tony smiled at the familiar voice. "Good morning to you, too, smart ass. How are things in your neck of the woods?"

"Quieter than yours," Brian retorted before adding, "you ok?"

"Yep. Got lucky." Tony thought, *Very lucky.*

Brian glanced down at the newspaper he was looking at and said, "Paper says you fell from the platform. Somehow I find that hard to believe."

Tony snorted. "Fell, huh? I don't think so. Guy behind me got shoved, lost his balance, and we both landed rather unceremoniously on the tracks. End of story," Tony summed up succinctly.

"The story says it was a miracle you were both uninjured. Care to let me know how you managed that?"

Tony heard the concern through the bantering in Brian's voice and said, "I was able to roll off the tracks along with the guy that fell with me."

Brian thought about what Tony said. He had seen her in action and she defied imagination. He had the utmost respect for her and considered her a friend. "Okay. Just checking to make sure you were all right. When are you guys coming over for dinner? Shannon's been asking and the kids are really excited about meeting a real live FBI agent," Brian said chuckling. "They're at that hero worship age."

Oh, hell. I'm gonna have to turn him down again. "I'm working on a case that involves shift work right now. How about I give you a call when it breaks?"

"Sounds good," Brian said. He was looking forward to having Tony and Megan over.

"See ya." Tony had just set the phone down, when it rang again. Frowning, she picked it up. "Hello."

"Tony?" David asked, hesitantly. He'd only spoken on the phone with Tony once and wanted to make sure it was her.

"Yeah," Tony said, resting her weight on her uninjured leg.

"This is David. I just wanted to make sure you were ok. The paper said..."

"I know. I'm fine. The paper exaggerated the accident," Tony ad-libbed, having no idea what the paper said because she hadn't read it yet.

David smiled and said, "Oh, good. We were really worried."

"Thanks for calling, David," Tony said with mixed feelings. She wasn't used to having people care one way or the other what happened to her, except for Megan. She appreciated his concern but found it somewhat disconcerting.

"No, problem. Talk to you later," David said, relieved.

"Bye."

Tony opened the door figuring the wash should be about done when the phone rang again. Exasperated, she picked it up saying, "Hello."

Barbara was taken aback. She couldn't have misdialed. Megan's number was programmed into the memory. Tentatively, she asked, "Is Megan there?"

Not recognizing the voice, Tony forgot her irritation and said pleasantly, "She's not home right now. May I take a message?"

Why was someone else answering Megan's phone? "Yes. Would you tell her to call her mother?"

"Sure," Tony said, hoping her tone hadn't been too brusque when she answered the phone.

Hanging up the phone, Tony made it to the apartment door for the second time, when the shrill sound of the phone once again split the air. Ignoring it, she closed the apartment door firmly behind her.

* * * * * * * * * *

Megan took the grocery bags out of the trunk and loaded them into the elevator, holding it with the stop button. Arriving on the fourth floor, she pushed the stop button in, grabbed a couple of the bags, and went to the apartment. Tony heard her and opened the door, taking the bags and putting them in the kitchen. She walked to the elevator with Megan to get the rest of the groceries.

"Your Mom called and wants you to give her a call," Tony told Megan while they were putting the groceries away.

Megan looked up from putting a box of rice and some pasta in the cupboard. "Did she say anything else?"

"No. But I think she was surprised I answered the phone," Tony said, still looking through bags.

"This is going to be real interesting. You have no idea how nosey she is," Megan said, frowning. "Guess I'll call and see what she wants when we get done here."

Tony looked up and winked. "Just tell her you have a roommate."

"Well, that does happen to be true," Megan said, grinning at her partner. "Just don't make me laugh when I tell her that."

Tony drew an exaggerated "x" across her chest. "I promise to behave while you are talking to your mother." Smirking, she added, "But only until you get off the phone."

Megan's eyes twinkled, and she said, "Is that a promise?"

"Do you want it to be?" Tony parlayed back, grinning.

Chuckling, Megan said, "You are so bad."

Looking in another bag, Tony smiled when she saw the peach pie. Walking over to Megan, she kissed her and said, "Thanks." Opening the last bag, she glanced over at Megan. "You got Dove Bars."

Grinning, Megan said, "Don't tell me. You like those, too?"

"Well...a little," Tony said with twinkling eyes.

Walking into the living room to call her mother, Megan noticed the red light on the answering machine blinking.

"Someone else must have called when you were in the laundry room," she said, depressing the play message button.

Tony put the last few items away and arrived in the living room in time to hear the message. "Hi, Tony. This is Mom. If you have time, give me a call."

Megan looked at her partner and smiled. "Must be family day today."

Tony shook her head. "Yeah, I guess it is." *Some days you just couldn't win.* Sitting down on the couch, she extended her sore leg out along the side of the coffee table. It felt a little better that way.

Megan sat down next to Tony and dialed her parents' number. "Hi, Mom. You called?"

Barbara smiled at the sound of her daughter's voice. "Hi. I just wanted to remind you about Saturday. Who answered your phone?"

She sure didn't waste any time asking. "Tony." Glancing at her partner and winking, Megan said, "She lives here, too."

Well this is sure a surprise, Barbara thought. Walking out to the kitchen to get her tea, she asked, "Since when? You never mentioned having a roommate. How did you meet her?"

"I met her working on the Shadow case." Deciding to downplay it and hopefully satisfy her mother's curiosity, she continued, "Tony's lived here for a while now."

"Is she the FBI agent whose picture was in the paper with yours? The one you went on vacation with?" Barbara asked, raising her eyebrows.

"Yes," Megan said, correctly deducing that Ashley must have told her that, but offering no further explanation.

She couldn't have lived there that long then. The article about her in the paper said she was new to Cleveland. "Okay. It was just a bit of a shock to hear someone else answer your phone." A thought suddenly occurred to Barbara. "Megan...you know if you need any money we could help you out."

Megan frowned, wondering where her mother had gotten that idea. "Thanks Mom, but my money situation is fine."

"Well, I just thought since you had gotten a roommate..." Barbara trailed off.

Megan's brow furrowed and she pursed her lips. Holding her anger in check, she said, "Mom, I don't have a roommate because I'm short of money."

"Well, just remember we're here for you if you need some help. It's nothing to be ashamed of." Barbara couldn't think of any other reason her daughter would have a roommate. There had to be some problem. Since Megan had left home, she'd always lived by herself.

Megan's anger briefly surfaced, and her words flowed forth unchecked. "If my roommate was a guy, would you still think I needed money?"

Smacking her lips together in a disapproving sound, Barbara stated what she thought was obvious. "That's different."

Sighing, Megan said, "No, it's not." Deciding to end the conversation, she added, "I'll see you Saturday."

"Okay, dear. Bye." Barbara shook her head. She should have known better. Megan would never admit she needed help. She was too independent.

Megan glanced at Tony. "I can't believe she thinks you live here because I need money. That's my parents' answer to everything." Megan paused and met Tony's eyes. "One part of me wants to just tell them about us, but I know how narrow minded they are. They would never understand."

"If you think it would cause problems, there's really no need to say anything about it," Tony said. She didn't want Megan to do anything that would make her uncomfortable or further strain her relationship with her parents.

"I know. But I would like to tell them. It would be so nice if they would accept the fact that we are together, like your mother did." Shaking her head and looking down, she said, "Unfortunately, I just can't envision that."

Tony reached over and put her hand under Megan's chin urging her partner's head up. Looking into the troubled, hazel eyes, she said, "Hey. Come on. Don't worry about it. There will be plenty of time to tell them if you decide to." Smiling and winking at her, Tony added, "I don't plan on going anywhere."

Some of the stress faded from Megan's face and the corners of her mouth turned up. Tony certainly wasn't the most talkative person she'd ever met, but she sure knew how to make her words count. Leaning over, Megan kissed her and said, "Good."

Chapter
8

Megan peeled off the surgical gloves and dropped them in the garbage can, having just finished her only case for the day. The woman had been found dead in her home from unknown causes. Megan had quickly located the cause of death as an aneurysm in the brain. The woman had only been thirty-six years old. Megan had long ago realized you didn't take anything for granted, and it had been really driven home over the weekend.

She thought back over her conversation earlier with David. She had told him about Tony's accident and he had shaken his head in disbelief. He had commented that sometimes life was stranger than fiction, but it was amazing that no one had seen the impatient person who had caused the whole thing by shoving so hard. Considering how many people had been on the platform, Megan didn't find it unusual at all.

Megan went to the locker room and changed out of her scrubs into her street clothes. A quick check of her inbox revealed a message from Tony. Smiling, she picked up the phone and dialed her number.

When her lover answered, Megan smiled and said, "Hi. I just got your message."

"Do you have time for lunch? I can pick you up whenever you're free," Tony said, already missing Megan even though she hadn't started her new shift yet.

"Sounds great," Megan said, delighted at the chance to see her lover again today. "How about twelve-thirty?"

"I'll be there," Tony answered, pleased that Megan wasn't too busy to go to lunch.

David walked in and sat down. Megan looked up and said, "What's up?" knowing instinctively that her friend had something on his mind.

Flopping into the chair, David said, "Mike went to the doctor Friday."

"Is he ok?" Megan asked, concerned.

David smiled and said, "Yeah. But it turns out he's allergic to cats. He tested negative on everything else, but we're going to have to find a home for the kittens. So, I was wondering if you knew anyone who might like them? We want to place them together. We're going to miss them."

While he was talking, David pulled an envelope out of his pocket. Pulling a photograph out of it, he handed it to Megan saying, "I'm going to take this to Trading Times this afternoon. For just $10.00 extra they'll put the picture in."

Megan looked at the picture of the kittens. One of the kittens was black with a white face. It had a splash of white on the chest and white stockings extending halfway up the front legs. The other kitten looked like an artist had taken black, orange and beige, and just splotched them arbitrarily over her back. Her chest, face, and legs were all white. The mismatch of color extended up to the top of her head giving the appearance of a hat.

"Ooh. They're so cute!" All of a sudden Megan had an idea. "Can I borrow this picture until after lunch? I want to show it to Tony."

"Sure," David said, hoping this meant what he thought it might. "They're really good kittens. You wouldn't even know they were around." He paused, "Well, most of the time."

Megan laughed at the look on his face. She knew that the kittens were probably a hand-full. "Yeah, right," she said, smiling.

* * * * * * * * * *

Megan was waiting outside the building when Tony arrived. Walking over to the Buick, she opened the door and got in. Looking at Tony, she smiled and said, "Hi."

Tony smiled back at her partner. "Hi, yourself. Where do you want to go?"

Megan didn't really care where they went. She just wanted to enjoy some time with Tony. "How about Isabella's? That's close, and it'll give us more time."

"Okay," Tony said, maneuvering the car away from the building and merging with the traffic on the street. A few minutes later they arrived at the restaurant.

Following the hostess to a table, they sat down and ordered coffee before perusing the menu. "I'm going to have the chicken breast salad. That's always good," Megan said, laying down the menu.

Tony laid down her menu and said, "Then I'll have that, too."

After placing their orders, Megan looked at Tony and asked, "Is a dog the only pet you had when you were a kid?"

Setting her coffee down, Tony wondered what prompted this question. "Yes. Why?"

Smiling at the questioning look on Tony's face, Megan asked, "Do you like cats?"

Playing along, Tony said, "Yes. They're ok. I like most animals. Why? Do you want to get a cat?" She knew Megan must have some reason for asking.

Megan grinned and said, "Sort of." She took the picture of the kittens out of her purse and handed it to Tony. "Aren't they cute?"

Tony took the picture from her partner and looked at it. Glancing up, she said, "Yes, they are. Whose are they?"

"David and Mike's. Mike is allergic and they have to find a home for them." Megan paused and said, "I think we could give them a good home."

Tony quirked a half smile. "You do, huh?" Seeing the excitement on her partner's face, she thought, *You can have anything you want if it makes you happy.*

Stirring her coffee, Megan said, "Well, only if you want them, too."

Winking at her, Tony said, "Are you sure we want both of them?"

A warm smile lit up Megan's face. "David wanted to place them together and, besides, they wouldn't be lonely when we're at work. Are you sure you don't mind?"

Tony smiled at her partner. "No, I don't mind." *Like I could really mind.* "It'll be nice to have a couple of pets."

"Oh, good!" Megan said, excitedly. "I just knew you wouldn't mind. I'll go get them tonight." Pointing at the black and white kitten, she told Tony, "This one's name is Velcro and this one is Huggy."

"Velcro and Huggy?" Tony asked, amused. *Those are certainly original names.*

Megan grinned back. "I thought the names were kind of cute. David said he named them that because they were both so sweet and wanted to be close to them all the time."

Tony just shook her head. *I just might have to tease David about those names.* After they finished lunch, Tony dropped Megan off and said, "I should be home by midnight or at the latest twelve-thirty, so don't wait up. You have to get up too early."

Nodding her head, Megan said, "Okay. See you later," not looking forward to spending the evening alone. Well, at least she'd have the kittens to keep her company.

* * * * * * * * *

"So, Tony," Keith said waiting for her to look up. "How did you end up in Cleveland?"

Glancing at the other agent, Tony said, "I requested a transfer and this is where they happened to have an opening. How about you?"

"My family is here and I was engaged when I entered the academy. So when I heard there was an opening here, I put in for it." Keith pulled out his wallet, extracted a picture and handed it to Tony. "This is my wife."

Tony took the picture, looking at the attractive woman. Smiling, she said, "She's very pretty," and handed the picture back to him. It had been a very slow shift. There had been only one subject in the house they were conducting surveillance on all evening.

"What about you? You married?" Keith asked.

"No. I do have a significant other though," Tony said, not elaborating, but wishing she were at home instead of in the dingy apartment they were sitting in.

A black Chevy van pulled up in front the building across the street. "We have company," Tony said picking up the camera. Focusing in the wide-angle telescopic lens, she snapped off several pictures of the two men clad in jeans and T-shirts carrying briefcases. Once they entered the surveillance site, she took a few pictures of the van making sure the license plate was visible.

Keith was monitoring the receiver and tape recorder. Coming to life, it recorded the conversation between the new arrivals and the lone occupant of the dwelling. Picking up a tablet, he jotted down notes at strategic points in the conversation.

Tony kept her eyes trained on the doorway across the street. She wanted to see if they left with anything other than the briefcases they entered with. During the three days of surveillance, the agents had already picked up pertinent information on the destination of the money once it was turned in.

* * * * * * * * * *

Megan locked the door and walked down the hall to the elevator. She was looking forward to seeing David and Mike's new house and she was really excited about bringing the two kittens home. Megan loved animals and had brought many strays home as a child but her father had refused to let her keep any of them. These kittens would be her first pets. She grinned happily at the thought.

Locating the address, Megan pulled into the driveway behind Mike's Chevy Cavalier, leaving access to the two-car garage. The attractive colonial was white with gray trim and had a large front yard setting the house well back from the street. She got out of the car and walked to the side door, but before she could ring the doorbell, the door swung open.

David smiled at Megan. "Hi. Welcome to our abode." He stood aside so she could enter.

Megan smiled. "This is really nice, David."

"Wait until you see the inside," David said. They still had some boxes to unpack, but the house was mostly in order and he was anxious for his friend to see it. Mike walked into the room and greeted Megan.

"Hi." Megan smiled warmly. She didn't see Mike often but liked him. He was a little on the quiet side but was perfectly matched with David who was quite gregarious.

David and Mike gave Megan the grand tour. The house was decorated attractively and had a very relaxed, pleasant atmosphere. The curtains and blinds were color coordinated to match the area rugs that covered the hardwood floors. The windows maximized the outside light, and plants were generously scattered throughout the dining and living rooms. The kitchen was modernized with an abundance of wooden cupboards set against eggshell colored walls, offset by a bright yellow and blue border just under the ceiling.

"The kittens are in the den," David said. "Wait until you see them. I know you're going to love them." Leading the way, he opened the door just wide enough for him and Megan to squeeze in. "Every time I open the door they make a beeline for it. I don't think they like being locked up after having run of the house," David explained.

Megan knelt down on the floor and held out her hand to the kittens. Naturally curious Huggy walked over and sniffed her fingers. Taking a few more steps she bumped Megan's hand with her head and a quiet rumble began. Velcro, not wanting to miss out on the attention, came bounding over and pushed her body up against Huggy's purring loudly. When Megan lowered her other hand to Velcro, stroking her head and back, the kitten arched into it contentedly.

David grinned. "Looks like you're a hit."

"They are just adorable," Megan said, smiling up at David. "I don't think you have to worry about finding a home for them anymore. But I should get going so they can get used to their new home."

"Okay. It'll just take me a minute to get their things together," David said, before leaving the room. Putting their food and dishes into a bag, he got their carrier and litter out of the hall closet. David took the carrier into the den and then put both kittens in it. Securing the door, Megan picked up the carrier containing the bouncing kittens and walked out of the room. He retrieved the litter box and followed her out of the den. "Just a minute and I'll have this all ready for you."

Walking with Megan out to the car, he put the bag of food, litter and litter box into the trunk of her car. Megan sat the kittens on the back seat and fastened the seat belt around the carrier. It didn't hurt to be safe. If she had to stop quickly, she didn't want the kittens on the floor.

* * * * * * * * *

Tony drove the car along the familiar route singing along with an old Carpenters song. She had only one more day on second shift and then she'd be on the graveyard shift. While the prospect didn't thrill her, at least she would be able to spend some time with Megan. The evening had been unbearably long.

Passing the entrance ramp at Edgewater Park, Tony turned on her signal preparing to merge with the oncoming traffic, so she could move over to the right lane in time to exit. Moving skillfully between the two vehicles entering the expressway, she changed lanes. The car in front of her moved over into the left lane, and the one behind her followed suit.

Slowing as she approached the exit, the vehicle that had merged behind her pulled even and swerved into her lane. Tony jerked the steering wheel to the right moving the car onto the berm while simultaneously depressing the horn and thinking, *damn idiot. He never even looked.* But the thoughts barely had time to cross her mind before it registered that the truck was continuing to crowd her, forcing her further off the road. Suddenly the driver jerked hard to the right, violently slamming the heavy pickup into her car, before bouncing off and continuing down the street. The sound of the impact echoed through the still night.

Tony fought to regain control of her car. The force with which the pickup hit her car propelled it through the snow fence. The wildly spinning tires of her car could not find purchase on the grass and it slipped over the lip of the embankment.

While fighting fiercely to keep the car to the left, Tony's mind processed the fact that if the car slid over the incline, it would most likely flip. She instantaneously made a decision to try and stop the car against one of the two trees on a slight incline that her car was rapidly approaching.

The wheels of the car fought against the direction she attempted to steer the car and, with only seconds to spare, her desperate efforts were rewarded when her car impacted with one of the trees. Before her body had finished its momentum forward, she was thrown violently back against the seat, her head banging the headrest, when the air bag deployed.

Chapter
9

Sherman struggled for a moment before regaining control of the pickup truck. He heard the loud and satisfying bang from the impact of her car against the tree. Smiling, he exited at Clifton and made his way to a nearby bar where he planned to leave the truck. It was close to a bus stop that ran all night and it was an anonymous way of traveling back to his hotel.

Standing at the bus stop, he thought about the accident. His timing had been perfect. Sherman had selected the site the day before. It was the only stretch along her route home that had an embankment.

Sherman smirked. He would have rather her car gone over the embankment. But her car had hit the tree with such force it was unlikely she had survived. If Viglioni was alive, she would be seriously injured, and he would just visit the hospital and finish the job. Getting on the bus, he walked to the back and sat down. The police scanner in his room would furnish him the information he needed.

Back in his room, he turned on the scanner and picked up the disjointed conversation between the dispatcher and the police. There had been little traffic and it might be a while before she was discovered.

The scanner clicked to life. "Dispatch to Unit 28 and Ambulance 1. I have a motorist on the line calling from a cellular phone relaying an accident at the Route 2, Edgewater exit. MVA versus tree. Condition of occupant unknown."

"Unit 28 copy."

"Ambulance 1 en route."

Smiling, Sherman thought, *so far so good.*

* * * * * * * * * *

The whirling sound of a siren cut through the night. The ambulance slowed at each intersection before proceeding, the driver intent on arriving at the hospital safely. Pulling into the emergency entrance to the large community hospital well known for its trauma center, he swung the ambulance around, backing up to the emergency room doors. He got out of the ambulance, quickly walked around to the rear and assisted the other paramedic by helping her move the portable gurney to the edge of the ambulance, allowing the legs to drop and lock into place.

The emergency room personnel met them at the door and the driver gave the following report while the gurney was rolled into the trauma room. "This is a thirty year old woman who was driver of MVA versus tree. C-spine precautions, vital signs stable, no obvious blunt trauma, no LOC, extraction time was thirty minutes."

* * * * * * * * * *

Megan woke up feeling uneasy. She opened her eyes and looked into the green eyes of a purring kitten lying contentedly on her chest. Not fully awake, her mind processed several things and one of them was anxiety. Automatically sensing that Tony wasn't in the bed, she looked at the clock before sitting upright alarmed. Huggy meowed in protest at the sudden movement and loss of her comfortable bed.

It was one-thirty. Tony should have been home. She said she'd be home by midnight or twelve-thirty at the latest. Throwing the sheet off, Megan got up and walked into the living room and kitchen before proceeding to the bathroom wondering why Tony wasn't home. It was possible she could have gone out with guys after work or something. People did that all the time. *Yeah, but she would've called,* her mind answered. *Not if she didn't want to wake me. Really? And she would take the chance of worrying you instead? Not likely. She is only an hour late. Maybe the report took longer than normal, or maybe they moved in on the surveillance site. That was probably it.* But Megan didn't believe that. The internal argument she was having had little impact compared to the feeling in her gut. She *knew* something was wrong.

Megan thought over her options and realized there was little she could do. But she wasn't going to sit around and do nothing either. What if Tony needed her? Trusting her instincts, she decided to call the only person she knew who might be able to find out something quickly. She knew if this turned out to be a false alarm, she might be laughed at later, but she didn't care. The feeling that something was wrong was too strong to ignore.

"Hello," the deep, sleepy voice answered.

"Hi, Brian. This is Megan. I'm really sorry to bother you and it may be for nothing, but Tony's over an hour late and I have a bad feeling." Megan paused, knowing she probably sounded ridiculous.

Brian wakened fully as he listened to Megan. He liked the young Coroner and knew she was a sensible young woman. If she thought something was wrong, then he would check it out. She was not prone to hysterics. "Stay by the phone. I'll make a few calls and get back to you."

Megan paced back and forth in the kitchen. *Tony, where are you? Are you ok?* She was startled out of her thoughts ten minutes later, when the phone rang.

Wasting no words, Brian said, "I'll pick you up in fifteen minutes. Tony's been in a car accident. She's at Metro."

Megan went through the motions of putting her clothes on, occupied with trying to keep terrifying images from appearing in her mind. Shutting her eyes tightly with her hands balled into fists, she finally won the battle. She would accomplish nothing by panicking.

Megan stood in the lobby of the apartment building waiting for Brian to arrive. What could have happened? Tony was an expert driver.

Trying to focus her thoughts elsewhere, Megan looked at one of the pictures in the lobby. It was a portrait of a woman from the Victorian era, but the picture began transforming. In her mind's eye, she saw Tony sitting across from her, smiling the special smile that Megan knew was reserved only for her. Scenes from the last time she saw her lover continued to play through her mind in slow motion. She saw incredibly blue, mirth-filled eyes, shining out of a perfectly sculpted face, and the quirky little half smile when Tony learned the kittens' names. She felt the strong, soft hand gently squeeze her own and heard the softly spoken words, "See you later, love," when Tony dropped her off after lunch. Choking back a sob, Megan thought, *She has to be ok. She just has to.*

The reflection of headlights against the lobby doors drew her attention from the picture, and she hurried out the doors and got into Brian's car. Megan was already asking, "What did you find out?" before the door was even shut.

Briefly glancing at the drawn face of his friend, and wishing he had something positive to tell her, Brian said, "Not much. The patrolman on the scene is still in the ER and I didn't want to wait for him to call me."

Megan took a deep, calming breath and looked at Brian. His short hair was disheveled from sleeping, and his unshaven face showed heavy stubble. Suddenly realizing just how quickly he had arrived, she said, "Brian, thanks."

Hearing the emotion in the young woman's voice, Brian said, "No thanks are needed. You two are friends. I'm just glad you called me." He sped through the streets, the siren blaring and the blue and white light on his car creating strobe effects in the darkness.

For Megan, the ride lasted an eternity, her mind tormented with the thought that *she would have called if she could.*

Brian, in an attempt to make Megan feel better, said, "You know Tony's a real tough customer."

Megan smiled ruefully. "Yeah. I know. But this doesn't make sense. Lately she's had the worst luck. Two days ago she got pushed in front of a train, and now she's in a car accident."

"It is unusual," Brian agreed, his mind processing the information and not liking the direction his thoughts were taking.

* * * * * * * * *

Tony looked at the lights overhead. With her neck secured in the uncomfortable collar, that was about all she could do. At least she was on a regular gurney now instead of the hard board the paramedics had insisted on moving her on. She knew they had only been doing their jobs, but all she had done was rub her neck and comment that she had a headache when they had finally freed her. It had taken them half an hour and the Jaws of Life to get her out of the car. *Who wouldn't have had a headache?*

The emergency room team examined Tony and determined there were no obvious injuries. They told her they would take an x-ray just to make sure her neck was ok. If the films were negative, they would take the collar off.

Tony felt ok, all things considered. She had already checked herself out and could move her arms and legs without any pain. She figured she probably sported a few bruises from the airbag, but other than that she had come out relatively unscathed.

Her thoughts turned to Megan and she fervently hoped her partner did not know she wasn't home yet. It would worry Megan too much. *Please be sleeping. love.* Once the x-ray technician had finished taking the x-rays, Tony told the nurse, "I need to notify someone I'm here."

"Whom do you want me to call and what's the number?" the nurse asked.

Tony gave her the information and the nurse said. "It may be a little while because we're really busy right now."

"Just make sure she knows I'm all right," Tony said. It was bad enough she couldn't call Megan herself, and she wanted her partner to know she was ok.

An hour passed and no one had been back to her cubicle. Tony's thoughts had alternated between the accident and her partner. She was tired of trying to figure out why that idiot had swerved his truck into her. *All I want to do is get out of here and go home.* Her thoughts turning dark, she thought, *I'd like to get a hold of the guy driving that pick up.*

All of a sudden Tony's patience ended. She was sure there was nothing wrong with her neck. She felt fine. Megan should have been here by now. It would never have taken her this long, and she wanted to see her partner now. No matter how crazy her life had become lately, the one thing that was sure and comfortable and right was Megan.

Tony slowly sat up. Feeling no pain, she swung her legs over the side of the gurney and slid to the floor. Standing next to the gurney for a moment she decided her first instinct had been right, and she had somehow escaped serious injury. Walking over to the privacy curtain, she pulled it opened and looked down the aisle. There was a desk centered in the middle of the row of cubicles and it was there that Tony saw a phone. While walking to the desk, the doctors and nurses were busy with other patients and did not notice her. *So far, so good.* Picking up the phone, she began dialing.

"What are you doing up?"

The high collar prevented natural movement, and Tony had to turn sideways to face the woman talking to her. The irritated face of a very angry nurse confronted her.

The nurse's reaction never even fazed Tony, and she said, quite reasonably, "Sorry, but I need to let someone know where I am. I gave the number to the other nurse an hour ago and since Megan is not here, my guess is it was never called."

The nurse said emphatically, "You need to lie down right now. You have not been cleared. Do you know the damage you could be doing to your neck?"

Tony's persona changed. In a low assertive voice, she said, "I will lay down once I call Megan," ignoring the nurse who continued to berate her for being on her feet. She had to dial the number over again and this time tried nine first to get an outside line. The phone rang. On the fourth ring the answering machine picked up. Tony hung up the phone, thinking, *Megan must be on the way,* and followed the frustrated nurse back to her cubicle.

Brian parked in the emergency room parking lot and they entered the hospital together. Hurrying over to the information desk, Megan said, "I'm looking for Antonia Viglioni. She was brought here after a car accident."

"Are you a relative?" asked the woman behind the glass partition in a bored tone of voice.

Megan narrowed her eyes and said, "I'm her doctor."

"Oh. Come on back," she said, releasing the lock of the door that led to the emergency room bay.

Brian said, "Go on. I want to talk to the cop that was at the scene."

Megan quickly walked to the cubicle she had been directed to. Taking a deep breath, not knowing what to expect, she pushed aside the curtain entering the private cubicle. She saw the tall form of her partner lying flat on a gurney with a c-spine collar around her neck.

Walking over to the gurney she looked down at Tony, her mind quickly processing the fact that there were a few bruises on her arms but otherwise no obvious signs of injury except for the cervical collar. But that could be very serious. She looked into the deep blue eyes gazing up at her.

"I'm ok," Tony said smiling ruefully. "This is just a precaution." Megan placed a hand on her lover's forehead and breathed an audible sigh of relief, the tight control she had put on her emotions finally dissolving.

Tony watched the expressions of fear, worry, concern, and relief flicker across Megan's face. Her stomach tightened at the thought of all the anguish this had caused her partner. Taking hold of Megan's hand and looking into the concerned hazel eyes, she said, "Sorry, love. I wanted to call you myself and let you know I was ok but they wouldn't let me. When I finally did, you had already left."

"It's not your fault," Megan said. "I just can't bear the thought of anything happening to you and lately..." Megan stopped and looked at Tony questioningly. "No one called me."

Tony's brow furrowed slightly. "Then how did you know?"

"I woke up, you weren't there and I just knew something was wrong. So I called Brian, and he found out you'd been in an accident and were brought here," Megan answered.

Megan's simple answer left Tony speechless. *She just knew?* Looking at her partner, Tony's words conveyed the depth of her feeling. "You just knew?"

"Well, yeah," Megan said, the corners of her mouth turning up into a smile.

Tony looked into the hazel eyes watching her. Megan was always surprising her with her insight on things, but this was really unbelievable. *I am so lucky.* Squeezing her partner's hand, she said, "You're the best thing that ever happened to me. I'm so lucky I found you."

Megan felt the warm sense of well being that only Tony could elicit in her. Leaning down, she met Tony's lips for a fleeting kiss. "I'm just as lucky. Let's get you out of here. I'll be right back."

Leaving the cubicle and walking to the desk, Megan found a doctor talking on the phone. Waiting until he was finished, she said, "I'm Dr. Donnovan. Who is handling the patient in the last cubicle on the right?"

"You mean the MVA?" When Megan nodded affirmatively, he said, "I am."

"What's her status?" Megan asked.

"We're waiting on the results of the cervical films. I'll check on them. They should have been read by now." Megan stood next to him while he called the radiologist. Hanging up the phone, he said, "They're negative. I'll write her release orders."

Tony and Megan walked out into the emergency room waiting area a short time later looking for Brian. Spotting him, they walked over. Brian stood to greet his friends. Tony looked ok. The patrolman had said the car was probably totaled. This was one lucky woman...again.

"Well?" Brian asked, brusquely.

Smiling at her tall friend, Tony said, "I'm ok."

Shaking his head, in an exaggerated show of exasperation, Brian said, "I can see that. What happened?"

Tony chuckled at the expression on Brian's face. Shrugging her shoulders, she said, "You know, Brian, I don't understand it myself. A guy in a pick up truck deliberately swerved into my car. Just doesn't make sense."

Brian thought about what Tony had said. *I don't like the sound of this.* "I'm glad you're ok," Brian said underplaying his concern. "But, Tony, I have to tell you...this is getting old."

"Tell me about it," Tony said glancing at Megan.

"I want to talk to you tomorrow. You can give your official statement then," Brian said. Tony smiled her appreciation, as they left the hospital.

Chapter
10

Tony opened her eyes and was greeted by the filtered sunlight streaming through the curtain on the window. The familiar feel of Megan's body against hers felt so comforting. Lately it seemed like the events in her life were out of control. It was almost as if whatever cosmic forces there might be were angry with her, and she was being punished for some unknown transgression. The two accidents elicited a feeling of coincidence in her that made her uneasy. Unfortunately, she had nothing to base her suspicion on, except a well-developed survival instinct.

But right now, here, with her lover wrapped in her arms, all the events of the last few days took a back seat. Tony lightly ran her hand through Megan's hair, enjoying the feel of the silky strands against her hand. *I wonder if you know just how important you are to me? I love you so much. Have I told you that lately?*

Looking at the peaceful face of her partner, she hoped things would settle down in their lives. Megan didn't deserve to be put through so much. The thought, *I hope it's over,* floated through her mind, but that didn't make sense. *Nothing was going on...or was it?*

Megan's awoke to the comforting feel of even breathing and a steady heartbeat echoing in her ear. Her mouth curved up into a smile and snuggling a little closer, she thought, *She's right here and she's ok. I love waking up next to her like this.* Her thoughts were interrupted by a soft, rich voice. "Morning, beautiful. You finally awake?"

A contented smile appeared on her face. "I was hoping you wouldn't notice. I'm not sure I want to get up yet," Megan said, leaving her head on its soft pillow.

Tony grinned, loving this part of their morning ritual. In a minute or two, Megan would look up at her with those beautiful eyes and a lazy smile on her face. She knew her heart would flutter, like it did every time she saw her feelings reflected back at her through the eyes of her partner.

Megan raised her head and looked at her lover. "How do you feel?"

Tony looked into the sleepy, hazel eyes peering up at her, and unable to resist, she leaned over gently kissing the soft, sensuous lips before answering. "Fine. No headache or sore neck or anything."

Noticing how light it was, Megan said, "I guess we better get up. We've got a lot to do today."

"Yeah," Tony said, reluctantly releasing her hold on Megan. She stopped in the bathroom and then walked into the kitchen to turn on the coffee. As was customary, Megan had prepared it for brewing the night before.

Her progress was impeded by two meowing kittens waiting impatiently for their food while trying very hard to trip her by winding between her legs. Bending down and petting them both, she smiled at the loud purrs her stroke elicited. "Aren't you two cute? I guess you must be hungry."

A quick search of the cupboards revealed a few cans of food and Tony opened one, scraping the contents of the can onto a saucer for the two kittens and placing it on the floor.

Walking into the bedroom, she drew her sleeping shirt over her head and tossed it on the bed. Opening the closet, she took out a pair of jeans and a pullover top.

Megan called work and told Dr. Whitehouse she was taking a vacation day due to a personal emergency. *I can't believe he didn't give me a hard time. Not that it would have done him any good anyway.*

Walking into the bedroom, Megan felt her heart flutter at the sight of her naked partner. She was gorgeous even with the additional bruises marring her body. Crossing the room, she stood in front of Tony, her eyes running lasciviously down the length of her lover's body.

Tony's breath caught in her throat. *Oh. God.* The sultry look on her partner's face sent a jolt through her body. *She was so sexy...so Megan.* Her heart racing, she bent her head and kissed the full, soft lips turned up toward hers, while her body shivered at the light feathery touches of Megan's hands.

Megan pulled back and took off her sleeping shirt basking in the appreciative look on her partner's face. Tony's raised a hand to Megan's face, her eyes dark with passion. "You're so beautiful," she said in a low, throaty voice.

Taking Megan's hand, she led her to the bed and lowered her body over that of her partner's. Megan guided Tony's head down, kissing her deeply. Her desire escalated and goose bumps formed on her body when one of Tony's hands found a breast and her fingers teased the nipple. All their plans for the day were forgotten.

* * * * * * * * *

Sherman worked the stair stepper steadily, his thoughts on the events of the previous night. He had called the hospital to find out Viglioni's condition. They had told him she was still in triage and her status was unknown. He had gone to bed comfortable in the knowledge that she couldn't have walked away from the accident uninjured, and he'd just pay her a visit in the hospital today.

After a leisurely breakfast, he called the hospital to find out what room she was in. He had been told they had no patient by that name. He just figured she was dead. But never one to leave anything to chance, he had called the hospital morgue. He was advised his "sister" had not been admitted to the morgue. Perhaps he had the wrong hospital. Calling the emergency room once again, playing the part of a very concerned brother, he was able to learn that she had been released the night before.

While this was only a minor setback, he wasn't going to waste any more time trying to stage an accident. It was time to go buy a voice-activated tape recorder. He could listen to it at his convenience and be sure of not missing anything pertinent. He also needed to retrieve the tracking device from her car. That should be easy enough. FBI badges were quite handy for things like that.

Sherman continued mulling over different options. He had thought about taking her out at the surveillance site, but she always traveled there with another agent. It was too chancy to do it at the FBI lot.

Leaving his thought behind, he decided to go sightseeing. After all, he was on vacation. Viglioni could wait for a while. An opportunity would present itself and, when it did, he would act on it.

* * * * * * * * *

Tony and Megan were sitting at the kitchen table eating chicken salad sandwiches. In another hour Tony was due to leave for work. Megan had wanted her to stay home, but Tony had convinced her that all they did was sit around anyway and she had the next day off.

"What did the insurance company say?" Megan asked.

"They're going to have someone look at my car today or tomorrow. Personally, I think it's totaled." Quirking a half smile, she added, "I think we need to go car shopping soon."

Grinning Megan said, "You like that Jeep you rented don't you?"

"Well, it is kind of nice," Tony said, nonchalantly.

Megan laughed at the disinterested look her partner was trying to get her to buy. "Uh huh. Nice enough we had to ride around in it for an hour," Megan teased.

"I didn't hear you complaining," Tony said, her eyes twinkling.

Megan's face turned pensive. "No. You didn't. It was an opportunity to spend time with you, and the way things have been going lately, I'm almost afraid to let you out of my sight."

Tony felt her stomach tighten. *We shouldn't have to live like this.* Reaching across the table, she placed her hand on Megan's, not saying anything.

Her thoughts turned to the accident. There were so many unanswered questions. Why had the guy in the pick up deliberately rammed her? Was it just a drunk or a crazy? Had she just been in the wrong place at the wrong time? She might be more inclined to believe that if it hadn't been for incident at the train station. How could she make Megan feel better?

Comforted by the contact, but watching her lover drift off, Megan said, "Earth to Tony." When the deep blue eyes met her own, she continued, "What are you thinking about?"

"Everything that's been going on. It is so strange. I've never been prone to accidents and all of a sudden there are two in three days. Doesn't make sense. I feel like I'm missing something. I just don't know what," Tony said, looking at Megan.

Megan's sober expression mirrored her partner's. "I've been thinking about it a lot, too. When I woke up last night, I knew something was wrong. I don't know why, but I just did."

Megan's thoughts turned reflective. "The night you got stabbed in the flats...I remember thinking how it almost seemed like it had been deliberate." Her troubled eyes met Tony's. "We found out later it was. I feel like that now." She squeezed Tony's hand.

Tony saw the worry reflected in Megan's eyes. *What could she say? She didn't understand it either.* It was very troubling that Megan felt that way. Hopefully she was wrong and it was just the stress of the two accidents. "Nothing else is going to happen. It was just a coincidence" Tony didn't really believe that, but she wanted to allay Megan's concerns.

Megan squeezed Tony's hand and looked into her eyes, saying, "I hope you're right."

The phone rang. Tony let go of Megan's hand, stood up, and walked over to the phone. Picking it up, she said, "Hello."

"Hi. Brian, here. What time do you get off tonight?"

"11pm. Why?" Tony asked, curious.

Brian thought to himself, *Here goes nothing.* "I'm still concerned that this may not have been an accident."

"Yeah, I know. We talked about that earlier. I agree with you, but there's not a whole lot I can do about it," Tony said, wondering why he was bringing it up again.

Plunging ahead, Brian said, "I'm going to have a patrol car follow you from the surveillance site to the garage to get your car and then home."

"Come on, Brian," Tony said, amused that Brian would even suggest such a ludicrous idea. "You got to be kidding. It was probably an isolated incident by a crazy. I was just in the wrong place at the wrong time." Tony snorted when another thought crossed her mind. *How the hell would she explain to Keith why she was being escorted around by the local cops?*

Brian ignored her reaction and continued, "How about humoring me? What's the harm?" He hadn't expected Tony to accept the offer and knew he would have to work at it.

Megan looked at Tony while listening to her end of the conversation. *Wonder what's up? She doesn't seem very pleased whatever it is.*

Tony glanced at Megan and saw the curious expression on her face. Suddenly her ego didn't matter that much. There was something more important to consider, like Megan's feelings. *It would make her feel better, even if I think it's ridiculous.*

Wondering how she was going to explain this to the other agents, she said, "Okay. You already have the address. It's on the report I filled out. I'll wait until the car shows up before leaving," Tony said.

Brian couldn't believe she'd agreed. "Good. I'll have someone there at 11pm," he said, hanging up. He didn't want to give her a chance to change her mind.

Tony hung up the phone and sat back down at the table. Smiling at Megan, she said, "If it makes you feel any better, Brian is going to have a patrol car follow me home tonight."

Megan felt like a tremendous weight was lifted off of her shoulders. She hadn't known how she was going to get through the evening. She would have done nothing but worry. The relief evident by the warm smile that covered her face, she said, "It does make me feel better." The thought crossed Megan's mind that she would still worry some, until Tony was home safe that night.

* * * * * * * * * *

Sherman sat slouched in the seat of the car, cleaning his fingernails with his knife. It wasn't that he needed to, it was just something to pass the time. The streetlight reflected off the stainless steel Smith & Wesson 357 magnum lying on the seat next to him. It wasn't his weapon of choice, but it would do the job. It was loaded with .38 caliber hollow points. *Hollow points were such a nice invention. They go in small and come out big.* Sherman smiled to himself. *Wouldn't be much left of her head once the bullet had completed its trajectory.*

Sherman saw the agency car enter the garage at the same time his peripheral vision noticed a patrol car pull into a parking place across the street. *Probably taking a break from patrol.*

He sat up straighter and trained his eyes on the exit, waiting for his target to emerge in her new Jeep. He grinned sardonically. *It was so nice of her apartment to have the parking places numbered for the tenants.* Once he knew she was in the apartment, he had gone to the garage to see what vehicle was in the parking space. Leaving nothing to chance, he had doubled checked later by parking in the same space he was in now, waiting for her to arrive for her shift.

When the sienna Jeep Grand Cherokee Limited exited the garage, Sherman shifted the car into drive prepared to move in behind her once an adequate space had passed. He felt a brief flicker of surprise when the patrol car pulled in behind the Jeep. That was no coincidence. A slow smile covered his face. She was running scared. Just as he had suspected, all the rumors he heard about her over the years were exaggerated. Shifting his car into gear, he pulled out and drove back to the hotel strangely disappointed. *So this wasn't going to be such a challenge after all. Scared people make mistakes.*

* * * * * * * * *

Tony turned on the coffee pot and took out a couple of bagels. Megan had to work today and was getting ready. Tony was supposed to meet with the insurance adjuster, but other than that had no plans. She was just glad things seemed to be getting back to normal.

She had already fed the kittens, and they were contentedly sitting next to each other meticulously cleaning themselves and occasionally each other. Tony smiled at them. It really was nice having the kittens here. They had slept on the bed with them last night, Huggy next to Megan and Velcro next to her. Huggy seemed to be the more mischievous of the two, not that Velcro wasn't quick to join in whatever trouble her buddy found.

Tony smiled at the lovely sight that greeted her eyes when Megan walked into the kitchen. Her partner was dressed in a casual, sapphire blue suit with the jacket worn open over the matching skirt and off white blouse. The rich blue color offset Megan's blonde hair and highlighted the gold specks in her eyes. "You look really nice," Tony said, quite taken with her partner's beauty.

Cocking her head and smiling at Tony, Megan said, "This is just my work clothes."

"So. You look nice no matter what you wear," Tony said, walking over and kissing Megan before adding, "Coffee's ready. Want some orange juice?"

Megan gave her partner a hug and said, "You're so sweet," waiting for her lover's cheeks to redden like they did every time she told her that. Watching Tony's face darken a few shades, she continued, "Orange juice sounds good. You're really spoiling me having breakfast ready every morning." Grinning wickedly, she added, "You know you really are cute when you blush."

Tony rolled her eyes, the action in contrast with the warm glow she felt at her partner's words. Fleetingly kissing Megan before releasing her, Tony got the orange juice out of the refrigerator and poured them both a glass.

"What are you going to do today?" Megan asked, wishing she had another day off.

"Wait for you to get off," Tony answered, and grinned at the surprised look on Megan's face. *Gotcha.*

"Very funny. I meant really," Megan said, laughing while looking into her partner's twinkling blue eyes.

"That is *really* what I'm going to do," Tony said winking at Megan. "But while I'm waiting, I'm going to call the insurance adjuster and then probably kitten proof the apartment."

"Good. Those two are too curious for their own good."

Megan finished her breakfast and got ready to leave. Kissing her lover before departing, she said, "I'll call you later."

Tony savored the short kiss and said, "I'll be waiting."

* * * * * * * * * *

They were still doing construction on the innerbelt, and it was the usual bumper-to-bumper traffic, moving at a crawl. The slow drive did not affect Megan's extremely good mood. It had been so nice to have a normal morning for a change. That was the way she wanted to start every morning...feeling secure and very loved. She wondered if this was something everyone in love experienced. It was such a wonderful sensation, and one she would never willingly let go of.

Arriving at work, there was no more time for the warm thoughts. They were backed up on cases and, before she knew it, the morning had passed and it was lunchtime. Telling David they would finish the other cases after lunch, she shed her gloves and smock, returning to her office in her scrubs.

Opening the door, all thoughts of the cases she had just finished left her mind. There in the middle of her desk was a slender glass vase containing a dozen long stem roses. They were a beautiful scarlet red. She walked over to her desk and picked up the small envelope secured in their midst. The words written on the card tucked inside the envelop filled her heart with a giddy happiness. "I love you," and it was signed simply, "Tony."

Holding the card tightly in her hand, she bent over to smell the sweet pleasant odor they emitted. *I love you so much. Tony.* Warm fuzzy thoughts flowed through her mind intermingled with the image of her smiling partner. Oh, she'd gotten flowers before. But none would ever hold the special meaning these did. Tony had never given her flowers before.

Megan sighed happily and sat down in her chair, her emotions still running rampant. Picking up the phone, she dialed home.

"Hello."

Megan loved listening to the rich low tenor of her lover's voice. Smiling into the phone, she said, "I love you. They're so beautiful. You are so sweet."

"I love you, too," Tony said, smiling into the phone feeling a deep sense of satisfaction at the happiness she could hear in Megan's voice. "I guess you like them."

"Like them? Are you kidding? I love them! They're beautiful." Megan paused, momentarily at a loss for words.

The silence lengthened because a very pleased Tony was grinning into the phone. "No more beautiful than you."

Megan felt her heart flutter at the words. "Thank you, sweetie, but I better go now or I may decide to come home and I don't think the boss would like that."

"Sweetie!"

Megan laughed and said, "See you when I get home."

"Bye."

Tony hung up the phone shaking her head. *Sweetie? What was with that?* She grudgingly admitted that it did sound kind of nice the way Megan said it. But she'd just die of embarrassment if Megan ever called her that in front of anyone.

Tony opened the oven door and looked at the lasagna. It would be done in about ten minutes. She had gotten the recipe Sunday when she talked to her mother. Thinking about the conversation, she smiled. Her mother wanted to come and visit. Tony knew Megan liked her mother and had repeated the question for her partner's benefit. Megan had smiled and...well, she really didn't need to say anything. The expression on her face was all Tony needed to see. Her mother had sounded so pleased when she told her she was more than welcome to visit. So many things had changed in such a short time, first meeting Megan, and then the reconciliation with her mother. Life was good.

Her thoughts turned briefly to the inexplicable accidents. The bruise on her leg was still painful, and probably would be for a while. At least it didn't hurt to walk on it anymore. Tony still couldn't make any sense of the bizarre events and just wanted to get their lives back to normal.

Last night, while on surveillance, she had decided to surprise Megan with the roses and a nice dinner, then spend a quiet evening together and maybe watch a movie or something. Lately it seemed like all they did was manage crisis after crisis and then the aftermath of each. She could do without all the excitement and knew Megan could, too.

Once Tony had everything ready, she walked into the living room to check on the whereabouts of the rambunctious kittens. She spotted them curled up against each other sleeping in the recliner.

Megan had informed her that cats slept twenty hours a day. She wanted to know twenty hours of *what* day. The kittens seemed to have unlimited energy, and it was a job sometimes to keep them out of things. Not that she minded. Tony was actually quite taken with the kittens. It was really funny that each kitten had seemed to gravitate toward one of them. Velcro always sought out Tony. Huggy seemed to adore Megan, and you could tell she felt the same way.

Tony looked around the apartment once more after meeting with the insurance adjuster. She had spent the better part of the day kitten proofing the apartment, and Huggy and Velcro had been only too happy to help. For some reason cords seemed to hold a special interest for the kittens. Well, at least now they wouldn't have to worry about them hurting themselves while they were at work.

Tony turned toward the door when she heard the key in the lock. Wearing a smile that lit up her whole face, Megan walked in carrying the vase of roses. Walking over to her partner she wrapped her arms around her still clutching the vase in one of her hands. "I missed you. I really love the roses," Megan said relaxing against the tall familiar body.

Tony returned the hug, enjoying the feel of her partner wrapped comfortably in her arms. Looking into the sparkling hazel eyes, she said, "I missed you, too." Lowering her head, she met her lover's lips and enjoyed a sweet, very satisfying kiss.

Megan laid her head against Tony's chest smiling contentedly. "I guess I should set the roses down."

Smiling Tony said, "That might be a good idea. They are kind of prickly."

"Oops. Didn't think about that," Megan said, releasing her partner.

Noticing the dining room table was set, she raised her eyebrows and walked into the kitchen to set the vase down on the table in there. She and Tony usually ate in the kitchen and she was surprised to see the dining room table prepared for dinner. Turning to face her partner, she asked, "What's the occasion? Are we having company?"

Tony looked at the curious expression on Megan's face and smiled. "No. I just thought it would be nice to eat in the dining room tonight. Just something a little different."

Tony was sure full of surprises today. "Umm...smells good in here. What did you make?" Megan asked, her mouth watering.

"Mom's lasagna," Tony said, her smile widening at the delighted look on Megan's face. "I thought you really liked it."

"Oooh good! I loved it," Megan said, giving Tony a big hug.

Tony kissed Megan, and then released her saying, "It should be ready by the time you change clothes."

* * * * * * * * * *

A short time later, Megan sighed happily and sat back in her chair. Smiling at her partner, she said, "That was delicious."

A warm smile covered Tony's face and she said, "Thanks, love. Ready for dessert?"

Placing her hands over her stomach and widening her eyes, Megan said, "You're kidding, right? I'm stuffed!"

Tony laughed at the expression on her partner's face. "I am, too. Want to watch a movie? We haven't done that in a long time."

Megan grinned and said, "Sounds good. Do you have one in mind?"

Tony smiled back at her partner. Megan looked relaxed and happy, the stress of the last few days gone from her face. A sudden thought occurred to her, *It's a simple equation really. When Megan is happy, so am I.* With that thought in mind, she said, "Why don't you pick one?"

Megan's forehead creased momentarily and she turned her eyes upward as she feigned deep thought. "Hmm...a comedy, huh?" Laughing at the amused look on Tony's face, she said, "How about *Sister Act*? I love that movie."

Teasingly, with her eyebrow raised, Tony said, "I'm so glad you could think of one."

Megan sat in her favorite position, relaxing on the couch against Tony with her lover's arm resting on her shoulders. She could watch this movie a million times and never tire of it. And somehow it was even more enjoyable watching it with her partner.

She loved the rich sound of Tony's laughter and she had been pleasantly surprised when Tony joined in with the songs. *I just love her voice.* Lately there had been so little time for the simple things in their life. She had really missed this part of their relationship, and it felt really good to have it back.

Tony wasn't sure if she was laughing more at the movie or at Megan's delighted laughter. This felt so right. All the tension of the last few days was finally gone. One of her most frequent thoughts made an appearance in her mind. *How did I ever get so lucky?*

When the movie ended, with a smile still etched on her face, Megan said, "I just love the first time she leads the choir in church. The look on the Mother Superior's face is too much."

Tony grinned and said, "Yeah. And the part when they're cleaning up the neighborhood is really funny, too."

Looking at the mellow, contented expression on her partner's face, Tony felt a sense of peace. She leaned over and kissed Megan, "How about dessert?"

"You mean that wasn't dessert?" Megan asked, grinning.

Tony quirked a half smile and drawled, "Well..."

Megan winked at her partner and said, "I think I want to save the best for last. So what dessert did you have in mind?"

Tony shrugged nonchalantly. "Just something I thought you might like." Standing up, she said, "I'll go get it."

"I'll help. I want to see what it is anyway," Megan said.

Tony opened the refrigerator and took out two pieces of carrot cake specially made by the bakery at the Giant Eagle grocery store. Each piece was totally covered with the rich cream cheese frosting that so enhanced the taste of the moist cake.

"Ooh. My favorite. How did you know? I never told you," Megan said, surprised.

Tony winked and said, "I have my sources." Actually Ashley had told her last time she happened to answer the phone when her partner was out on a case.

Megan sat at the table and pulled the plate in front of her, taking a bite of the delicious cake. "Let eat in here." Tony chuckled and joined her partner at the table.

Megan savored each bite of the rich cake. "Feel like some tea? It'll only take a couple of minutes to make some," she offered when she was finished.

Before Tony had a chance to answer, they heard a dull thud coming from the living room. Tony rolled her eyes and grinned. "I'll go see what they did now."

Megan chuckled at the expression on Tony's face. The kittens were always into something. "Okay. I'll put the tea on."

Chapter
11

Huggy sat on the coffee table looking at the silk flower arrangement. A white paw hesitantly hit the green leaf before quickly pulling it back. The eyes watched the quivering leaf and the paw reached out, more confidently now, and batted the leaf harder. Her head tracked the movement of the leaf and when it slowed, she struck it again.

Velcro crouched on the floor, body motionless, watching the movement of the leaf, her tail twitching back and forth. Suddenly, the black and white fur ball streaked across the floor and leaped up onto the coffee table. Sliding across the smooth surface of the table unable to get purchase, she slid into the basket housing the silk flower arrangement propelling it across the table and onto the floor before following it with an ungraceful landing. Standing up, looking indignant, she batted the offending leaves.

The original culprit, startled by the unexpected arrival of her playmate, jumped straight up into the air before landing on her toes back on the table. Crabbing sideways, all the hair on her tail standing on end, she danced across the table and looked over the edge. She watched Velcro playing with the leaves for only a moment before jumping to the floor and joining in the fun.

* * * * * * * * * *

Tony walked into the living room and shook her head when she saw the two kittens happily playing with the leaves of the silk plant in the middle of the floor. Shooing them away, she picked up the basket and the plant, putting it back together in a semblance of the way it had been before the kittens had attacked it.

Setting it up on a shelf, Tony started to walk back to the kitchen when she stepped on something. Lifting her bare foot, she plucked the offending item off of it, smiling when she saw what it was. The arrangement was realistic, but she never realized it had a ladybug in it. Just as Tony was about to place it on one of the silk leaves, she stopped, all senses on alert.

Placing the ladybug in the palm of her hand, she looked at it closely. Something was odd about it. All of a sudden it hit her. There were three antennas protruding from it. The extra one was slightly longer and thinner than the other two. Narrowing her eyes, she placed it back in the basket, her thoughts turning dark.

Tony walked into the kitchen and raised a finger to the center of her pursed lips signaling for quiet. Looking at Megan, her eyes imploring her partner to play along with her, she said, "I'm going to take a shower now. The kittens trashed the silk flower planter but I've put it back together again. Why don't you put the darlings into one of the bedrooms?"

Mouthing, "Come with me," she left the kitchen and walked into the bathroom, Megan right behind her. Closing the door, she pulled the shower curtain and turned on the water. Turning and looking at her puzzled partner, Tony said, "We're being bugged."

"Bugged? You mean someone's been listening to us? Why?" Megan asked perplexed. "Who would want to bug us?"

Tony's brow creased in thought. "I don't know. I've got a bug detector in my bag in the closet. I'll check the apartment and find out if there are any more and, if there are, where they are. I don't want to get rid of them yet because that'll alert whoever put them here that we found them. Once I get done, let's go for a ride. Then we can try and figure it out."

Megan placed her hand on Tony's arm, delaying her departure. "How did you find out?" Her knowledge of bugs was limited to what she saw on TV or in the movies, but she knew they were not easy to find. She was also angry at the invasion of their privacy.

Tony smiled for the first time since they entered the bathroom. "It turns out that noise we heard was Huggy and Velcro playing with the planter on the coffee table. They got a little rambunctious and knocked it to the floor."

The lines of her face-hardened and she continued, "I stepped on something when I was picking it up. It was a little ladybug. Something about it seemed odd, and then I realized it had three antennas. The third antenna was a little longer and thinner than the other two."

The irony was not lost on Megan. She mused aloud, "Real clever. A bug in a bug." Glancing up at her partner, she asked, "How did you know?"

Tony shrugged. "I've used similar ones in some of my cases. I'll double check it, but I am sure that's what it is."

Megan looked off into space and spoke her thoughts aloud, "Something is going on. I knew it."

Tony placed a hand on Megan's shoulder, the contact drawing her lover's eyes to hers. She smiled ruefully at Megan and said, "I hoped you were wrong."

Shaking her head, Megan said, "So did I."

"I put it back, so watch what you say in the living room. The running water will keep whoever is listening from hearing our conversation even if there is one in here."

Tony explained. "The main thing right now is to act normally. Come on. I'll show you how the bug detector works. The one I've got is nice because it has a setting on it that allows it to vibrate like a pager instead of beeping, so if anyone is listening right now, they won't know what we're doing."

After turning off the water, Megan followed her partner into the bedroom. Opening the closet door, Tony pulled out one of her suitcases and took out a small accessory bag. Unzipping it, she removed various small devices. Settling on one that looked something like a remote control, but was smaller, she put the other items back in the bag.

Picking up the bug detector, she turned it on to the vibrate setting and watched the red light. It would flashed if it detected a bug. The closer it got to the bug the faster the light flashed.

Megan stood out of the way watching Tony. The planes of her face had sharpened and there was no wasted movement in her actions. The few times she had watched Tony at work, she was always struck that this warm, loving woman was also a very competent and, when necessary, very deadly FBI agent. Certainly not someone anyone with any sense would antagonize.

A complete scan of the apartment revealed only two bugs, one in the kitchen and the one in the living room. Tony smiled grimly. They knew what they were doing. Not coincidentally, both rooms had phones and most of their conversation took place in one or the other.

* * * * * * * * *

Tony and Megan sat in a booth in the back of Diana's. She was sure they had not been followed, and she was an expert at detecting tails. No one had ever succeeded in following the agent unless she wanted to be followed.

After ordering a coffee and tea respectively, Tony said, "I don't get it. I think it's fairly safe to assume I am the

target. Coroner's apartments are not likely to get bugged."
She smiled at Megan.

Megan sighed. "Just when I thought everything was
back to normal for a change. You know, Tony, I could
really do without all this excitement," Megan said in a
bantering voice but was actually very serious.

"You and me both. I was willing to write off the accidents even though that guy deliberately swerved into my
car. I know you had a feeling about them and I thought it
was one hell of a coincidence, too, but I was hoping he
could've been a drunk or a weirdo of some kind."

"Do you have any idea why someone would want to,"
Megan paused, unable to bring herself to say kill, and finished with, "hurt you?"

"No. I have gone over everything I've done in the past
several months, and I can't think of any reason anyone
would want to...bug our apartment." Tony pushed her hair
away from her face and continued, "It has to be a pro. The
bugs are very cleverly disguised."

Megan spent each day sifting through evidence and
finding clues that were almost nonexistent. Moving the
stir around in her tea, deep in thought, the analytical portion of her brain sorted through everything Tony had done
since she met her. An idea formed in Megan's mind.

Tony watched her partner, worried. Megan absently
played with the stir in her tea, her eyes trained on the cup.
Tony was just about to interrupt her thoughts, when the
hazel eyes met her own.

"What about when we were in D.C. and you talked to
Huey? Any possibility someone could have found out
about that? You mentioned Huey said you might have to
testify. Maybe someone doesn't want you to."

Tony looked at Megan thoughtfully. Nothing she
could come up with made any sense. That was a possibility, even though it was kind of far fetched. "You might
have something there. It's worth a shot. I'll call Huey
tomorrow. It just seems so extreme." Sighing Tony added,

"If it is related to that, they must know the chances of uncovering the perpetrator is very small, so why bother?"

"Maybe there's more to it than you think," Megan said. "I can't think of any other reason someone would be after you unless it has to do with some case you did before we met."

Tony shook her head. "No. You could be right. On the few cases my cover was blown, we ended up busting all the leaders and they are still doing hard time."

Tony took a sip of her coffee and continued, "We have to remember to act normally when we are in the living room or kitchen. Since the rest of the apartment is not bugged we can talk behind closed doors in the bedroom or bathroom. Now that we know there is a bug, we can use it to our advantage to lure whoever it is in."

"You're not going to do anything dangerous are you?" Megan asked, becoming even more worried than she was.

Tony saw the worry on Megan's face and said, "No. I'm just going to talk to Huey first and then Brian. I know I can count on them. I'd like to set a trap with Brian's help." Smiling reassuringly at Megan, she continued, "I won't do anything on my own. But I think we both need to be very careful."

"I'm not the target here, you are," Megan said, relaxing a little since her partner wasn't going to try to handle this herself.

"We don't know that for sure. I just don't want to take any chances, ok?" Tony asked, her concern reflected in her eyes.

"Does this mean you're going to take me to work again?" Megan asked, a small smile forming on her face.

"Yes. If you don't mind," Tony said, relieved that Megan had suggested this.

"Mind...not hardly. Well, in that case, ok," Megan said smiling, hoping to ease some of the worry from her partner's face.

* * * * * * * * * *

Tony dropped Megan off at work and headed home. She treated her surroundings with even more care than usual. *There will be no more accidents,* she thought, grimly.

Arriving home, she exchanged the line from the jack to the phone with a twenty-five foot one and walked into the bedroom. Attaching a scrambling device to the phone, she made the first of two calls. Since phone monitoring was most often done remotely, she had no idea if the phone was tapped and wasn't taking any chances.

Sitting on the bed, Tony said, "Hi, Huey," when he answered the phone.

"Hi, Tony. What's on your mind?" Huey asked, surprised by the call. The phone was propped on his shoulder and he was looking at the messages that he had received.

Deciding to get right to the point, Tony asked, "How's the investigation going?"

"I turned it over to Internal Affairs the same day you were here. Why?" Huey sat back in his chair, his full attention on the conversation now.

Tony stood up and walked around the bedroom. "I have suddenly become accident prone and I found a bug in my apartment. Both of the accidents were a little too close for comfort. There is nothing I am involved in here that should elicit this kind of action. The only other thing I can think of is that it has something to do with your investigation."

"Anything is possible, but it doesn't make sense. Internal Affairs runs a fairly tight operation and your current assignment is only available through your personnel file."

"Well how about humoring me and checking to see if my personnel file has been pulled?" Tony asked knowing the record could not be accessed unless a log was signed. Standing in front of the window, she continued, "I know it's a long shot but I'd like to know so I can eliminate the possibility."

"Okay. I'll check on it today."

* * * * * * * * * *

Megan sat at her desk going through her inbox. She had already finished her only case for the day. Some of the results were back from the lab and she was pleased to see that her suspicion on the drowning victim had been right. He had been dead prior to entering the water.

David walked in and sat down, draping a leg over the arm of the chair. "Hi, boss," he said, grinning.

Megan chuckled. While it was true that she was his boss, their friendship extended to their work relationship. "Hi. You want me to tell you what happened over the weekend, right?" she asked, smiling warmly at her friend.

"Well, it would be nice since we were too busy yesterday, and I did see Tony drop you off in that gorgeous Jeep, and you just happened to tell me enough yesterday to worry me," David said, settling back in the chair and crossing his arms.

"Yeah. Guess I did. Relax, it's a long story." Megan smiled ruefully at her friend and began relating the events of the weekend.

* * * * * * * * * *

Tony dialed Brian's number and waited for him to pick up. Wasting no time, she said, "I need to see you. When would be a good time?"

Brian listened to the terse statement and knew something must have happened.

"Come on down now. I'll make time."

"I'll be there in twenty minutes," Tony said, relieved that he had time to see her so quickly.

* * * * * * * * *

Tony quickly walked across the squad room oblivious to the admiring looks from the occupants. Arriving at Brian's desk, she said, "Hi," and sat down in the chair adjoining the desk, stretching her legs out in front of her and crossing them at the ankles.

Brian took in the controlled look on Tony's face and leaned back in his chair and crossed his arms. He answered her greeting by asking, "What's going on?"

Tony looked at Brian and said, "I found a couple of bugs in the apartment last night. Apparently, someone is very interested in what I am doing. I'd like to set up a sting operation to lure this guy into the open, but I'm going to need some help."

"How do you know it's a guy and how do you know there is only one person involved?" Brian asked.

"I don't know if more than one person is involved, but I don't think I'd be sitting here talking to you now if he had help." Tony paused, gathering her thoughts. Turning slightly in the chair, she rested her elbows on the desk. "Call it a gut feeling, but the type of incidents makes me think that he probably acted independently. I'm thinking it is the driver of the pick up that rammed me. I did get enough of a look to know it was a man."

Brian nodded his head. *He had forgotten she had mentioned that in her report.* He had also learned long ago to always trust your gut. "I take it you have something in mind?"

Tony smiled grimly. "Yeah, I do. I want to stage a meeting in my apartment where we set up a phony bust scenario for the surveillance case I'm working on. We can make it seem authentic by mentioning that some information has been leaked and that Braxton gave me the authority to call in you guys to prevent anyone from being tipped off about the bust. This guy obviously knows a lot about me and has to know I just finished working a case with you, so he should buy it."

Tony paused to brush the hair away from her face with her hand. She knew she needed help, but it seemed funny to be asking for it. She had always handled her own problems.

Brian waited quietly for her to continue. He knew her well enough to know that she was unaccustomed to asking for help and was pleased at the show of trust.

"The only way I can make this work is to have some of your people help. I want to set myself up as bait to draw him out. But I don't want to be a sitting duck. I need to be covered by your guys," Tony said, watching Brian closely trying to gauge his reaction.

Brian was more than willing to help Tony out. He knew he'd have to call on his friends, since this was certainly an unofficial request. But he felt she was putting herself at too much risk. "I don't like the idea of you as bait. It's too chancy. What if my guys don't see him in time? I'd feel personally responsible if anything happened to you."

Tony sat up straight in the chair, and crossed her arms. "Whoever is doing this is definitely a pro. If I don't set myself up, he'll never show."

Brian still wasn't convinced this was the best plan and decided to try another tactic. "Does Megan know about this?" he asked, pointedly.

Biting off her initial retort, which was to tell him that was between her and Megan, she said, "Not yet." Meeting Brian's gaze, she continued, "There didn't seem much point in telling her until I knew if you were going to help."

Shaking his head, he said, "Tony, you've got someone else to think about. We'll figure out something else."

Frowning, Tony looked pointedly at Brian and said, "I know that. I'm worried about her. What if he gets frustrated and tries to get at me through her? I can't take that chance. She's too important to me. There isn't any other way. I have to do this."

Brian made a decision. "I'll help you. But I got a feeling Megan is going to be pissed off at both of us."

Tony nodded her head in agreement. Explaining her plan to Megan was not something she was looking forward to.

Brian took a pen out of his pocket and jott notes on a pad of paper. "What's the time line?"

"If you can get the others together in time, I'd like for everyone to come to my apartment this evening. I thought we could set up the sting for tomorrow night," Tony said, knowing what she was asking would be difficult to accomplish.

Brian looked up from the pad of paper and met Tony's eyes. "Moving kind of fast, aren't you?"

Deep blue eyes met steel gray ones. "I have to. I have a feeling the attacks are going to intensify, and I don't want Megan or anyone else I know jeopardized."

After a moment's thought, Brian said, "Okay. I'll start notifying people. How about we show up at seven?"

Tony smiled and said, "Sounds good. And Brian...thanks."

"No problem," Brian said, hoping he had made the right decision.

* * * * * * * * *

Huey hung up the phone and sat there thoughtfully, his elbows resting on the desk and his chin supported on a bridge formed with his hands. He had been concerned about Tony's accusation and the ramifications of it since she had reported it to him. If her file had been pulled, then this was bigger than he had first thought.

Walking out of his office, he said to Jean, "I'm going over to Human Resources."

He arrived at the Records Room and walked up to Sarah who was stood behind the sign-in desk. Looking at the older woman fondly, he said, "Hi, Sarah. I need the personnel record on Antonia Viglioni."

Pushing the login form across the desk, Sarah smiled and said, "Hi, Huey. Just sign for it here. That record's been kind of popular lately."

Huey looked up from the log. "What do you mean?"

"I just pulled it for someone else last week," Sarah said, a little puzzled by his reaction.

Taking the log back, she flipped a few pages back and ran her finger down the entries. Finding the one for Viglioni she murmured, "That's strange."

"What's strange?" Huey asked, trying to see what Sarah was pointing to on the log.

Looking up, Sarah said, "This isn't the name of the agent who signed for the file. This has the Director of Quality Control's name. The agent who signed for it was a young guy I've seen around. That's why I didn't question it. Can't think of his name right now. Nice young man. I can't believe I missed that. Oh, well. Maybe he was just signing the name of the person he was getting the information for."

"Let me see that," Huey said. Taking the log from Sarah and looking at the entry, he asked, "Did he remove the file?"

Frowning at Huey, she said, "No, of course not. You know that's against our policy. I pulled it for him and he looked at it in the file room. He returned it within fifteen minutes."

"If you remember who the agent was, call me," Huey said, before leaving. This was very odd. Regulations stipulated that the individual signing out the record sign the log no matter what the reason was for pulling it.

Walking back into his office, he said, "Jean, would you get Ed in Quality Control for me?"

Jean smiled and said, "Sure." Once she got the Director on the phone, she put him on hold and dialed Huey. "He's on three, Mr. Straton."

"Thanks," Huey said, before picking up the call. "Hey, Ed, how's it going?"

"Same as usual. What's up?" he asked, knowing Huey did not make arbitrary phone calls.

Drumming his fingers on the desk, Huey asked, "Did you request the personnel record on Antonia Viglioni last week?"

Wondering what prompted the question, Ed said, "No. She's not working covert anymore. I'd have no reason to."

"That's what I thought, too. Thought you might like to know an agent signed out her file and used your name on the log."

"Do you know who?" Ed asked, suddenly very interested in the conversation.

Huey sighed. "No. But Sarah has worked in the Records Room forever and she said she's seen him around. I may have her look through some pictures of the agents assigned here if she doesn't remember who it was. She said he was young so that should cut down the list some."

"Keep me informed. I'd like a few words with whoever it was," Ed said, his voice hard.

"Will do," Huey said, before hanging up the phone. Settling back in his chair, he looked out the window. Sarah held the key to the investigation. He would go back to records and talk to her.

Chapter 12

Megan walked to the waiting Jeep, opened the door and got in. Smiling at the woman she loved, she said, "Hi."

Tony looked at the bright warm smile lighting up her partner's face and her heart sank. She knew her plan was going to upset Megan. If there was any other way, she would do it rather than put Megan through the worry she knew this was going to cause her. "Hi." She was unable to match her partner's engaging smile with one of her own.

Looking at her lover, a feeling of trepidation came over Megan. Placing her hand on Tony's thigh, she asked, "What's wrong?"

Tony placed her hand over Megan's and squeezed it, before shifting the car into drive and pulling out of the parking lot into the street. "I need to discuss something with you. I figured we could stop at Friends, get something to eat, and talk there."

"Why do I get the feeling I'm not going to like this discussion?" Megan asked, her uneasiness growing.

Tony didn't have an answer and changed the subject. "How was work?"

Watching her partner's face, Megan went along with the subject change. Alarm bells were going off and she wasn't looking forward to the "discussion" Tony wanted to have. "Work was fine. I told David about the latest adventures of Huggy and Velcro. He wants to stop over and see the kittens. He and Mike are going to look at puppies this weekend."

"Did he mention what kind they were going to get?" Tony asked, happy Megan had gone along with her.

"He's not sure. They're thinking about a medium sized dog. Although, he did mention that they're going to check both kennels, and the Animal Protective League first, to see if they can find a puppy there."

After being seated at Friends, they both ordered coffee and the sautéed seafood with linguini. Megan looked at the serious expression on her partner's face and waited patiently for Tony to tell her what was on her mind. When it became apparent Tony was in no hurry to begin the conversation, she decided her partner needed a nudge and said, "So what's going on?"

Sighing, Tony said, "I talked to Huey today. He's going to check and see if my personnel file has been pulled."

"Okay," Megan said puzzled. They'd talked about this last night. "Did he say anything else?"

"No." Tony was still trying to figure out how to approach her role in the sting operation with her partner. Deciding to be blunt, she continued, "I went to see Brian today."

"What for?" Megan asked, sensing this meeting had something to do with whatever Tony was reluctant to tell her.

Looking at Megan, Tony said, "I suggested we set up a sting operation to draw this guy out."

Megan knew there had to be more to it than this and asked, "How's the sting going to work?"

Her face expressionless, Tony said. "We decided to set it up at the Leaning Ledge. Brian said a lot of cops from fifth district go there to eat, and if we run into trouble we'd probably have extra help."

"Tony," Megan waited until her lover met her eyes, "how do you fit into this?" *And why do I know I'm not going to like it?*

Glancing away from the piercing hazel eyes, Tony said, "I'm going to be outside in a parking lot across the street covering the front door of the restaurant. I'll be parked in the Shopper's Mart. He should feel fairly secure because of the traffic from the store and make his move."

Megan's eyes narrowed, and she said, "You're purposely setting yourself up," already knowing the answer.

Tony looked at her partner earnestly. "I have to. If it's not realistic, it'll never work."

Megan sat back in her chair and crossed her arms. Capturing her partner's deep blue eyes with her flashing hazel ones, she said, "No."

Tony sighed. There was no mistaking Megan's anger. She couldn't blame her partner for not liking the idea, and it was nice to know how much she cared, but she was going to have to make her understand. She leaned forward. "Megan, listen to me. I know it's dangerous. But don't forget, this is what I am trained for. It'll be ok."

Megan looked at her partner sitting across the table. She knew Tony was highly trained and very capable, but this left too much to chance. "There has to be some other way. What if he tries to take you out from a distance? No one can protect you then because no one will see him," Megan said, unable to hide her concern.

That thought had occurred to Tony, but she really felt he would want to make sure she was the one in the car. She now believed he had been behind both accidents and would be much less willing to leave things to chance. Trying to allay Megan's concern, Tony said, "I don't think he'll do that. It leaves too much to chance."

Megan glanced out the window. *This was just too dangerous.* "That's not good enough. What if you're wrong?" She captured her partner's eyes with her own. "I love you.

Twice in the past week I could have lost you. I couldn't do anything about those times, but I can about this. I don't want you to do this."

"I love you, too. And that's why I have to do this." Tony then voiced her worst fear. " What if he tries to get at me through you? I'm not willing to take that risk. If anything happened to you because of me I could never live with myself."

"What about how I would feel if something happened to you? Doesn't that matter at all?" Megan asked, momentarily hurt until a thought pushed its way to the forefront of her mind. *This doesn't make sense. We are sitting here arguing and the thing we are both trying to do is protect each other. We need to work together on this.*

Tony saw the hurt expression flicker across her lover's face. That was the last thing she wanted to do. *I am really blowing this.* "Of course it does." Tony sighed. "I just want this to be over and our lives to get back to normal, and I don't know any other way to do that."

The waitress removed the uneaten salads and served their dinner. Both women had lost their appetite.

Megan pushed her food around on her plate trying to think of likely alternatives and not having any success. *Would this dangerous plan really put an end to this nightmare? Or would she end up losing her partner?*

Tony felt guilty because she knew she was asking more than was fair of her partner but felt she had no choice. The last thing she had wanted to do was hurt Megan's feelings. She had to end this and the only way to do that was take the offensive.

Megan looked up from her food. "When is this supposed to happen?"

Relieved that Megan had broken the silence, Tony said, "Brian's going to bring some of his friends over tonight and we're planning to have a staged conversation."

"There's no guarantee this will draw him out," Megan mused. "You really think this will work?"

Tony breathed a silent sigh of relief. Megan didn't seem so upset. "I think there's a good possibility it could."

Making a decision and praying it was the right one, Megan said, "Okay. What time are we going?"

Tony met Megan's eyes and said gently, "We aren't going. I am."

"If you're going, so am I," Megan said, emphatically.

"You're not trained for this. I am," Tony said, her eyes imploring her partner to understand.

"I didn't say I would participate. I said I was going. And you can just stop right now, because if you think there is any way I am letting you put yourself in danger without being there if you need me, you better think again."

Tony looked at her partner and raised an eyebrow. She ruefully thought, *I guess I didn't convince her.*

Megan never gave her lover a chance to respond and continued, "So when do we do this?" There was no way she was letting Tony do this by herself. It was bad enough she was going to do it at all.

Tony gazed at her partner. She captured the hazel eyes with her blue ones and watched the gold flecks whirling around angrily. *How can I ask her to do something I would not?* This might not be such a bad idea. There was always the possibility the sting would not work. If Megan went, at least she would know she was safe. She'd just have to do her best to make sure she was out of harm's way. Maybe Brian could assign someone to her during the sting.

Tony rested her elbow on the table and supported her chin in her palm. Quirking a half smile, she said, "Tomorrow night."

* * * * * * * * *

Tony sat on the couch next to Megan and looked at Brian and the other four officers gathered in her living room. Brian had briefed the others back at the station, and each knew that this meeting was simply to set up the trap they had devised. Each of the officers present had worked with Tony on the Shadow case, and had volunteered to help out.

"We just got word that one of the big players in a money laundering operation we've been doing surveillance on is going to be meeting with the local head of the operation. The meet is at the Leaning Ledge," Tony explained. "We're meeting here to discuss a sting operation between the FBI and local police. The reason we are asking you to help is because some pertinent information has been compromised. To avoid any other leaks, my boss set it up with Brian."

Nodding her head at Brian, Tony turned the briefing over to him. She wanted to give the impression that the plan would be all his idea.

Brian said, "Okay, guys, this is what we're going to do."

* * * * * * * * *

Sherman sat in his hotel room listening to the tape. Not expecting to hear anything useful, his ears perked up when the conversation turned to the sting operation. This had real potential. This had real potential. He rewound that part of the tape and replayed it.

This just might be the opportunity he was waiting for. He got out the phone book and looked up the Leaning Ledge. He located the street on his map and decided to check the area out the next morning. If the location fit his needs, he would take advantage of this unexpected break.

* * * * * * * * *

Megan looked at the "watch" on her wrist that Tony had given her to wear before she went to work. It was really neat. Her partner had told her that if she pressed the stem an alarm would go directly to Brian, who would have the receiver with him.

It did make her feel a little uneasy. She hadn't really thought about any danger to herself, even though she knew Tony was worried about that, but somehow, wearing this little gadget made it very real.

Preparing for bed, she realized this would be the first time she had to spend the night alone. Even the night Tony was in the car accident, she hadn't spent the entire night by herself. She chuckled to herself. *Geez, it is only for the next two nights. I'll sure be glad when that case she's working on is over.*

Megan's thoughts turned to tomorrow. She hoped the guy never showed up. The idea of Tony setting herself up as a target was very scary. And that scared the hell out of her. There had to be another way, but she didn't know what it was.

Sighing, Megan got into bed. Huggy and Velcro soon joined her and she slept fitfully, waking several times against the backdrop of loud purring.

* * * * * * * * * *

Tony arrived home with her usual patrol car escort. She got off the elevator and walked into the apartment. Megan sat in the kitchen drinking coffee. After laying her gun down, she walked into the kitchen and poured a cup of coffee. Joining her partner at the table, she said, "You look tired."

"I didn't get much sleep," Megan answered, smiling wanly.

Tony reached across the table and took hold of Megan's hand and squeezed it. Ad-libbing for the sake of the bug, she said, "Is it because of the sting tonight?"

Megan sighed. "That's part of it. I hate sleeping alone," she blurted out.

Tony almost spewed coffee all over the table. She certainly hadn't expected that comment, especially since her lover knew there was a bug in the kitchen. She stood up and walked around the table. Leaning down, she kissed her partner on the forehead. Holding out her hand for Megan to grasp, she led the way out of the kitchen and into the bedroom. Tony closed the door.

Tony put her arms around Megan and pulled her close. "I hate sleeping alone, too, love. Hopefully this case will be over soon. We've got enough to move in on them any-time. It's just a matter of waiting on Braxton to figure that out. He's a little slow on the uptake." After gently kissing her lover, she said, "If we're really lucky, the sting will work tonight, and Braxton will order us to move in on the money launderers over the weekend."

Megan relaxed against her partner, the contact lifting her spirits. She smiled at Tony's attempt to make her feel better. Looking up at her lover, she said, "You're a real dreamer, too," in an attempt at levity.

"Me?" Tony said, winking at her partner, happy to see the smile on her face. "Not really."

Megan hugged Tony and said, "Well, I hope you're right." Reluctantly she released the tall woman. "You ready?"

"Yeah."

When Tony returned from taking Megan to work, the phone was ringing. She walked into the kitchen and picked it up. "Hello."

A familiar voice asked, "Are you busy?"

Tony smiled grimly. This was a simple code they'd set up indicating she should go to a secure phone. "Yes. Can I get back to you later?"

"Sure," Huey said, standing in his office looking out the window.

After hanging up, Tony carried the phone into the bed-room and attached the scrambling device. She knew it would be a lot easier to use the portable phone but they were notorious for being intercepted and the scrambler might not be totally effective.

After dialing Huey's number, she waited patiently for him to come to the phone. When he answered, she asked, "What's up?"

"Your record has been accessed and it's not clear who pulled it or why. It may just be a coincidence. I am still checking things out at this end," Huey said.

Tony's eyes narrowed and anger briefly flickered across her face. "I don't think it's a coincidence. So I'm going to go on the assumption that it's another agent, or someone from the inside hired a mercenary."

There wasn't much Huey could say. He happened to agree with her. "Be careful, Tony. I'll call you when I know more."

Hanging up the phone, Tony was glad that she had decided not to include any of her FBI coworkers, because she had no way of knowing if they were connected to the attacks on her.

After taking a shower, Tony retrieved her gun and placed it on the nightstand. She fell into a light sleep, her subconscious mind tuned to wake her at any odd sound. Velcro and Huggy joined her a short time later.

* * * * * * * * *

Megan sat at her desk unable to concentrate on the lab reports she was looking at. Setting them down, her thoughts turned to the sting operation planned for that night. There was so much being left to chance and she was very worried about Tony's safety.

When the phone rang, she welcomed the interruption. "Dr. Donnovan."

"Hi. Sorry it took me so long to get back to you. With the deadline for people who filed extensions drawing near, work has been unreal," Ashley said.

Megan smiled, glad to hear from her sister. "No problem. I figured you were just busy."

"Any chance you can get away for lunch today? Two appointments I had scheduled canceled and I've finally got a little free time," Ashley said, hoping Megan would be able to get away. It seemed like ages since she had seen her younger sister.

Glad for the diversion and wanting to see Ashley, Megan smiled and said, "I'd love to. Where?"

"How about the Boarding House at eleven-thirty?" Ashley chose a place close to where Megan worked figuring they would be able to take a little longer lunch that way.

"That'll work. See you then," Megan said, looking forward to lunch.

Chapter
13

Tony set the bag of Chinese food on the table. Megan was changing clothes. Neither of them had wanted to cook tonight, so they had stopped at their favorite take out place.

Her thoughts turned briefly to their plans for tonight. She wasn't supposed to make an appearance until nine even though Brian and the others would be there earlier to get in place.

Kris was going to pick up Megan at eight. Brian thought very highly of the policewoman. She had not come to the apartment for the meeting, so her identity, if they had been observed, would be unknown to Tony's antagonist.

The tall woman planned on leaving at eight-thirty. She was going to drive her jeep because it would be easy to spot. Tony grimly smiled and her thoughts turned dark. *Let the game begin.*

* * * * * * * * *

John casually leaned against the building near the mouth of the alley. He was hidden from the casual observer, but his position allowed him an unobstructed view of the sienna Jeep in the parking lot across the street. Should anyone see him, he looked every bit the part of someone waiting for a friend, and he added to the illusion by occasionally raising his wrist to peer at his watch.

All the volunteers knew that the chance of a successful conclusion to this operation was small. It had not deterred any of them, though. Every officer involved in the sting considered Tony one of their own. The fact that she was an FBI agent no longer mattered. She had earned her place among them and they would do their best to protect her. They had all been at their posts for over an hour and John knew that the likelihood of their target showing up now was slim.

John shifted his weight to his other foot and suddenly felt a blinding pain crash through his head before everything went dark.

Sherman put the blackjack back in his pocket and smiled, satisfied that his first objective had been reached. He pulled a roll of duct tape out of his cargo pocket. The cop shouldn't wake up for a couple of minutes and when he did, Sherman wanted to make sure he couldn't give an alarm. If everything went according to plan, he would be leaving the area by the time he woke up anyway, but he would leave no room for error.

He tore off a strip of the duct tape and slapped it over the unconscious man's mouth, making sure it was tightly adhered to the skin. After rolling the cop over, he secured the man's hands behind him by winding the tape around his wrists. Satisfied that he would not be able to get loose, he tore the tape and moved down to his feet, quickly and efficiently binding his ankles together in the same manner. Back on his feet, he put the duct tape back in one of his cargo pockets. The whole procedure took less than two minutes.

Grabbing a hold of the cop under his arms, Sherman dragged him further back into the alley behind a dumpster. He had already ascertained that they were on radio silence so he shouldn't be missed anytime soon. Completing his task, Sherman melted back into the shadows intent on seeking out his next target.

Sherman had been in place since early afternoon and had waited for the police to arrive. Their operation had been organized and planned well. The cops were strategically placed in and around the restaurant and were well hidden. The officers inside the restaurant and the adjoining buildings would not hinder his effort. He would only concern himself with the cops stationed outside because of the potential for interference.

Tony sat in her car, all senses tuned to her surroundings. Brian and two other officers were in commandeered second floor locations on both sides of the street watching everyone who approached her car. If anyone got too close or looked suspicious, they were to key the radio once. There had already been three false alarms.

Sherman sauntered down the street toward the Shopper's Mart with his hands in his pockets. Entering the parking lot from the street, he casually ambled across the blacktop in the general direction of the Jeep. Noting nothing out of the ordinary, he moved up to the blind spot on the vehicle, just standing there nonchalantly looking around. Satisfied that no one was watching him, Sherman moved silently up the side of the vehicle. He was pleased to note that Viglioni had her eyes trained on the restaurant across the street.

Tony heard the radio key a moment before her acute hearing picked up the sounds of stealthy movement. Using her peripheral vision she saw a casually dressed man slowly moving forward from the rear of the Jeep. Watching his progress in the side mirror, she saw him pull a gun from his pocket and raise it.

Waiting until precisely the right moment, Tony lifted the door handle and simultaneously slammed her weight against the door, hoping to dislodge the gun. She was rewarded with a grunt of pain and the dull thud of metal impacting against blacktop.

In one fluid motion, she grabbed her nine-millimeter and exited the car. The force of the blow had backed her assailant away, and she knew she would have to use the small advantage she had gained very quickly.

Sherman had just begun to turn toward Tony, when the door caught him squarely in the stomach and he doubled over in pain, muttering, "Fucking bitch." At a distinct disadvantage, he knew he needed to get the gun from the ground, but she was getting out of the car way too quickly. Rising up from his bent over position, Sherman balled up his right fist and drove it upward into her chin.

Watching her stumble backward and hit her head against the doorframe of the Jeep, he snarled, "You've met your match this time."

Bending over and reaching for the gun, he was startled to hear, "Stop. Police," accompanied by the sound of running footsteps. Growling a curse, escape foremost in his mind, he forgot about retrieving the gun and ran down the street with Brian and another officer close behind him.

Momentarily stunned by a combination of the vicious sucker punch and the impact of her head against the doorframe, Tony saw an amazing multicolored light display in front of her eyes. Right after Sherman voiced his threat, she heard someone shout, "Stop. Police," and saw her assailant take off running, with Brian and one of the locals in hot pursuit.

Megan was inside the store furtively watching Tony. Her view blocked by the Jeep, all she could see was the top of her partner's head when she exited the vehicle. When Tony fell back against the car, Megan bolted through the door of the store, any thought of danger to herself secondary to the automatic response to her lover's distress.

Pushing off the car, Tony barely regained her balance before she was off and running. She heard the sound of shoes hitting pavement behind her and knew another officer had joined in the chase. Her long legs ate up the ground quickly, and within seconds she left the sound behind, steadily gaining on Brian and the other officer pounding down the street in Sherman's wake.

Megan got to the Jeep in time to see the back of her partner as she raced off down the street. She called out to her partner to stop but the plea met deaf ears. Megan shook her head and leaned against the vehicle. *At least she must not be hurt too bad. Did I really think I was going to stop her?* Shaking her head at the silly notion, she walked to the door of the jeep that was still hanging ajar and sat down in the front seat.

* * * * * * * * * *

Tony lengthened her stride and her adrenaline-filled body responded to her demands with a burst of speed. She drew even with Brian and the other cop and surged ahead closing the distance between her and her target. Dodging people walking down the sidewalk and focused solely on the man in front of her, she could no longer hear the other pursuers.

Sherman had purposely stayed on the well traveled street darting around the people out for a stroll on the warm, humid night. He needed to increase his distance from his pursuers and knew they wouldn't take a chance of firing their weapons at him because of the civilians on the street.

Taking a quick look over his shoulder, he was startled to see the tall, dark woman rapidly closing the distance between them. The cops had been left far behind. Sherman thought quickly. She still had the gun in her hand, and while he was confident he could disarm her, he couldn't take the chance of locals catching up and overwhelming him by sheer numbers.

Seeing a group of civilians across the street oblivious to the ongoing chase, he ran out into the middle of the traffic dodging and cars running directly into the group of people. He brutally shoved his way to the center of the group, grabbed the arm of a young woman and yanked her

forward then kicked her feet out from under her before
forcefully shoving her to the ground.   After savagely
elbowing his way past the others, he broke into a dead run,
knowing that the chaos he had caused should slow the
other agent down.

Tony followed close behind losing a couple steps
while dodging cars in the busy street amidst the sound of
squealing brakes and honking horns.   Her eyes narrowed
when she saw Sherman knock the woman down, but she
was already being helped to her feet by one of the other
women in the group.   Dodging the innocent bystanders who
had been drawn into the drama on the street, but losing a
few precious feet in the process, she once again delved
deeply within herself, demanding more from her body and
closed the distance that remained between her and the man
she was chasing.

Sherman looked back over his shoulder and felt a brief
flicker of concern.   Raising his hand and wiping the sweat
from his face, he thought, *Damn woman just keeps coming.*
He suddenly smiled at a gift fate handed him.   Two boys
were riding their bicycles toward him.   Running between
them, he grabbed the smaller of the two, jerking him off
his bike and kicking the bicycle into the other youth causing him to fall.

Sherman savagely smacked the kid hard across the
face stunning him.   With his large hand gripping the thin
arm of the youngster, he half carried and half dragged him
to the curb.   Picking up the kid by his T-shirt and the
waistband of his shorts, he heaved him into the street with
enough force the boy stumbled, unable to get his balance
and fell into the path of the oncoming traffic.   The boy lay
there frozen, his eyes wide with terror, as cars slammed on
their brakes, burning rubber into the road, as they
attempted to avoid the living obstacle in their path.   The
angry honking of horns broke the silence of the evening
and pedestrians screamed and yelled when they realized
the kid was petrified and unable to move.

Sherman faded behind the gathering group of civilians, too caught up in the terror in the street to notice him. Making sure he caught Tony's eye as she altered her path, he nodded, giving her a cocky two finger salute before turning and sprinting down the street.

Cursing silently at the ruthless maneuver, Tony reacted instantly and altered her path into the street. After several near misses while dodging the moving cars, she grabbed the kid by the arm and pulled him to his feet shielding him from the oncoming traffic with her body until they reached the safety of the sidewalk.

Leaning over, placing her hand on his shoulder, Tony asked, "You ok?" Sherman had slapped him pretty hard and there was a trickle of blood at the corner of his mouth. Shaking, the kid looked at her with awe-filled eyes and shook his head up and down.

Satisfied that he was just scared and not hurt, she raced off down the street. Brian and the other two cops had caught up, but their target was gone. He could have turned down any one of a number of alleys or side streets. Not willing to give up, she loped along at an easy pace, the locals joining her, as she ran up the street glancing down each opening she passed, hoping against hope to catch some glimpse of him. The few minutes it had taken her to rescue the child and make sure he was all right was all the head start her adversary had needed. Finally giving up the futile search, she slowed to a walk, the evening breeze cooling the thin sheen of sweat covering her body.

* * * * * * * * *

Sherman had reconnoitered the area earlier and planned several avenues of escape should they become necessary. When he finally succeeded in delaying Viglioni, he turned down the first alley he came to. Sherman ran across several backyards, vaulting several fences in the process until he came to the mouth of another alley. Running down the alley, he approached the rear of a three-story apartment building. With practiced ease, he jumped up and grabbed the bottom rung of the fire escape quickly making his way to the roof.

Sherman lay flat for a half hour to make sure he wasn't being observed. When he was satisfied, he took off his jacket and then removed the thin surgical gloves he was wearing. Pulling a cap out of the jacket pocket and put it on his head. After thoroughly checking the area again, he exited the roof.

Sherman walked nonchalantly up the alley in his base- ball cap and T-shirt and turned onto Fleet. He walked some of the very same ground he had run down earlier, giving every indication of being one of the locals on his way to the bus stop.

* * * * * * * * *

Tony and Brian walked side-by-side back toward the Leaning Ledge restaurant. Brian was concerned about the whereabouts of two of his men that had not joined in the pursuit.

Taking his radio off his belt, he said, "Unit one to Unit three. Come in." He was relieved a moment later to hear, "Unit one, this is Unit three. Over."

The big man asked, "What's your 10-20?"

"Parking lot across from the Leaning Ledge. Units five and six are with me," the officer reported.

Brian said, "Unit One, out." He took a handkerchief out of his pocket and wiped the sweat from his face. Mus- ing out loud, he said, "Doesn't make sense. What in the hell are they doing back there? Kris is the only one who was supposed to stay behind."

Tony had no idea and shrugged her shoulders. Her thoughts were on her assailant. *Ruthless bastard. What kind of lowlife places a child in jeopardy just to save their own ass? What if she hadn't got there in time?* It was common practice to use diversionary tactics when being pursued, but there were certain lines a professional just did not cross and Tony knew she was dealing with a professional of some kind. Her eyes narrowed, and she smiled grimly thinking about what she'd like to do when she got a hold of him.

Brian looked over at Tony and felt a chill. She had a professional aura that was frightening, even to him. And right now, she oozed danger. He'd only seen this persona once before, and still remembered the fear he'd felt when she'd literally dragged him from his chair, blaming him for placing Megan into the hands of a madman. Looking away, Brian almost felt sorry for their protagonist. Almost, but not quite.

* * * * * * * * * *

Megan, Kris and the other two officers saw Tony and Brian approaching. Megan left the group and quickly walked toward her partner, feeling a sense of relief. Tony appeared to be fine. But she was not prepared for the cold faraway look in her partner's eyes and felt a chill when she gazed into them.

Softly, she asked, "Tony, what's wrong?" and tentatively placed a hand on her forearm. She had been listening to the radio conversation between Kris and one of the other officers and knew the guy had gotten away, but normally her partner would've just taken that in stride. Something must have happened to elicit this kind of reaction, and Megan found it frightening.

Tony shoved her dark thoughts aside and looked at her concerned lover. The dangerous glint faded from Tony's eyes and she said, "The bastard tossed a kid into the middle of the street to get away." Tony looked away for a moment. "I expect that from the lowlife's I usually deal with, but he is supposed to be a professional."

No wonder her partner was angry. Worried, Megan asked, "Is the child ok?"

Tony placed her hand on Megan's shoulder needing the comfort the contact afforded her. Meeting her partner's worried eyes, she said, "Yes. He's ok. Two of Brian's guys are with him now getting a statement. They'll contact his mother and make sure he gets home ok."

Remembering Brian's comment about the officers that were left behind, she asked, "What's with Kevin and John? How come they stayed here? Kris was the only one that was supposed to stay behind."

Megan narrowed her eyes. She had her own suspicions about that. When she asked the officer why she wasn't joining in the chase, Kris had told her she wanted to make sure he didn't circle back to the restaurant. "She stayed behind because of me, didn't she?"

Tony looked at her lover, a small smile appearing on her face. "You didn't think I was going to leave you out here alone with this guy on the loose, did you?" she asked, gently squeezing Megan's shoulder.

The irritation Megan had initially felt faded. She knew on occasion Tony could be overprotective, but it was so comforting to know she could always count on her partner. No, Tony wouldn't leave her alone if she thought there was any chance of danger and she loved that feeling. Smiling wryly at her partner, she said, "No. Don't guess you would."

Tony grinned and said, "Glad you see it my way. So, why did the other two stay behind?"

Megan looked at her partner shaking her head. "You're not going to believe this. After you guys took off, Kris came over to the Jeep where I was sitting. She asked me if I'd seen John or Kevin. When I told her no, she tried to raise them on the radio and couldn't get an answer. So then we both went to their posts." Megan brushed a stray hair out of her face and continued, "We found both of them bound with duct tape. The last thing they remembered was being hit on the head. Neither one heard a thing. I checked them out and they're ok."

Tony listened silently. He had the advantage by knowing what they looked like. Had he been suspicious it was a setup or was he just being extremely cautious and not taking any chances? She didn't know, but then it really didn't matter any way. The operation had failed.

Just then Brian stalked over, his face dark with anger. Looking at Tony, he said, "Do you know what that bastard did?"

Tony met his gaze and said, "Yeah. Megan just told me. He had a trump card and he played it. He knows what we look like. That gave him an advantage."

Brian nodded, still angry. "Well, this was a total bust. Now what?"

Tony ran a hand through her hair and looked off into the distance. *Good question. Now what, was right?* Turning back to face Brian, she said, "We wait for him to make the next move. The ball is in his court. Since it was dark, and we didn't get a good look at him, and know little else about him except he is probably a professional, we just wait."

Brian sighed. "All we can do really. Watch your ass," Brian said and walked away. Turning around looking pointedly at Megan, he added, "Both of you."

Megan felt a chill. Lifting her head and meeting Tony's eyes, she said, "I really needed to hear that."

Tony felt a flicker of fear for her partner. After what she had witnessed tonight, she knew her pursuer would stop at nothing to get to her. It greatly distressed her that Megan had been inadvertently drawn into this mess. Concerned she met her partner's gaze. "He's right. Do you think you could stay at Ashley's tonight? I don't want you staying at the apartment all night by yourself."

"Probably. I'll call her." Megan felt a sense of relief at the suggestion. The idea of spending another night in the apartment alone was not appealing at all. Megan pulled the cellular phone out of her purse. After extending the antenna, she pushed the on button and dialed her sister's number, relieved when she heard the familiar, "Hello."

"Hi, Ashley. Would you mind if I stayed at your place tonight?" Megan asked.

Ashley set down the glass she was holding, her attention completely on what her sister was saying. "You know you can stay here any time. What's wrong?" Megan had never called at ten at night wanting to stay at her place. Something had to be going on.

"Remember what we were talking about at lunch?" Megan didn't want to elaborate over the phone.

"You mean about Tony's accidents?" Ashley asked, remembering how distraught her sister had been. "Are you both ok?"

Hearing the worry in her sister's voice, Megan said reassuringly, "Yeah, we're fine and it's about that. I'll fill you in when I get there."

"Okay. See you in a few," Ashley said, before hanging up. *At least they were both ok.*

Megan turned off the phone, lowered the antenna and put it back in her purse. Looking up at Tony, she said, "I guess you're going to work."

Tony looked at her partner, puzzled. "Why wouldn't I be?"

"I just thought with everything going on... you did get punched in the face...and let me see your head. You hit it pretty hard. From what I could see it looked like you almost got knocked out." Megan reached up and felt the back of Tony's head. "Yeah, you got a welt back here, all right."

Tony grinned at her partner. "Nice try, love, but a little bump on the head isn't any reason for me to call off."

Megan had figured it might be worth a shot and smiled back at her partner. "Wait until you look in the mirror and see that nice bruise on your jaw," Megan quipped, exaggerating the injury.

Tony ran her fingers along her jaw. "It's not very swollen. Can't be too bad."

Megan's eyes twinkled, and she said, "It's not. I was just kidding. I thought maybe I could get you to stay home."

Tony smiled. "Now there's a thought. Wish I could, but you can bet I'll be by to pick you up first thing in the morning." Tony paused and then added, "Unless you'd rather sleep in. Ashley could probably bring you home later."

"You better be there when you get off," Megan said, grinning, but only partially joking. Tony had to work evenings tomorrow and would have very little time to sleep, and Megan intended to keep an eye on things while she did.

Tony chuckled and said, "Yes, Ma'am. Let's go see if Kris can take you to Ashley's. I don't want to take any chances just in case he's still around and follows me when I leave."

"What about you? You still have to get to work," Megan said, worried.

Tony met Megan's eyes. "Don't worry. I'll have my usual escort. I'll be fine."

"There's Kris," Tony said, spotting the policewoman. "Let's see if she can take you over there now."

* * * * * * * * * *

Sherman lay stretched out on his bed in the hotel room, his head resting on his hands. He felt invigorated. Damn that had been fun. It had been so long since any of his cases offered a challenge, they had become almost boring. But not tonight. He couldn't remember the last time he had felt so alive. What a rush! He'd been set up and they still couldn't catch him.

He had to give Viglioni a little credit. She wasn't too bad after all. At least she offered up a challenge. But the local cops were so inept, and talk about out of shape. They had been left in the dust.

His thoughts turned to the tape he'd listened to. He knew she was working second shift tomorrow, and she was still being escorted to and from the surveillance site by the local cops.

A plan formed in his mind. The more he thought about it the more he liked it. Why shouldn't he have some fun with this case? He deserved it. Who knows how long it would be before he found another worthy adversary.

Sitting up, he played different scenarios through his mind. *Yep. It was perfect. Chancy and bold, but plausible.* This would definitely be a challenge to pull off, and it would make the thrill of the kill so much more satisfying.

Chapter
14

Tony unlocked the apartment door and opened it. Once they were inside, she locked it and walked straight into the kitchen. Megan followed her. The kittens appeared from parts unknown meowing loudly.

Megan smiled at them. "Oh. Poor babies. You probably thought we deserted you. Are you hungry?" She took a can of cat food out of the cupboard and emptied it into their dish. Placing it on the floor, she chuckled when the kittens attacked the food with relish. She put fresh water in their dish and after placing it on the floor turned to watch Tony.

Pulling a chair away from the table Tony kneeled down looking under the table. She reached for the tiny bug that had been secured there. Once she had it, she stood up and walked into the living room and plucked the ladybug off the silk plant. Megan followed her into the bathroom and watched as she flushed them both down the toilet.

"I'm so glad those are gone," Megan said, relieved.

"So am I. I'm going to check and make sure he didn't put any more in here," Tony said, walking out of the bathroom toward the bedroom. A thorough scan with the bug detector revealed no other bugs, much to Megan's relief.

Megan walked over and hugged Tony. "You need to get some sleep."

"I will. I'm going to take a shower first," Tony said, meeting Megan's lips for a fleeting kiss.

Megan made a pot of coffee. She would put off errands until tomorrow when Tony was off. She was not about to leave the apartment while her partner was sleeping.

Looking at her "watch," she felt better. One press of the small button and help would be on the way. Megan hoped he had been scared off after last night. She knew Tony didn't think so, but she could hope couldn't she?

The ringing of the phone surprised her. Who would be calling this early on Saturday? She picked up the phone and said, "Hello."

Huey had expected to hear Tony's voice and paused for a moment before speaking, prompting Megan to say, "Hello," again. "Is Tony there?" Huey enjoyed the sound of the pleasant voice.

"She's a little busy right now. May I take a message?" Megan asked, wondering who the caller was.

"Yes. Tell her to call the shop."

"Okay," Megan said, before hanging up the phone. Tony had explained the phone code to her and when he had mentioned the shop, she knew the caller was Huey.

When Tony got out of the shower, Megan said, "Huey called. Isn't it kind of unusual for him to be calling on a Saturday?"

"Yeah, it is. He must have found out something," Tony said as she picked up the phone and attached the scrambling device before dialing Huey's number.

When he answered, she said, "Viglioni here. I'm secure."

Huey wasted no time filling Tony in. "All hell has broken loose here. Sarah remembered who pulled your record, and when we put the screws to him, he sang. You have a very deadly wet agent after you. His name is Jess

Sherman and he is good. Thought you'd better know whom you're dealing with. I'll fax his picture to you."

Tony digested the information. She wasn't really surprised. She knew her assailant was professionally trained, even though he had ceased to be a professional in her mind. "Any idea what this is all about?"

"He doesn't want you to testify. He has a personal stake in this case. That's all I can tell you right now." Huey had full confidence in Tony's ability to take care of herself and knew she would use this information to her advantage.

"Thanks, Huey. I appreciate it," Tony said, before hanging up the phone. So it was another agent and not a mercenary. In Tony's mind, the worst thing an agent could do was to turn against one of their own. There was an unwritten code of honor among the agents.

Megan looked at the far away expression in Tony's eyes and asked, "What's wrong?"

Leaving her thoughts behind, Tony said, "It seems our 'friend' is a rogue agent. I had hoped I was wrong about that."

Megan looked at the pensive expression on Tony's face. "You seem...disappointed or something," Megan said, watching her partner closely.

"I am. Agents don't go after each other because of personal agendas," Tony said, before adding very quietly, "no matter what."

Megan didn't know what to say to that. "There's nothing you can do about it right now. Why don't you go lay down? We can talk about it when you get up. I'll get you up if anything unusual happens."

Tony knew there wasn't anything she could do right now, but she had one more thing on her agenda for the day. "Would you mind calling Brian and getting the name of the best locksmith he knows? I want an electronic lock installed today. We also need to call the security company and see if they can upgrade our alarm and change the code. Tell them it's an emergency and it has to be done today."

Megan was once again hit with the seriousness of their situation. They had no idea when or how he might strike again. "Don't worry, I'll take care of it," she said, happy to have something to keep her busy so she wouldn't have as much time to worry.

Seeing the worried expression on Megan's face, she did not have the heart to tell her that it probably wouldn't do any good. With the right equipment, a lock or an alarm could be disabled in seconds. Her hope was that since Sherman was acting on his own, he might not have the latest equipment. Until Sherman was apprehended, she would just make sure Megan was never in the apartment by herself.

"Thanks, love." Leaning over and softly kissing her partner, Tony said, "I'm going to bed now."

* * * * * * * * * *

Megan smiled at David and Mike and said, "That was fun. I better get going now. I don't want to be late."

"You're a good player," David said, grinning at her. It had been fun having Megan over. They didn't see her much now that she had met Tony. He was very happy for both of them, but he did miss her visits.

"Nah. No better that you guys. We all won once," Megan said, chuckling. She'd always liked Pictionary. It was fun to see who could guess what you were drawing.

David and Mike walked with her to the door. "See you Monday," David said.

Smiling, Megan said, "Okay. Bye."

Pulling out of the drive and into the street, Megan looked around her. Tony had followed her to David and Mike's house to make sure she wasn't followed. Her partner had assured her no one had followed them, but the fact that Tony had thought it was necessary made her nervous.

* * * * * * * * * *

Megan arrived at her parents' house, got out of her car and walked to the side door of the two-story colonial. The house sat on a large lot with the deck facing a large pond and woods bordering the back yard. The front yard was gorgeously landscaped with flowers adorning the front of the house and bordered by decorative stones.

With a light touch to the doorbell to announce her arrival, she opened the door and walked in.

Barbara walked into the foyer, smiled and said, "Hi, Megan," and then hugged her. "It's good to see you."

"It's good to see you, too, Mom," Megan said, returning the hug with a smile.

"Your father's in the living room. Why don't you go join him while I finish dinner? It should be ready in about a half-hour. Would you like something to drink?"

Megan grinned, caught up in her mother's cheerfulness. "Do you have any iced tea?"

"Made some just for you," her mother said, unable to wipe the smile from her face. She had missed her daughter. "Go on. I'll bring it in."

"Thanks."

Megan walked into the living room. Her father sat in the recliner in an upright position. Even when he was off work, he had a professional appearance about him. He wore khakis and a sports shirt with the creases still intact. "Hi, Dad."

"Hello, Megan." Waving his arm toward the couch, he said, "Make yourself comfortable."

Megan walked over and sat down. Knowing her father lived for his job, she asked, "How's work?"

"Very busy. We've had to add some associates because the firm is in such high demand," Charles said, proudly.

"That's great. I know you've wanted to expand for a while now. What do Ken and Gene think about the new associates?" Megan knew the other two senior partners had been reluctant to add more associates. They were concerned about their own profit margins.

"They're ok with it. We've picked up some major new clients, and it allows us time to properly set them up. The associates can handle the routine clients."

Megan's mother walked in and handed her a glass of iced tea. "Here you go."

"Thanks, Mom."

"You're welcome." Looking at her husband and daughter, Barbara said, "Dinner will be ready in about fifteen minutes," before turning around and walking back to the kitchen. Barbara was pleased. It looked like Megan and her father were doing just fine.

"I saw your picture in the paper. That was quite an impressive write up. It seems like a hard way to get a little recognition, though," Charles said, thinking of his personal agenda for his daughter.

"I like my job, Dad. It's challenging to try and find evidence and clues to link together what happened to the victim." Megan smiled, warming to a topic she enjoyed. "It's never boring, and I never stop learning." She had decided to elaborate so her father would understand what she found fascinating about her job. Maybe then he would realize that she really was doing what she liked.

Charles looked at his daughter. She did seem happy. How could he make her understand that the Donnovans just didn't work in public service? That detracted from the powerful image he had spent years developing. *It was a constant source of embarrassment to him that his daughter was a pathologist. If she had to choose medicine, she could have at least chosen a field that was respected like surgery.*

Charles stated his argument eloquently, the same way he addressed the court. "But Megan, that's a gruesome job. I don't see why you would want to work as a public servant for a pittance of money and little recognition, when you could be sitting in a nice clean office meeting with clients and making real money. It's not too late to go back to school. With your brains you could probably finish in three years."

Megan looked at the earnest expression on her father's face. "Dad, I don't want to be a lawyer," Megan smiled and continued, "I'd rather do the behind the scenes work. My picture getting in the paper was more of a fluke than anything else."

"If you call almost getting killed a fluke, then yes, it was. You put your life at risk helping to solve that case. You don't make enough money to be put in that situation," Charles retorted.

"That was an exception. For the most part, my job is quite safe. A sociopath could just as easily target a lawyer," Megan said, watching her father intently.

Before Charles had time to formulate an answer, Barbara called from the dining room, "Dinner's ready."

Charles and Megan walked into the dining room, and Charles assumed his seat at the head of the table.

Megan looked at the lavishly set table and delicious entrees her mother had made and smiled. There was stuffed Cornish hens, wild rice, asparagus, and cucumber salad. "This looks great!" Megan said, smiling at her mother.

"I thought you might like it," Barbara said, pleased.

Megan ate, thoroughly enjoying the meal. She knew her mother spent a lot of time and effort in preparing savory meals and was an accomplished cook. She always enjoyed her mother's creations. Megan realized how much she missed this part of her relationship with her parents. Serious talk had always been avoided at the dinner table and the conversation revolved around their friends and family. She listened to her mother talking about her plans for redecorating the den and offered her opinion. Even her father had a few ideas to contribute. Megan relaxed and enjoyed herself.

After dinner, Megan insisted on helping her mother clear the table and put things away while Charles returned to the living room. Barbara looked at her daughter. "I'm glad you could make it today. We seem to have such a hard time getting together."

Megan had enjoyed the nice quiet dinner so much, and being an eternal optimist, she had to stop a minute to remember why she avoided visiting her parents. "I know I haven't been over much, and I miss seeing you both. But, Mom, you know why."

"Your father's only looking out for what he considers your best interests," Barbara said, smiling. "I know you don't agree on that. But he really just wants the best for you."

"Yeah. I know, but what he thinks is best for me isn't what I want to do, and I hate to cause hard feelings, so the alternative is to stay away." Looking at her mother and smiling, Megan added, "But I will try to do better."

Barbara smiled back at her daughter. "Good. Besides he'll eventually come around. Just give him some time."

Megan chuckled ruefully. "Mom, I'm going to be twenty-eight soon. I think if he was going to come around, he'd have done it by now."

Barbara sighed. She knew Megan was probably right. "Well, you never know. It still could happen." The two women walked into the living room carrying coffee cups. Barbara gave one to Charles, and then sat down on the couch with Megan. "Have you talked to Taylor lately? She just found out she's pregnant," Barbara said, looking completely like the happy grandmother she was.

"Oh, that's great! I know they wanted to start a family. When's she due?" Megan asked grinning.

"March 18th. Ashley, you and I need to get together and plan a shower for her. I thought January might be a good time to do it."

Due to their various schedules, Megan didn't get a chance to see her sisters very often and the idea of helping plan Taylor's shower really appealed to her. With a warm smile lighting up her face, she said, "Okay. That'll be fun."

Charles took a sip of his coffee and asked, "What about you, Megan? Have you been dating anyone?"

How did I know this would come up? Dating any-one...hum...not really, I'm already taken. Leaving her thoughts behind, Megan said, "No, I'm not dating anyone."

Charles looked pointedly at his daughter and said, "You're not getting any younger. If you wait too much longer all the suitable young men will be gone."

Barbara looked at her daughter. She was so attractive. She just didn't understand why the men weren't flocking after her. The problem was she just spent too much time at work to go out and enjoy herself. "You know, Megan, your father has a point. You really should spend more time socially and less at your job. If you don't go out you can't meet people."

Megan took a deep breath. She wasn't in the mood for this conversation right now. There had been too much hap-pening in her life lately, and it wasn't over. Her partner had put her life on the line last night so that their own lives could return to normal and she just didn't want to play this particular game with her parents right now. With those thoughts in mind, she decided to put an end to the topic.

Looking her father in the eyes, she said, "I am very happy with my life the way it is. So can we please talk about something else?"

Charles was angered by what he perceived as a disre-spectful remark from his daughter. "You don't run this house, and it would behoove you to listen to your mother and me on this. I expect you to show a little respect, and when I'm ready to change the subject, I will."

"Charles," Barbara said, hoping to avoid a potential showdown, "if she doesn't want to talk about this right now..."

Charles was not about to be deterred. "Well, when are we going to talk about it? She hardly ever comes over. I think this is as good a time as any."

Megan looked sadly from one parent to the other. This just didn't make any sense. They were talking about her like she wasn't even in the room. Standing up, Megan

said, "I'm going to go now. Thanks for dinner. It was
great..."

Rising to his feet, Charles said, "And just where do
you think you're going? I want to know when you are
going to start acting like a Donnovan? It's bad enough you
have that public servant job, so the least you can do is
marry into our class of people."

Charles paused, unsuccessfully trying to calm down.
"I know it's not because there aren't plenty of eligible
young men interested in you. I introduced you to Eric and
Jeffrey at the last party we had. They both asked you out,
and you turned them down."

The stress of the last week had taken its toll and
Megan's eyes flashed and her temper flared. Words fell
freely from her mouth before she could stop them. "I've
already met someone. She's a wonderful woman that I
love more than I ever thought was possible."

Megan realized what she'd said when she saw the
shocked expressions on her parents' faces. *I wanted to tell
them, but not like this, and not today.* Resigning herself to
the explosion she knew was coming, she met her father's
widened eyes.

"You're telling me you're a lesbian? You like
women?" Charles sputtered incredulously. Looking at Barbara, he asked, "What did we do wrong?"

Megan looked at her father and said, "Dad, it's not
about that. It's about love." Shifting her gaze back and
forth between her parents, Megan continued, hoping she
could help them understand her feelings. "I am happier
than I've ever been. When I met her, I knew there was
something special about her. I never felt that way about
anyone before."

Barbara didn't know what to say. Her daughter's face
softened when she talked about her feelings. This was just
such a shock.

Charles still couldn't believe his ears. "You're going
to disgrace the entire family. How could you do this to
us?"

"No, I'm not, Dad. You are respected and liked in the community. That's not going to change, and besides, how would any of your associates know anyway?" Megan said, reasonably.

Barbara thought about the few conversations she'd had with Megan lately. Some of the things her daughter had said, now made more sense. She just hadn't been paying attention. "It's that FBI agent, isn't it?"

Megan looked at her mother and said, "Yes, Mom. She really is great. You'd like her."

Charles' face reddened, anger replacing the shock. "You are wrong. I will not allow you to disgrace the family like this. Until you come to your senses, you are not welcome in this house any more."

"Charles," Barbara said, warningly. "Megan, he doesn't mean that."

Megan felt her stomach tighten and fought to control her emotions. Looking at her mother, she said, "I had hoped you might understand."

Turning to her angry father, she said, "I'm sorry you feel that way," and then she turned and walked to the side door, letting herself out.

Barbara tried to follow, but Charles grabbed her arm and stopped her. "I meant what I said."

Barbara glared at her husband. "Charles, you're wrong. She's our daughter."

Charles unflinchingly met his wife's eyes. "This is my house, and I will not allow her to disgrace it with her deviant behavior."

****

Megan got into her car very depressed. It shouldn't have come to this. She knew she should have reined in her temper, but they would have had to know sooner or later anyway. Tony was too important to her. But she'd never expected her father to ban her from the house.

Putting the car into gear and pulling into the street, Megan was unaware of the tears falling down her face until she had to pull over, no longer able to see clearly. A little while later, her tears in check, she pulled back onto the road and drove across town.

Megan turned the car toward the place she had always found solace, the shores of Lake Erie. It was still light out and the beach was not crowded, but populated enough to be safe. Megan parked the car and walked along the beach, the ever-present shells crunching under her feet.

Leaving the beach in favor of one of the docks, she walked across the warped, uneven boards, passing all the people that were fishing. When she got to the end of the dock, she stood for a moment looking out over the lake, before sitting down on the hard surface near the end.

The tears started again, and she let them flow unchecked. Mostly she felt so incredibly sad. She longed for the comforting feel of Tony's arm around her. She knew her father could be very intolerant, but she'd just had not expected that reaction. Megan had always justified his actions by convincing herself, that in his own way, he was looking out for her. After today, she could no longer pretend that was true.

Megan stayed until the moon was visible and the other patrons began leaving before she finally got up and walked back to her car. A brief smile appeared when she remembered that Tony was off tomorrow.

Megan thought back to her conversation with Tony that afternoon, before she had followed her over to David's house. Her partner had insisted she go to Ashley's house until she got home from work and had a chance to check out the apartment. Tony had assured her that she would be home by midnight, but to call first, just to make sure she was there.

Looking at her watch, Megan sighed. It was ten o'clock. She loved her sister dearly, but she just didn't want to see her tonight. Ashley had known she was having dinner with their parents' and would want to know how it

went, and she just didn't want to talk about it. Her emotions were still too raw. The only person she wanted to see
was Tony.

Sitting in the car, lightly drumming her fingers on the
wheel, she decided to go home. She knew Tony would be
mad, but with the new lock and alarm system installed, it
should be safe enough. Megan really didn't think Sherman
would come to the apartment any way. If he wanted to
confront Tony in the apartment, he could already have
done so.

Chapter
15

Sherman leaned against the vanity waiting for someone to get home. The closet door was already open so he could quickly and quietly move into it. He had known the girlfriend would be at her parents' house, and Tony would be working evenings from information he had gleaned from the tapes. He didn't even bother checking for a tape today. After last night, it was obvious she knew about the bugs.

His thoughts turned to his target. He acknowledged a grudging respect for her. The sting operation had been cleverly set up and executed. It would have trapped anyone less skilled than he was. He chuckled softly. *I never even suspected it was a setup.*

The faint noise attracted the attention of the kittens and they wandered back to the bedroom, looking at the strange man curiously. He had chased them out of the room once and they were leery of him, and poised for flight. Sherman stood up and stomped his foot down hard on the floor, frightening both kittens and grinning coldly when they ran. *They come back again and I just might take some target practice.*

* * * * * * * * *

Shifting the car into gear, Megan pulled out of the parking area and drove the short distance to the apartment. Parking in her usual spot, she took the elevator to the fourth floor. Punching in the numbers to open the electronic lock, she entered the apartment and was greeted by two meowing kittens. Stepping around them, she walked over to the alarm and deactivated it. Stooping down to pet the kittens, she smiled at the loud purrs.

"Did you two miss me? I missed you." Glancing around, Megan asked the kittens, "What did you two get in to while I was gone?" Huggy and Velcro continued rubbing up against her legs and purring contentedly. Chuckling, Megan said, "Guess I'd better go look around."

She stood and walked into the dining room and then to the living room, dodging the kittens that were accompanying her. Everything looked fine. Megan walked down the hall glancing in the bathroom, surprised that the door was open. She thought she'd closed it when she left. One time of cleaning up toilet paper strewn all over the apartment was enough for anyone. At least she'd gotten lucky and they hadn't attacked the new roll.

As Megan was closing the door, Huggy ran into the bathroom and jumped up on the toilet seat. "Oh, no, you don't," Megan said and lifted the kitten up, carried her out of the bathroom, and closed the door.

After setting Huggy down, Megan walked over to the balcony. She opened the sliding glass door, stepped outside and walked to the railing. The warm breeze felt good, and Megan looked up at the sky. The moon and stars were already visible, but tonight she took little joy in the sight.

Megan just wanted it to be time for Tony to get home. She bent down and absently stroked the soft fur of the two kittens that had joined her on the balcony.

Megan thought back over the events that had transpired at her parents' house. She had done a lot of soul searching at the beach and felt she had done the right thing by telling her parents about her and Tony. She did acknowledge she could have handled it better, but the outcome would probably have been the same.

It wouldn't do any good to dwell on it, but she really hadn't wanted to estrange her parents either. *Why is everything so complicated?* Megan knew there was no obvious answer to that question the moment it crossed her mind. She also knew that she was not willing to sacrifice the love she had found by living a lie, just to please her family.

Tony was the most important person in her life. She was her best friend, confidante, lover, and partner. Her life would not be complete without her. The love and happiness she'd found was not something she was willing to let go of, nor did she want to. In time, maybe she could help her parents to understand that.

Suddenly uneasy, Megan turned around and looked back into the apartment. Goose bumps had formed on her arms and the hair on the back of her neck was standing up. She'd felt for a moment like she was being watched. Shaking off the sudden chill, she decided she was probably just overreacting to all the stress of the evening.

Sherman barely ducked his head back into the hallway in time. He'd only been watching her for a minute when she suddenly turned around. He'd have to be more careful. He didn't want to reveal his presence yet.

After walking back inside, Megan closed and latched the balcony door. Even though she remembered locking the door when she got home, Megan walked over to the door and double-checked the lock. It was bolted. Her overactive imagination was obviously at work here. The door had been locked when she got home and the alarm had been set. No one could have gotten in. But still uneasy, she walked down the hall and looked into both bedrooms, before returning to the one they shared.

Megan sat on the bed. It would be another hour at least before Tony got home. She might as well take a shower while she was waiting for her partner to get off. The warm, soothing water would help relax her. She took her nightshirt off the hook on the door and walked down the hall to the bathroom. She quickly entered and closed the door before the kittens could run in.

Megan took a towel out of the linen cupboard and turned on the shower, adjusting the water. Afetr undressing, she stepped into the shower and let the warm water cascade over her. She felt some of the tension melt away.

Sherman opened the closet door. He was extremely glad they were louvered. It not only allowed him a partial view of the room, he could hear better. He'd always had high energy, and staying out of sight in the closet was very confining. Grinning, knowing she couldn't hear him, Sherman stepped into the hallway and looked at the bathroom door.

Megan turned off the shower and pulled the curtain simultaneously letting out a blood-curdling scream when she realized someone was standing there.

Tony jumped, startled when her partner screamed, and quickly moved forward wrapping her arms around her. "What's wrong? It's only me. I knocked on the door first so you would hear me," Tony said, trying to comfort her shaken partner.

She'd been surprised to see Megan's car in the garage and figured something must be wrong since she had come home instead of going to Ashley's house like they'd agreed on.

Megan felt her thundering heart slow down. "Sorry. I've been a little jumpy tonight. I didn't hear you knock and you're really early," Megan said, clinging tightly to her partner, so relieved that her words came in a rush.

Tony continued to hold her partner, waiting for her breathing to return to normal. Megan, much calmer, looked up into the concerned blue eyes gazing at her. Smiling ruefully and releasing her partner, she said, "Oh, look. I've gotten you all wet."

Tony picked up the towel and handed it to Megan. "Here you go. I'll go make us something to drink. Want some tea?"

Megan took the towel, still relieved to see her, and smiled. "That would be great."

Tony's keen hearing had picked up a background noise when Megan screamed. That, combined with the fact that her partner was jumpy put Tony in a very dangerous mode. She knew the kittens could have made the noise she heard, but she wasn't taking any chances.

Putting her finger up to her lips signaling for quiet, she waited for Megan to towel off and put her sleeping shirt on. Tony pointed toward the kitchen and waited until her partner walked down the hall and disappeared into the doorway.

Tony had set her gun down on the toilet tank when she entered the bathroom. For some reason she had wanted to keep it near. The thought crossed her mind that it was a good thing she had. She picked up the gun and flipped the safety off. Walking slowly and quietly down the hall, her hairpin reflexes were ready to react at the slightest provocation.

Sherman cursed silently. He had been surprised to hear the apartment door open, knowing Tony wasn't due home yet, and had moved back into the bedroom. Just when he was backing into the closet, a piercing scream had penetrated the air. Startled, he bumped his head on the doorframe.

He stood in the closet with his gun in his hand, listening for any sound that might indicate he'd been heard. Sherman still preferred the element of surprise and would rather wait until Tony had settled in. The chances of her having her gun near then would be slim. He had already looked around the apartment and hadn't seen any weapons. This led him to believe that she probably only had the weapons she carried on her person.

Megan walked into the kitchen, her heart pounding painfully. Tony thought he was in the apartment. The idea that someone could be in the apartment...or was in the apartment gave her the creeps, and a chill coursed through her body.

Her sudden chill turned to fear for her partner. *Please be careful.* The metamorphosis her partner had gone through was still imprinted on her mind, and she still found it amazing that the aura surrounding her partner changed instantaneously the moment she sensed danger. But that didn't diminish the fear she felt for her. If this guy was in the apartment, he had the advantage. Tony would have no idea where he was and what if she didn't see him until it was too late?

Standing just inside the kitchen, Megan strained her ears listening for anything that would let her know what was happening. She didn't want to get in Tony's way, but she had to see what was going on. She would be ready if Tony needed her help. Poking her head around the doorway, she took a quick look down the hallway.

Tony kept her back at the wall walking sideways to present the smallest possible target. She knew he was in the apartment. Her body was screaming warnings. Once she had gotten over the shock of Megan screaming and the odd sound had registered in her mind, her body had reacted instinctively and all her fine tuned senses kicked into gear.

Arriving at the bedroom doorway, she took a quick look inside before pulling her head back, not wanting to give her assailant a target. Quickly kneeling, her weight supported on one knee, she trained her eyes on the space under the bed. Thankful for the light cast by the lamp, she could make out no unnatural shadows. She straightened and took a step through the doorway her back against the open door.

Velcro was following her favorite mom. This was a new game. Her mom was acting very funny. Slinking down the hall she stopped near Tony's feet and crouched down, her tail twitching.

Quickly boring of the game, Velcro ran down the hallway and into the other bedroom. Braver now that her mom was home, she walked over to the closet door and batted it with her paw.

Sherman silently cursed again. That damn kitten was back again. His view was limited through the louvers and he couldn't see the entire room but he could see the kitten sitting in front of the door trying to get her paw through one of the louvers.

It was extremely quiet in the apartment, but that didn't mean anything. Both women could be in the front part of the apartment.

Periodically peering around the doorway and watching Tony's progress down the hall, Megan suddenly realized she had left her "watch" in the bathroom. Knowing instinctively that they might need it if that guy really was in the apartment, she looked down the hallway to see where Tony was. Megan saw her partner look into their bedroom. Taking a deep breath and moving very quietly, she started down the hallway to the bathroom.

Tony caught movement in her peripheral vision and saw Megan walking down the hall toward the bathroom. Her heart beat faster and she thought, *No, no. What are you doing? Get back in the kitchen. It's not safe.* Waving her back, she saw Megan hold up a finger in a "just a minute" signal. *Go back,* Tony pleaded silently. Keeping her eyes peeled for any movement from the bedroom, Tony stayed where she was and breathed a silent sigh of relief, when she saw Megan hold up the watch and retreat back to the kitchen.

Now that her partner was out of immediate danger, Tony quirked a small grin. That was a good idea. It wouldn't hurt to have help if they needed it. The thought surprised her. Nice to know her world had grown to include people she could count on.

Stealthily walking further into the bedroom, she looked at the closet. It was the most logical place of concealment. Tony moved next to the closet door and pressed her body against the wall.

In a sudden quick movement, she flung the door open before plastering herself back against the wall, her gun trained on the entrance. There was no movement, and she instinctively knew no one was hiding in there. Moving away from the wall to the front of the closet, her body was poised to jump out of the way at any indication of danger. She looked in the closet. It was empty.

Sherman slowly turned the doorknob. The kitten quit trying to put a paw through the louvers and looked up at the moving handle. When the door slowly opened, the kitten bolted out the room and into the hallway running past Tony and into the kitchen.

Tony noticed the kitten's flight and stopped outside the other bedroom door. Totally focused she listened for any sound coming from the room.

Megan paced back and forth in the kitchen. It seemed like Tony had been back there forever when, in fact, it had only been a couple of minutes. She almost jumped when Velcro came sliding across the floor, coming to a stop near Huggy.

Walking to the doorway she looked down the hall and saw Tony standing outside the second bedroom door before quickly pulling her head back into the kitchen. Maybe this was just a false alarm. Obviously there had been no one in the first bedroom. *Yeah, right.*

Sherman was pressed against the wall in the bedroom next to the door. Hearing nothing, he eased around the door only to bump into an equally startled tall, dark woman.

Tony reacted a millisecond faster and grabbed the arm holding the gun pointed at her, shoving it up and simultaneously pressing hard on a nerve in the wrist. Sherman had squeezed the trigger and the gun went off, the bullet imbedding in the wall.

Megan's heart almost stopped when she heard the gunfire. She immediately activated the button on the watch and ran to the apartment door to unlock it. Running back into the kitchen, she looked down the hallway, quickly pulling her head back when she saw that Tony seemed to be unharmed.

Sherman was unable to stop his hand from opening and the gun fell to the floor. Brutally driving his other elbow into Tony, he threw his weight against her propelling them across the hall, their momentum stopped when their bodies impacted against the opposite wall.

Having a slight advantage now, Sherman grabbed Tony's arm and slammed it against the wall, causing the gun to fall from her hand.

Tony had finally got her breath back from the blow to her solar plexus, and she pushed away from the wall attempting to free herself, while simultaneously drawing her knee up in an attempt to incapacitate Sherman with a groin hit.

Expecting the move, Sherman jumped back out of the way and while Tony was off balance, he once against threw his weight against her driving her into the wall, raising his hands to her neck and choking her.

His grip was like iron and Tony resisted the urge to grab his wrists and attempt to dislodge his hands. Already feeling the lack of oxygen, she raised her arms and forcefully smacked her open hands against his ears with strength fortified by adrenaline. The blow caused a slight loosening of the choke hold and, sucking in some much needed air, she brought her arms up between his with an outward sweeping motion and broke his hold on her neck. At the moment his hands loosened, Tony drove her head into his face, her forehead impacting with his nose, followed by a crushing blow to his chin with her elbow.

Sherman jumped back, tears blinding him. In excruciating pain, his hands involuntarily covering his bloody nose, he backed away from her trying to stay out of her reach in the narrow confines of the hallway. He lowered a hand to his pocket, extracted a switchblade, and pressed the button that snapped the blade into place. Extending his arm in a slashing motion with the knife, he moved toward her, his vision slowly improving.

Quickly back peddling, Tony circled him, staying clear of the reach of the knife, looking for an opportunity to disarm him and deliver a crippling blow. But Sherman protected himself and countered her attempts to get closer by leading with the knife. Turning sideways to present a smaller target, he circled warily; the dance of the two adversaries well underway.

Megan continued to observe the battle knowing it was best if she stayed out of the way. She had already started down the hallway once, before Tony broke the chokehold around her neck. She had watched Tony in action before and had full confidence in her ability to protect herself. But this guy was heavier than she was, and it was obvious he was also very highly trained.

When Sherman pulled the knife Megan's temper flared. She'd be damned if he was going to harm her lover if she could do anything about it. Tony didn't have anything to protect herself with. Looking around the kitchen for a weapon, her eyes settled on the heavy, round paperweight sitting on the table. It was about the size of a baseball except it was flat on the bottom. A pretty yellow flower was suspended in the middle of it.

Grabbing the paperweight off the table, she waited until Sherman's back was toward her, and then stepped into the mouth of the hallway. Waiting until Tony noticed her, she hefted the paperweight in her hand, and drew her arm back sending it forcefully through the air, satisfied when it landed solidly in the middle of Sherman's back.

Megan knew it wouldn't really hurt him, but her intent was to distract him so that Tony could disarm him. Sherman was unable to check the automatic impulse to turn his head at the sharp pain that shot through his back when the paperweight hit him.

Tony immediately threw her leg up into a front kick, connecting solidly with his wrist. Sherman grunted in pain, both of them hearing the snap of a bone as the knife fell to the floor.

Holding his injured wrist against his chest, Sherman threw a brutal sidekick toward Tony. She danced out of the way and let go of a roundhouse that snapped his head back and stunned him. Immediately followed up with a solid kick to the groin, Sherman dropped to the ground.

Tony reached down and picked up her gun and trained it on the other agent. Her thoughts were dark, the image of a terror stricken boy laying in the middle of a busy street flickering in slow motion through her mind. Her finger tightened against the trigger.

Suddenly she felt a warm hand on her arm, and a concerned voice asked, "Tony...are you ok?"

Taking a deep breath, Tony said, "Yeah, I'm fine."

Just then the front door banged open and two uniformed cops entered the apartment with their guns drawn.

Megan called out, "Down there," and the two officers quickly walked down the hallway, taking in the scene.

Not knowing either patrolman, Tony said, "FBI. Would you cuff this guy to something?"

One of the officers grabbed Sherman, hauled him to his feet and took him into the living room. He fastened the cuff to Sherman's uninjured wrist and fastened the other end around the metal frame of the heavy computer table. After putting his gun away, he pulled out his radio and called for an ambulance.

The other officer asked Tony to surrender her gun. Knowing this was just routine procedure, she handed it to him. The patrolman tookl her weapon, put his gun in his holster, and questioned Tony and Megan.

Brian arrived and walked into the apartment. Taking over the questioning, he quickly had a summary of the events. When Tony got to the end of her statement she mentioned her gun had been confiscated. "You never fired your gun, right?" Brian asked.

"No. Never had a chance to," Tony said, her face grim.

Brian had no doubt she would have liked to, though. Turning to the officer that had her weapon, he said, "Give her back her gun. She's an FBI agent and they have jurisdiction on this case."

Tony picked up the phone and called the number she had been given to reach Huey after hours. When he answered, she said, "We got him."

"You ok?"

"I'm fine. But Sherman managed to break his wrist in the scuffle," she paused and then added, "and probably his nose, too."

"With some help from you, I'm sure," Huey quipped back.

"A little," Tony said, smiling. "The local cops are going to take him to the hospital and then hold him until you can get someone here to pick him up."

"I'll have someone there tomorrow morning."

* * * * * * * * * *

When the apartment finally cleared out, Tony walked over and hugged Megan. Returning the hug, Megan asked, "I'm so glad you're ok. How did you get home so early?"

"Braxton finally gave the word to move in. All the principal players were gathered at the site and when we let him know that, he realized it was too good of an opportunity to pass up."

"It's finally, really over?"

"Um hum. You know you got a real mean fastball, love. That was a good idea. Thanks," Tony said, smiling at her lover.

"I had to do something...when he pulled that knife..." Megan trailed off remembering the anger and fear she had felt.

Tony bent her head placing a soft kiss on Megan's lips. "And you did."

Cocking her head to the side and raising an eyebrow, Tony said, "I'd like to ask you something." She gazed into Megan eyes. "Why are you home instead of at Ashley's?"

Megan took in the serious expression on Tony's face and looked away. She figured Tony would be upset about her coming home, and considering what had happened, she was surprised she wasn't angrier. "I didn't want to go to Ashley's. I figured you would be home soon and we had just put on the new lock, so I thought it would be ok."

Damn. I should have warned her about the lock. "Megan." Tony waited until her lover looked at her. Looking at the expression on her partner's face, she asked, "What's wrong? Why didn't you want to go to Ashley's? Did something happen at your parents'?"

Megan sighed and answered the last question. "Yeah, it did." Releasing Tony, she asked, "Want something to drink?" and then she turned around and walked toward the kitchen.

Tony watched her partner walk away and then followed her. It was obvious Megan was upset.

Megan put water in the teakettle and asked, "Is tea ok?"

"Sounds great," Tony said, watching her partner closely, trying to read the expression on her face. The closest read Tony could come up with was sadness. She walked over to her partner, looked into the troubled hazel eyes, and asked, "Want to talk about it?"

Megan peered into the warm blue eyes and felt the love and concern they reflected. Giving Tony a quick hug before releasing her, she said, "Yeah. I do."

The teakettle whistled and Megan quickly made two cups of tea handing one to Tony. "Let's talk in the living room." Settling on the couch, Megan snuggled close to Tony. She wanted and needed the contact. Tony put her arm around her partner and waited for her to begin.

By the time Megan had finished relating the events of the evening, her eyes were moist again, but no tears fell. She had already been through the gamut emotionally between her parents and fear for Tony's life when she was fighting the other agent. There just weren't any more left.

Tony had listened quietly while Megan talked. Not knowing how to make her lover feel better, she said, "I'm sorry. But Megan it sounds more to me like your dad had the biggest problem with it, not your mom."

"Yeah, I know. But ever since we were little, she always supported his decisions. She never stuck up for us." Megan paused to gather her thoughts. "But you know what? I'm glad I told them. I love you, and if they can't accept that, then maybe it's better this way."

The depth of feeling she felt for the smaller woman snuggled against her suddenly impacted on Tony. Capturing her partner's eyes with her own, she said, "Do you have any idea how much I love you?"

A warm smile covered Megan's face, and she said, "Yes, I do. Because I love you just as much."

Chapter
16

Megan walked into the kitchen trailed closely by two meowing kittens. Opening the canister containing the select Colombian blend, she carefully measured three-and-a-half level scoops into the filtered basket and filled the pot to the five-cup level. After turning it on, she took a can of cat food out of the cupboard and emptied it into the kittens' dish. "You know you two could eat a little dry food once in a while."

She unlocked the apartment door, retrieved the paper, re-locked the door, and returned to the kitchen. Seated at the kitchen table, Megan opened the paper and perused the news.

She wasn't surprised she had awakened before Tony. She had entertained the idea of just staying in bed waiting for her lover to wake up, but she'd had to go to the bathroom and figured she might as well stay up rather than take a chance and wake Tony. She'd only had a few hours of sleep on Saturday, and with everything that had happened Friday night and then last night, she had to be exhausted.

Tony woke up to the smell of coffee wafting into the bedroom. She loved the smell of brewing coffee, but she was surprised she had not heard her partner get up.

Walking into the kitchen after a stop at the bathroom, she smiled and said, "Morning, love."

Megan looked up when Tony walked into the room. Her eyes twinkling, she said, "Hi, sleepy head."

Tony grinned. "Sleepy head, huh. Look who's talking." She walked over to Megan and bent down and kissed her. After getting a cup of coffee, she sat down at the table. "Anything interesting in the paper?"

"Not really," Megan said handing Tony the part she had already looked at.

Megan stood up, walked over to the refrigerator and opened the door insearch of the can of orange juice she had taken out to thaw yesterday. *Where had she put it anyway?*

Tony took in the sight of her partner bending over looking for something in the refrigerator. She had an unobstructed view of her lovely muscular legs. Not interested in the newspaper anymore, she got up and walked over to the refrigerator and leaned over Megan asking, "What're you looking for?"

Megan had sensed Tony behind her and wondered why her partner was so interested in what she was looking for. "I thought I took out some orange juice yesterday and I can't find it."

Tony placed her arms around Megan's waist and pulled her against her body. Moving her mouth next to her partner's ear, she breathed, "You have gorgeous legs." Stepping backward, still holding Megan around the waist, she placed warm moist kisses on the side of her neck. Feeling the chair behind her, she sat down pulling Megan onto her lap.

Goose bumps ran up and down Megan's body at the feel of the soft, moist lips against her neck. When Tony sat down, she turned sideways on her lap and raised both of her arms placing her hands in her partner's thick, soft hair, pulling her head down meeting her slightly parted lips with her own. Thrusting her tongue deeply into Tony's mouth, she felt her desire escalating with the answering plunge of her partner's.

The passionate kiss was sent shivers up and down Tony's body. Keeping her mouth locked on her lover's, she lifted the edge of Megan's sleeping shirt and moved her hand under it finding the breast she was seeking. Kneading it softly she felt her partner's intake of breath and thrust her tongue deeply into her mouth, her fingers lightly caressing a nipple.

Megan moaned and placed a hand on Tony's chest and pushed back, breaking the sensuous kiss. "Tony...wait."

Tony stilled her hands and looked into her lover's passion-filled eyes. Her voice throaty with desire, she said, "I want to make love to you, Megan."

Megan's heart was already racing and the sound of the low sensuous voice sent another shiver down her body. "I want to make love to you, too," Megan said. Standing up on shaky knees, she extended her hand to her partner, "Come on."

Tony took hold of Megan's hand and followed her into their bedroom. Tony pulled her sleeping shirt over her head and tossed it out of the way, watching Megan do the same with hers. Tony felt a jolt to her core when she raked her eyes down the length of Megan's body, from the full firm breasts, to the small waist and muscular abdomen, to the curly golden hair and the shapely muscular legs.

Megan felt every nerve in her body reacting to the way Tony was looking at her. Unable to hold back any longer, she stepped toward Tony and wrapped her arms around her.

Tony placed her hands on Megan's buttocks and pulled her closer running her hands over the round, firm skin. Megan moved her mouth to a dark nipple and sucked on it gently. Hearing her partner groan, she moved her other hand up and kneaded the other breast while she caressed the nipple that her mouth had captured lightly with her teeth.

Tony didn't know how much longer she could stand there under the sensuous onslaught of her partner. She guided them toward the bed and laid down pulling Megan down with her.

Maneuvering herself over her lover, Tony lowered herself until she was supported with her elbows on either side of Megan. The swirling gold specks in the emerald green eyes that were darkened by desire captivated her. Lowering her lips to her partner's, she kissed her deeply before moving her mouth to her neck, placing warm, moist kisses along it until she found the pulse point where she stopped and sucked lightly.

When Megan returned to an earthly plane and was able to speak, she turned to her partner. "You are so good."

"Only because I have a great partner," Tony said smiling at the woman she loved.

Megan raised a hand to Tony's face and caressed the soft skin with her fingers. "I love you."

"I love you, too, love."

Megan ran her fingers lightly across the silky skin of Tony's abdomen before moving her hand upward and tracing invisible designs on the perfectly formed full breasts.

Tony felt her heart racing again and the throbbing between her legs increased in intensity. Megan smiled at her partner, her hands never stopping. Leaning over, she ran her tongue around one of the nipples before capturing it with her mouth and the lovers continued to explore the physical side of their love.

* * * * * * * * * *

A week had passed since Tony's assailant had been captured and their lives had finally returned to normal. Tony and Megan were watching the news after work. When it was over, Tony said, "Huey called today."

"Oh, really? Are you going to have to testify?"

"He doesn't think so. They have so much evidence against what he is calling a vigilante group that he said I will only have to give a deposition, which I can do here."

"That's good. I'm just glad it's over," Megan said smiling at her partner. The phone rang and Megan picked it up.

"Hello."

"Hi, Megan," Barbara said, "It's mom," she added unnecessarily.

Megan raised her eyebrows surprised. "Hi, Mom," she said, not knowing what to expect.

It sounded so good to hear her daughter's voice. Even though it had only been a week since she had seen her, it felt so much longer. Barbara did not agree with Charles and had decided regardless of how he felt, she was not going to ignore her daughter. She had always supported him, even when she didn't agree with his decisions. This was one time she couldn't do that.

And she had to admit she was a little curious. Well, ok, very curious about the FBI agent that had apparently stolen her daughter's heart. What was so special about her that she would risk her father's wrath? Surely she'd known what his reaction would be.

"Mom...you still there?"

"Yes, dear, I'm here. I was wondering when we could go to dinner?" Barbara paused and then added, "I mean all three of us. You and me and your friend. I'd like to meet her if she wants to come."

The small smile on Megan's face grew in intensity, and she said, "Just a minute. Let me ask her." She held her hand over the mouthpiece. "My mother wants to meet you and thought it would be nice if we could all go to dinner together."

Tony smiled warmly at her partner and said, "Sure. Whenever you want, love."

Coming next from
RENAISSANCE ALLIANCE

Forces of Evil
By Trish Kocialski

This is an action adventure story that involves several government agencies pursuing the same target unbeknownst to each other. Two of the central characters discover each other's cover and team up to stop the evil plot from occurring. Forces of Evil takes place predominantly in the Catskill's region of New York State and in New York City. The plot includes through a variety of means, attempts to assassinate many world leaders in an effort to take over the world. Can the forces of evil be stopped in time?

Available November 2000.

Available soon from

RENAISSANCE ALLIANCE

Jacob's Fire
By Devin Centis

Jacob, a university professor/scientist, has found a formula for a cure for AIDS, but if the formula is improp-
erly used, it causes mass destruction. The government
and a private pharmaceutical firm want Jacob's formula, and will go to murderous means to get it. However, the pharmaceutical rep who is supposed to cajole
him into selling the formula to her firm is a Christian
who won't exert unethical means. In fact, she and
Jacob become friends during a time when war is breaking out with Russia and China allied against Israel.
The rep tries telling Jacob that what is taking place in
the world follows biblical prophecy and he should
covert from Judiasm to Christianity.

The formula does fall into the wrong hands, and
plague-like devastation is wreaked on the world. In the
meantime, both Jacob and his new found female friend
find they must escape from the government who wants
the formula to use in battle.

Jacob's Fire intertwines mystery with politics and
attempts to form a "New World Order" on the political,
religious, and economical levels. Jacob accidentally
gets caught up in this web of shadow secret organizations through his daughter marrying a young man who
works for the Vatican as well as the new global president.

Out of Darkness
By Mary Draganis

In a most troublesome period of human history, subjugated by the might of Nazi Germany, two women meet under extraordinary circumstances. This is the story of Eva Muller, the daughter of a German major, the commander of the occupying force in Larissa, Greece in 1944. Through the intervention of the village priest she meets Zoe Lambros. Zoe is a young Greek woman with vengence in her heart and a faith in God that's been shattered by the death of her family. They develop a friendship borne out of this dark time, and they help each other to learn to live and love again.

You Must Remember This
By Mary Draganis

You Must Remember This is the sequel to Out of Darkness. With the help of Alberta Haralambos, Eva's stepmother, Eva manages to get out of the factory and use her language skills in the ever busy interpreter division while Zoe Lambros sets out to fulfill a dream of studying for her arts degree. From out of Eva's past comes a woman, Greta, that threatens their happiness. Greta hides a secret that when revealed will lead to extraordinary measures being taken to bring this woman to justice.

And Those Who Trespass Against Us
By H. M. Macpherson

Sister Katherine Flynn is an Irish nun, sent by her order to work in the Australian outback. Katherine is a prideful woman who originally joined her order to escape the shame of being left at the altar. She had found herself getting married only because society dictated it for a young woman her age, and she was not exactly heartbroken when it didn't take place. Yet, her mother could not be consoled and talked of nothing except the disgrace that she had brought to the Flynn name. So, she finds great relief in escaping the cold Victorian Ireland of 1872.

Catriona Pelham is a member of the reasonably affluent farming gentry within the district. Her relationship with the hardworking townspeople and its farmers is one of genuine and mutual respect. The town's wealthy, however, have ostracized her due to her unorthodox ways and refusal to conform to society's expectations of a woman of the 1870's.

As a bond between Katherine and Catriona develops, Catriona finds herself wanting more than friendship from the Irishwoman. However, she fears pursuing her feelings lest they not be reciprocated. And so the journey begins for these two strong-willed women. For Katherine it is a journey of self-discovery and of what life holds outside the cloistered walls of the convent. For Catriona it is bittersweet, as feelings she has kept hidden for years resurface in her growing interest in Katherine.

Vendetta
By Talaran

Nicole Stone is a narcotics detective with a painful past
that still haunts her. Extremely attractive, yet reclu-
sive, she has closed her heart to love and concentrates
solely on her career. After someone tries to kill her
partner in cold blood, she meets her partner's sister,
Carly Jamison. An unmistakable attraction catches
both of these women off guard. Can Nic protect her
partner and Carly from the clutches of a ruthless drug
lord bent on revenge and still open her heart to the one
woman who could change her life forever?

Printed in the United States
6279